THE
WHOLE MESS
AND OTHER STORIES

OTHER BOOKS BY JACK SKILLINGSTEAD

The Chaos Function
Life on the Preservation
Are You There and Other Stories
Harbinger

Praise for
The Whole Mess and Other Stories

"Equally at home depicting adventures in the multiverse and outer space, these stories are pre-eminently about real people making their hardest choices. A master of the many worlds of science fiction, Jack Skillingstead is also one of our most humane writers."
— James Patrick Kelly, author of *Think Like a Dinosaur*

"*The Whole Mess* is a beautifully crafted exploration of the human heart told through the broad palette of science fiction."
— Brenda Cooper, author of *Edge of Dark*

"This is a wonderful collection of stories about people caught in challenging situations who desperately need to both figure what's going on and how to extricate themselves from their dire and disorienting circumstances. Jack Skillingstead has an amazing ability to bring us right into the thoughts of his characters and make us feel they are our own. While these include the doubts and insecurities, they also include those dawning moments of realization and triumphs. I find myself convinced that it's me who is lost in a dream or a game or some other terrifying or perplexing adventure. My own survival seems to depend on the character's. It's me who breathes a sigh of tense relief when the characters find their way home."
— Sheila Williams, editor of *Asimov's Science Fiction*

"I'm reminded again that Jack is truly one of the living masters of the short form. He's honed science fiction to its sharpest cutting edge . . . Beautiful, daring, imaginative—this collection secures Jack's legacy as one of the masters of modern science fiction."
— Ted Kosmatka, author of *The Flicker Men*

"[Skillingstead's] a craftsman. His sentences are spare and clean, the paragraphs balanced, yet there are so many moments that rise toward poetry. He has a gift for finding new, graceful ways to describe things we've all experienced and seen in print a thousand times."
— Daryl Gregory, author of *Spoonbenders* and *Revelator*

"Jack Skillingstead's stories are challenging and intriguing, often touching, always fascinating. He's a writer who proves that science fiction can have heart. I can't recommend this collection highly enough."
— Louisa Morgan, author of *A Secret History of Witches*

"Jack Skillingstead explores how we experience reality, parallel realities, artificial intelligence, and the slippery nature of the heart in this important and thought-provoking addition to the SF library. Along the way he tells banging good stories, one after another, like a string of narrative firecrackers."
— James Van Pelt, author of *Summer of the Apocalypse*

"The tradeoff of our coming transparent world [is in] Jack Skillingstead's 'Yours, Mine, Ours.' The many gains and poignant losses. The stark choices, whether to live as grownups, awash in the kind of light that would have seared every god of Olympus."
— David Brin, author of *Startide Rising* and *Existence*

THE
WHOLE MESS
AND OTHER STORIES

JACK
SKILLINGSTEAD

FAIRWOOD PRESS
Bonney Lake, WA

THE WHOLE MESS AND OTHER STORIES
A Fairwood Press Book
November 2023
Copyright © 2023 Jack Skillingstead
All Rights Reserved

First Edition

Fairwood Press
21528 104th Street Court East
Bonney Lake, WA 98391
www.fairwoodpress.com

Cover art © Vincent Chong
Cover and book design by Patrick Swenson

ISBN: 978-1-958880-12-8
First Fairwood Press Edition: November 2023

For Nancy

CONTENTS

An Introduction to Daryl Gregory (Featuring Jack Skillingstead)

Here's how I tell the story:

The most important day of Jack Skillingstead's life was the day he met me, his new best friend. It was May 5, 2006, at the Nebula Weekend in Tempe, Arizona. And yes, okay, that was also the day he met Ted Kosmatka, runner-up best friend (Ted can write his own essay if he wants to argue the rankings), and Nancy Kress, the woman he'd someday marry. But I know—know—that it was meeting me that changed the trajectory of his life, because meeting Jack changed mine—that's just physics. We smacked into each other like two billiard balls, flew back to our respective corners of the country, and then kept bouncing into each other for the next seventeen years.

At first Jack was just an excellent hang. He's one of those rare people I can riff with effortlessly, so my first move upon entering a science fiction convention is always to find Jack at the bar and pull up a stool. There we'd sit, topping each other's jokes, taking tangents into gossip, puns, absurdism, mock outrage, and wordplay for wordplay's sake. Jack's a comedy sniper. He sits still, speaks quietly, and fires off jokes that are dry as vermouth. Civilians are thrown off by his deadpan delivery and mistake him for a sincere gentleman, which only makes the comedy more hilarious (for me).

What a relief it was when it turned out this guy could out-and-out *write*. There's a particular hell known to writers when they discover that some perfectly pleasant person they've met writes sentences that grate like clichéd nails on a hackneyed chalkboard. Jack is not that guy. He's a craftsman. His sentences are spare and clean, the paragraphs balanced, yet there are so many moments that rise toward poetry. He has a gift for finding new, graceful ways to describe things we've all experienced and seen in print a thousand times. I've read many descriptions of being drunk, but this line from "Einstein's Theory," one of my favorite stories in this collection, knocked me out: "Absinthe trickled into the convolutions of Albert's brain." So efficient, so apt.

There's not a wasted word in that story, which is typical of Jack. He never overreaches. He also never tells the reader how to feel—and that restraint makes the stories come alive. He makes room for you, and trusts you to understand the emotion behind the things left unsaid, the uncompleted gestures, or something as simple as a description of a man walking down a late-night city street toward home. That's the final image in "Einstein's Theory." I won't insert the paragraph here, because I want you to see how the whole story builds toward that moment.

Jack became not only my favorite writer, but my favorite person to talk with about the craft of writing, and to bitch about the business of writing (two very different things). It turned out we were enamored with the difficulty of writing well, the taking of pains, even when no reader might notice the effort. (Yes, this suffering artist routine makes us feel superior, but please allow us to camp on this small patch of moral high ground.) We had to invest ourselves in the act of writing, because if we relied on the publishing business to provide self-esteem or satisfaction, we'd throw ourselves off a fucking cliff.

When my third novel tanked and my publisher dumped me, I was too embarrassed to talk to anyone in the field about it—except Jack. Later I had a publisher drop an entire series before I could write more than the first book, and he was there for that too, and many other setbacks and rejections and disappointments over the years. I tell people new to the field that they should become friends with other writers; that way, instead of feeling like some solitary loser, you feel like the member of a losing team.

But it can be hard for writers to manage their envy when teammates start winning without them. With Jack I've never felt a twinge of jealousy. This is not because I'm a saint, free of pettiness (ask my family). It's because I admire his writing so much that I'm thrilled when others recognize it, too. I was in the car with him when he got the email that his novel *The Chaos Function* had sold to Houghton Mifflin Harcourt, and I had only two thoughts: One, why is Jack reading his phone while driving? Two, damn straight they bought the book—it's terrific.[1]

I'm always reluctant to share my own good news. As a Midwesterner, I grew up believing that if you were ever caught bragging, God would send a tornado to destroy your house. So whenever something positive happens in my career, Jack's one of the few people I can whisper the news to. He kindly gives the impression of being genuinely happy for me.

Jack became, in short, the guy I could talk to about everything. Not only our professions, but everything important: kids, relationships, divorce, aging, death . . . no topic too grim. He has the constitution for driving through the dark.

When my marriage broke up and I found myself planning to move across the country, Jack volunteered to ride with me from Pennsylvania to California. In a Mini Cooper. In winter. At night we drank in dive bars and ate in sketchy restaurants. We slept in ancient motels alongside Route 66, sharing a room, even though I snore like a backhoe scraping rock. We drove nine, ten, eleven hours a day, for four days, and for much of that time I was swerving all over the emotional road. Reader, I hope you have someone in your life who will cross the continent with you in a tiny British vehicle, and not only *not* murder you, but buy you several suspiciously cheap margaritas in a Mexican restaurant in Barstow. I arrived in Oakland hungover, but alive, and grateful.

I'm sorry. I know you were expecting an essay that was more about Jack than me. But the embarrassing and not-so-secret secret about writers is that everything we write is really about ourselves. That's as true in fiction as non-fiction, though in stories we try to disguise ourselves. We put our words into the mouths of characters who don't look like us, or live in locations far away from us, or belong to a different species or form of life. Science fiction, our preferred genre, is built for writers to hide themselves in.

But the truth leaks out. And when I read the stories in this book, I see Jack.

---

[1] Jack has informed me that he received an acceptance email before we entered the car and only told me about it while driving. That may be true, but my version is funnier.

Jack's always been a loner at heart, but in his fiction he takes those feelings of isolation and amplifies them, clarifies them, and fleshes them out. He's a master at writing about the Eleanor Rigbys and Father Mackenzies of the world—the sole survivors, the dispossessed, the alienated. You'll find many of those lonesome souls in his first collection, *Are You There and Other Stories*. Many are in this collection, too. Take Amrita, the protagonist of "The Sum of Her Expectations," whose only companion is Tripp, an android. A catastrophe strands them on an alien planet inhabited only by runaway nano-builders creating a vast, empty city. Tripp abandons Amrita to join his robotic brethren. Late in the story, when Amrita fears she'll never escape the planet, Jack gives us this:

> Tripp visited her in a dream. He was his old self, undamaged and companionable. His blank face swiveled toward her. *I've got your back*, he said, but it was just Amrita's deep architect of loneliness trying to manufacture the loyalty that Tripp, in the end, had been incapable of.

Deep architect of loneliness. I felt that Jack had outed himself with that one. He takes the raw materials of speculative fiction—multiple universes, AI, space travel, aliens, magic—and builds beautiful structures where his characters can live. There are men and women thrown into alternate realities, like the characters in "Dream Interpretation," and those who recognize, like the protagonist of "Einstein's Theory," that they've lived in the wrong universe all along.

And some are outsiders in their own world. In "Mine, Yours, Ours," a woman is trapped in a surveillance state of "neighbors" who know everything about her, and will judge her for everything she does, but don't know her at all. The willfully oblivious main character of "Destination" is kidnapped by a self-driving car and driven out of the comfort of the privileged exclusion zone, into a world he doesn't want to be a part of.

But when I compare the stories in this collection to the ones in *Are You There*, I detect a shift in approach, or at least tone. It seems to me that in these stories, Jack's ready to let in a little light.

The lead story, "The Whole Mess," takes a typically Skilling-steadian riff on multiple realities, but adds properly pulpish Love-craftian monsters, plus a touching, romantic relationship. Jack, doing romance! "Straconia," about a man pulled into a mean-ingless, Kafkaesque universe, should be relentlessly sad, but instead evolves into something beautiful. "Arlington," another story about a lone pilot, is full of Jack's love of flying (see his story notes at the end of the book) and ends with a turn toward friendship and something close to joy.

And sometimes he takes on the darkest themes and plays them for comedy. "Salvage Opportunity," to pick one example from several in the book, is a funhouse mirror about loneliness, which could be read almost as a vaudeville sketch about three actors playing the same man, or one actor playing three characters.

I don't mean to suggest that Jack's gone soft. There are tough-minded stories here, and some, like "Steel Lake," are as devastat-ing as anything he's ever written. But many of the stories in this book that seem headed for some bleak cliff, instead rise at the end and take flight. The lift-off is almost always made possible by a character finally reaching out to others, making a connection, or trying one last time for reconnection. Jack, a natural-born solo flyer, keeps reminding us that we need co-pilots.

One more thing about me, if you'll indulge me. Last month I was in Tennessee, spending time at my mother's bedside, reading through Jack's collection again. She was at home, in hospice care, mostly sleeping, which means there were a lot of empty hours. Jack texted frequently, checking in on me. I was grateful for that, and grateful that I had his stories to keep me company. I hope you love them as much as I do.

— *Daryl Gregory*
June 8, 2023

THE WHOLE MESS

The kid in the duck-hunting hat reached across my desk with a folded sheet of yellow graph paper in his fingers. "I think you will find this interesting, Professor Dunn."

I took the paper and opened it. A mathematical equation, meticulously printed in black pencil, marched across the sheet. It began: {C-cosmo} + {C-astro} and at first glance appeared to be headed towards Gleiser's multiverse modification of the Drake equation. But it diverged wildly and without resolution.

"What is it, Mr. Whitfield?" I asked, not quite looking at him.

"Something I believe only you can finish."

"I see. Stump the prof. I'm not a cosmologist, you know."

He shook his head, rejecting my rejection. Daniel Whitfield was big as a linebacker though nothing about him suggested athleticism. Freshman-aged but not a freshman, he had been auditing my combinatorial topology class at the University of Washington, and he was becoming a distraction. Each day he showed up in his absurd red and black duck-hunting hat with the ear flaps turned down, sat in the front row, and stared at me. Whitfield never removed his hat or his camel hair coat. A silver ballpoint pen protruded from the outside breast pocket, and feathery gray streaks stained the lapels of the coat. Cigarette ash, I guessed, smelling tobacco now that he was sitting so near.

"I'm not trying to stump you," he said. "You're looking at the most important work you will ever do."

"Is that right?"

"You want to know what it is?"

"Not especially." I resumed placing folders into my briefcase, which is what I'd been doing when Whitfield entered.

"It's an incantation," he said.

"A what?" I met his eyes briefly and looked away.

"You concede Tegmark's mathematical universe hypothesis?"

"No."

"You don't concede it? That's in direct contradiction to what you've—"

"I concede the MUH, but I don't agree to this discussion."

"I risked my life to bring this to you."

"Mr. Whitfield, please."

Whitfield pointed at the paper. "It's ancient. When they found it, the final expression was missing, deliberately removed. Once that expression is restored, the world changes. I'm confident it won't defeat you, Professor Dunn. I've studied everything you've published since your student days at Harvard. Very unorthodox. This problem requires a particular genius."

I was inclined to laugh, but Whitfield's intense and utterly humorless stare "defeated" me, as he might have put it. Genius. I hated that word.

"Very interesting," I said. "In any case, I'm late for class."

I tried to hand the paper back but he waved it away. "That's yours." He stood, almost knocking his chair over. "Goodbye," he said, hunching his shoulders and turning away. His brown Oxfords, so big they were almost clown shoes, scuffed across the carpet. He left the door open on his way out. A certain percentage of my students fell within the Asperger's spectrum, a common affliction found in the narrow population of mathematical obsessives, prodigies, and, especially, "geniuses." Whitfield's apparent insanity made him an outlier, though. I started to crumple his silly paper but stopped, gave it another look, and slipped it into my briefcase.

Daniel Whitfield did not return to class. But his equation, or as he called it, his *incantation*, became my hobby and then my obsession. And of course Whitfield had known it would happen that way. Night after night I sat up late in my West Seattle townhouse drinking endless cups of lemon tea (I'd long ago put aside the single malt Scotch that had led me astray in my university days and afterwards) while scribbling out my attempts to solve the Whitfield equation. At every impasse, and there were many,

I reached for the guitar I kept leaning against the bookcase next to my desk. Music, like everything else, is mathematical. Fingering random scale variations sometimes loosened that part of my mind seeking non-linear solutions.

My obsession became relentless. For the first time in my experience I saw more than the purity of mathematics. The equation was trying to *tell* me something, a story, almost in the manner of ancient hieroglyphs.

In a dream I found myself standing before a blackboard, my back to the classroom. My hand worked furiously, the nub of chalk clicking against the slate. As always, the final expression eluded me, and I threw the chalk down in disgust. An odor of brine and corruption, half sea and half sewer, filled the classroom. I felt a looming presence and became afraid to turn around and face my student. Instead I picked up the chalk and resumed work. That was the message of the dream: Finish.

The next day I was crossing the lower campus with my briefcase and coffee, walking quickly to make my first class. Lisa, a young woman whom I liked but knew only slightly, an administrative assistant in the dean's office, was walking toward me on the otherwise deserted path. A brisk October wind swept maple leaves into the air between us. "Hello, professor," Lisa said. I met her eyes glancingly, started to reply, and the solution to Whitfield's equation appeared in my mind with all the urgency of a fire alarm. It happened that way sometimes. I stopped, put my briefcase down, and fumbled for a notepad and mechanical pencil. The solution felt tenuous and I didn't want to lose it.

Lisa said, "Are you all right, professor? Here, give me that."

She took the coffee from my hand. I mumbled something, my head down. Printing quickly, I transcribed the completed equation in tightly crabbed symbols and numbers then reviewed the result, moving my lips and thus speaking the incantation. It was solid.

The wind dropped as if a plug had been pulled. I looked up. A maple leaf sea-sawed out of the air and landed on the others.

The atmosphere became electric. Lisa looked at me. I saw fear in her eyes before I quickly glanced away. Behind her on the path a ragged hole opened like a rough doorway or the mouth of a tunnel. Its face rippled with an oily iridescent sheen. The hole expanded and acquired depth. An elephant could have passed through it.

For a moment I couldn't credit what I was seeing. The brine-and-sewer stench familiar from my dream wafted out of the tunnel. Instinctively, I took Lisa's arm and pulled her back, only to stumble over my own briefcase. She grabbed my arm to keep me from falling, and we ended in an awkward embrace.

A shape moved inside the tunnel, something huge, dragging itself towards us. My flight response seized me but I couldn't move. Lisa and I held onto to each other like children. The ground shifted then, like an elevator that stops too sharply inches below the next floor. The sensation was so startling I looked at our feet, expecting to find us standing in a sinkhole. But we stood on the ordinary path, and the air was moving again. When I looked up, the tunnel and whatever had been about to emerge was gone.

"What was *that*?" Lisa said.

I shook my head. A monumental change had occurred but I couldn't identify it.

Lisa patted my sleeve. "You can let go of me now."

"What? Oh—"

She handed me the coffee. My hand was shaking, and I hoped she didn't notice. I looked at my watch and received another shock. The watch I had strapped around my wrist that morning had been a simple drugstore Timex. Now I wore a stainless steel Mont Blanc with Arabic numerals and three sub dials. I had never seen the thing before—except that I *had* seen it before. Of course I had. It had been a gift from, from . . .

"Professor?"

"Something strange is happening."

She laughed shortly, a response I couldn't interpret. But I never was good at decoding human beings, looking into their eyes, unraveling human motivations. Only the reliability of numbers had ever made sense to me.

"Do you feel all right?" I asked.

She thought about it. "All right, but different."

"Different how?"

"This is going to sound odd."

"Go ahead, please."

"I feel like I don't know whether I should tell my insurance company about the scrape I put on the fender of my Fiat in the parking garage this morning."

"I don't understand."

"Professor Dunn, I don't own a car."

Now I made myself look into her eyes. "I'm sorry?"

"*I don't own a car.*"

I looked away again, my mind trying to bend around oblique corners. It failed. "I'm going to my class."

"What about what just happened?"

"I don't know." I walked away, disoriented and more frightened than I would have liked to admit. Lisa came after me.

"I'm staying with you," she said.

Teaching was out of the question. My students would be elated when I dismissed them. Lisa hovered at my elbow when I entered the lecture hall. It was a large class, almost a hundred undergraduates—and they were all listening to a man I did not recognize lecture from the podium. He noticed me in the back and lifted his chin, as if to ask my business. I thought I must be in the wrong place. But when I withdrew to the corridor I saw that I'd opened the correct door.

"What's wrong?" Lisa said.

"I'm not sure."

I slipped on my glasses and read the schedule attached to the wall. It was my number theory class at my hour, but someone named Ethan Kriegel was teaching it.

I leaned against the wall and closed my eyes.

"Professor Dunn?"

"I have to think."

The door to the lecture hall opened. Ethan Kriegel, I presumed, stepped out and addressed me. "Dr. Dunn, did you need to speak with me?"

"No. Yes. Why are you teaching my class?"

"Your class? But you assigned it to me."

"I don't assign classes. What are you talking about?"

Kriegel smiled uncertainly. "I'm sorry, Dr. Dunn, but—"

"I want to know what the hell is happening," I said, my fear translating to anger. Kriegel stepped back.

Lisa touched my shoulder and said, "Let's get out of here."

"Wait."

An identity began to surface on Kriegel's features, like a face slowly floating to the surface of a murky pond. Of course I knew Ethan Kriegel. I was head of the math department and he was one of my best people. This *was* his class to teach. I ought to know, since I had assigned it to him myself. I lightly touched my forehead with my fingertips, as if the answer to this mystery might be written there in braille. Somehow I had moved into a different life, one that still belonged to me but diverged significantly from the one I'd known.

"I apologize, Professor Kriegel. Please return to your class."

Feeling nauseous, I turned and walked away before he could reply. Lisa stayed with me and I was glad of it. Outside I sat on the steps and took deep breaths. Lisa sat beside me.

"I feel sick to my stomach," she said.

"Me, too."

"It's like a different life happening to me," she said. "I'm remembering all kinds of stuff that I know isn't true, but somehow it *is* true. The car thing is just one of them. What's happening to us?"

"I don't know but I think he's going to tell us." I pointed at a man crossing the quad and heading straight for us. It was Daniel Whitfield, still wearing his duck-hunting hat and camel hair coat. He was grinning like a demon. Maybe he *was* a demon.

Whitfield climbed the steps and stood before us. "You did it," he said. "Congratulations."

"He did what?" Lisa said.

"Unlocked eternity. The New Age of the Masters is already spreading across the infinite."

"Your damn equation," I said.

"I knew you wouldn't be able to resist it. And once the incantation is expressed there is no un-expressing it."

"All we want is to get back to the place we started," I said.

"Oh, you wouldn't like that one anymore. It's already very much transformed. There's been a regime change. But don't worry, it will catch up with you here soon enough. In fact . . ."

He swept his arm toward the quad. A dozen or so students crossed on their way to or from class, backpacks slung over shoulders and cell phones in hand. The air became still as the air inside a sealed tomb. An oily black oval rippled into existence above the bricks. It acquired depth, became a tunnel. Lisa and I stood up. A purple and pink tentacle unrolled from the tunnel, picked up a co-ed in a red sweater, and flung her screaming into the air. The other students scattered, screaming and shouting. Lisa said, "Oh my God, oh my God," and ran back into Maier Hall.

Daniel Whitfield climbed the last steps and stood before me, unconcerned by the chaos. "It's pointless to run. The Masters will appear in every iteration, eventually. You've provided the access that was lost for so long."

I was barely listening. A nightmare had dragged itself out of the tunnel and into the light. More of its kind crowded the tunnel's mouth. The first to emerge made directly for me, using its tentacles to pull and hump forward at surprising speed. I stumbled back, terrified, and seemed to step into a depression that hadn't been there a moment before. I flung my arms out for balance. And with the abruptness of a channel change, the quad resumed its mundane aspect. A dozen students crossed the bricks with backpacks and cell phones—including the co-ed in the red sweater whom I'd seen die only moments before.

Daniel Whitfield had vanished. I stood alone at the top of the stairs.

And I didn't belong there. The University of Washington had been my home (some would have called it my hideout) for fifteen years. Yet now I felt like an intruder, and I knew I had side-slipped into another "iteration," one very far from the world I was used to. My Timex was back, but this time my clothes had changed. Instead of my customary tweed jacket I wore a brown leather coat over a gray hooded sweatshirt. I reached up and removed the baseball cap I hadn't been wearing a moment ago and stared at the Seahawks logo. I touched my face and discovered I now wore a full beard.

After a moment I replaced the hat and descended the steps in a daze, my dirty white sneakers feeling strange after years of loafers. This iteration's identity slowly rose to the surface. By the time I reached University Avenue and the six-year-old Ford Focus I'd left parked there, I knew perfectly well that I didn't belong on campus, except as the slightly sad figure I now inhabited, a man well past thirty ignorantly in search of entry into the higher-education structure. My appointment with the admissions counselor hadn't gone well. I was woefully under-qualified, and my paltry community college credits were non-transferable.

The whole thing was an ironic counterpoint to my original arrival, a decade and a few iterations ago, when I was the over-qualified applicant for a teaching position that would ensure insulation from the cries of *Genius!* that had hectored me since grade school. Now I fell short even as an aging freshman looking for validation in the form of a degree in the humanities.

Yes, the *humanities*.

In this sorry version of myself I no longer possessed (or was possessed by, as I used to think) the special aptitude for mathematics that had defined my expectations and my misery for as long as I could remember.

I still lived in West Seattle, but no longer in a townhouse with a view of Puget Sound. The Ford took me home, like a dog who finds his way back from the wilderness. My *body* knew where it lived, even if my migrant identity remained largely lost. Presently I found myself parked before a tan building with three cracked concrete steps leading to the lobby door. Flaking gold letters on the glass spelled Franklin Apartments. I turned the engine off and held the little bundle of keys in my open hand, waiting to recognize the proper one. Eventually I did.

The deeper I penetrated this iteration the more familiar it became. The studio apartment enclosed me like the arms of a sisterly spouse in a sexless marriage. The trestle kitchen with its old-fashioned appliances and stale odors refreshed memories of countless Campbell and Totino's feasts. The unmade sofa bed told its story of grim bachelorhood. I'd lived alone in my townhouse, too, but those rooms had been neatly (obsessively so) maintained, and my rich intellectual life acted as counter-balance to my inevitable loneliness.

When I saw the computer I had to wonder whether I'd time traveled as well as side-slipped. Instead of the sleek Macbook Pro

I was used to, a boxy anachronism sat on my Ikea desk. The CRT monitor alone must have weighed forty pounds. I reached for my cell phone but it wasn't in my pocket. A Swedish Health Cooperative calendar on the kitchen wall informed me I still occupied the year 2017. Looking at it, I remembered why I had the calendar. SHCC employed me as a phlebotomist. That is, I spent my workdays drawing blood from the arms of patients sent to the lab by their physicians. I shuddered at the thought, while simultaneously feeling cranky gratitude for the job. After all, I'd gone to school for the certification (my untransferable credits) and was lucky to be making $17 an hour. Never mind the periodic panic that I was wasting my life, the kind of panic that had sent me to the UW campus that morning.

The land line began ringing, startling me with its piercing electronic trill. I lifted the handset from its wall-mounted cradle.

"Please, God," Lisa said, "tell me this is Professor Dunn."

For a moment, I almost couldn't breathe. Emotion compressed the air out of my lungs.

"Hello?" Lisa said.

I swallowed. "It's Dunn," I said, "but I'm not a professor anymore."

Lisa sat on my sofa. The bed, with its dirty bachelor sheets, was folded inside and hidden under swaybacked cushions.

"My i-Phone is gone," she said, staring at me as if I had stolen it (which, in a way, I suppose, I had). "*Everybody's* phone is gone. I'm back to not having a car, and there's a student discount Metro Pass in my wallet. Get this, I don't work in the dean's office anymore. I'm a *freshman* and I've got loans and Pell grants up my ass. And there's this." She pushed up her sleeve. A tattoo of a winged serpent, red forked tongue wickedly extended, wrapped around her forearm.

I cleared my throat. "That's . . . new?"

She laughed shortly, and this time I didn't have any trouble interpreting her meaning. "New? I used to ride the dragon. You don't know what that means? Heroin. Dragons are kind of like flying serpents, and serpents symbolize the devil. So okay it sounds dumb saying it out loud. Every idiot wants to tell the story of her tattoo. But this serpent on my arm is a reminder. The dragon is patient. It's always waiting for the needle. I got the tat a month after I should have been dead. It cost three hundred dollars. The money was in a paper bag, which had been in the lap of my boyfriend, who had passed out next to me in his car. Only he wasn't passed out. We were sitting there because we were going to buy drugs in the parking lot of a Tukwila strip mall. I thought my boyfriend passed out, but he was dead. That was my big turning point, right? I grabbed the bag and ran. Sweated out detox, joined NA, and got the serpent—as a reminder. That's my story. There's only one problem. None of it happened to me—I mean, none of it happened to the real me. But in this nutty place it's exactly what happened. I got clean, and I got motivated, and I went back to school. Professor Dunn, what the *hell* is going on?"

I sighed, rubbed my eyes. "You probably won't believe this."

"Are you kidding? Did you hear what I just said?"

"I heard you. All right, listen."

I told her the whole thing, Whitfield and his equation that was really an incantation, the parallel iterations.

"I don't understand what you mean when you say 'iteration.'"

"That's Whitfield's term. Substitute bubble universe, if you prefer. The theory is every decision creates a bubble universe of its own. Big decisions, little decisions—it doesn't matter. If space and time are infinite, then the variety of alternate realities is also infinite. When I expressed the completed Whitfield equation, it acted as a key to let through what Whitfield called the 'The Masters.' According to him, these things will populate across all realities. But I think the equation did something else, too. It opened pathways between the parallel universes, between these bubble worlds. Chutes and ladders. Escape routes. Of course, according to Mr. Whitfield, escape is ultimately impossible."

"You mean everybody goes into alternate lives, like what we're doing?"

I shook my head. "No. Probably just me, since I solved the equation. And maybe you get carried along because we were together, holding onto each other, at the exact moment the key turned."

After a long pause, Lisa said, "What are we going to do?"

I found myself wanting with everything I had to give her a

hopeful answer, but I didn't have one.

"I don't know. Maybe if I could find Daniel Whitfield, he could tell us."

"Is there a way to get us back to where we started?"

"We wouldn't want to go back to our first world. It's already overrun by the Masters. And from what I saw, they do not promise a benevolent dictatorship."

Lisa's shoulders slumped. "Can I have a glass of water?"

"Of course."

I held a water glass under the kitchen tap, then remembered I kept a bottle of cold spring water in the refrigerator. I opened the door. Beer bottles rattled. The spring water was there—next to an economy-sized bottle of Smirnoff. I stared at the vodka for a long moment, then reached for the spring water and closed the door.

"Thanks," Lisa said when I handed her the bottle. She drank half the water then looked around my apartment, which was just this side of shabby. "I didn't think a professor would live in such a . . . small place."

"I told you. I'm not a professor in this bubble. I'm a med tech at Swedish."

"Why?"

"Why? I told you, every decision creates a different—"

"But do you know what decision you made to go from full professor to medical tech?"

I blushed, acutely and illogically embarrassed. "I think different aptitudes dictated different choices. In this world I've lost my talent for mathematics. It's odd, really. My whole life people called me a genius because of what I could do. At Harvard they expected me to shine like a new star. I resented it, to be honest. Resented the expectations. That's how I wound up at UW. I wanted to be normal. I didn't like the pressure. Besides, I like teaching. I had an aptitude for that, too. Maybe even a little genius for it."

"That's nutty," Lisa said.

"What is?"

"Resenting an incredible gift because you want to be limited like everyone else. It's even kind of insulting, when you think about it."

"Don't forget, it's my 'incredible gift' that let the Masters in and exiled us from our lives."

"Well, maybe if you still had the gift you could fix things."

"I doubt it."

"How would you know, now that you're one of us?" She stood up and went to the window. It had started to rain. "Professor Dunn?"

"Yes?" I didn't bother to correct her again.

"I don't want to be alone. Can I stay here? Just for tonight? I know I'm supposed to be a different me, but I still feel a lot like the old me. I don't belong here yet."

I knew the feeling. "Of course you can stay."

She turned away from the window. "I don't mean I want to sleep with you. That's not what I'm saying."

Ridiculously, I blushed again. "I understand."

"I just don't want to go home yet."

"Absolutely."

I cooked a frozen pizza. We talked about our lives in the previous and present iterations, locating the points of commonality and tracing where the iterations diverged. The process of investigation, analysis, and revelation was similar to what I used to do with numbers and equations, only here I was exploring a human equation, and it was exhilarating. For me, a whole new field of discovery.

Lisa fell asleep on the sofa. I spread a blanket over her and settled back in my lounger with my feet up on the coffee table and a blanket of my own pulled to my chin. Rain ticked against the window. My thoughts followed divergent paths. During our long conversation I had frequently found myself looking directly into Lisa's expressive eyes, responding to personality cues. Losing the curse of my so-called genius seemed also to have relieved me of my social awkwardness. Except for the End Of Humanity In All Worlds, it felt almost like an decent tradeoff.

As I drifted further toward sleep, I entered the realm of intuitive fantasy and insight, of auditory and visual hallucination rising from the borderland of consciousness. I quite distinctly heard Lisa say *Maybe if you still had it you could fix things*, and I startled out of near-sleep, knocking the empty pizza box off the coffee table. I stood up and paced around the room, feeling the kind of excitement I'd only ever felt when the solution to a particularly difficult problem presented itself. Too excited to keep the insight to myself, I shook Lisa awake.

"What's wrong?"

"Nothing. I just—I think I can fix it."

She squinted, still groggy. "Fix—?"

"The Masters, all of it. Listen to me. Every time the tunnel opens it's right in front of me, and the first Master comes straight at me. Add to that, Whitfield went out of his way to assure me there was nothing I could do to cancel the incantation, and what does that tell you?"

She blinked. "I don't know?"

"It tells me there *is* a way to cancel the equation, and I'm the only one who can do it. Makes perfect sense, if you let it. The fact that the incantation existed in the first place means it must have been used—used and then canceled by an equation of equal but opposing power. Otherwise we would already have been living in a world dominated by the Masters, correct?"

"Oh my God."

"There is just one problem."

She fell back on the sofa cushion. "You can't fix it, because now you're one of us instead of a genius."

"Yes."

"I wish you hadn't woken me up."

"No, it's still good. The Masters are going to appear in every iteration, every bubble world, including this one. So all we have to do is wait until they come. Their arrival will trigger my flight response, and we'll shuffle across to a bubble where I've retained my special aptitude."

"Your genius."

"If that's what you prefer."

"How long for that to happen?"

I lifted my empty hands. "I have no idea."

In the morning Lisa went home to face her life and I reported to the Swedish Clinic on California Avenue, only a few blocks from my apartment. Throughout that first morning I was on edge, expecting at any moment to be confronted by the tunnel and the questing tentacles of a Master intent on crushing me.

But it didn't happen.

Instead, I changed into my blue scrubs, greeted my co-workers, collected the day's first blood-draw orders, and started work. I looked at the top sheet and thought, as I always did: *It's show time*, and called into the waiting room, "Jonas Beckwith?" A large man with wispy white hair and a potato nose stood up. I led him to Room 3 and asked him to roll up his sleeve.

By lunch I was as much my new self as my former self. The routines and habits of my circumscribed life asserted themselves. Memories long ago formed in the current bubble pushed aside memories I'd carried over in side-slip flight. My ten years teaching at the University of Washington appeared almost as the structure of a life lived not by me but by a particularly adept memoirist whose journals I'd read.

The last patient of the day, a young blonde woman named Jo Kaye, stood up when I called her name. She was wearing a red and black Pendleton coat. The sight of it sent a disorienting wave through my head, and I had to lean against the wall. The Pendleton reminded me of Daniel Whitfield's duck-hunting hat; it reminded me of who I had been, and I realized my 'Professor Dunn' identity, in one short day, had submerged into the memory pond and stranded me in a life that already felt comfortably lived-in. It was a startling realization, though perhaps no more startling than the knowledge that I might find contentment here. Could the fleeting panic of a 'wasted' life be nothing more than a ripple from a lost iteration?

As if I were sleepwalking, I brought Jo Kaye to an unoccupied phlebotomy room, drew three tubes of her blood, properly capped and labeled them, and told Jo to have a nice day.

Have a nice day.

The minute my shift ended I ran back to my apartment, frightened and cursing the current iteration, a world where personal computing and cell phone technology lagged twenty years behind what I had been used to. What if I forgot who I was before I could reach the phone in my kitchen and call Lisa, the only person in the world who could anchor me to my former identity? I'd written her number down but didn't bring it with me.

I came winded and anxious onto my street. Lisa was sitting on the steps leading to the lobby of the Franklin Apartments. I halted on the sidewalk, breathing hard. She saw me and stood up. The moment suspended between us, almost dropped, then she said, "Professor Dunn," and her voice cracked. I went to her. And this time I did hold and comfort her, though I still had no legitimate comfort to offer.

"I started forgetting, disappearing," she sobbed into my shoulder.

"Me, too."

"Why haven't they come? You said they would come and then you could fix everything."

"They'll come. But. . ."

"But what?"

"It might not be like I said."

She drew back, wiped her eyes. "What do you mean?"

"The other two times, the tunnel opened right in front of us and a Master came for me immediately. I think it's because I was a treat—as long as I possessed the potential, at least, of expressing the counter equation and slamming the door shut on them again. But in this bubble I'm—"

"One of us."

"Yes. Not a priority target."

"So it's hopeless."

"Not as long as I remember my first iteration."

"What good does remembering it do us? We're better off forgetting." She started to turn away.

"No," I said, "we're not." I touched her shoulder. She wouldn't look at me, but she was listening. "When the Masters arrive, however long that takes, I have to be ready. I have to remember how it all started and my part in it. Their arrival might still trigger the side-slip flight reaction, even if I'm not the primary target anymore. But moving to a different bubble, even one where my ability is intact, won't help if I don't remember who I was and what I have to do."

She looked at me. "My day has been a nightmare. I have roommates and I don't like them. We're all college girls, even though I've got five years on both of them. There are all these little microaggressions. Even that word, "microaggression"? I'd never normally use a buzz word like that. Now it comes naturally. All day, since I left here, I've felt myself rising into this life and fading out of the one I came from."

"We need a constant reminder, like your serpent tattoo."

I looked into her eyes, that simple act that had eluded me in my so-called genius life, and she returned my gaze. This was communication on a wordless level, a level that maybe other people, normal people, took for granted but which I hadn't previously known. Now the words didn't even have to be said, but Lisa said them anyway.

"Professor Dunn? I'm moving in with you."

That night I said, "You can have the bed."

"No. This is your apartment. I'll make do with the sofa."

"Okay. But, Lisa? The sofa is the bed."

"Oh, jeez. Look, I'll go home."

"No, no, it's okay. I'll buy a trundle bed tomorrow. If it goes on very long, we could rent a bigger place. Tonight I'll sleep in the bathtub."

"In the bathtub?"

"You know, padded with blankets and pillows. One night isn't going to kill me."

She looked doubtful.

"Honestly," I said.

She nodded slowly. "So, this is one of those sofas that opens up?"

"Yeah."

I showed her how it opened up. As soon as it was a bed, I hastily stripped off the dirty sheets.

"I'll get you fresh," I said.

Except my only other set of sheets were already in the laundry hamper.

"I'll wash them," I said.

"Where's the washer and dryer?"

"In the building's basement."

Later, while the sheets tumbled in the dryer and I sat in a hard plastic chair reading a book under fluorescent light, Lisa came down the steps with a couple of white paper bags.

"Cheeseburgers," she said. "We forgot to eat."

"I didn't forget. There just wasn't anything in the apartment."

"Well. Burgers."

We sat next to each other, ate our cheeseburgers, and watched the laundry tumble. It was nice.

"This is more domestic than I like to get," Lisa said.

"Oh, yes?"

"I don't mean it's bad or anything."

"No?"

"No."

The bathtub made a lousy bed. A *lousy* bed. It was too short, or I was too long. And no amount of cushioning made it any more comfortable, and I didn't have much to cushion it with anyway. But my shift at Swedish started early, so I tried to make the best of it, pulling my elbows in and my knees up. I dozed fitfully, then opened my eyes. I'd left the bathroom door open, in case blood-thirsty Masters from the fifth dimension made an appearance and I had to get out fast. Lamp light shone out in the main room, and I could hear the saggy springs of the sofa bed squeak and groan under Lisa's restless body. I cleared my throat and called out softly, "Are you all right?"

The bed stopped making noise. After a few moments Lisa replied. "Yes. I'm sorry. Did I wake you up? I can't sleep."

"You didn't wake me up."

"I keep thinking about them."

"Them who?"

"You know. *Them.*"

"The Masters."

"Whatever they are. Do you have any Ambien?"

"No. Wait a minute, I don't know if I have any or not. Let me look."

"Don't get up."

"I want to get out of this stupid bathtub anyway."

In the process, I bumped the cold-water handle with my knee. The faucet gushed before I could crank it off. "God damn it."

"What's happening?"

"Just flooded my blankets with cold water."

Lisa stood in the doorway, looking frowzy in her misbuttoned shirt and uncombed hair. I felt ridiculous and exposed in my boxers and T-shirt.

"Let's see what I've got." I opened the medicine cabinet. "No Ambien, but here's Lunesta."

"That works."

I opened the box. It was mostly empty. Then I remembered I took one almost every night and that it was a habit that had begun to worry me but which I was not yet prepared to break. Pretty often I washed the Lunesta down with vodka and spring water.

"What's wrong?" Lisa said.

"Nothing. Those early shifts are hard. I just remembered I've been taking pills for months. Maybe that's why I'm having so much trouble getting to sleep tonight."

"Or else it's being all scrunched up in a bathtub."

"Or that, yes."

I tore a pill off the foil template and handed it to her.

"Professor?"

"You're going to have to stop calling me that."

"I don't want to. It helps me remember."

"Good. Don't stop."

"Professor Dunn, would you mind sitting next to me until this pill knocks me out? I'm really spooked and I feel massively insecure. Is it okay?"

"Of course."

I pulled on a pair of pants and sat in a chair next to the sofa bed. Lisa lay on the bed under her covers. She looked over at me and after a while said:

"What I really need is a little human contact."

Without moving a muscle I turned into a gawky thirteen-year-old boy.

"Could you come over here?"

"Yes."

"I don't mean sex."

"The answer is still yes."

I stretched out beside her and put my arm around her. She rested her head on my chest.

"What if they come and we can't slip away to another bubble?"

"That won't happen."

"I can't believe any of this is real."

The Lunasta turned out her lights in a matter of minutes, but I didn't return to my soggy bathtub bed. I held Lisa for what remained of the night, and once in a while I kissed the soft wave of her hair.

*

The building shook violently. One moment I was standing in the kitchen filling the kettle with water for coffee, the next I was flat on my back. The cupboard flew open and a stack of dishes crashed onto the counter, shattering. I rolled away and covered my face. Sharp fragments bounced off my shoulder, rained onto the floor around me. The shaking paused. I held my breath. Lisa cried out from the other room. I gained my feet and stumbled out of the kitchen. She stood at the west-facing window, hands braced on the frame, her body rigid. There was a long gash on her right calf.

"Earthquake," I said. "We need to get out of here."

She turned and gave me the look a cement wall gives a speeding car. I knew what she was going to say before she said it: "No. It's them. And we're still here. Look at the sky, Professor Dunn. Look at it."

I approached the window. The sky boiled with sulfurous yellow clouds. Wind-smudged pillars of smoke rose from fires too numerous to count. Already the invasion was well under way, and the Masters had taken no notice of me.

"*Damn* it."

I turned around. In the kitchen doorway Lisa stood holding the phone. "It's dead." She dropped the handset and it dangled at the end of its cord. She pulled on her pants and jammed her feet into flats. She was halfway out the door when I said, "Where are you going?"

"My parents live in Northgate. I want to see them before it ends."

"Lisa—"

She waited.

I lifted my empty hands. "I'm sorry."

"Goodbye, professor."

I stood there in shock. Then I forced myself to move, to go after her. We might still survive this. At the least I could help her reach her parents. I ran into the hall. She was just turning the corner for the stairs. Another violent jolt hit the building. I bounced off the wall like a pinball. The lights flickered out and plaster dust sifted from the ceiling. I rubbed it out of my eyes. Lisa was gone. It was my fault. Completing the equation was what my mind had been designed to do. When Whitfield handed me the paper the solution was as good as accomplished. Because I had to keep proving to myself that I really was the genius I continually told myself I didn't want to be.

I staggered out of the building. The air was thick with that brine-and-death stink of the Masters. I stood on the sidewalk, looking for Lisa. She didn't own a car. It was mad to think she could make it to Northgate alone on foot, more than ten miles through a devastated urban landscape. Smoke rose above the townhouses and apartment buildings. A woman screamed on the next block. Gunfire popped rapidly. I ran toward the sound.

A tunnel opened above the main intersection of Alaska and California. A cop stood before it, fumbling with his handgun, trying to reload. I saw Lisa. She cowered in the doorway of Cupcake Royale. A three-story brick facade loomed above her. A Master emerged from the tunnel, its pink and black tentacles flailing excitedly. One seized the cop in a boa-coil grip. His gun clattered to the street. The Master lofted him into the air, shook him violently, and dashed him down, his head bursting like a melon. The Master unleashed a piercing ululation, something between a siren and a wolf howl. Other Masters came humping out of the tunnel. One casually whipped a tentacle as thick as a fire hose into the face of the building Lisa cowered against. I yelled "No!" as the bricks tumbled in a deafening avalanche that buried her. One naked foot extended from the rubble, hazed in cloud of masonry dust.

My throat burned. I couldn't breathe. The flight response fluttered in my chest. But it wasn't self-preservation, escape from the Masters. I simply couldn't absorb what I'd done, my responsibility for the whole mess. I took a step toward Lisa, as if I could do anything for her, and the ground seemed to fall away. Not a crack in the pavement but that elevator-drop feeling of a side-slip across worlds.

And found myself on California Avenue pushing a shopping cart loaded with hobo possessions (musty cloth sleeping bag; a collection of empty soda cans rattling tinnily against the cart's wire frame; a lamp shade pointlessly salvaged out of the garbage, and, most importantly, a broken guitar). My alcohol-saturated brain seethed with numbers. In this iteration I was a drunk, and a madman, and, once again, a mathematical savant, albeit who had no knowledge of the Whitfield equation.

But I remembered. And I remembered what I owed.

Night fell. I drew the guitar from my shopping cart. On the headstock, faded and chipped gold letters spelled YAMAHA. The high e string was missing, and a ragged hole gaped in the body, where someone had put their boot through it.

I arranged myself in the doorway of Cupcake Royale, the spot where, in another world, Lisa had died, and began fingering the strings of the Yamaha. A few people dropped coins into my Starbucks begging cup. Notes picked on the remaining five strings of the guitar teased order from the maelstrom inside my head. I listened for Whitfield's equation and finally began to see it. A long string of numbers and symbols unwound before my interior vision. Now that I'd recovered the equation that had opened the door to the Masters, what incantatory solution sealed it shut again?

Someone kicked the bottom of my shoe. I opened my eyes and blinked at Daniel Whitfield. He stood over me, still wearing his camel hair coat and ear-flapped duck-hunting hat. A cigarette jutted from his lips. He removed it.

"We meet again," Whitfield said.

"Keep away from me," I said. My fingers continued to pick significant patterns up and down the fretboard. I was close.

"Stop that and pay attention." Whitfield yanked the guitar out of my hands.

"Don't—"

"I'm sorry, Professor Dunn, but you suck on this thing."

The closing equation was right there, its completion just out of sight. I needed my strings. But when I started to get up and reach for the guitar, Whitfield easily shoved me down.

"Let's wait for the Masters together, shall we, professor?"

"I don't understand why you want them," I said.

He spread his hands. Ash dropped from the tip of his cigarette into my begging cup. "I am a humble servant of the New Order."

On cue, a tunnel drilled open behind him. Shortly the involuntary mechanism buried within me would side-slip me to another bubble. If I lost my genius again it would be a meaningless reprieve. And I was so close to solving the closing equation.

I got on my feet and fought Whitfield for the guitar. He laughed. "You're just a pathetic drunk." He pushed me away, took the Yamaha by the neck with both hands, and swung it at the sidewalk. The body burst apart with an outraged twang of strings and crack of wood. He dropped the pieces.

The stink of brine and corruption rolled out of the tunnel. I thought, madly enough, *One equation to rule them all*. But the closing equation wasn't to rule anything. All I wanted was to shut the door. I had momentum. Maybe I could finish it without the guitar. A ballpoint pen stuck out of Whitfield's outside breast pocket. I grabbed it, then with both hands I shoved Whitfield in the chest, knocking him backwards into the tunnel. His surprised cry skirled away as if down a well. I turned and hunkered in the doorway. No paper, so I ripped my shirt sleeve open, clicked the pen, and began printing out the closing equation on the inside of my forearm. I'd had most of it before Whitfield ripped the guitar out of my hands. Now came the rest in a smeary blue intaglio. Something fluttered in my chest, and I fought against the flight response. The brine-and-death stink became overpowering.

A chain of numbers and mathematical symbols stretched from the crux of my elbow to the branching blue veins at my wrist. A tentacle slipped around my ribs, coiled tight, and jerked me off my feet even as I completed the final expression. My ribs snapped like branches. Blood gurgled up my throat . . . and then I felt the elevator drop. The unbearable pressure ceased. Briefly, I hovered in the dark, the closing equation repeating across my mind.

And like *that*, it was over.

The kid in the duck-hunting hat reached across my desk with a folded sheet of yellow graph paper in his fingers. "I think you will find this interesting."

I ignored the paper and looked into Daniel Whitfield's eyes. "Thank you, Mr. Whitfield. I did."

A deep vertical crease appeared between his eyes. I finished packing my briefcase and closed it, smartly snapping the latches. Whitfield placed the paper on my desk blotter.

"This is intended for you."

"Of course it is. Meanwhile, I'm late for class."

Whitfield stood up and walked out of my office. I waited a minute, then picked up the paper, unfolded it without looking directly at what was written on it, and fed the thing into my document shredder.

In the hall, I pulled the door shut behind me, giving the knob a brisk shake to make sure it was securely locked. Then I headed not to class but to the Dean's office.

I had to know how much Lisa remembered.

Mine, Yours, Ours

They wanted a piece of her body.

Emily was collating tax documents for a client when an urgent alert flashed red in her Corneal Window where, like so many things, it was impossible to ignore: an exclamation point in the shape of a stylized caduceus with the letters I.O.E beneath it.

Emily's heart fluttered and her breathing went shallow with anxiety. She pushed back from the workstation. Regardless of her exaggerated anxiety level, as Dr. Schafer called it, the alert from I.O.E. triggered an anxiety *spike*. How foolish she had been ever to submit her profile.

She wouldn't be able to resume work until she responded. Emily closed her eyes. It flashed in the dark.

"Emily?"

She looked up. Sindhu Mahre, the department head, stood behind her. "Are you all right."

"I—I have to go home."

"What's wrong?"

"It's illness. In the family. My mother."

"Oh, I'm sorry. Is it serious?"

"Yes."

Hypertrophic cardiomyopathy killed Emily's mother, but that was long ago. A transplant organ might have saved her. Emily never forgot her mother's sudden absence, never forgot the empty body, a *thing* under the hospital sheet, not her mother but all that remained. Now it was Emily's genetic inheritance, a terror that *might* happen, even if it probably wouldn't.

"I'll log you out on Family Leave," Sindhu said, being kind.

"Thank you."

Emily had joined the I.O.E. to alleviate her "irrational fear," as Dr. Schafer described it. *Irrational but altogether genuine—one* of his stock phrases. *His* solution was the anxiolytic, Nardil. "A mild one, Emily. It leaves you in charge, just better able to relax a bit. Evaluate." When she declined, the prescription processed through anyway and appeared in her mailbox. Angry, she threw it in the kitchen cupboard, where she kept her vitamins.

Of course, Dr. Schafer did not approve of her joining I.O.E. But Emily was an adult, regardless of her anxiety assessments. Should she require a heart transplant, the International Organ Exchange would guarantee a donor. *Guarantee* she not become, like her mother, a thing under white hospital sheets in a room where the machines had stopped. But that guarantee required Emily to be a donor of at least one organ, should a recipient in need be a convenient match—a somewhat less remote possibility than Emily's heart failure. Two terrifying prospects . . .

. . . and now the second one was happening. She could hear Dr. Schafer telling her, *You shouldn't have joined I.O.E, not in your state of mind.*

But she had. And Emily never imagined her call to donate would arise so soon.

The alert continued to flash as Emily made her way home on the rail. She could not disable it without severing everything else, friends, news feeds, all the world that came through her Window: Jenny's cat danced on one foot; Treva was outraged about Sudan (and everything else, it seemed); David had a weird dream; ten things you didn't know about drones; blink-link this quiz! The International Organ Exchange planted a red alert in the middle of all that.

Safe in her apartment, Emily removed her CW lenses. Immediately she activated the vapor screen in her nook by the kitchen. Jewel light projectors twinkled. An Aladdin's plume of digital smoke resolved into her feed—and here was the alert again, urgent, red, stabbing. But also friends, information, the world outside her head and beyond her walls.

Emily turned away and made a cheese sandwich. Simply knowing her feed was running—that soothed her. The same way her I.O.E. contract had comforted her the moment she submitted her signature. But when she turned back to the vapor screen, there was only the insistent, pulsing red caduceus. Emily whimpered, a sound she almost didn't recognize as coming from her own throat. She tossed the butter knife into the sink, the sharp metal-on-metal clatter like the externalization of her impatience. "All right, all right."

She sat down and stirred her finger under the alert, which promptly vanished, replaced by the blue I.O.E. logo ringed by images of happy people around the globe exchanging toothy smiles with white-coated surgeons. A male voice spoke to Emily in a business-like tone.

"Good day, neighbor Emily Vega."

Emily didn't bother replying, since it was impossible to tell whether the voice was human, recorded, or contrived by machines. *Identify what you are*, she wanted to say, but even that seemed a burden of inquiry she shouldn't be pressured to make.

After a pause, the voice continued. "Emily Vega, are you there?"

She sighed. It could still be a machine. "I'm here, yes. What is it you need from me?"

"Your right lung for transplantation."

Alvaro Samano's pulmonary fibrosis was no fault of his own. The agent from the Exchange made sure Emily understood that, but she didn't care, it didn't matter. "Alvaro's condition is idiopathic." the agent said, as if to assure Emily that Alvaro was *deserving* of the violation about to be inflicted upon Emily's body.

Emily smiled tightly. All she could think about was the operating table, like a slab on which they would lay her out and deprive her of consciousness, deprive her of identity while they cut her. Oh, she had reviewed all the details of the procedure. She was required to review them. "I don't need to know about that," Emily said, meaning Alvaro's innocence and the grisly details of surgically removing her lung.

"I.O.E. pledges full transparency."

Thank you, no.

Alvaro Samano was twenty-seven years old, married, a father, a participating member of society—fully invested in the social contract, Emily supposed, like her former classmates, like her co-workers. Not that she ever craved that sort of inclusion. She had her life, a perfectly valid life, with routines and privacy into which she did not want to invite strangers, be they neighbors or otherwise. Another catchphrase. *You depend on your neighbors, so your neighbors can depend on you!*

"I wonder," Emily said to the young woman in the business suit who had just told her about the pledge of transparency, who had just provided, unasked for, a biographical and exculpatory sketch of Alvaro Samano. "I wonder if a delay is possible."

"A delay?"

"A postponement, I mean. Of the surgery."

The interviewer turned her empty hands palm up and smiled understandingly. "It's normal to be anxious."

Tell that to Dr. Schafer. Emily said, "You see, I never—"

"And I'm certain you can appreciate Alvaro's own anxiety."

"Of course."

"Participating in the International Organ Exchange is a cooperative investment in humanity, and I think it's wonderful that you've joined us."

"Yes, yes." Emily looked at her knees. "But. . ."

"But?"

"Is it, I mean—the urgency. Is the urgency necessary?"

It was.

Emily arranged for leave from her position at Moss-Waters LLP. They were very understanding. Sindhu congratulated Emily on her worthy participation in a vital program. "I'm so glad your mother is better, and now you're doing your part for a neighbor." Emily cringed inwardly, the lie rebounding in her face. One lie always led to another. Better to say nothing at all. Sindhu arranged the time off without depleting Emily's earned vacation days. "You'll be back in no time, the way these procedures are performed now. And you get a booster implant for your one good lung. Too bad the booster can't operate alone. Anyway, it's barely more than an office visit. My sister . . ."

*

Emily presented herself at Swedish Hospital the evening before the transplantation procedure. She believed she could do it,
fulfill her requirement. But a lung, it was serious. A contribution
that would restore quality of life to a stranger named Alvaro Samano. At least that's all the Exchange would ask of her. She had
merely to endure it, and then a heart would be available if and
when she required it. A heart was the most serious thing of all.
Others in the Exchange, whose demands were less grave, were not
required to offer up a selection from their living bodies.

When the nurse and the I.O.E. rep came into Emily's room to
go over preparations, on her last night with two complete lungs,
she said, "It's funny to be doing this for a stranger."

"But Alvaro isn't a stranger," the Exchange woman said, and
the unspoken but fully understood and agreed upon addendum
attached: *No one is.* The world is now a village. Emily had never
believed that. Did that make her so odd? She had her feed, enclosed within her chosen privacy. What more did they want of her?

"Of course not." Emily tried to smile.

"He's your neighbor."

"I know."

Information, questions, answers, assurances—and good luck.
Then they left her alone. Emily lay on the hospital bed under
tightly stretched sheets. On the slab, hovering, it seemed, over
the same abyss that had swallowed her mother's light. Her fear
was irrational, Dr. Schafer would have told her. Emily *knew* that.
Couldn't she be allowed her irrationalities? She wanted her mother to come and tell her it was all right, she wanted to be held. So
foolish, a grown woman wanting her mother's comfort. But Emily
hadn't anyone, no family, her friends existent only on her feed.
She didn't even allow herself a pet.

In the hospital bed, Emily reached for her hand-held device, a
slim keyboard no bigger than her palm. She thumbed a post, and
her words appeared in her CW, bracketed by a flow of information.

—you'll never guess where I am—

When responses began to appear, Emily hesitated. She didn't
want to tell them.

—i'm on vacation is all—

—oh where—

—that's my secret / someplace warm and happy and wonderful i can tell you—

—wonderful—

—fantastic emily—

Of course anyone who actually investigated . . . who unleashed a curiosity worm into the mesh . . . could find out the
truth, where Emily was at this moment. What was going on. The
fact that no one even cared enough to poke at her privacy façade,
well, it hurt a little, even though it was the life she chose.

*I have friends, but superficial ones. Sociable, but at arm's
length. The sort of friend I am, to others.*

Alvaro *was* a stranger. They all were. Of course, I.O.E wanted
her to meet Alvaro, and of course she declined. She was meeting
her responsibility, that would have to be sufficient. She refused
even to view an image of the man. Let him remain nothing to
her. That way she could direct her fear and resentment toward an
abstraction, rather than a man. Alvaro, the abstraction, of course
knew all about Emily.

In I.O.E. you exchanged more than organs. All the world
was like that. Each level of participation in community, in convenience, demanded you surrender a larger portion of your identity. Was it any different than trading a piece of your body for the
assurance you would continue to exist? Everyone remembered,
or was supposed to remember, the bad times, the times when
unidentified voices wielded disproportionate social leverage. The
enemy had long been identified, and its name was anonymity.

Now there were no deep secrets, only the slim privacy that
citizens gave each other out of courtesy. That seemed to suffice,
for most—a "village" of reciprocal respect. But Emily looked
back, with longing, at those vast, anonymous cities of old, where
you might live forever a stranger, and possibly die alone, but it
was no one's business.

And yet . . . no one forced you to sign the I.O.E. contract, she
chided. *You made your own body part of the village.*

Emily folded her hands over her keypad device, over her
chest, and closed her eyes. The illuminated feed scrolled against
the screen of her eyelids. In a corner, time rolled over, and Emily felt a weight upon her chest. She opened her eyes, her focus
adjusting beyond the feed to the antiseptic details of her hospital

room. She could hardly breathe, the weight was so tremendous.

Emily peeled back the covers before she even knew she was going to do it. She found her clothes in the closet and quickly dressed, afraid someone would interrupt her. As each layer of clothing covered more flesh, her anxiety subsided. No one accosted her on her way out. She had a right to not be there, after all. Or maybe no one noticed. In her life, people frequently failed to notice Emily.

Emily was eating lunch outdoors, holding the cheese-and-onion sandwich between the fingers of both hands, taking small bites. It was such a nice spring afternoon. She sat on a stone bench in the urban park between the building containing the offices of Moss-Waters LLC and two other office towers. The small green leaves of decorative trees flickered in the breeze. Then a man's shadow appeared on the pavement, and Emily looked up. The man was young and well-dressed, wearing a tie. He was also wearing a stylish pair of Window glasses. Some people didn't like the corneal lenses.

"Hello," he said.

"I'm sorry, do I know you?"

"I'm Alvaro Samano's brother. My name is Thiago."

Emily nodded, waiting for words.

"May I speak with you?" Thiago said.

"I suppose so, but I'm not changing my mind."

He waved her objection aside. "Another donor has already been selected."

"Good."

"Your canceling, it wasn't right. It was unconscionable, and that's putting it charitably."

"But it worked out." Emily's voice was as small as she felt.

The man stared her, like he was staring at a strange bug he'd discovered in his garden. Emily looked at her sandwich, which she couldn't imagine finishing. She said, "It's just, at the last minute I couldn't go through with it. I wanted to, but it wasn't a choice. It didn't feel like one, I mean. I don't expect that to matter to you or your brother. For whatever it's worth, I've been punished."

"Expulsion from the Exchange, yes."

Of course, everybody knew everything. It didn't take a curiosity worm to find out about a major broken promise. A village sin.

"I can't blame them," she said. Sometimes Emily thought that without secrets a person wasn't really herself but simply what her neighbors thought she was, vocalized she was. Alvaro's brother was still standing there, staring at her from behind his Window glasses in that strange, almost predatory way, so she asked, "Is there something else?"

"Alvaro was very upset. You should know that. He's not as strong as some people. He's frightened, and will be until the operation is over."

"I can understand."

"Oh, can you? You never met, since you wouldn't allow him that courtesy, but for Alvaro it felt like he'd gotten to know you. And then for you, a neighbor, to disappoint him like that."

"I'm sorry." *But he doesn't know me and neither do you.*

"I have upset you?"

"I'm not upset." She was, though. And now she was distracted by a post on her private feed:

—em, did you really duck out on that guy like they're saying—

"Goodbye, then," Thiago said, but she wasn't listening. Messages had begun to cascade down her feed.

—that poor man—

—i heard he died—

—my god em by now aren't you even an adult—

Emily's feed was *clotted* with messages from critical strangers. They overwhelmed her friends, until her friends became strangers themselves.

—is it true you did that—

Emily was relieved to return to her cubicle, where she surrendered her CW lenses to the orderly, impersonal repetitiveness of assembling tax documents.

At five o'clock it was time to stop. She had hopes that *it* would be over. Hesitantly, she switched back to her private feed, and the onslaught resumed. Emily discovered, to her horror, that she was *trending*. Her perfidy was trending. Was she the first person ever to withdraw from the International Organ Exchange, for goodness sake? Hadn't her neighbors anything better to talk about?

Again, a tremendous weight of anxiety pressed upon Emily's chest. Her lungs, *her* lungs, labored for breath.

We all breathe the same air, was the ubiquitous slogan, suggesting the planet's atmosphere was the common ocean in which they all swam, all the world's neighbors. The shared pride of nine billion souls who—as a village—worked together to repair the atmosphere, the seas, the land. A better world, for the most part . . . *but not for people like me.*

"I do my own breathing, thank you," Emily sometimes said, alone and unheard in her apartment, listening to the phrase in her mind, or out of her feed, sometimes unable to make a distinction between the auditory memory and the streaming admonition.

She stumbled to the rail station. Thiago Amano tagged her in a post that blink-linked to a video loop recorded from his Window glasses. The clip showed Emily sitting on her bench with her sandwich held delicately between the fingers of both hands: ". . . I'm not changing my mind . . . I'm not changing my mind . . ."

—so callous—

—honestly em—

—never really knew you I guess—

That was true. No one really knew her. Why did they think they had to? The flood of critical comments created tributaries off the main topic, surging with uninformed opinions. At home, unable to stop looking, Emily witnessed the final indignity: Dr. Schafer's self-interview on the general subject of mood and anxiety disorders, intended, he said, as a public service. Though he never mentioned her by name, Dr. Schafer's tag represented him as Emily Vega's Personal Therapist. Of course, that's what guaranteed a million blink-links.

Emily interrupted the feed and removed her Window lenses, popping them out like coins into a beggar's cupped hand. What was she begging for, except to be left alone?

A month passed. Emily wore her CWs at work and removed them immediately afterwards. Poison ran through her feed and she never looked at it anymore. She could not create another. Each individual was allowed one identity, their own true name.

Everything attached to it, flowed to it. What if she read what the poisoners said about her and become what they believed she was?

But what she never expected—the thing that hurt the most—was pity. The latest wave to crest across her feed. Generous villagers, grownups, expressing charity, chiding the chiders.

—leave her alone, can't you see she's not all there?—

—look, she's refused to take even mild anxiolytics. That's dumb, but it's part of the syndrome, clinging to depression like an addict—

—did you watch that compilation about her mother? How sad! You bullies better back off, or we can look closer at YOU—

Trend lines shifted. The decent villagers were winning . . . and their pity hurt worse than anything, hurling Emily even deeper into a pit.

She rumbled home on the rail, one among her neighbors, in the middle of the world but separated from it. The train rocked and swayed. Faces stared under jaundiced light, eyes seeing what she did not see, their feeds active. A young man in a black sweater sat on the seat across the aisle, watching her—*her*, not his feed. Emily couldn't interpret his expression. But Emily never could interpret expressions, the nuances, could never complete the translation, never answer the question: *what is he thinking?* This man appeared unhealthy, too thin, weak, taking shallow, consciously measured breathes.

Her stop slid into place outside the train and halted. The doors opened. Emily stood up. The man's gaze followed her. What did he imagine he knew about her? "Yes," Emily said as she passed him, "I'm that awful, awful person. Doesn't that make you happy?"

"I don't think you're awful. I'm—"

But she stepped onto the platform and quickly walked along the body of the train, back toward the stairs to the street level. The train hummed out of the station. Following after it, a hot breath of air adjusted Emily's blouse, flipped her bangs—a mother's invisible hand fussing with her appearance.

Behind her, someone wheezed, "Slow down, please wait."

Emily looked back. The sickly man in the black sweater was walking toward her, breathing with difficulty, something in his hand. Of course she knew who he was. He and his brother looked very much alike. Did it mean there was nothing she could do, no separation she could effect? Was this the beginning, would they now follow her out of her feed and into the real world of her everyday aloneness? If true, she couldn't bear it. Emily fled up the stairs and home to her apartment.

She stood in her kitchen, the Nardil container in her hand. Why hadn't she returned the pills to Dr. Schafer, as she had intended, or thrown them away? "Why don't I ever know which is what?" Emily asked the empty room. Maybe she *did* know. Hadn't she read somewhere, a blink-link off her feed, about the idea that conscious decisions were illusions and all one's true decisions formulated under the surface, where something that was you but not *you* sorted reality? What if the not-you was part of a lot of other not-yous inhabiting the unconscious, and so it was your *neighbors* all over again, a community, or a mob—and a mob of Emilys within, the cavewoman, the terrified child, the pre-sapient animal, the mourning daughter—and *they* had all decided that, yes, keep the Nardil and by all means use it.

By all means *take* it. Take all of it.

When she had said no to the prescription, Dr. Schafer told her she might want it, if not today, then someday. "Pay attention to the dosage," he had said. Dr. Schafer's risk assessment, his evaluation and session notes, were available to the greater medical establishment. Key words flagged, authorizing deeper investigation of risk factors, "harm to oneself or others," the details of her treatment *collated* like so many 1040s, itemized deduction declarations, and W-2s. Finally, a human assessor, not unlike Dr. Schafer himself, reviewed the information (if a human ever did review it) and directed the prescription be filled "in the interests of the individual and the society at large," as they liked to put it. At least no one would make her actually *swallow* the Nardil; that was up to Emily.

She struggled with the cap, scattering pills across the counter like seeds. Twenty seeds for her eternal garden. Emily stared at the pills, her breathing gone shallow with dread, her lungs ready to betray her, as she had betrayed Alvaro before everyone turned on her.

A musical tone sounded through the apartment—someone pressing the button next to her name outside the building's lobby door. The chimes sounded again, like a prod, like a finger poking her shoulder. Was she supposed to *let* them decide for her?

Angry, Emily swept the pills into the sink and washed them down the drain.

On the screen in the living room the man in the black sweater gazed back at her. "Hello?" he said, sounding out of breath. "Emily Vega?"

She didn't expect to reply, but apparently the words had already been selected. She managed to twist them to her advantage even as they blurted past her lips. "It didn't work. I washed them all down the drain. All of them."

"I don't understand."

"Of course you don't."

"You left your keypad on the train."

"My—?"

He held up something that might have been Emily's device, though it was hard to tell, just as it was hard to tell whether this man was Alvaro Samano, though she had been positive, or nearly positive, only minutes ago. She checked her pockets, looked around the room, but didn't see her keypad. "I'm coming down."

The man in the black sweater stood on the porch outside her building. Emily opened the door as he was triggering a medical inhaler into his mouth. He put it back in his pocket, looking sheepish. "Asthma," he said.

"You're not who I thought you were."

"I couldn't catch up to you, and you didn't respond to messages. I guess you couldn't without this." He held out her device. "I knew who you were, so I searched your address and routed it. My name's Caleb."

Emily accepted the device and turned it over in her hands.

The neighbor in the black sweater, Caleb, frowned. "I'm sorry, did I interrupt something?"

"No, you didn't interrupt anything. I did."

He looked puzzled. There were so many of them in the world, so many puzzled people. They flailed at each other, told each other who they thought they were supposed to be, every interaction a validating performance entangled in a safety net of crisscrossing feeds, not even suspecting they had fallen off the high-wire, or were afraid to climb for it in the first place. But not Emily, finally not Emily. She was alone, balancing across the sky, where you had to be a little crazy.

She preferred it that way, didn't she? Preferred to be alone?

Later she found the Nardil, one capsule that hadn't gone down the drain. She held it in the palm of her hand, and asked herself the question again.

ASSASSINS

with BURT COURTIER

I t will be a particularly brutal kill, even by her standards.

She sat in warm shade at an outdoor café along the Calle de las Huertes, not far from the Prado Museum. Sonia needed to work in public spaces, needed to witness the human cost. Tourists, students, illegals and the unemployed crowded the surrounding tables—all strangers. But that was nothing new. She could touch them only by wounding them, as she had been wounded. What would millions of Experiencers think if they knew a coward lurked behind Simone The Slayer?

Black-shirted waiters circulated between the tables. A few feet away a woman in a white sundress laughed. About thirty years old, she wore Experiencer glasses, the lenses polarized for the sun, and a headscarf. The bearded young man sharing her table kissed her neck playfully, and she laughed again. Of the hundred or so people visible to Sonia, maybe two-thirds of them wore Experiencer glasses, and many of them were fully immersed, the lenses gone a dully-reflective silver, like drawing a screen between the outer world and *Labyrinthiad*. Holding hands, an older couple in matching tropical shirts strolled out of the umbrella shade of the cafe and crossed the sun-struck plaza. Pigeons swooped and plunged, their black shadows gliding over the bricks. Motorbikes threaded through the moving crowds, their two-stroke engines making a lawn-mower racket.

"Hasta luego." It was the bearded man. He stood up and blew a kiss at the woman in the white sundress. She laughed and waved at him, like she was brushing off a fly. Walking backwards from their table, he bumped into Sonia. She jerked away. "Perdón," he said, turning and bowing. She scowled at him; Sonia didn't like to be touched. He shrugged and left her alone. His girlfriend touched the right temple of her Experiencer glasses. The lenses turned silver. Sonia looked away.

It was time.

Sonia placed her Cube next to her napkin, leaned forward and whispered the unlocking code. Glowing symbols floated above the table. Her long fingers made slight, almost imperceptible motions as she manipulated content, combining and recombining intricate patterns. The military-grade throat mic picked up her sub-vocal directions and voiceovers. Sonia's custom software reshaped her tonal qualities to create her character's signature voice—a voice that had insinuated itself into a million nightmares. Simone.

It was ready.

Sonia reached for her neglected macchiato. She sipped, absently licked bitter foam from her lips, set the cup down. Taking a pause. Virtual murder was still murder—the murder of emotional attachments. She ought to know. Sonia had cherished the character Emi Nakano, until the Editors discontinued Emi's existence on the grounds of inadequate popularity scores. When Emi suffered death by Editor, something died in Sonia, too. Now she felt connected only to the pain she caused. Maybe she had replaced her Emi Nakano obsession with her own meta assassin—but so what? Call it the failed transfiguration of revenge.

All right.

She uploaded her data to a rendering engine that converted her C-sym programming into a finished scene. A final hesitant pause . . . and she slipped the module undetected into the vast meta story that was *Labyrinthiad*. Like slipping a dagger between ribs to pierce the heart of a created world. In a moment, Ellis Ng would "die." Was Sonia the only one who recognized Ellis as nothing more than an emotional trap for the self-deluded?

Sonia's hands shook as she reached for her coffee. She emptied the cup and set it down. A cigarette would have helped her nerves, but they were banned now even in Europe.

Mileva Kosich, sitting on a bench across from the Office of Public Affairs, eye-flicked behind her Experiencer glasses. It was her lunch-break and she just had time to meet her virtual friend, Ellis Ng. Belgrade disappeared, and Mileva was gliding in a sun-

boat over a crystal blue pond. Ellis approached in his own sunboat, its solar net billowing like a gossamer shell. Of course, Ellis was legion, and millions of Experiencers considered him a friend, but that didn't undercut Mileva's joy at the sight of his approach. Everyone enjoyed their own personal Ellis. He stood up and waved with two fingers extended (his customary greeting), making the boat rock. A black-winged personal flying suit swept down out of the empty sky. Mileva caught her breath. Simone! The assassin fired a projectile and Ellis Ng's sunboat exploded in a plume of flesh and fiberglass. Shocked, Mileva fumbled her glasses off. She sat on the bench, too upset to move.

Sonia killed only the popular characters. Five so far. And once slain, they resisted the Editor's attempts to resurrect them. Sonia's killing routines remained with a character and haunted them even in virtual death. The resurrected were lifeless zombies compared to their former selves. Their popularity, as defined continuously by the Experiencers, plummeted and they were quickly edited out. Of course, "life" in *Labyrinthiad* was an oxymoron, perpetuated by the mock-divine spark of rudimentary AI. Characters like Ng became the perfect companions because they analyzed your personality and speech and fed you tailor-made conversation. Nevertheless, waves of real despair followed the death of young eCelebs. Taking down beloved characters and the income streams they represented to the Publishers was dangerous. Real world dangerous.

Hachiro Jin, closed inside an egg-shaped Sleep Pod in the Helsinki Airport, touched the temple of his glasses and went full-immersion. It would be pleasant to pass a few minutes with Ellis Ng. The virtue of a virtual friend was availability without complications. Hachiro's layover was four hours, more than enough time to catch up on sleep and conversation with a friend who seemed perfectly to understand the worries of a forty-three-year-old businessman. Ellis, waiting for Hachiro on a red footbridge in the Sankeien Gardens, smiled and raised his hand—and then collapsed, a shaft protruding from the back of his head. Simone The Slayer stood a moment in his place. "Gomen-nasai, Hachiro-kun," she said, flashing a lifeless smile before flickering out of existence. In the Sleep Pod, Hachiro ripped off his glasses, swearing.

Sonia waited for the reaction. Any moment now. Then a waiter stepped in front of her, blocking her view. He bent forward, reaching for her empty cup, his eyes a turquoise gleam. Just like the eyes of Sonia's character-killer, Simone. So many people affected body modifications that emulated favorite *Labyrinthiad* personalities. This waiter had even added Simone's signature scar, like a back-slash setting off the corner of his mouth.

"Would you like something else?" he asked.

"No."

Annoyingly, he lingered, staring into her with his faux-Simone eyes. Sonia squirmed in her seat. Hadn't she seen this man before, on the sidewalk near her apartment? Was he even a waiter? His shirt didn't exactly match the other waiters' shirts.

She forced herself to return his stare. "What do you want?"

The waiter grinned, said, "Stay as long as you like," and walked away, leaving her empty cup on another table.

Juanita Torres' physical body reclined in the passenger seat of her self-driving Elon IV. The car negotiated Chicago traffic on its way to the law offices of Ferguson & Torres. Behind her Experiencer glasses Juanita had eye-flicked herself to a virtual tent pitched in the high desert of New Mexico, where she lay quietly with Ellis. Sometimes Juanita simply needed to be alone with her friend, without words. It was a meditation, a stress-reliever. A timer would call her back to the car when they approached the office. Beyond the open tent flap pink and yellow layers of sunrise set off the jagged line of the Sangre de Christo Mountains. Then a figure appeared, blocking the view. Simone The Slayer in a panther-black body suit ducked into the tent, expertly wound a shiny garroting wire around Ellis Ng's neck and snapped it taut. Blood sheeted over Juanita, splattered the tent fabric, making a sound like rain. Juanita slapped her Experiencer glasses off and sat up in the car, screaming. Simone's muffled laughter drifted up from the floorboards near her feet.

*

A collective shudder swept through the café and across the open plaza. Random people stumbled to a stop. Sonia winced, feeling their pain—her connection to other people. What would she be without this shared suffering? She wasn't brave enough to find out. She had never been brave enough. The pain she caused was her only tie to others.

The woman in the white sundress and headscarf a few tables away began weeping, her shoulders visibly shaking, and then slammed her glasses hard on the tabletop, even as others hastily donned theirs. Sonia's segment was loose in *Labyrinthiad*. You could *feel* it. Like a sudden pressure drop before a coming storm.

Only one man failed to react.

At a table across the open café space, his Experiencer glasses parked on top of his bald head, he never took his eyes off Sonia. A broad, stocky man in a dark blue collarless over-shirt. Two University girls, awkwardly holding each other in grief, crossed in front of him. When Sonia could see again, the table was empty.

Quickly, Sonia pocketed her Cube and dropped five euros on the table. She stood, rattling her chair back, and walked quickly away from the café.

She cut through a narrow cobblestone alley, intending to double back and make her way to the Arguelles neighborhood. There she kept a safe room unconnected to her Sonia Andrijeski identity—a name with shallow roots. In Arguelles she would hide in the camouflage of rowdy students and jangling nightlife.

The yellow walls of the alley loomed over her. Dead vines trailed from boxes under shuttered windows. Sonia quickened her pace, and then stopped, gasping, when the bald man stepped around the corner and stood in her way. She scuffed back, glanced over her shoulder. She could run but he would easily catch her. They both knew it. He grinned.

"For an assassin," he said, "you're a mousy thing."

She retreated another step, and he moved toward her. A little dance.

"I'll scream," she said.

"You won't."

A pink cloud boiled out of a device in his hand. Sonia heard herself cough, as if the cough were un-synced with her collapse. The cobblestones came up and slammed her shoulder. The bald man stood over her. He tucked his device away, started to bend down. The sound of a motor ripped into the alley. She seemed to hear it after the bald man had already turned in reaction—Sonia's pink cloud reality.

The bald man fell, his body landing next to Sonia with a sickening and off-timed thud. She blinked heavy lids. A red puddle oozed away from the fallen man and began investigating the channels between cobble stones. Sonia managed to push herself back before it touched her. She looked up. A man holding a gun dismounted a blue Vespa and approached her. The waiter from the café, the one with Simone-The-Slayer's eyes and scar. He tucked his gun into his waistband, pulled his shirt over it, and hunkered next to her.

"He would have taken you back to the States," the waiter said, his words almost-but-not-quite in sync with his lips. "But I don't take people back." He shrugged. "Private contractors, right? Some are more full service than others."

Sonia squinted, trying to interpret what he'd said as anything other than an obvious threat. She struggled to get up. The waiter watched her, like he was watching a representative of an unrelated species. A true killer's coldness reflected in a virtual killer's eyes. God, he was a *fan*. Sonia grasped at self-control. Her voice barely broke when she said, "Don't hurt me, please."

He pressed his hand to his chest, as if he couldn't believe what she was suggesting. "I would never. I admire you too much. At least, I admire Simone. Professional respect crosses worlds." He reached out quickly and picked something up. Her cube. Sonia's hand twitched involuntarily. And the gun was back in the waiter's hand and leveled at her.

"I'll make you a deal," he said. "Give me your key, promise to never upload to *Labyrinthiad* again, and you can go."

"What?"

"I've been watching you for days. I could've taken you out any time. Giving you a chance to walk away, that's me showing respect for what you created." He held the cube up. It contained Simone's unique code, all her untraceable killing routines. "Decide now."

Sonia tried to rub the fogginess out of her eyes. "You want to be *her*. Simone."

"The key. Deal or not?"

"What if I don't want to?"

"Then I hurt you."

Numbly, she recited the code.

The waiter held the cube in the palm of his hand. He voice-entered the code. The cube glowed blue, ghostware deploying raw content for manipulation. He stared avidly at the display—Simone The Slayer in utero—then turned the Cube off, pocketed it, and, without another word, walked away.

Never upload to *Labyrinthiad* again? Impossible. But without Simone to connect to the common suffering, who was she? What was her *purpose*?

The killer mounted his Vespa and zipped out of the alley, leaving Sonia standing next to the dead man. A trace of motor exhaust lingered. She cringed, alone and exposed, and stumbled back the way she'd come, her head throbbing. Soon she found herself in the anonymous safety of the crowded plaza, surrounded by people she could no longer hurt. Woozy, she stopped and covered her eyes. A wave of pink-cloud dizziness swept through her and she started to fall, barely catching herself. Someone took her arm, steadied her. Sonia stiffened.

"Are you all right?" It was the woman from the café, the one so upset by Simone's kill that she had slammed down her Experiencer glasses. Others stopped, concerned. *Is she sick? Give her some room.* A young man produced his phone. *Should I call for medical?*

Sonia shook her head. "No, don't."

The woman, still holding Sonia's arm, searched her face. "You're sure you're all right? You looked like you were going to faint."

"Just a little dizzy. I'll be okay."

"At least you ought to sit down. There's a table. I'll get you a glass of water. My name's Mia, by the way."

Why was she so kind? Why was anyone? After a too-long pause, Sonia said, "Thank you," and they sat at a table near the one from which Sonia had exploded an emotional bomb. A bomb that had wounded many people, including Mia and perhaps others who later paused out of concern, not knowing they were so-licitous of Simone's creator.

Sonia attempted a smile, "I'm not usually like this."

Mia stared back at her uncertainly. "Don't worry about it. I'm a bit of a mess myself. The Slayer struck again. Simone. That bitch."

Sonia picked up her lemon water, sipped, then held the cold, sweating glass in her hands. "Someone should take her down." Her words sounded odd to her, yet familiar. In a moment she re-alized: Simone.

Mia's eyes widened as she leaned back in her chair. "They . . . they've tried."

"Maybe it will be someone who knows her."

Sonia noted absently the sound of scrabbling chair legs on cobblestones. Standing now, backing away from the table, Mia said, "Nobody knows her."

Sonia nodded. Her head cleared. "Yes, of course. Nobody does."

THE SUM OF HER
EXPECTATIONS

Amrita stabilized the escape pod. Her hands were shaking; she had barely gotten out. The *Meghnad Saha*, a Class B planet surveyor she'd called home, retreated from the aft view screen, dropping rapidly from the orbital plane, pulled down by a force from the planet.

"Tripp?" Amrita said.

After a moment, a voice from the surveyor: "It doesn't appear I'm going to be able to stop this thing."

"You should have come with me in the pod."

"Hindsight. I'll keep trying. Here comes the blackout. Goodbye. Sorry . . ."

"Tripp?"

Nothing.

Amrita tracked the *Meghnad Saha* all the way to the surface. She tried repeatedly to resume contact but Tripp wouldn't answer. Transcyber Reactive Positronic Personality: Tripp, for short, and the only friend Amrita had, or wanted. If he survived the crash, she wasn't about to abandon him. She blinked tears away and began to configure her escape pod for decent.

The Kabbhan forbade landing on Trappist-1e, or even approaching the planet within a designated radius of three hundred thousand kilometers. Because the Kabbhan stargates had made interstellar travel possible for humans in the first place, everyone respected this single restriction. Everyone but Amrita, who was signatory to no such agreement.

A proximity alert began beeping in the escape pod. Amrita considered a quick burn for radical decent. Get down before anyone could stop her. But it was already too late.

The Kabbhan star cruiser emerged like a sperm whale from a shot glass. Above the planet's horizon an elongated node appeared, squeezed forth, and *popped*: the cruiser, bigger than anything Melville dreamed of, came alongside Amrita's two-seat escape pod in synchronous orbit one hundred and eighty kilometers above the planet's largest continental mass. Amrita put her nose to the viewport. A massive wall shut out the stars.

With the back of her hand she wiped sweat off her upper lip, and waited. Eventually, the alien spoke, via comlink—at least it appeared that way. The green comlink indicator blinked on Amrita's vaporware display, and she heard the expected transmission hiss. But she knew Kabbhan technology was not what it appeared to be. Even calling it technology was a mistake.

Earth ship. Prepare to receive Kabbhan personnel.

"What?"

Out of nowhere, a man appeared at her elbow, already strapped into the right seat. Amrita would have jumped out of her skin, if that were possible. Actually, it *was* possible; the Kabbhan had demonstrated as much by becoming the only known race to have achieved transphysical migration.

"Who the hell are you?" she demanded.

The man turned to her. "The sum of your expectations."

"I've heard that one before. You're a Kabbhan presentation?"

The Kabbhan probed minds to find materials with which to construct compatible presentations. A Kabbhanian presentation acted as a surrogate presence. No one had ever seen an actual Kabbhan and very few had seen their presentations. Those who *had* seen a presentation reported a disorienting experience. While the presentation existed only in the probed subject's mind, it activated all the necessary neural and sensory pathways to create an apparently physical manifestation. Apparent to the one being probed, at least. In short, the right seat was empty.

"You may regard me as Dad."

"Dad! I don't think so. Besides, you don't even look like him."

Not that Amrita remembered her father, her "dad," except as a degraded holo she'd discovered in a lockbox after her mother died. Among the few important documents still mandated to exist in physical form were scattered a handful of personal items, trinkets accumulated over a long life. Amrita used her thumbnail to pry open a silver locket stamped with an impression of Shiva—and *wham!* her father leaped out and stood flickering before her. She knew it was her father, because who else could it be? Old fashioned hololockets like this one had been romantic keepsakes when Amrita's mother was young, and she had only ever loved one man—as she frequently reiterated. In later years, after she found happiness with a microbiologist named Brenda on the colony world Deneb V1, she added: One was enough.

The holo had been that of a young man, handsome, after a predictable fashion. But there was a sly, cunning light in his eye that suggested a con man's motivations. *Eye*, not eyes. The holo's degradation had turned Amrita's young father into a puzzle of many missing pieces—including the piece with his right eye. A therapist had once suggested that Amrita had spent her life, unconsciously of course, searching for the missing pieces of dear old dad. It accounted for her lack of respect for rules and authority figures. Amrita responded: "You're joking, right?" She had been under court order to participate in ten therapeutic sessions. The court order came as a result of a juvenile misadventure involving a stolen moon skimmer and a high-speed chase across the Mare Serenitatis. Had she been eighteen instead of thirteen, the consequences would have been dire, not therapeutic. The "You're joking" remark had been in session number two. The next eight preceded unproductively.

This Kabbhan presentation didn't look anything like the holo. It was older, for one thing. A man of late middle age, with silver-streaked hair combed back in a pompadour, and wrinkles around his brown eyes.

"There is no error," he said.

"I hope you don't think you're going to stop me. Because I'm telling you right now, I *am* going down there to get my friend."

"Stopping you isn't my intention. I'm here to assure your survival. We Kabbhan feel a certain responsibility towards less evolved species endangered by our discarded artifacts, even though our warnings have been explicit. Shall we descend now? If you are prepared, of course."

"I'm prepared. *Dad.*"

Amrita manipulated vaporware toggles, like twiddling fingers in a particularly well-organized steam cloud. The pod altered orbital trajectory, and Trappist-1e's very large horizon became larger still. Amrita glanced at the rearview screen. The Kabbhan starship was gone, as if it had never been there. And it hadn't been. Like Dad, the ship had been the sum of Amrita's expectations, this time in regards to alien spacecraft. The Kabbhan thought that beings stuck in the physical required corresponding illusions. Maybe they were right.

Amrita's escape pod burned through the atmosphere at hypersonic speed. Curtains of fire fluttered across the ports, then blew away, revealing an expanse of salmon-colored twilight. It was midday on Trappist-1e and as bright as it ever got. Six more alphabet planets hung in the sky like a god's game of crescents and balls.

From altitude, the self-expanding megalopolis looked like a continent-covering *crust*, an eczema salted with glittering lights.

"What a sight," Amrita said.

Dad nodded. "When the last of us migrated out of the physical, the automated city-builders on this colony planet ran amok. That was more than a hundred Sol years ago, by your time measure."

"There's so *much*."

"Indeed. Construction has proceeded unchecked, consuming every available mineral resource, husking out the planet even as it gradually covers its surface with an abandoned-before-built city."

"What happens when the builders run out of land?"

"They continue into the sea, erecting piers and floating platforms on the surface, and submerged suburbs of pressure domes and interlinking tubular passageways. They can and do build anything."

Amrita banked the escape pod and dropped several thousand meters, slipping across the sky at dizzying speed. She felt it in her gut, the swoop of gravity-assisted acceleration. Dad sat placidly, watching out the port. As they drew nearer, details emerged from the crust. Towers, blocks, domes, heptagons, pyramids, complex ribbons of transportation infrastructure . . .

"There," Dad said.

A trench of smoldering destruction. Amrita slowed the pod's descent, swooped in close, and hovered. Machines, like giant stalk-legged spiders, swarmed the trench, collecting into piles the remains of shattered buildings. Energy beams fired from the spiders' underbellies. Brilliant flashes, like small nuclear detonations, burst upon Amrita's eyeballs. She looked away and spent a few seconds blinking the blue-white afterimages out of her eyes. When she looked back, the debris had been reduced to slag.

"The city-builders will digest the material," Dad said, "and recycle it into the construction matrix."

The builders, or nanoswarms, grew buildings from the ground up. Even now, the trench gradually filled with new growth, like an invisible surgeon knitting a wound.

Amrita flew her pod over the trench. At the end of it lay the *Meghnad Saha*, broken-backed and nose up. Smoke trailed from rents in the engine compartment and crew cabin, while instruments of the city proceeded with dissection. Giant mechanical mantises peeled off titanium plates, like strips of bark from a fallen tree. They cast the plates down for the spiders to gather, evaluate, and slag.

Amrita loitered above the spectacle. She opened a channel. "Tripp?"

White noise.

Dad said, "He may not have survived."

"Or he may *have* survived."

Dad put his hand over hers. Amrita's parietal lobe received nerve impulses, as though someone was actually touching her skin. Dad's eyes swam with empathy, which she didn't trust. "I need to know for certain," Amrita said, and pushed her hand forward. The illusion of Dad's fingers slid away. She reached into the vaporware display, activated the sensor array, and swept the wreckage.

"He's not there. I don't read his power core's signature."

"Perhaps he has been digested."

"The radioactive core would still register."

Amrita broadened the search, scanning the surrounding area as rapidly as possible, worried that the builders would take notice and pull her down with tractor beams, just as they'd done to the *Meghnad Saha*. Then Tripp's signature appeared. "Got him! He's on the move."

She locked down the location and deactivated the sensor array. "Do you think the builders know I'm here?" Her pod was shielded from sensor examination, but then the *Meghnad Saha* had been, too.

"I'm afraid they do now, Pumpkin."

Pumpkin?

That was the color of the Martian sky above Burroughsville, the main Cydonia colony, where Amrita spent her first six years. Her real dad had never called her 'Pumpkin' or anything else that she recalled. She had only one vague and retreating memory of him walking out the door of their hab. She didn't remember *him*; she remembered his back as he walked away. She remembered the door sliding closed, leaving her fatherless. She remembered her mother's tears. And anger. Not long after that her mother requested reassignment to Luna, dragging Amrita along to the land of stark desert contrasts and no friends. The moon skimmer incident was inevitable, and would have happened sooner if Amrita had been tall enough to reach the controls.

Pumpkin was what *Ideal Dad* called her—back when she was five years old and in need of a father who called her something, anything. Ideal Dad: AKA made-up-dad: AKA Kabbhan presentation. From the quantum flux the Kabbhan had probed her mind and found a ghost who had never lived. Amrita now recognized the physical template: the silvered pompadour, the kind eyes. They belonged to a man she used to see walking around the buried corridors between Burroughsville habs. Some kind of maintenance man, originally from New Delhi, on Earth.

"Please," she said to the presentation, "don't call me that again."

Dad nodded. "All right, Amrita."

"Nobody in my life has ever called me 'Pumpkin.'"

Dad listened respectfully.

"And don't look at me that way, either," Amrita said.

"I'm sorry. Am I looking at you incorrectly?"

Amrita narrowed her eyes. "Are you being funny?"

"I doubt it. Before the Great Migration I was considered by my friends to be on the dour side. Also, in the quantum flux, no one tells jokes. We Kabbhan no longer exist as individuals, except when it becomes necessary to create a presentation. Telling jokes in the flux would be like telling jokes to a mirror."

"I don't know if you're being serious."

"Then I am a poor communicator, which is a failing I was *not* accused of prior to migration."

"Okay, that's plenty."

"Plenty?"

"Of you talking."

Amrita looked for a place to set down. She flexed her hands, worried. "The builders won't attack?"

"Attack? The builders don't *attack* anything. They're hungry for building material, that's all."

"It looked like they were attacking the *Meghnad Saha*."

"Preparing it for digestion," Dad said. "Local resources are finite. The builders hunt constantly for materials. When your surveyer skimmed the atmosphere it became a potential resource. You were warned of this, were you not?"

"I shielded the ship. It should have been invisible." Amrita had been attracted to Trappist-1e *by* its forbiddenness. She had wanted to see what no human had seen, and she wanted to see it because everyone from the Kabbhan themselves to the Gate Authority in the Epsilon Cygni system had told her she couldn't.

"Insufficient," Dad said. "Your sensor scan revealed you."

"All right. Will the builders try to *digest* me?"

"Of course not. They don't digest living organisms."

"That's great for me, but Tripp isn't a living organism."

Amrita concentrated on her maneuvering controls. She lowered the pod between soaring towers that reduced even the twilight to full night. Landing lights planted cones on a pristine avenue no Kabbhan (or human, for that matter) had ever trod. Gear extended, and moments later pneumatic suspension units absorbed the pod's touchdown.

Amrita idled the engines and unstrapped. "Tripp is close. I'll go get him. When I come back, you'll have to give up your seat."

Dad nodded. "Of course. I'm not actually in the seat, anyway. But I don't think you should leave the pod."

"Why not?"

"The builders won't harm a living organism, but once you climb out, the pod will become a construction resource. They seized your planet surveyor only after you abandoned ship."

Amrita bristled. "I didn't abandon anything. Tripp shoved me into the pod. He overreacted to the builder's tractor beam."

"Yes. It wouldn't have pulled the ship down, not while you were aboard."

"Tripp was trying to protect me."

Dad regarded her empathetically. "I see."

Amrita switched on her comlink. "Tripp? You're out there. Answer me."

He didn't reply.

"He's probably turned off his communication device. Receiving your signal might direct the builders to him. Amrita, remaining here is dangerous."

"You said the builders wouldn't digest a living organism."

"No. But once you walk away, your ship becomes a resource. I suggest you fly us out of the city. I will give you a safe destination."

"I'm not leaving Tripp."

"Hmm." Dad tilted his head. "He's artificial, isn't he?"

"What's that got to do with anything?"

"Nothing, I suppose."

Dad tapped two fingers against his lower lip. It's something Amrita herself used to do when she was little, a pensive tick that she transferred to Ideal Dad to help make him more real. It really irritated her that the Kabbhan presentation had adopted it. The maintenance worker from New Delhi had probably had ticks and mannerisms of his own, but Amrita pointedly avoided learning what they were. She wanted only to see him in the corridor sometimes and think, *My dad's going to work.* But at night she hoarded his image and turned it into a wonderful father. He wasn't a maintenance man but a gardener. Like Ideal Dad himself, the garden didn't exist. Amrita liked to imagine it in a vast underground vault with a pretend sky adrift with fluffy white clouds. She liked to imagine tall sunflowers (she'd seen pictures in school) nodding on their stalks. Dad played a game with her, telling stories of the sunflowers, which were special Martian sunflowers and could think and had personalities because they contained the lost souls of the vanished inhabitants of Mars.

Amrita put her helmet on. "He's inside that tower. I'm going to get him. I'll remote-fly the pod, set it to execute an evasive pattern to avoid the tractor beams, and then return. That should work, if I make the pattern tricky enough."

"It might. For a short time."

"It's going to work."

Dad sighed.

Amrita programmed the maneuver, then belted on her side-arm and climbed out of the pod. She felt the planet's pull, the gravity twice that of Mars but significantly less than Earth's. She had lived on both worlds. Earth was prettier, but Mars (and Luna) was easier on her spine. The heating coils in her suit warmed her against the outside temperature, which hung just above freezing. How was anybody supposed to live on this planet?

When she turned, Dad already stood in the street. She said, "Please don't do that anymore, either."

"Don't do what anymore?"

"Pop in and out. If you're going to act physical, act it all the way."

Dad nodded. "If it makes you happy."

"Nothing makes me happy. Hold on."

She used her wrist controller to spin up the pod's engines. Dad watched her impassively, tapping his lower lip.

"Stop doing that," Amrita said.

Dad stopped.

Amrita focused on the pod. It began to rise. The speed of its ascent increased. Amrita held her breath, waiting for the invisible lasso of a tractor beam to grab the pod and smash it down. But the pod climbed above the skyline and darted away—safe, for now.

"If it doesn't come back," Amrita said, "We're all marooned here."

"I'm not here in the first place," Dad said. "But leave that aside. You are marooned whether or not the pod returns."

"What are you talking about?"

"Your pod cannot withstand the forces found within our gate."

The Kabbhan stargates linked distant locations within the Milky Way. When humans discovered the gate shimmering in Jupiter space, it had opened the galaxy to human exploration. Only the gate in the Epsilon Cygni system was forbidden. Entering it, Amrita had been instantly transported across nearly twelve parsecs to the Trappist-1 system.

Amrita's heart beat faster. She had suspected the escape pod was insufficiently sturdy for the stargate, but she had intended to chance it, anyway. Now she didn't know what to do. Taking a risk was one thing, suicide was another. "Another ship will come," she said.

"No ships come here."

"Mine did."

"Amrita, no one *wants* to come here."

"I'll figure something out."

Dad nodded, as though he were nodding at a child who had just vowed to *stay up all night*.

"I will help you settle on this world. There is a lovely island situated on the terminator, where the temperature range is more compatible for your human physiology. In your remaining lifespan the builders will not reach it. Conditions may be challenging at first."

"Well, shit," Amrita said.

"Everything is going to be okay . . ."

Pumpkin.

With her dad, Amrita walked alone down the broad Kabbhan avenue. From deep in the city came the creaking, groaning sounds of nano construction.

"What a waste of time this place is," Amrita said. "All these buildings and no one to live in them or work in them."

"Time," Dad said, shaking his head. "An odd concept."

Amrita looked at him, unable to ignore what she rationally knew wasn't there. "What's odd about it?"

Dad said, "First of all, 'time' is an artificial construct. How do you waste a construct? In the Flux—"

"Dad? I'm not in the mood."

"Of course, sorry. In the Flux we aren't influenced by moods."

"*Okay.*" Amrita stopped walking and turned on him. "If it's so wonderful in the Flux, what are you even doing here?"

"I'm not here."

Amrita closed her eyes briefly. "You know what I mean."

"I told you. I came to help you survive."

"Right. Because you feel responsible. Now what's the other reason?"

Dad shrugged. "I happen to enjoy inhabiting a presentation. Among my fellow Kabbhan that makes me unusual."

"I hope you're having a wonderful time."

"I am."

"That's great." Amrita looked around at the buildings. "He should be right here. Tripp, it's me! Tripp!"

Her words echoed down the canyon of tall buildings, all of them black and shiny-smooth and hollow. She approached the nearest, a tower that rose hundreds of meters, an immense heptagonal spear ending in a rounded point. The entrance to the lobby, or whatever the Kabbhan called it, stood open and doorless. Her helmet lights revealed the empty interior. She stepped inside and tilted her head back. Load-bearing supports crisscrossed all the way to the point. That was all.

"It's called a shell," Dad said. "I knew you were wondering."

She didn't say anything.

"The builders execute the architect's plan, create basic structures, the interiors to be added later, according to the wishes of future inhabitants. As there are no future inhabitants, the city itself is now, and will remain, a shell."

"I don't care," Amrita said. "I just want to find my friend."

From far away, a small voice, almost inaudible, said, "I'm here."

Amrita squinted. The voice was so faint, she wasn't sure she'd even heard it. Wasn't sure whether it was outside of her head, or inside of it, another Kabbhan illusion, or what. She turned up the gain on her headset.

"Tripp?"

"Over here."

She swung her headlamps in his direction. Tripp stood in a far corner of the shell, his back against the wall. He looked more or less human—well, less—but he had two arms and two legs and one oval-shaped head. She walked toward him, her footsteps echoing.

"What happened to you?"

"My leg was damaged in the crash. I barely managed to hobble this far. They almost got me. Now I can't move without falling."

"They won't get you," Amrita said. "I won't let them."

Dad cleared his throat. Amrita ignored him.

"You can't stop them," Tripp said.

Amrita crouched and began examining the damaged leg. At

the knee, a couple of carbon fiber rods bent in the wrong direction, inhibiting articulation.

"Don't be afraid," she said.

"Oh, I'm not really. It's just my positronic brain pretending to feel human emotions, so I will seem more companionable."

She looked up. "We've discussed your honesty on this topic before."

"Sorry."

Amrita produced a multi-tool and began fiddling with the leg.

"The weird thing is," Tripp said, "I'm not even sure I want you to."

She looked up. "Want me to what?"

"Stop them."

Amrita stopped fiddling. "Why the Hell are you saying that?"

"It's strangely compelling."

"*What's* strangely compelling?"

"To become part of the city," Tripp said. "I don't know. Would it be so bad? Maybe it's because I'm already artificial, but these last hours, pretending to feel so afraid even when you were not here, hiding, getting my apparent dread of extinction organized to display when you showed up—it's really made me think. My whole existence has been nothing but a performance."

"Tripp!"

"I'm serious. If I simply walked out there, exposed myself, let them slag me, allowed myself to be digested and my elements to be recombined into the building matrix, wouldn't I be part of something greater than myself?"

"Tripp, please be quiet now." Listening to him made her feel lonely. "I think the crash must have damaged more than your poor leg."

"No, my brain is fully functional. You know, I was in communication with the *Meghnad Saha* even as the instrumentality dismantled her. She didn't display fear, because that isn't part of her reactive programming mask. But she *was* excited. I'm certain of that. This may sound strange to you, but in the end she believed that to be digested was the greatest adventure. At least, that's what she said."

"She did not."

"I suppose she may have been regurgitating something from the library that got mixed up in her damaged memory core. Anyway . . .

"Hold still, please." Amrita loosened the bolt that attached the bent rods to Tripp's knee swivels. The bolt dropped to the ground. Gritting her teeth, she got a firm grip on one of the bent rods, wrenched it back and forth until it suddenly came loose. She fell on her ass, still holding the rod.

"He's right," Dad said. "We Kabbhan, like all physical beings of limited duration, lived our lives in fear. After the Great Migration, fear vanished—along with our individual personalities, of course. It may be the same for artificial beings when faced with the prospect of joining the greater reality of the city."

Amrita rolled to her knees. "Have either of you even considered the virtue of silence?"

"Either of you?" Tripp said. "Who else are you talking to?"

"Nobody. My dad."

"Which is it?"

"They're the same thing."

Amrita resumed work on the second bent rod. She twisted and wrenched and pulled. It came free of its upper swivel but not the lower. Finally she gave up and let it dangle.

"Try that," she said.

Tripp moved his good leg forward, planted it, then moved his damaged leg. The dangling bar tapped against the other rods and the knee wobbled slightly side-to-side. Tripp waved his arms for balance. Amrita scrambled to her feet to catch him, but he managed to remain upright without her.

"How is it?" she asked.

"Unstable. I'm not sure this will work."

"Keep practicing, walk around."

"All right." Tripp walked away into the shadows, the dangling carbon rod making a tap-tapping sound like a blind man's cane.

"The builders will very probably take him," Dad said.

Amrita turned on him, annoyed with herself for accepting his presence outside her head, where it wasn't. "I could use a little optimism around here. You're supposed to be helping me, right? Well, do some helping, why don't you? Get us away from where Tripp is in danger. Get us to that island."

"I can take you there. The builders have no interest in a biological. But Tripp will inevitably be noticed."

Amrita paced around, working her hands together, thinking. "What if I turn the builders off? Isn't that what your people should have done before the Great Migration?"

"That isn't possible. In the absence of Kabbhan oversight, the builders have adapted and become self-motivated to complete the architect's plan. Only the architect can cancel the build."

"Who's the architect?"

"Since they were left running, the builders devised their own plan."

"The builders are their own architect?"

"Exactly." Dad spread his arms and turned in a circle. "They build. It's what they do. It's all they do. When the original plan was complete, they simply extended the parameters to include the entire planet. That way they will remain busy and fulfil the dictates of their primary function. But they are not sentient. No amount of logical persuasion will convince them to abandon their own plan."

"That leaves Terminator Island, or whatever you call it."

"The island has no name. Nothing here does."

"Let's just go. Tripp!"

They emerged from the building in time to witness the arrival of a ten-meter-tall spider. Moments later, the pod came zigzagging out of the sky and settled onto the same spot it had previously occupied. The spider stalked toward the pod.

Amrita yelled, "Run!"

Since she was the only one with working legs, she ran alone—though Dad appeared to be running beside her.

"How am I doing?" he said.

"What?"

"You said you wanted me to be physically consistent."

Behind her, Tripp's dangling carbon rod clicked and knocked against his leg, like a syncopated timer.

Amrita ripped her sidearm out of the holster but hesitated. "Dad, you're sure that thing won't attack me?"

"Yes."

Amrita triggered her weapon. A pulsing white particle discharge cut across one of the spider's legs, severing it above the first joint. The spider stumbled and began tracking left. Amrita ran back to Tripp, pulled his arm across her shoulders, and helped him walk the remainder of the distance to the pod. He was light for an artificial.

"Stand here." Amrita climbed the ladder and reached down. "Give me your hand, I'll pull you up."

But Tripp wasn't looking at her. He watched the spider circling itself, partially hobbled, and, to Amrita's horror, Tripp began limping towards it.

"Tripp, what are you doing! Stop."

Without looking at her, Tripp said, "You should fly away now. It's important that I serve a larger function. While the *Meghnad Saha* existed, my part of the larger function was assured. There is no larger function on your island."

"Our friendship is a larger function." Amrita felt an ache in her chest.

Tripp didn't speak again but limped, loose rod tapping, over to the spider and held up his arms. The spider took notice, stopped chasing itself around in a circle, and slagged him.

The ache in Amrita's chest intensified and became unbearable. "*Why?*"

From the right seat, already strapped in, Dad laid a comforting illusion on her shoulder. Her brain told her it was a father giving her a reassuring squeeze.

"We best go now, Pumpkin."

She buckled herself into the pilot's seat, roughly wiped her eyes, spun up the engines, and sped into the sky, reaching maximum thrust within seconds. They achieved altitude and raced toward the sea.

On tidally locked Trappist-1e, Terminator Island stood on the edge of eternal night. Amrita knelt in the powdery blue sand, breathing inside her helmet. "I don't see any builders."

"They exist everywhere but are too small to see."

"If they're on the island, why aren't they already building their damned city?"

"It would be disorderly. The builders follow the architect's plan, in this case their own plan. And the plan is to build contiguously outward from the main continental mass. These builders would not become activated until the project arrived after crossing the ocean. That is a distant occurrence. In the meantime you can use the builders for your own project, once I tell you how to activate them according to your deeper architectural desires."

"I don't have any deep architectural desires," Amrita grumbled.

Dad, standing over her, said, "Of course you do."

Amrita was not Kabbhan. The nanobuilders did not naturally synch with her inner architect. But, because she was the only game in town, at least until the city arrived, eventually they made a connection. A good thing. The Trappist atmosphere was unbreathable, at least for humans. Sooner or later (probably sooner) the pod's emergency atmospheric conversion processor would break down.

The builders started . . . building. Amrita had been dozing in the pod, lulled to unconsciousness by the wheeze and huff of the processor, which sucked in air and displaced most of the carbon dioxide with an artificially produced mixture of nitrogen and oxygen. The conversion unit was designed as a temporary stopgap. The replicating oxygen / nitrogen molecules on board would soon be depleted, and that would be the end of Amrita.

A creaking, groaning sound plucked at her awareness, and she opened heavy eyelids. The atmosphere in the pod was thin, just barely enough to support her life. But like *that* she was wide awake. Around the pod, for a radius of fifty meters or more, walls built themselves up, gradually creating an enclosed space. At the same time invisible builders filled the still-exposed interior space with walls and corridors and furniture and apparatus familiar to Amrita, including a large atmospheric conversion unit. Fascinated, Amrita tore into a packet of emergency rations and watched the show. The builders worked quickly.

At the point when she knew exactly what the builders were creating, Amrita turned to Dad, who was always at her side.

"I didn't ask for this," she said.

"Your architect is a deep expectation, beyond your conscious control. I'm sorry. The builders are designed to synch with Kabbhan brains, which were more limber, not human brains. This is what you get, I'm afraid. At least it is life, yes?"

Outside the pod, a copy of Amrita's Burroughsville habitat took shape.

*

Black. Inside the hab, if she wandered too far, the soothing blue and gold tones of her remembered home in Burroughs-ville segued into the shiny, smooth, black "shell" material of the Kabbhan city. Mostly, Amrita stayed in her room, reading her way through the pod's mirror library from when it was attached to the *Meghnad Saha*. A couple of times a day she left the hab and crossed to the farm. The walls of the farm enclosed a space twice the size of the hab. Using seeds and fertilizer packets from the escape pod's long-term planetary survival stores, Amrita had begun to grow her future diet of bland vegetables. Already leafy shoots had emerged. The sight both encouraged and depressed her. How long would she be stuck here?

Sometimes, on her way back to the hab, she paused to gaze out over the sea. Beyond the horizon, the builders continued their work on the continent and beneath the waves. Tripp was now part of that building matrix. If he could pretend fear why couldn't he have pretended loyalty and stayed with her? Tripp was part of the city, but what was Amrita part of? She had spent her life devising ways to separate herself from her fellow humans. Now, for the first time, regret wormed into her heart.

"I don't understand why he did it," she said one evening when Dad came in to say goodnight. "I thought we were friends."

Dad sat on the bed. It was a perfect duplicate of Amrita's childhood bed. When she lay down to sleep, her legs extended beyond the mattress. "Perhaps the friendship was more one-sided than you like to believe."

"You didn't even know him," Amrita said.

"Was there something to know? He was artificial. Kabbhan could not have created a presentation from him, even. Tripp had more in common with the builders than with you."

"Stop talking to me," Amrita said. "Can't you stop and go away? I don't need you anymore."

Dad held her hand. "Do you really want me to leave, Pumpkin?"

By force of will, Amrita almost convinced herself that she couldn't feel the hand gently squeezing hers. She would have pulled free, except she *could* see, in her mind's eye, the grim comedy of her lying alone on the bed, talking to herself while twisting and pulling away from someone who wasn't there. It was easier to accept the illusion. Just as it had become easier to accept the illusion calling her "Pumpkin." Was there any point in fighting it? Besides, it would be too lonely without Dad, even though Dad wasn't really there.

"At least make yourself appear in your original Kabbhan form." she said. "The Dad thing bothers me."

"Oh, I couldn't do that. I no longer possess a self-image. To appear Kabbhan now would require a living Kabbhan mind from which to draw."

"You won't try?"

"I'm afraid it would be pointless." Dad shook his head and chuckled. "You know, I'm really enjoying my temporary individuality."

"That's wonderful." Amrita turned away.

"But—"

"But what?" She turned her head and looked at him.

"Nothing." Dad smiled kindly. "I went to the underground garden today." He gave her ankle a fatherly squeeze.

Amrita groaned. Not this again. She turned away, facing the wall. "There is no underground garden."

"The sunflower people want to tell their story, the story of old Mars."

"I don't want to talk anymore," Amrita said.

"Why don't I tell you a little of it?" Dad suggested.

"Jesus. I just said—"

"It's fascinating, the story of old Mars."

"Stop *talking* now."

"Don't be sharp with me, Pumpkin."

Amrita rolled over and sat up. "It bothers me that you won't stop talking when I tell you to stop. You used to stop."

Dad folded his hands in his lap and looked at them. "I appreciate," he said, starting slowly, seeming to hunt carefully for the right words, "that I sometimes make you uncomfortable. But I hope *you* can appreciate that I'm not a mere thing, a device, you can choose to turn off and on at will. I'm not an artificial, like your so-called friend, Tripp."

"Leave Tripp out of it."

"I would like to," Dad said. "But I find your morbid attachment disturbing."

"Disturbing." Amrita's childhood room seemed too small, the air too thin. Childish and colorful drawings she'd once created on a Play-And-Swirl pallet adorned the walls, primitive renderings of her little Burroughsville family. Mom and Ideal Dad. The goddamn maintenance man. Amrita stood up. She felt crowded—which was ridiculous, when you thought about it. "I'm going outside."

"A walk sounds nice, Pumpkin. I'll come with you."

"Please don't."

Amrita suited up, cycled through the airlock. Dad stayed with her every step of the way, acting the part of a physical presence without interruption, just as she'd once requested. She walked along the shore until she began to feel tired. Dad never stopped talking.

"The Sunflower Martians lived thousands of years ago, back when sparkling blue water filled the canals and riverboats propelled by solar sails navigated from community to community, trading goods and stories."

Amrita kicked at the powdery sand. "There were never any canals on Mars."

"Nonsense!" Ideal Dad said.

She stopped and looked back. Ideal Dad kept talking, but she was getting better at ignoring him. From this distance, the hab and farm buildings appeared small and generic—except in scope, no different than the shells of the city.

I found some shells on the beach, she thought, a little hysterically. And then she realized something.

Ideal Dad was saying, "The Martians chose sunflowers because the flowers are so bright and sunny and optimistic, just like the Martians themselves used to be."

"Hold up," Amrita said."

"What is it, Pumpkin?"

"If the builders can recreate my old Burroughsville hab, why can't they recreate the *Meghnad Saha*?"

For the first time in days, it seemed, Ideal Dad became quiet.

"Well?" Amrita said.

"We should be getting back home now."

"Answer my question."

"A spaceship is very complicated."

"The hab is complicated, too."

"The interiors exist as a deeply imprinted memory with an emotional toggle from your childhood."

"Tripp and I lived together on the surveyor for a long time. That's imprinted, too."

"It's not the same." Dad's tone suggested the conversation was over. He turned and walked away, back toward the hab, kicking up no sand, leaving no footprints. After a few meters, he disappeared. Amrita stood there, as if trying to catch a glimpse of a mirage. It had been a long time since Dad had last pulled his disappearing act.

She woke on her hab bed and lay still, listening. Somebody was in the corridor outside her room. She got up and padded over to the door, slid it open a few inches. A man, his back to her, walked away toward where the corridor curved. A *different* man. Carrying a long-handled static duster, he was dressed in the green jumpsuit worn by maintenance workers in Burroughsville, a long time ago. Amrita slipped into the corridor and followed him. He rounded the corner. She ran to catch up.

"Hey."

He paused and turned his head, his face in partial profile. It was Ideal Dad, and it wasn't Ideal Dad.

"What are you doing?" Amrita said.

"It's late for you, kid. Where's your mother?"

"I don't like this." Amrita stepped back. "Don't do this."

The maintenance man grunted and continued on his way, toward the next bend in the corridor, occasionally swiping the walls with his duster. Around that next bend the shiny black shell material replaced the phony representation of Amrita's hab. She didn't follow him. She was afraid to.

That day on the beach, it was the last time Ideal Dad appeared. Amrita spent her days alone in the hab. A heavy lethargy came over her, and she stopped going to the farm. The process of suiting up and cycling through the airlock made her tired even to think of it. She barely left her room, where she slept a lot and nibbled on the last of the pod's emergency rations. Every night she heard the heavy shoes of the maintenance man clocking down the corridor, but after that first time she stopped going out to investigate. It was all inside her head anyway.

One night, lying in the dark, on the precipice of sleep, Amrita heard something, a minute creaking, groaning. The sounds of nano builders at work. She sat up and waved her hand over the bedside lamp sensor. The light came up. In a corner of the room, a child's desk took shape. It was a fully interactive FunDesk. Amrita's eyes widened. Up to now the room had duplicated her childhood hab, recreating what had actually been in it. But she had never had a FunDesk, though she'd repeatedly begged her mother for one.

Amrita swung her legs off the too-short bed. She wriggled her toes in the carpet—then stopped when she realized it was the same thing she used to do when she was five years old. The desk finished building itself. Cherry apple red swept away the shell-black look. What next, duckies on her underwear? The room was infantilizing her. Only it wasn't the room.

Footsteps crossed the floor on the other side of the wall common to the family quarters. Not the heavy tread of the maintenance worker. Amrita, suddenly terrified, approached the curtain between her bedroom and the family's common space. In all these weeks, no one had appeared in the family space. Amrita lifted the curtain aside in time to see a man pass into the corridor, his back to Amrita, a young man with squared shoulders.

"Wait," Amrita said, her hand reaching out.

The door slid shut behind him.

Half dressed, barefoot, she pursued him, but was afraid to catch up. They followed the curving corridor and came to the airlock.

Amrita found her voice. "You can't do this to me."

The man turned. A piece of his face that included his right eye was missing.

"All I ever wanted to do was stay," he said, "but you won't have it." His voice sounded garbled, as if he were talking around a mouth full of mud. It wasn't a human voice at all, but maybe the voice of a creature that had stopped physically existing a very long time ago. As he opened the airlock's inner door, his face began to melt. He shuffled into the airlock. The inner door closed with a decisive *clunk*. Amrita rushed to the little round window. The airlock was empty, with the outer door never having opened. She was alone again, but hadn't she always been?

Amrita moved out of both the infantilizing room and the false representation of her old Cydonia family quarters. She dragged everything she needed down the corridor and around the second bend, and there she made a place for herself enclosed by the shiny black shell material. She craved the inconvenience of reality. She *needed* it, if she was going to have a chance.

Amrita resumed tending the farm. She required food, enough to go beyond the limits of her pod rations. It would take a long time to accomplish what she intended to accomplish—if she ever did accomplish it.

She mind-sifted nanos in the blue sand, and worked doggedly to reconstruct the *Meghnad Saha*. Hours and hours she spent remembering every detail of her lost surveyor. She started in the morning and ended at night, curled on the hard shell material, concentrating until her mind went slack with fatigue. On the beach—slowly, slowly—the ship began to rise. First the landing struts and feet and then a skeletal approximation of the superstructure. She wouldn't need the whole thing, just the essentials. Structural integrity. Ion propulsion engines. One pressurized cabin . . .

Tripp visited her in a dream. He was his old self, undamaged and companionable. His blank face swiveled toward her. *I've got your back*, he said, but it was just Amrita's deep architect of loneliness trying to manufacture the loyalty that Tripp, in the end, had been incapable of. She sat up and angrily wiped away tears. "I don't *need* you anymore. I'm getting out of here." By "here" she meant more than Trappist-1e.

She wanted so badly to abandon the abandoned part of herself.

Amrita tried something new. Before sleep she focused hard on the missing pieces of her space ship reconstruction, the pieces that eluded her conscious efforts. She woke with fresh details of the *Meghnad Saha*, details that had always been there just beyond her grasp.

The builders resumed work and they worked rapidly.

*

"Ready to fly," Amrita said, standing by the surveyor, her gloved hand flat against the hull. She turned back to the hab and saw nothing more than a collection of black shells. Of course, it was different on the inside. But she would never visit the inside again. After a minute she turned away and opened the hatch on the underside of the reconstructed ship and hauled herself up. Minutes later the *Meghnad Saha*, streaked out of Trappist 1-e's atmosphere and towards the Khabban gate. She was going home.

DESTINATION

B rad, I'd like you to get out of the office for a few hours."

"Why?" Brad Ott had been sunk so deep in his design template that he hadn't noticed his manager enter. Now he looked up at Adelina Serna in her neat business suit and perfect makeup, standing before him hip-cocked with her arms crossed under her breasts, and he began to sweat. Brad liked to be left alone. He did good work. His apps came pre-loaded on every 3-D printed phone the government distributed to the masses outside the exclusive zones.

"Don't look so scared," Adelina said. "I just want you to play a game."

Brad was lost. "A . . . game?"

"Real world. Have you heard of Destination?"

"Where the car drives you around and you don't know where?"

"That's it."

"It doesn't sound like my thing."

"Today it's your thing."

"I have a lot of work to do here." He could smell his own sweat and wondered, embarrassed, if Adelina smelled it, too.

"This is about work, Brad."

"I don't—"

"You and some of the other creatives never leave the building. Brad, I don't think I've ever seen you go outside. Today I want you to get out there."

"But I don't like it out there. I like it in here."

Adelina smiled. It looked a little forced, the strain showing around her eyes. "It won't hurt. Besides, it comes straight from corporate. TTP initiative."

"Oh." That was that. TTP—Training Temperament Priorities—superseded everything.

"Corporate feels it will improve morale, shake out the cobwebs."

Until Adelina walked through the door, Brad's morale had been fine. "When do I have to play?"

"Right now."

Brad sighed, touched the jewel light on the corner of his desk. The design template folded up and dropped down the illusion of a bottomless shaft, then the surface of his desk assumed the appearance of a solid oak slab.

Brad stood up." I don't know much about Destination. How do I start?"

"Surrender your lendings."

"What?"

"It's a phrase, part of Destination. It means give up your stuff, basically. Your ID, credit pass, phone—all that stuff."

"Do I have to?"

Adelina stared at him without blinking. "Okay," Brad said, "okay."

It was hard to remove his wristband, which contained all the "lendings" Adelina mentioned. Not *hard* hard; simply difficult to part with.

"This makes me pretty uncomfortable."

"I know. That's part of it." She held her hand out, the mauve nails perfectly filed. Brad dropped his wristband into her palm and watched her tuck it into the slash pocket of her skirt.

"Now we go for a drive," she said.

"We're going . . . together?"

"A figure of speech, Brad."

In the garage under the AirVision tower, a row of jaunty white-and-blue, egg-shaped vehicles sat parked at the curb. Fully electric, as much window as body frame, the Destination cars were common driverless vehicles intended strictly for transport within the city. Thousands of them hummed around the streets of selected metropolitan areas, at least they did inside the exclusive zones. Beyond the barricades things were less orderly. Less clean.

Brad's fellow "creatives" stood talking to their department managers, or staring around the garage with bewildered expressions. Others already sat in their assigned vehicles, waiting for Destination to begin.

Brad rubbed his wrist, missing his lendings. In a way, what Adelina had said about never leaving the building was true. Brad spent all day at his desk. When he went home at night he rode the elevator down to the transit depot. From there, a train carried him across town to his conapt, where he rode *another* elevator to the thirty-third floor. There wasn't any need to go outside, he had everything he needed *inside*. Whatever Amazon couldn't deliver (virtually nothing) he could order sent up from neighborhood restaurants or whatever.

"It's like a scavenger hunt," Adelina was telling him. "The car takes you to a random destination. You bring something back to prove you were there. An artifact. It has to be a thing specific to the place, identifiable as belonging there."

"Like a T-shirt with the name of the neighborhood on it?" Brad thought in terms of neighborhoods because he never left the barricaded exclusive zone. It was like the thing about never going outside. But outside within the city was still *inside* as far as the greater world was concerned. The greater world where his AirVision apps proliferated, entertaining the masses and creating revenue streams. "But without my wristband I don't have any money," he said. "How am I supposed to bring something back?"

"You have to *talk* to people, Brad. You have to interact. Destination is a social challenge game. It's supposed to take you out of your comfort arena. And I hope you will be more creative than a T-shirt."

Brad envisioned the awkwardness of procuring an "artifact," without the aid of his wristband, from somebody else's neighborhood. "I don't know—"

"It'll be fun. Besides, the Destination car won't return you without an artifact."

"Have you ever played?"

"God, no."

Brad doubted it would be fun. On the other hand, it wouldn't be difficult. Destination was a popular game, and there were only so many neighborhoods inside the exclusive zone. People must be used to scavengers piling out of eggs and, essentially, begging for stuff. Some more high-minded types complained that Destination mocked actual poor people. Brad could see the point. While his parents had certainly not been beggars, they *had* been working class, living well outside the exclusive zones, surviving on factory pay. Until age nine, when Aptitude Assessment placed him in the top percentile and he was whisked off to an education inside the Seattle exclusive zone, Brad had lived with them in a government housing block. Not like the old-style tenements. A decent place, or decent enough.

"How do I win?"

"Win?"

"The game. Destination."

"You don't win. You play. Winning isn't the goal. It's social. It takes you—"

"I know. Out of my comfort arena."

The other eggs began to pull away from the curb.

"Better get going now," Adelina said.

He reluctantly got into the vehicle. The door locks engaged. He swallowed, waved at his manager, who turned briskly away. Adelina could be a pain, but he didn't blame her for making him play Destination. When TTP issued marching orders, you marched. Period.

The car rolled up to the surface streets and accelerated. It was raining. For a couple of blocks Brad's electric egg traveled in a parallel lane next to an identical vehicle. Ted Lee, from AirVision's art department, looked across at him. His face behind the fogged glass appeared confused, nervous. Ted was a stone introvert. Destination was going to be tough on him. Brad waved, then his vehicle made an abrupt left turn, and he never saw Ted Lee again, except in a video capture that made Brad sick every time he thought of it.

Inside the Destination car, Brad closed his eyes and tried to relax. In a couple of hours he would be back in his office working on the RATATTACK! upgrade. RATATTACK! was a real game, not a pointless driving-around exercise designed to make people uncomfortable. Part of the Urban Legends Series, the RATAT-TACK player scored by "shooting" real-life rats with their government-distributed phone. Of course, if your home turf was short on real rats you could substitute cats, or dogs, or crows, or whatever, and the app would score those as rat kills. Naturally, you weren't really killing anything. RATATTACK! overlaid a targeting sight on the phone's camera. The screen flashed red when you scored a kill. The real creature scurried away, albeit marked in the phone by the physical characteristics recognition software, so you couldn't score on the same rat twice.

The upgrade would make the chosen species *look* like big fat urban rats—on the screen, at least. The kickass thing about RATATTACK! was how it interfaced with the real world. Millions of players around the world competed for the highest score within regional and species parameters.

Brad closed his eyes and tried to sort out a coding problem. Time passed. The egg's electric motor hummed. Rain rattled on the roof. He lost track of time. A rough patch of road surface shuddered the car. Brad looked up out of his thoughts. He used his shirt sleeve to wipe fog off the window. Dingy stone buildings, none higher than ten stories, slipped by. Metal grates covered shop windows. An old Black woman in a rain-saggy sweater and knit hat pushed a rusty shopping cart piled high with junk. She leaned into it, like Sisyphus and his rock. A panel truck with a human operator passed him.

Fuck. He had departed the exclusive zone.

Annoyingly, the GPS display was blank. Was that part of the game, or was it simply broken? Either way, Brad didn't like it. If the former, then why? Was it so hard to maintain equipment? Brad did his job, why couldn't others do theirs?

He had passed through the barricades without even knowing it. No one stopped you going out; getting back in, without his wristband, that was going to be a pain.

"Hey," Brad said, "there's something wrong here."

The egg jolted over uneven pavement. It wasn't built for driving outside the well-maintained city streets. The car had *little* tires.

"You need to turn back," Brad said. "Turn back now. Are you hearing me?"

The car did not reply. Every car Brad had ever been in since moving to the exclusive zone replied to passenger voice inquires, if not commands.

A freeway sign swept past. The Destination car swung onto

the ramp. Both gas and electric-powered vehicles, all much larger than Brad's fragile egg, soon crowded him into an aggressive traffic flow. It was a mixed highway, driverless intermingled with human operators. Brad shrank down in his seat as tractor-trailer rigs rumbled past like dinosaurs.

"Take me back, take me home," Brad said. Then he shouted, "What's *wrong* with you?"

Humming to itself, the Destination car kept going.

Hours later, beyond the great exurban sprawl, traffic thinned out. For a while the scenery turned green. Brad wiped another hole in the constantly-fogging side window. A dilapidated barn stood in a field of high, wet grass, half its roof collapsed into the hayloft. By the time night fell, Brad had given up any hope that the car would turn back. The headlights made shallow penetration into the dark.

Brad was hungry and thirsty. He racked his seat back as far as it would go, folded his arms, and tried to sleep. In an anxious dream he found himself, a child, buried under empty soda cans, broken appliances, and assorted junk in the old woman's shopping cart. He tried to tell her to stop, but his weak and frightened child's voice couldn't be heard over the jiggling of aluminum cans and the cart's squealing wheels. He clawed frantically to get out. The old woman pushed him back down. When had her face become his father's?

Brad started to cry, just as a jolt through the floor of the Destination car brought him out of the dream. He rubbed his eyes and looked around. He was stopped at a re-charging station. There were no other vehicles. The Destination car had mounted the charging-stud, and that was the jolt that had awakened Brad. Immediately he pulled on the door handle, but the lock was still engaged.

"Car, unlock the door."

The car went on re-charging and did not unlock any doors. In the window of a little pillbox structure, a man in a baseball cap stood talking on a phone. Brad waved, trying to get his attention. The man waved back, enthusiastically. He looked really happy, and he was talking animatedly into his phone.

Brad yelled, "Hey, I can't get out! Help me!"

The man began laughing. Brad drew back. What the hell? There was a clunk when the charger uncoupled. The engine started, and seconds later the charging station and the crazy person in the pillbox retreated into the dark.

The car drove all night. Early the next morning it exited the freeway. Brad sat forward, suddenly wide awake. His stomach started cramping when he passed the WELCOME TO DUPREE, CALIFORNIA sign. Dupree was his hometown, where he'd lived until he was nine, when Aptitude Assessment hoisted him away to better times. His parents had worked in the tire factory, two jobs being necessary to maintain even their modest circumstances. This wasn't a random destination. If the car stopped, Brad planned to kick the window out.

A horse stood at the top of Main Street shaking its head, like an old man who couldn't remember where he was supposed to be. Out here, for some, horses had come back in service. The Destination car swerved around it, continued down the street, then tucked itself into the curb behind a large fossil-fuel pickup truck with rusted wheel hubs and a broken taillight. The engine turned off, the instrument panel went black, and the door locks clacked open.

Brad climbed out and stretched. He felt stiff, hungry, and thirsty. Also desperately in need of coffee. His caffeine headache was like a little hand squeezing his eyeball. The stomach cramps probably resulted from hunger. It didn't mean anything that they felt like those cramps that had doubled him over when his mother sent him outside to wait while his father "unwound." Unwinding had been the family code for a process that ended when his dad passed out. Brad used to imagine a tight spring in the middle of his father's chest gradually uncoiling, as if his father had been a robot with a faulty mechanism, the loosening spring making him talk too loud, stumble around, sing weepy songs, break plates, lapse into sullen and distant gazes. When the spring unwound all the way, Dad slumped over. Brad used to wait outside in the cold and dark until his mother called him in. Why had she let it take so long? Of course, she had no choice.

In the early stages of unwinding, Brad's father had once taken a swing at a policeman and was beaten badly. It was a beating from which he never fully recovered.

It felt unreal, standing on the main street of Dupree. He never been back, not since Aptitude Assessment. His parents had received passes to visit him in the exclusive zone, so there was no need. His AA had created a bubble of privilege, and he especially wanted his father to see it. But his father had never come. And now both his parents were long dead.

Across the street, a door banged shut. Brad turned toward the sound. Locals sat in the plate-glass window of the Sunshine Diner. Brad rubbed his naked wrist. Without his wristband he couldn't even buy a cup of coffee. He started across the street anyway. The Sunshine Diner had always been there.

Standing inside the doorway, conspicuous in his expensive, if rumpled, suit, Brad felt at a loss. There were maybe ten customers in the café—eleven, if you included the dog, an unkempt-looking animal with muddy paws. It lay panting on its side next to an empty bar stool, as if it were waiting for someone, or had maybe fallen off the stool.

"Coffee, mister?"

A middle-aged woman with curly gray-and-black hair held up a pot of coffee. Brad's reflexive response was out of his mouth before he could modify it to include his financial circumstances, which probably wouldn't have helped, anyway. He doubted Dupree got a lot of Destination gamers. "Yes. I mean—"

She held the pot poised above a thick mug and looked a question at him.

"Yes," Brad finished. "Coffee."

She filled the mug and turned away. Brad sat on the red vinyl stool. There was a tear in the seat repaired with duct tape. He added cream and sugar to the coffee and took his first sip. He have to run out on the tab or beg poverty, but how much could a cup of coffee be? When he got back to the city, he would send them the money. He wasn't a thief. But he couldn't bring himself to beg, not in Dupree. This place was behind him, and outside of the exclusive zones begging wasn't a game.

He needed a salvage artifact so the car would take him back. Brad cast his gaze around the diner for matches, or paper napkins, or anything that might bear the name of the town on it. A menu would have been perfect. But there weren't any, just slow-scrolling video displays embedded in the counter under cloudy Lucite.

A glass-fronted case next to the register displayed racks of pastries, cookies, and cakes. It would be so easy to reach around the counter and take one. On top of the case, a single dried-out Danish stood propped on a little easel, as if it were a work of art. Next to it was a slate chalkboard, about the size of a tablet device, with a cheerful red border. "No one saves us but ourselves" was written on the board, "so what are you waiting for?"

"That's our Buddha," the waitress said.

"Your Buddha?"

"Look at it."

Brad looked at it.

"He's got his own Flutter account," the waitress said.

"Who does?"

"The Danish—Buddha. At Dupree Buddha."

Brad squinted at the pastry. It did look a little bit like a Buddha figure.

"A customer saw what it was and showed Al, the guy who runs this place? Al gave the customer a chocolate croissant and kept the Danish. The Dupree Buddha is famous, at least on Flutter. Check it out."

She retrieved her government-issued phone and showed him the screen. Flutter was an approved media that encouraged social bonding while actually effecting isolation. @dupreebuddha posted a *lot*. Probably it was a random quote-generator. Brad recognized some quotes from historical figures, including JFK and Malcolm X. Some of the quotes looked legitimate, others had been modified. (*Ask not what you can do for your country, because your country won't listen to you anyway*). @dupreebuddha had eight hundred thousand followers. Was that even possible for a pastry? There was a picture of @dupreebuddha propped on its easel.

"This one's Emerson," Brad said.

"Which?"

"'*Life is not a destination but a journey, so why aren't you moving against the ones who want you to stay in one spot?*' That's Emerson, not Buddha. The first part is, anyway." Brad smiled to show he wasn't being an asshole. The partial Emerson quote struck Brad as providential. Here was his Destination artifact, a Flutter-famous artifact tied to a specific location. Of course, this wasn't an ordinary game of Destination. But he could sort that out once he was home.

"No kidding," the waitress said, sounding as though she didn't care whether he was kidding or not.

Three teenage boys in a booth by the window started laughing. The waitress shouted past Brad, "What's so funny, you kids?"

One of them held up his phone, a video playing on the screen. Hardly able to get the words past his cackling, he said, "The scared-looking dude is in some serious shit!"

"Oh, yeah?" She quickly tapped up a different screen on her phone, stared for a few seconds, and chuckled. "I guess he is."

"You ever play RATATTACK on that thing?" Brad asked.

"Yeah, sure."

"I hear there's an upgrade coming."

"Got it already."

"What—? You can't have it already." He wanted to add, *Because I'm still working on it*, but didn't. The waitress fiddled with her phone again and handed it to him. An ad for LitesOut sleeping pills ran, the Git-It-Now buy-button blinking so urgently Brad almost tapped it, as he had once been conditioned to do. Then the screen cleared to the familiar RATATTACK gun site. Since the lens on the back of the phone was pointed at the waitress, she appeared as the target. The software transformed her out of her waitress uniform into a fashionable business suit and changed the background to a luxurious conference room—tricks the current version of RATATTACK! certainly could not do. Even Brad's upgrade wouldn't be capable of *that*.

"Go ahead," the waitress said. "Take your kill."

Brad pushed the physical button under the screen. The business-suit version of the waitress exploded in a burst of blood and wriggling guts. Jesus Christ, it was vicious. He handed the phone back. "Did that download from the regular network?" It was a stupid question. Everything on the gov-ish phones downloaded automatically from the same network. That was the whole point.

The waitress looked at him. "Sure. The regular network."

Brad unconsciously rubbed his left wrist. No one inside the

barricades bothered with phones anymore. The wristband projected an interactive Ghostware cloud which was much neater and more convenient. Inside the zones, everything was better.

More raucous laughter broke out from the teenagers in the booth. One of them said, "That scared-looking guy is *doomed*!"

When the waitress retreated into the kitchen, Brad checked that no one was looking, then leaned over the counter and grabbed a Danish out of the display cabinet. He swapped it with the Buddha, which he slipped under his jacket. His heart was racing. He had never stolen anything. He never *needed* to.

Outside, he all but ran for the Destination car. Halfway across the street, he stopped. Someone was already sitting in the car. Brad looked around. Probably he appeared as lost as the horse still loitering at the end of the street. Since there was nothing else to do, Brad finished crossing the street and opened the car door. A scruffy-looking kid, maybe twenty years old, sat in the right seat. His Levi's had a hole in the knee, but not a stylish one.

"Who are you?" Brad said.

The kid pushed a flop of glossy black hair off his forehead. "You can call me Xavier. You better get in, before someone finds out what you did. Don't bother lying. I know you have the Danish."

Brad looked back at the diner, then got into the car and pulled the door shut. The Destination car stood out in the same way his suit did, marking him as an outsider. He wanted to be gone out of there, and fast.

"Go on," Xavier said, "start this thing up and let's get rolling."

Sheepishly, Brad withdrew his hand from inside his jacket, clutching the Buddha. The pastry was hard as cement. Brad's stomach growled. As long as he was stealing stuff, he should have filched something edible out of the display case, too. He held the Buddha up to the dashboard. A thread of red laser light slipped over the stale pastry, scanning it, and for the first time the car spoke: "Artifact authenticated."

The engine hummed to life and they started moving.

Brad turned to Xavier. "How you know? Who *are* you?"

"I'm your driver."

"This car doesn't need a human operator."

Xavier shook his head. "Not the car. I'm *your* driver. If you decide to join the cause, I'll be the guy that guides you in the right direction. I'll be your manager, if you want to look at it that way."

"My manager." A picture of Adelina appeared in Brad's mind. Xavier did not exactly match up.

"You think we're kidding around?" Xavier said.

We?

"What do you think you're doing here, bro? Playing Destination? We hacked the cars and *gave* them destinations. I personally gave you *this* destination."

"I don't think you can do that."

"Man, it's done."

"How?"

"The Network is vulnerable. Sure, they got sophisticated firewall protection, but we find our way through cracks so small they aren't even noticed. I got into the Destination server by, you know, collapsing my skeleton and squeezing through—like a rat. Hey, Brad. It's a freaking rat-attack!"

Brad went cold. "How do you know me?"

The Destination car swerved around the horse.

"I know all about you, Brad. We've been inside AirVision's servers for months."

A couple of dogs ran alongside the car, barking and snarling, then fell back. A boy, maybe eight years old, picked an aluminum can out of the gutter and dropped it in a paper shopping bag. He glanced up when the car hummed past him.

Xavier nudged Brad's shoulder. "Anywhere you can score a couple of nickels, huh, Brad?"

"What?"

"Seventeen-buck universal minimum wage outside the privileged zones is crap if every job is a minimum wage job, and the Network sets the prices and tells you what you to buy. Pay before content, and everybody's hooked on content. You know what I'm saying?"

"I don't think you should be in this car."

"But I *am* in this car. Where we are now, Brad, is that people are pissed. Even the ones who don't know they're pissed, are pissed. The situation is going to be addressed, and that can go a couple of ways. Let me show you something."

Xavier held out a 3D-printed government-issued phone. The case had been cracked (supposedly impossible to do), the back plate removed, and the original unit mounted on brackets attached to a larger board. Xavier touched the screen and a video started to play—without the Git-It-Now button flashing. Police drone footage of some kind of chaotic street scene. The drone swept down on a seething mob. The mob dispersed, revealing a white-and-blue Destination car, the windows smashed, the egg-shaped vehicle rolled on its roof and—my God!—Ted Lee, the AirVision art department guy, crawled out of the windshield frame, blood on his white shirt. *The scared-looking dude is in some shit!*

Brad shook his head, disbelieving. "Where's that, where that happen?"

Xavier wore a vicious little smile. "Your friend wound up in Oakland. That wasn't my call, by the way. I don't want violence."

Don't you, Brad thought. That smile said something different.

Xavier shoved the phone in Brad's face. "This is an example of the wrong direction. The barricades are gonna fall, Brad. And not everyone wants it to be . . . orderly. Pissed, remember? An inside man with your talent could help things go easier."

"Let me see that phone."

Xavier handed it over. Brad examined it. "You shouldn't have been able to do this modification. That's not supposed to happen. And there's no public feed on police drone video. *We* don't even see those."

A second video started playing, this one a citizen upload. Brad stared at himself waving frantically from a re-charging car, the word-crawl under his face spelling, *Hey, I can't get out! Help me!*

The little fist squeezed Brad's eyeball.

Xavier plucked the phone out of Brad's fingers. "We, huh? Well, we minimums out here in the world are not all as dumb as you want to think. And we don't like your definition of "inappropriate" technology. We can selectively distribute videos, software upgrades, whatever, and the Network can't detect it."

"How you trick AirVision into sending us out in Destination cars? That was a TTP directive."

"Bro. We *are* TTP."

"What?"

"We have been for the last couple of years. We've got tunnels all through AirVision. In a couple of years we'll own the Network, not that anyone inside will know it. And we're making rat tunnels into the multinationals, too. It can come down in blood, or it can come down like a dream—you know, the way reality shifts around you when you're right in the middle of it? Brad, I'm offering you a position with our revolution. You can get in on the ground floor and help make the dream version happen, or you can hide behind the barricades and wait for chaos and blood. We need people with your skills, working on the inside. What do you say?"

"I don't believe any of it. Okay, you hacked the Destination server, but that's not a revolution. It's just . . . a glitch."

Xavier laughed. "Oh, you believe it, all right. You believe all of it. You just don't want to." Xavier glanced out the windshield. They were approaching the freeway ramp, slowing for the Yield. Xavier quickly put his phone away. "I'm gonna be in touch," he said. "It won't be that obvious, but keep your eyes open. You know, a long time ago in France they chopped heads off. Let's try to minimize that shit." The left front tire of the Destination car jolted into a pothole so deep it almost didn't roll out. "Fucking infrastructure. We're gonna get to that."

The car started to turn onto the ramp. Startlingly, Xavier shoved open the door and jumped out. Brad wrenched around. A fossil fuel sedan swung in front of Xavier, he climbed in, and the car sped away.

As he approached Seattle, heavy traffic, big trucks and cars, hemmed in the little white-and-blue egg, and Brad could taste the exhaust of fossil fuel behemoths like a film on his tongue—like a taste out of the past, when he'd lived in Dupree. A poisonous memory toggle. They had beaten his father. Resisting arrest, according to reports. And Brad could believe it. From the security and distance of the exclusive zone, it was easy to remember his father as a loud trouble-maker who drank and made everyone unhappy. Easy to tell himself the beating had been more-or-less deserved. Hadn't Brad himself, as a kid, harbored a secret fury toward his father?

Xavier probably thought he was being clever, kidnapping Brad and bringing him back to Dupree, where memories might awaken. Well, they had. So what?

At the barricades, they took Brad aside to verify his identity. He had expected it but after twenty hours on the road he wasn't happy about it. Even when the retinal scan ID him, the black-uniformed border agents seemed put-out, even angry, about the inconvenience. *We've got better things to do. Who goes outside without his wristband?* It was an ugly little room that smelled like sweat. The raw fluorescent light exacerbated Brad's headache. His mood was at least as ugly as the room.

"You know what?" Brad said to the agent with the long gray sideburns. "You guys are dicks."

A muscle jumped at the agent's jaw, and for a moment Brad thought the man was going to slug him. He didn't, though. He opened the door and stood aside. Almost disappointed, Brad stepped out. He used to imagine his father's beat-down, an event he hadn't witnessed. Policemen swinging truncheons, his father curled in a fetal position. What a dumb thing, trying to provoke a border agent. Brad didn't know what had come over him.

He climbed back into the ridiculous egg-shaped car. What was wrong with him?

The Destination car descended to the garage beneath the Air-Vision tower. As Brad climbed stiffly out of the vehicle, another Destination car's engine started and pulled out. Adelina Serna sat in the passenger seat, a tense, frightened expression on her face. It was the middle of the night. But when TTP issued marching orders . . .

In France they used to chop heads off. Let's minimize that shit.

Back in the office, Brad dropped into his chair. He should have been starving, but the empty sickness in the pit of his stomach didn't want food. He still had the stupid Buddha Danish. He tossed it on the desk. Virtual ripples radiated away. Brad passed his hand over the jewel light on the corner of the desk, and a Ghostware cloud formed. He navigated to @dupreebudha's Flutter feed. Despite its theft from the diner, the Danish's posts had continued uninterrupted. Brad scrolled through them, reading mangled quotes. He came upon what he'd been looking for without even realizing, before that moment, that he *had* been looking for it.

@dupreebudha: "Thousands of candles can be lighted from a single candle, and it looks like you need a new manager."

Brad turned off his desk and stared out the window. Adelina Serna wasn't his favorite person, but she didn't deserve whatever Xavier's people had in mind for her. All those candles could light up a dark place—or set it on fire and burn everything and everyone to ashes. Once the candles were lit, it could go either way. Brad thought of Xavier's vicious smile. For a certain type of person, once you *could* burn something down, wasn't it inevitable that you would?

"I just want to go home," Brad muttered.

But where was that?

DREAM INTERPRETATION

The hour was done and they'd gotten nowhere. David Grant closed Elena Navarro's file and set the device aside. "I think we're finished for today." He began to stand.

Elena's chin came up. "We have to get out. Tomorrow night is our last chance."

He paused, half out of his chair, then settled back down. For the last hour she had sat across from him, clearly agitated but unresponsive to his questions. He glanced at the clock. "I'm afraid the time—"

"You better *listen* to me, Doctor Grant."

It was late. Ava was expecting him home. She wanted to *have it out.* Tell him the reasons she was leaving. But Grant didn't want it out. He wanted it in, where he didn't have to feel those reasons directly. Compartmentalization, keeping his emotions in a box, made sense to him. But not to Ava. *Having it out* is what made sense to her. Grant's stomach muscles clenched at the thought of it. And what was the point? Ava wasn't changing her mind about leaving. She made that clear. Meanwhile, his client needed his attention.

He calmly opened Elena's file again. "I'm listening."

"You don't need to write this down," she said. "Just remember what I'm telling you. If you haven't already, you're going to have a dream. It will seem more real than your actual life. That's because this *isn't* your actual life. The dream is."

Where was this coming from? "Go on."

"This room, the entire world outside the door, everything you can see from the window. It's not your real world. No, that isn't right. This world is real, but it's not where you started. It's not where you belong."

Elena's left eye twitched. That was new. Grant took note.

"When you have the dream," she said, "*accept* it. Stay with it. Don't go to sleep. It's your only chance."

He studied her face. Elena had come to therapy as a last resort. Her attitude was sarcastic, dismissive of the process, self-mocking—all a front she wore to mask her fear. But her grip on reality had never been in doubt.

"But if I'm dreaming," Grant said, "aren't I already asleep?"

She stared hard at him. "You're not listening. *This* is the dream. What we're in right now. Only it isn't a dream. It's an alternate probability, a mass effect caused by Nakamura."

Grant stroked his chin, giving himself a moment. "What's Nakamura?"

"Of course you wouldn't know. It doesn't exist here."

"Elena, really. I—"

She stood up abruptly, and Grant's body tensed. It was involuntary. Elena had struck her boyfriend, a major in the astronaut corps, with a heavy glass vase, sent him to the hospital. She told Grant that in her first session.

Elena paced back and forth, her face stretched tight, like a thin rubber mask. He watched her, warily. Then she stopped and faced him.

"Okay," she said. "You won't believe me, but I have to have this out."

"Go ahead."

"Nakamura? It's an alien artifact. Named after the astronomer who discovered it. He and everyone else thought it was an asteroid from outside the solar system. An interstellar object. That was eighteen months ago. I was a senior scientist at JPL, working with CNEOS. That's the Center for Near Earth Object Studies."

"I've never heard of it." Grant wondered if she had made it up on the spot. Her declarations felt improvisational.

"Most people haven't. But a week ago we became famous for identifying what Nakamura really is."

She shook her head, started pacing again, muttering.

"Elena, why don't you sit down. Please."

She looked at him, as if weighing whether it was worth it, then came back to the sofa and sat. Grant told his clients to sit where they were most comfortable, in either of the two chairs or the sofa. Most chose the sofa. He poured a glass of ice water from the silver urn and handed it to her. She took several deep swallows and set the glass down.

"I wasn't going to say anything," Elena said. "When I woke up this morning, I couldn't accept what was happening, even though I knew it was true. My whole day, it's going through the motions, following the routine. The routine brought me here for my Wednesday session. It was on the schedule."

Grant folded his hands in his lap and listened closely. Elena Navarro was not a scientist working at JPL. She was a NASA administration specialist based right here in Houston. She had held the position for five years.

"But all I've been thinking," she said, "is how do I make sure I don't wake up here again. The obvious solution is to not have a body to wake up in. Doesn't that make sense?"

Very carefully, Grant asked, "Have you been thinking about hurting yourself?"

Elena leaned back. After a beat, she said, "You have no idea what I'm talking about. You think I'm crazy. Or you think I have a brain tumor. You've always thought that."

"No, not at all. But we—"

"Nakamura is producing a distortion field. We don't know the reason, or if there is a reason. We call it the Nakamura Effect, for lack of anything better. It's what's causing all this."

Grant picked up his stylus pen and turned it with his fingers like a miniature baton. "Can you elaborate? What do you mean when you say 'all this'?"

"Never mind. I warned you. It's all I can do."

She got up and opened the door, then looked back. "Doctor Grant, I hope you'll think about what I've said. You deserve to go home. We all do."

He spent half an hour dictating his notes. Elena Navarro had come to him three weeks ago. Thirty-nine years old with a stressful job at NASA. She complained of anxiety, difficulty with concentration, memory lapses, and sudden, violent outbursts. All of it new. Elena claimed previously to have never lost her temper. Yet lately she found herself subject to sudden rages, smashing dinner plates, bruising her knuckles against the wall, screaming in frustration, as if that would help her recall the name that had disappeared down a memory hole, or the location of a missing key. And there was the vase incident.

Elena didn't want drugs and she resisted neurological imaging. It was some kind of stress-crisis, she told him. That's all. The violent outbursts worried Grant. He had told her an MRI would rule out oncological explanations. She refused. Like many people, Elena Navarro wanted to pretend that not-knowing was the same as not-having. But reality eventually caught up to everyone.

Grant's car turned onto Nagle Street. The townhouse looked, appropriately, like an empty box. The garage door was rolled up, Ava's Mercedes gone. Grant almost told his car to keep going. Classic avoidance. He kept quiet, and the car swung into the driveway.

Two years ago they had paid nine hundred and seventy thousand dollars for this address in the EaDo—east downtown Houston. Grant flipped on every light switch. Hardwood floors and marble countertops gleamed. A cleaning service kept the townhouse spotless. White vaulted space enclosed him with an autopsy room's sterility.

She hadn't waited for him to come home, after all.

He knew where Ava had gone. Knew *his* name—the man without emotional compartments. Max Stone, a partner in Ava's law firm.

Grant felt her absence in every room. Most of her clothes still hung in the closet, but her Maxwell-Scott travel bag was missing. He lingered in the walk-in closet, as did her scent, and tried to determine what she had taken, which outfits and accessories, which shoes. That might tell him if she had left for good, or for a break, or even just to make a point. In the master bath, the basket Ava kept her makeup in was empty and her toothbrush was gone. He stared at the empty basket and felt hollowed out. Unbearable grief rushed in to fill the cavity.

After too many glasses of ten-year-old Laphroaig scotch whisky, he went to bed and lay on top of the covers, fully clothed except for his shoes. A wedding picture stood on Ava's dresser. One of the things she'd left. Grant remembered their wedding day, how the threatened rain hadn't come and they were able to have the ceremony in the garden, after all. He had taken this as a positive sign, an approving nod from the matrimonial gods.

He got up and brought the picture back to the bed. Grant's head buzzed, but it wasn't the scotch. The sensation was peculiar, like standing next to a powerful generator. Above the skylight an airliner tracked west, position lights blinking, almost lost among the stars. The wedding picture slipped from his fingers.

He slept.

And woke in the wrong bed.

The room was small, the ceiling too low, the walls beige and cracked. A shirt draped untidily over the dresser. The sliding closet door stood half open. A rumpled blazer sagged between empty wire hangers. Under the window a portable air-conditioning unit rattled nosily, disturbing the pages of a *Psychology Today* on the bedside table. The room was so cramped that Grant could have opened the dresser drawers without getting out of bed.

A frightening sense of dislocation surged through him. His heart beat too fast. Cold sweat broke out on his forehead, and panic clawed up his throat. "*Help.*" Grant's voice cracked. He threw the sheet aside, swung his legs off the mattress, and sat breathing the dry, stale air. His hands were shaking. Then, as quickly as it had come, the panic subsided. The room became familiar. There was nothing unusual, except that Grant knew he was in a dream. A lucid dream that encompassed a life he had always, somewhere, been living.

A dream that felt more real than his life in the EaDo.

He dried his face with the sheet, picked up his watch, and squinted at the dial. 7:00 AM. After a quick shower he pulled on a pair of tan Dockers. All but one of Grant's shirts were in the laundry hamper, so he grabbed the one off the dresser, sniffed the armpits, and put it on. His movements felt routine, coded into muscle-memory. Was this really a dream? "I want to wake up," he said, but nothing happened. He could only go along with the body while it proceeded through its day. What had Elena said about the dream? *Accept it . . . stay with it. Don't sleep.*

An hour and two bus rides later Grant walked through the door of the Mental Health Alliance on the south side of Houston. By eight-thirty he was in his shoe-box-sized office with a cup of strong coffee and his first client.

Denny was twenty-two years old, a recovering drug addict who had lived rough on the streets of Houston for a year before getting clean. Now he washed dishes in a barbeque joint called The Devil's Tongue and spent the rest of his time between Narcotics Anonymous meetings and a rented room that probably made Grant's apartment look like Downton Abby. The state of Texas subsidized Denny's counseling, a condition of his probation. Without it he would probably be back on the streets, or in jail, or dead.

The kid was typical of Grant's clients in this life, a person on the margins of a society that had no use for him. In his real practice, Grant's clients were well-off men and women, but mostly men, who moved in his own socioeconomic sphere or higher. Usually higher. Elena Navarro hadn't quite fit that profile.

Working with state-dependent clients like Denny was grueling but satisfying in a way that Grant's real practice rarely was. Denny depended on him for his survival. But Grant's well-heeled clients too often hired him as they would a mechanic with specialized knowledge to fine-tune their self-absorbed psyches.

Back in college he had made a decision that brought him here. The same decision had cost him his future with Ava Conway.

On Grant's lunch break he walked across the street to a little park, marveling at the detailed perfection of the dream. He sat on a bench scrawled with gang tags and ate a tuna fish sandwich. In the broiling shadows homeless men lay like murder victims. Pigeons swarmed and cooed for crumbs. A mail-carrier in USPO regulation shorts sat on a bench across the way, where she always sat at the noon hour, sipping an iced coffee from Starbucks and eating a bagel. She waved at him, and Grant waved back. It was part of the work-day routine.

Of course, it was impossible. No dream was so vivid, so organized in sequential time. Grant's instincts told him this alternate life was as real as the one he had left behind. Perhaps more real. How could that be? Grant was shocked to realize he'd already stopped thinking of the life he had with Ava as being the real life. Now it was just the *other* life. If this dream lasted much longer, would he regard it as real and the other as a dream? And which was true?

In college Ava had envisioned herself and Grant as a couple propelled into the future on the rocket fuel of dual ambitions. She had thought Grant's aim to become a psychiatric social worker—a "do gooder"—was an insane waste of talent and earning potential. In the other world Grant had changed the trajectory of his education for the sake of keeping Ava. At twenty years old, his attraction to her had been more intense than his career ambitions.

In this lucid dream he no longer knew Ava. After the breakup they hadn't kept in touch. She presumably rode the ambition rocket into the future, while Grant caught a smelly bus ride to the Mental Health Alliance.

Sitting on the park bench with his tuna fish sandwich, Grant decided to try something. So far he had experienced the do-gooder version of himself like a passenger along for the ride. Did he have any control? He slipped out his phone. According to Google, six Ava Conways lived in the state of Texas. None resided in Houston, but the Ava Conway in Austin was a lawyer with a boutique firm specializing in intellectual property law. And she had attended Texas A&M during the years Grant had been there.

He touched her profile. A face appeared. Copper hair styled short, strong chin, nose and cheeks dusted with freckles. The red-framed glasses were new, but the eyes were the same. Intelligent, penetrating, blue. Grant felt a tingle of excitement. He had never stopped thinking about Ava. Had it been the same for her? He could still hear her whispering in his ear: *I've got your number, David.* Meaning she knew who he really was. Not a do-gooder determined on a vow of poverty, but an exceptional student with a brilliant, ambitious future—a future they would share. But Ava had been wrong about his ambitions.

Had the passage of ten years made a difference? In this alternate life, Grant had followed his own path, not the one Ava wanted for him. But here he was, past thirty and alone. As unscientific as it was to contemplate, what if two people really were meant for each other and subverting that fate was a mistake? Maybe this dream, as real as it felt, was a thought experiment constructed by his unconscious. Why not test it?

After work he composed a message: HEY, YOU! IT'S BEEN A LONG TIME, HASN'T IT? WE WERE GOOD TOGETHER, BACK IN COLLEGE. WONDER IF YOU LIKE TO HAVE

LUNCH AND CATCH UP. Etcetera. He labored over the message for an hour before hitting send, still unsatisfied. Then he spent the balance of the evening checking every fifteen minutes for a reply. One finally arrived after he was already in bed.

SORRY. I DON'T REMEMBER YOU.

Grant stared at the words. Suddenly his dingy little apartment seemed even dingier. Imprudently, he tapped out a reply. She might have forgotten his name. It was possible. Ava probably dated a lot in college. She needed to be reminded of who he had been to her beyond his name. He hit send. The email bounced back. Undeliverable.

Blocked.

He stared at the screen, feeling wounded. His thumb swiped away the block alert, leaving a news stream. The word Nakamura caught his eye. It had been in the news off-and-on. A huge asteroid passing by Earth. At the sight of the word, cold fear prickled up his spine. Grant put the phone face-down and pushed it away. This world no longer felt like a dream but the grinding reality he had chosen for himself. He clicked off the lamp, and rolled over. *Don't sleep*, Elena Navarro had said. *Don't dream.* But how else would he escape these feelings?

The city sang him to sleep with wailing sirens.

Grant opened his eyes in the East Houston townhouse. He lay on his back in the same position he'd gone to sleep. His mouth felt dry, his tongue thick. A gilded cloud slowly came apart above the skylight. The room felt spacious, luxurious. Grant knew where he was but it felt slightly unreal. The dream world of stuffy apartments, buses, social work, and loneliness stood in his mind with clarity greater even than a living memory. And the details did not grow muddled with the passing minutes.

Before leaving the townhouse, he called Ava's number. One ring and then nothing. Grant flinched. She had blocked him, just as her counterpart had done in the dream.

His first client was at nine o'clock. Marty Jepson, an oil executive who wanted to resolve his anger issues, or said he did. A large, florid man, Jepson was typical of the kind of client Grant regularly treated. Successful, motivated, late middle-aged extroverts seeking solutions to buried trauma and absolution for their sins. Sometimes the trauma didn't exist. Sometimes—many times, to be honest—the anger grew out of a core personality defect. Had Grant's lucid dream job as a psychiatric social worker been a morally superior position? Did the needs of Denny-the-junkie supersede those of Marty-the-executive?

Ultimately, both paths had led Grant to empty rooms.

This morning Marty Jepson didn't want to talk about the priest he believed abused him. He didn't want to talk about the slap he'd given his wife and the reasons why he might have done such a despicable thing (reasons other than the ones readily found in a bottle of Makers Mark and a bully's disposition).

"Last night I had a troubling dream, Dr. Grant."

Grant looked up. Jepson had never mentioned dreams, or anything else that strayed even slightly from the straight path between his altar-boy encounters with the parish priest and Jepson's increasingly violent temper.

"Go on, Mr. Jepson."

"It was like a whole 'nother life. Like what would have happened if I'd told my daddy about Father Devlin when I was thirteen, instead of keeping it bottled up all these years. Daddy had a real bad temper, and he let it go on Father Devlin. Killed him dead. I don't think he meant to go that far, but it happened. And it changed my whole life. Daddy went to prison, and our family lost everything. You know, doc, that secret between me and Devlin, it was like a rusty spur constantly jabbing me from the inside. It drove me hard and made me a fighter. Made me go *after* things. All that was changed in the dream. I never amounted to much at all, just a first-level manager at BP."

"Your dream sounds extraordinarily detailed."

"You being funny, doctor? It didn't play like any dream at all. I dropped into it like hitting the seat of my Cadillac already rolling down the 69. Jesus Christ, all that stuff I just told you? It was in the past by the time I got there. It was a *life*, already happening. The strange thing is, I felt more at home there than I do here. Now what the hell does that mean? Dr. Grant?"

Grant felt unmoored. His office, the chair he sat in, were both familiar and foreign. He closed his eyes against a wave of dizziness.

"Are you all right, doc?"

Grant opened his eyes. "I'm fine. But I can't tell you why you felt more at home in your dream than you do here."

Here, Grant thought, as if reality were a location.

"Now look," Jepson said. "Right before going to bed I had something like a headache. Not an ache, a buzz. Like a vibration in my skull. What I want to hear, is do you think there's a chance of tumor activity, and that's what made it so real?"

"I don't think so, but it's possible. I'll arrange an MRI."

"Hold off on that for now." Jepson picked up his hat, a fawn-colored Stetson, and stood. "I'll call you." He stood in front of Grant, a tall, physically imposing man, turning his hat in his fingers. "There's this other thing and it probably doesn't mean much. I didn't amount to a hill of beans in that dream, but I didn't have that priest thing hanging over my head, either. Didn't have that secret shame. And I was a better man, I think. I was the kind of man who would never get drunk and slap his wife."

That day, every client Grant talked to had a dream to report. Most of them had never before mentioned dreams. These dreams, these other lives, varied. Some were better than the client's waking life, others were worse, and still others were merely different—a wash. Another commonality was the buzzing before sleep, the headache upon awaking.

After his last client left, Grant sat alone in his office, stunned. And scared.

He called Elena Navarro's number. Somehow she had known about the dreams. Unless it was a coincidence too fantastical to be believed. Elena didn't answer. He pulled up her file, copied her home address, and told his car to take him there. On the way, he called three more times, without luck. He also tried Ava again, but he was still blocked.

It was a white stucco bungalow a couple of miles from the Johnson Space Center. A stunted palm tree stood in the yard, fronds drooping in the heat. The blinds were closed. Grant knocked, rang the bell. Nothing. He removed his hat, blotted his forehead with his sleeve, put the hat back on.

A man came out of the house next door, crossed tan, muscular arms, and stared at Grant. The man's polo shirt had the NASA insignia over the left breast. "Help you with something?" he asked.

"I'm looking for Elena Navarro."

"She's not here."

"I can see that. I'm her doctor. David Grant."

The man removed his aviators and stepped closer. A two-inch stitched wound ran diagonally above his left eye, where Elena struck him with the vase. "Elena's talked about you."

"You're Major Coontz?"

"I see she's talked about me, too. Yeah, I'm Ted Coontz. Making a house call, doctor?"

Grant smiled, as if he found that amusing. "I guess I am. She's not answering her phone. Do you know where she is?"

"I might."

"I need to talk to her."

Coontz looked troubled, reluctant. He put his glasses back on.

"What's going on, Major?"

"I have a trailer out in the Chihuahuan desert," Coontz said. "I took Elena there a couple of times. She loved it. Said if the apocalypse ever came, that's where she wanted to be."

We have to get out, tomorrow night is our last chance.

"And that's where she is?"

"Yes."

"How far is this place?"

"A few hours." Coontz scratched under his chin with his thumb. "Listen, doc. She said something you should know."

"What?"

"She said if you showed up here, I should bring you out to the desert. But I don't think it's a good idea."

Grant felt like he was following a script from which he couldn't deviate. His mouth was dry. He swallowed. "Tell me where this trailer is and I'll go myself."

"By the time you get there, it'll be dark. Besides, you'd never find it without me." Coontz looked at the ground and shook his head. "Shit. I'll drive."

They sped down Highway 87 in Coontz's Jeep, flashing past cars like they were standing still.

Grant looked at the speedometer. "Aren't you worried about speeding tickets?"

"Nope. The troopers *love* astronauts."

"Major, I want to ask you a strange question. Have you been having particularly vivid dreams?"

Coontz shot him a hard look. "I don't remember dreams. And I hope to God you aren't going to bother Elena about that shit. She's obsessed enough."

Neither of them spoke again until twenty miles southeast of Comfort, with daylight long gone. Coontz let up on the gas and said, "There it is."

Grant leaned forward. An unmarked dirt road came up fast. Coontz tapped the brakes and turned the wheel. The Jeep jolted off the paved highway. Even with his lap belt, Grant bounced out of his seat. From there, Coontz took it slow, following the sketchy track through a dense sea of creosote scrub.

After nearly an hour the headlights splashed over a silver Airstream trailer and solar panel array. A red sport utility vehicle was parked next to the trailer.

"That's her rig." Coontz pulled his Jeep up to the trailer, tires crunching. He cut the engine and tucked the keys under the sun visor. He and Grant climbed out of the Jeep and slammed the doors.

Under the Airstream's retractable awning, a figure stood up.

"El?" Coontz said.

Elena stepped into the starlight. She wore cargo shorts and a white sleeveless top. In her right hand was a tumbler half filled with clear liquid. Ice clicked against the glass.

"I brought your doctor," Coontz said.

"Doctor Grant." Elena stepped closer. "I'm glad you're here."

Grant smelled gin. "I came because of the dreams."

Coontz frowned at him.

Elena said, "I thought you would. Don't be afraid. We're all going to get through this." She put her hand on her hip and looked at the stars, as if she were expecting a delivery. "I have a plan."

Grant and Coontz looked at each other.

"What plan?" Coontz asked.

"That's a secret. Suffice to say, my head's clear."

The temperature had dropped into the low fifties. Elena didn't seem to mind the cold, even in her shorts. She had the door of the Airstream propped open. "It's hot in there," she said. "I'm airing it out. Let's sit down." She retreated back under the awning.

Coontz whispered, "Don't encourage her, for Christ's sake."

They sat in director's chairs. Under the awning it was too dark to see faces. Maybe it was hot inside the trailer but it was uncomfortably chilly outside. Grant crossed his arms and wished he'd brought a jacket.

"I can share my Hendrick's, if I have to," Elena said. "But I found Ted's beer stash and put it on ice, in case you boys showed up thirsty. So you got your dream, Dr. Grant."

"Yes. How did you know?"

"It's what I said in your office. We're in a probability dream caused by the Nakamura Effect. And the clock's ticking. Nakaumra's traveling at fifty-four miles per second. The field will release us in about six hours. Here, take a Lone Star."

A cold, wet bottle touched the back of Grant's hand.

"You too, Ted."

"I'll pass," Coontz said. "You got these trajectory numbers down, don't you."

"My team at CNEOS are good."

"You've never worked for CNEOS."

"In this world, that's true. But in the primary world, where our bodies lie dreaming right now, yes. I work at CNEOS."

Coontz grunted. "I can't understand you."

"And what happens when this asteroid or whatever it is gets out of range?" Grant asked.

"Nakamura is an alien artifact. What happens when it's gone? Anyone still here when that happens, stays here, I think." Ice cubes clicked against glass. "But if you're in the primary world, you stay *there*. Where you started. Where you belong."

They were all dim shapes in the dark, voices without mouths.

"So on top of everything else, consciousness is non-local?" Coontz said. "For God's sake, El, listen to yourself."

There was an edge in his voice, an edge honed on established grievance. Grant had heard the same tone coming from Ava . . . and past his own lips.

"Fuck it." Coontz shifted in his chair, making the hinged joints creak. "I can't believe you two are discussing this like it's a real thing. Like it's something that could be happening outside of Elena's head."

"I'm not delusional, Ted. You're angry because you're afraid. I understand."

"Like hell."

They stopped talking. Things chirruped in the desert. Grant leaned forward, trying to see Elena's face. Alien artifacts? Two worlds joined by dreams? It was a bridge too far. "This is fascinating," he said. "When we get back to Houston, I'd like to hear more about it." In a proper therapeutic environment, he added silently.

"Of course, doctor." She sounded almost amused. Like Ava all those years ago, she thought she had his number.

Coontz cleared his throat. "Anyway. Nobody's going back to Houston until morning. No point in risking a broken axle in the arroyo twice in one night. Let's pack it in."

The Major led them into his trailer. Despite the airing out, it was still explosively hot. Coontz flipped the light switch and nothing happened. "What gives?"

"I disconnected the collector cables and dragged the batts into the desert," Elena said.

"Why the hell did you do that?"

"It's better if we don't have any field interference."

A flashlight came on in Coontz' hand. He played it around the trailer. The light gleamed on aluminum foil covering the windows. "What'd you do to my Airstream?"

"I made a Faraday cage out of it," Elena said.

Coontz sighed heavily. "At this point, no fucking comment."

Elena and Coontz retired to the bed at the far end of the trailer. Grant removed his shoes and socks and stretched out on the hard leatherette sofa bench. They were arguing, keeping their voices down. Grant caught an occasional word. *Denial. Understand. Bullshit.* Eventually they stopped.

Grant lay sweating in the dark, unable to sleep. His client's dreams bothered him. His own, he could explain, or told himself that he could: the destruction of his marriage had been preying viciously on his mind. That Ava rejected him even in the lucid dream only supported Grant's own suppressed feelings of worthlessness.

But what about Marty Jepson and his other clients? They had all experienced similarly vivid dreams. For that, Grant had no convincing interpretation.

He rolled onto his side, pictured his Ambien prescription in the medicine cabinet of the EaDo townhouse. There was a buzzing in his head. He began to slip away. It seemed he heard traffic move in the street below a shabby Houston apartment. His eyelids trembled against morning light—then something interrupted the process. A disturbance from the other end of the trailer.

Grant's eyes snapped open and he stared into the dark, his breath gone shallow. After a few moments, he decided that he'd imagined the disturbance and tried again to sleep. Then the floor creaked under someone's footstep, and Grant was instantly alert.

"Who's there?" He could feel someone in the dark. Grant sat up. "Major Coontz? Elena?"

"It's me," Elena said.

"Oh."

"I was just coming to get a drink of water. I thought you were asleep. I'm sorry if I woke you."

"You didn't. I was thinking about what you said. About how this is all a false dream."

"Not a dream," Elena said. "An alternate probability. I know it's a lot to grasp."

To say the least, Grant thought. "Elena, It's not uncommon to think you made a wrong turn and aren't where you belong. Everyone's life feels counterfeit at some point. Or like a waking dream." His certainly had, ever since college.

"Is that how you feel, Dr. Grant?"

"What I feel isn't relevant. I'm talking about a psychological phenomenon."

"I understand."

They stopped talking. He could hear her breathing in the dark.

"Aren't you going to get your water?" Grant asked.

"You felt more at home in your dream, though. Didn't you, Dr. Grant?"

Grant hesitated to answer, then he did. "Not at home, no. It just seemed like the way I would have gone, if someone hadn't convinced me to go a different direction."

"And that made it better."

"Better? It felt like the life I deserved, I guess."

"More authentic," Elena said. "Dr. Grant? I'm sorry. But there's not much time left, and I think you'll be grateful."

"Grateful? It's hot in here. I have to get some air."

He started to stand, and Elena struck him with something high on the right side of his chest. He felt the blade scrape under his collarbone and plunge deep. Grant shoved her hard with both hands. The blade pulled out of his chest and Elena crashed against something and grunted.

He lunged across the trailer, groped for the door handle, found it and flung the door open. He fell off the steps, scrambled back to his feet, and blundered into the director's chairs. He threw them aside and ran into the desert.

The stiff fingers of creosote bushes snagged at his pants. He was sweating hard and couldn't draw a decent breath. Grant dropped to the ground, dragged himself under a clump of scrub, and lay there panting. Too late, he remembered that Coontz had tucked his keys under the Jeep's sun-visor. Now Elena was between him and his only chance of escape.

She called his name. Grant kept his head down and begged the deity he didn't believe in to keep her away.

"Dr. Grant! David! Don't be afraid. If you have a living body here, you might not be able to let go. Let me help you. I've worked it all out!"

Grant turned his head enough to see between the gnarled branches. Elena stood at the edge of the scrub, her left hand holding the back of her head, her right hand gripping the knife. Elena's white shirt glowed in cold starlight. What looked like ink splatters stained the shirt. *Not ink. Blood.*

She moved haltingly in his direction, the dry creosote tangles crackling against her bare legs. She tried to find a clear path, but there wasn't one. Grant pushed his white face into the dirt and kept still. The gritty sound of her boots scuffing the desert hardpan came closer, stopped, moved in a different direction, stopped again, then retreated. He looked up. Elena stood in front of the trailer staring into the desert. After a couple of minutes, she climbed inside.

Grant remained on the ground. The desert cold penetrated to his bones. The pain came forward, then. He had shredded the soles of his feet. The knife wound ached and felt hot, while the rest of his body rapidly turned to ice. Blood soaked through his shirt and stuck it to his chest. He couldn't draw a decent breath.

I'm going to die out here.

Grant pushed himself to his knees. He had been lying on his right arm so long it had gone numb. He held the arm close to his body and used only his left hand to shove away from the ground. His knees dragged forward and he rose to a shaky stance, shocked at how weak he'd become. Grant felt exposed, terrifyingly vulnerable. The Jeep was his only chance.

He hobbled forward. The closer he approached the trailer, the more his fear ratcheted up. He felt watched. Grant drew wheezing, insufficient breaths. A metallic-tasting fluid came up his throat and he spat it out. The taste made him nauseous.

He fell against the Jeep, opened the driver's door. The hinges creaked. He used the steering wheel to haul himself inside. He flipped down the sun visor, and the keys fell into his lap. Grant stared at them in a daze, then picked them up with his still-tingling right hand and tried to slot the ignition key. The keys slipped from his fingers and dropped into the foot well. The effort of reaching down seemed too great. Grant sat with his head hanging, wheezing like a torn bellows. But only for a moment. He made himself grope in the foot well until he found the keys. This time he got the ignition key slotted.

The engine cranked over and kicked in, loud. Grant popped the headlights on. Elena burst from the trailer and ran at him with the knife. He shoved the Jeep into gear and crushed the accelerator, gritting his teeth against the pain. Elena threw herself out of the way, and Grant rolled the steering wheel into a tight turn. The driver's door slammed and the vehicle jolted and careened into the desert. Grant fought the Jeep back to the dirt road. In the review mirror Elena stood with her arms at her sides, the knife blade catching star gleam.

Every dip and jolt made him gasp in pain. He went slow, worried about the Major's warning of a broken axle. Finally he came to Highway 87 and swung north, towards the town of Comfort. Twenty miles. His vision kept hazing in and out. He squeezed his eyes shut, shook his head, opened his eyes wide. Tried to focus, stay alert. The Jeep wandered with his attention. A car swerved around him, horn blaring. The shock galvanized Grant enough to reach the Comfort exit.

He removed his throbbing foot from the gas and veered toward the exit. The Jeep rolled off the ramp and onto the shoulder. Grant stomped on the brakes. The Jeep skidded and nosed into a ditch. The impact threw him against his shoulder restraint. The engine stuttered and quit.

Grant slumped against the door, too weak to move. Pain kept him conscious but foggy. For a while, it seemed Ava sat next to him and he spoke with her. She was very young, the Ava Conway he'd known at Texas A&M.

You have so much potential, David. Don't waste it.

"I'm hurt."

Whining about it won't help. Pull yourself up. Get moving.

"You don't understand." David closed his eyes, let his head droop.

I understand, Dr. Grant. I've got your number.

A whisper in his ear. A different voice. Grant opened his eyes—and recoiled. Elena Navarro leaned toward him, her eyes bright with her plan, her white blouse stiff with Major Coontz's blood.

"Jesus!"

Grant came fully awake. He was alone in the Jeep. Hot sunlight slanted through the windshield. Bells were tolling. Church bells. The engine wouldn't start. He gave up and started walking, every step on his bloodied feet exquisitely painful. He kept going. A car was bound to come by soon.

None did.

Comfort was a historical town with a population under three thousand. Many of the buildings dated back to the earliest years of the twentieth century, everything maintained to present a Simpler Times vision for tourists. Grant and Ava had once come up here on spring break. Now Main Street was empty. No tourists strolled the sidewalks and the antique shops and cafes all appeared closed. Only the tolling of the church bells indicated the town wasn't deserted.

Grant saw bright fluorescent light. He staggered under the red-and-white striped awning of an ice cream parlor. A man sat at one of the wire-frame tables, a shiny ice cream scoop in his hand. He was burly, with black hair thick on his forearms and a black mustache. The jaunty paper hat looked incongruous above his heavy features.

Grant stumbled through the doorway, leaving bloody foot-prints. A bright little bell dinged in counterpoint to the dolorous tolling of the church bells.

"I need help," Grant said.

The man in the paper hat came out of his chair and caught Grant before he collapsed.

"Did you try to do yourself?"

The man's words didn't make sense.

"What? I've been stabbed. A woman stabbed me."

"Yeah. Most died in their sleep. But I've heard stuff like that. You sit here a minute. I'll drive you to the hospital."

Grant slumped in a chair. He rested his head on his arms and sank into his pain and delirium.

He woke in a hospital bed, groggy with sedation. Grant had the room to himself. No one walked by the open door. No sounds reached him from the corridor. A cool stream of oxygen hissed into his nasal passages and an IV dripped something into his vein. He lay there listening to the beep and click of monitoring equipment until a male nurse came in. Big but running to fat, a chin like a shovel, prematurely balding. Bodine ("Call me Bo, everybody does"). Grant asked him what had happened.

"I guess half the world woke up dead yesterday," Bo said.

"What?"

"Like what I said."

Grant was stunned. "That's impossible."

"Is it? I wouldn't say so."

"Wait. You said yesterday. What day is this?"

Bo told him. Grant had lost twenty-four hours.

"You were exaggerating," Grant said. "It couldn't be half the population."

"That's what they were saying yesterday. Maybe it's more by now, or less. I can't bear to look. Lot of people who did wake up went on and killed themselves. That got to me even worse. Guess they couldn't take it. Or wished it was a dream. Maybe it is."

Grant stared at him, speechless. The world felt eggshell-fragile. Grief rose in him like poison waters. He looked away and wiped his eyes.

"Local man drove you up from Comfort," Bo told him. "Nice fella. All's they got down there is a clinic. Yesterday no staff showed up. It's the same here, mostly. I had a couple of doctors until this morning. Dr. Marsden, she fixed you up. Punctured lung. Oh, that's the morphine making you feel all weird. I'm supposed to take you off that today, but I don't know. Fixed it so you can self-administer."

Grant choked out the words, "I want to see the doctor."

"Like I said, she didn't come in. Nobody did. You're the only patient, and I'm the last nurse. Sounds like one of those crazy movies. That's okay, Mr. Grant. I cried my stupid eyes out all day. It's nothing to be ashamed of. I think I'll just leave you the morphine bag." Bo turned to leave the room.

"Wait. I want news. I want to know what's going on."

Bo scratched the side of his nose. "Cable TV's out. I don't know why. There's some internet left. I'll bring you a tablet."

The numbers were still being calculated, but the death toll was clearly going to be higher than Bo's "half the world." Survivors flailed for explanations, rational or otherwise. Most of the explanations populating across social media platforms were otherwise. The few official news sources still posting were no better. Grant kept scrolling until he couldn't take it anymore.

That night, Grant was tempted to disappear into the morphine. Instead he pressed the call button for Bo. It took a while for the nurse to respond. When Bo came in, he looked disheveled: shirt unbuttoned, face unshaven, eyes bloodshot.

"I want you to unhook me from the morphine," Grant said.

"Sure thing, Mr. Grant."

When Bo leaned over to remove the IV, Grant smelled whiskey and sweat.

"There you are," Bo said. "You need anything else, you push that call-button, like you just done. I'll be sleeping down the hall. Haven't got a home left to go to anymore. So this is it."

Grant came awake slowly, then all at once. Sunlight filled the room. How could it be so late? According to the institutional clock above the door it was almost noon. He rubbed sleep out of his eyes. A vague and ordinary dream faded behind them.

Nakaumra had moved on.

He pressed the call button. Bo did not respond. The medical monitor showed Grant's heart rate jag upward. He peeled off transdermal patches, removed the finger-clip sensor, and got up.

His bloody clothes were gone but he found a pair of gripper socks in the closet. Wincing, Grant carefully worked the socks onto his wrapped and swollen feet. The corridor was eerily silent, the nurse's station deserted. Papers in different colors—pink, blue, yellow—scattered across the floor.

"Bo? Anyone?"

Grant held his gown closed in the back, walked to the set of double swing-doors, and pushed through. Another empty corridor. But he heard voices and called out, "Hello?"

A teenage girl stuck her head out of the pharmacy. She didn't speak. Then she and a tall, skinny boy about the same age came out of the pharmacy together. They had the jittery look of some of Grant's clients from the Mental Health Alliance in his alternate life. The boy clutched the straps of a backpack. The three of them stared at each for a tense moment. Then the girl tugged on the boy's arm. He sniffed, wiped his nose on the back of his hand, and together they turned and ran away, their sneakers slapping the tile floor.

Grant returned to his room. His wallet and keys were in the drawer of the bedside table. He picked them up along with the tablet and wandered the hospital until he found a locker room for hospital staff. Some doctor had left a change of clothes in an unsecured locker. The chinos were too long and wide. He had to roll back the sleeves of the chambray shirt. In the mirror he looked like a well-dressed scarecrow.

From the lobby he called 911. The line was busy. He kept trying. Finally it started ringing. But no one picked up. After twenty rings, Grant cradled the receiver. All he wanted now was to go home, whatever that was to him anymore. The walk around the hospital had winded him and his poor feet were throbbing. He used the tablet to access his Uber account and request a ride. Five minutes later a driverless sedan pulled up. The system was automated, and autonomous vehicles didn't die in their sleep.

There was little traffic on Highway 290. A few autonomous cars carrying their own shell-shocked passengers. An old man with a grizzled beard raised his hand and gave Grant a little wave before the man's car dipped down an exit ramp.

Grant saw no police vehicles.

About halfway to Houston, a big Ford 250 with a human driver raced up alongside Grant's Uber. The driver, a young man with long stringy hair, pointed a revolver at Grant, mouthed *Bang*, then accelerated away. It left Grant shaken. The car made him a rolling target. He tinted the windows, crawled into the backseat, and kept his head down until he reached Houston.

A child's bike lay on its side in the middle of Nagle Street. The Uber deviated smoothly around it and stopped in front of Grant's townhouse. He almost wept at the sight, no matter that it was empty. He got out and he hobbled back to the bike and moved it to the sidewalk. It felt normal, like something he would have done two days ago. But it left him out of breath. A minute later he let himself in the front door. Ava was sitting on the sofa, a bottle of wine open on the coffee table. No glass.

"David," she said.

It was like a light coming on in a dark room. "You're *alive*."

"Max didn't wake up yesterday."

Max. The man without compartments. Sweet dreams.

Ava's next words caught in her throat the first time she tried to say them. "I didn't know where to go."

Grant said, "I'm glad you're here."

In the days that followed, they clung to each other like frightened children. At night they slept with the lights on, their bodies entwined. In the day they handled each other with kindness, patience, and, if not love, at least courtesy.

But it didn't last.

Old resentments lurked beneath a brittle surface. Grant and Ava argued about the past, the time wasted, petty grievances, who was at fault, whose character was deficient, what each had endured in the service of a marriage without wings. Everything had changed and nothing had changed.

"Let's not fight," Grant said.

"Why not? At least fighting involves emotion. You're so closed off, sometimes it's like living with a piece of driftwood. Fighting's better than nothing."

They were in bed, a yard of mattress between them, their backs to each other.

"It's hopeless with us," Ava said. "It always was."

"Don't say that."

"It's how I feel. Maybe I should . . ."

"Don't."

"Maybe it's time to move on," Ava said. "*Really* move on. I don't think I should have come back here. It was weak, and it's not fair to either of us."

"Like Max wasn't fair?"

"Max was a mistake, too. I needed the attention you couldn't give me. But cheating wasn't right. I'm sorry."

"It's crazy to move out, with everything that's happened."

"Maybe it's just as crazy to stay."

Fear came on like a fever. The moment stretched, until Ava said, "Tomorrow, I'll—"

"It's not pre-ordained." Grant's heart lugged heavily, more weight than pump. "I never told you about my dream."

They had discussed the dream phenomenon that seemed associated with the mass deaths, and Grant had told her everything he knew. Elena Navarro, Nakamura, the idea of probability dreams. He had told her everything, except the contents of his own dream.

"I didn't have one," Ava said. "Or if I did, I don't remember it."

"I remember mine. You were in it."

The mattress moved, the top sheet went slack between them. Ava had rolled over. He felt her looking at him, but he was still gazing out the window, his back to her.

We made different choices, he thought, rehearsing the words, moving his lips silently. *The marriage was strong. We didn't fight. I made you laugh. We had fun together. We just needed to find ourselves first. That's what we did in the dream, in the other reality. When we finally became a couple, we were older. The time was right. That proves we don't have to be hopeless in this life, because we weren't hopeless in that one.*

Then Grant rolled over and faced her and said the words out loud, with feeling borrowed from her eyes. If fighting was better than nothing, maybe a lie was better than fighting.

They finished the night spooned together.

*

More than three quarters of Earth's population had died in their sleep. Six billion gone. Then in grief and with the madness of hope, thousands more killed themselves. They believed death would release them back to their first lives, back to where their loved ones still lived. Mutual suicide pacts became common. For a while it was a thing to die while un-ironically live-streaming. The Grand Canyon enjoyed a brief vogue as everyone's favorite "Final Vacation" destination. Couples plummeted from lookout perches, sky divers without parachutes, holding hands and streaming video all the way to the bottom. They wanted the world they'd lost. But Nakamura had moved on, even if they couldn't.

Meanwhile, bulldozers plowed tons of earth into mass graves and crematorium furnaces ran hot as steel mills twenty-four hours a day.

None of Grant's old clients survived the first night. But once law and order was restored somewhat and it was safe to return to the office, Grant saw a significant influx of new clients. It didn't surprise him. They wanted to make sense of their lives, now more than ever. And everyone wanted their dreams interpreted. Had they been real, did their loved ones live on in some other reality? Why had the dreams stopped? Would death open a portal or an abyss? Grant didn't know. His clients needed to talk. They needed a sympathetic listener. Grant wasn't required to provide answers. Traditional therapy led clients to their own answers.

Ava went to bed early but Grant stayed up to organize notes for tomorrow's clients. Things were better between him and Ava, since he had lied about his dream. But Grant didn't trust the peace to hold. After all, it was built on a false foundation. And he was haunted by the idea that had he told her the truth, or said nothing, Ava would have left him again. Every day, the lie felt like something rotten he'd swallowed.

They sat on the balcony, drinking wine. It was a sultry night. The city was quieter than it had ever been in living memory. And the stars were brighter, almost as bright as you found them in the desert. The peace with Ava had held, but the knot in his gut twisted ever tighter. It wrung the pleasure out of everything, including the Pinot Grigio. Grant was trying to be done with emotional compartmentalization. Done with the boxes that had driven Ava away in the first place. But what was a lie, except a box to hide the truth in?

Grant put his glass down. "I have to tell you something."

"What is it?"

He fought a brigade of his worst fears, needing to get the words out.

"David?"

"I lied to you."

After a moment, she said, "Did you. What about?"

"My dream." He sighed. "It didn't happen the way I said. Instead, we split up in college and went our separate ways. Both of us were stubborn about what we wanted. I became a psychiatric social worker, like I used to talk about. You and I, we didn't know each other anymore at all. But it had been ten years, so I looked you up. I figured we would be more compatible now that we'd both established ourselves separately in the lives we'd wanted. But when I contacted you, it didn't work out."

"That's the whole lie?"

"Yes. I wanted you to believe we could be happy, that it was possible. I thought if you believed it had already happened, even in another reality, or even just in a dream, you might accept that it could happen in real life, too."

"David."

"I know it was cowardly. It's just, with everything that's happened, I couldn't stand it if you left me again."

"*David.*"

He blinked. "What?"

"I know you lied about the dream. I knew it as soon as you described it." She sipped her wine.

"What? How could you know that?"

"For one thing it was too, I don't know, pat."

"Pat?"

"Like what you thought a fairytale would be for us. A happy-ever-after."

"And you're not mad?" He felt the knot loosening.

"That you made up the dream?" She pursed her lips, considering. "No."

"Why not?"

"You don't do this human thing very well, do you?"

He showed her his open hands. "I don't know what that means."

"You were *trying*," Ava said. "I saw you trying. That's all I ever wanted, you know. For you to try, instead of pretending there was nothing wrong, or closing yourself off like you were scared all the time, like if you said one wrong word everything would fall apart. I could never read you, because you never showed me anything."

Grant thought about it. "Let me get this straight. You knew I lied about the dream but you didn't care because at least I was trying to make us work, even if it was by being dishonest?"

"That's right, more or less."

Grant picked up his glass. He felt relieved and confused, but mostly relieved. The Pino Grigio slipped crisp and cold over his tongue. They sat quietly for a while.

"So what really happened when you looked me up in your dream?" Ava asked. "You can tell me, it won't make me mad."

Grant shook his head. "You didn't even remember me."

Ava laughed.

"You were pretty huffy about it, too," Grant added. "What's so funny?"

"I don't know. Because it sounds so true this time?"

"Yeah. I guess things don't ever change, even in the dream version."

"Of course they do. Quit being gloomy. Look at us, having wine and a good laugh together. Huffy! Who says huffy anymore?"

She started laughing again. After a few defensive moments, Grant joined her. It felt pretty good. But something still bothered him.

"You're going gloomy again," Ava said. "Jesus, it's like an aura with you."

"What if it were true, what the suicides believe? That they die and then wake up in the other world?"

"You said it *isn't* true, because Nakamura is gone."

"But what if it were true. We go back to not knowing each other."

"Right."

"We might not even remember this world, or remember it only like a normal dream."

"I guess so. Who knows?"

"I just want to know what you would choose."

"Hypothetically?" Ava asked.

Grant nodded. "Hypothetically."

"I'd stay here."

"You don't really know that. You don't know what your real life was like, just what I told you. You don't remember a probability dream."

"This world's real enough for me."

"But you don't—"

"David. You're not the only liar around here."

He stared at her. "You mean you *do* remember? And you still want to stay here? Why?"

Ava shook her head. "You really are dense, aren't you. Why don't you open another bottle, and I'll explain it to you."

EINSTEIN'S THEORY

Albert Einstein sat on the edge of the bed and stared at his hands. Moonlight turned them into those of a younger man. *So now this is who I am.* The hotel room in Bern had become a tawdry dream. It was May 29, 1919, and he was forty years old.

Albert had a theory.

His hands, his soft belly, his problematical knees—they belonged to this *iteration* of Albert Einstein, but not to the optimal expression of his identity. *That* Einstein was elsewhere, living in a different avenue of time. Albert had come to believe there were many such *other* Albert Einsteins. But only one optimal version.

The Albert Einstein in the Stomberg Hotel was far from optimal.

He looked around at the sleeping woman. Thick black hair tumbled over her bare shoulders. Hilda. She was a young widow who had only recently come to work under his direction at the Swiss Patent Office. This situation in the hotel did not bode well for the future of harmonious working conditions. Albert reached out to touch her but pulled his hand back. Waking her would only complicate his departure. He stood up and drew on a pair of trousers.

Hilda said, "Where are you going?"

Albert sighed inwardly. "Nowhere. To the toilet."

"Hurry back."

When he returned the lamp was lighted and Hilda was standing at the window in her undergarment.

"You couldn't sleep?" she said.

"It's early."

She turned and held her arms open. Albert dutifully stepped into them and felt her breasts crushed against his chest, and his face was in her abundant hair. But the passion she had aroused earlier did not rekindle. He wanted only to get out of the hotel, to be alone. But he was too polite to say so.

"Would you like to go for a walk?" he said.

Still hugging him, she drew her face back and gave him a charmingly baffled look, a smile in front of her accordion chin.

"Now? At this hour?"

"Certainly. What has the hour to do with anything?"

"You're odder than you appear at the office."

"Everyone is odder in circumstances other than the familiar."

"I see."

"Where shall we walk?"

"You choose. Give me a minute to arrange myself."

Albert and Hilda crossed the narrow footbridge that spanned the Aare River and strolled along the *Gerechtigkeitsgasse* into the Old City. Albert kept his hands in his pockets. Hilda slid her arm possessively around his. They were among only a few nocturnal pedestrians. Albert told her about his theory, which for some reason was very much on his mind.

She laughed. "But why would you wish to be anyone but yourself?"

"Ha. Gernsback said practically the same thing."

"Who is Gernsback?"

"A man formerly from Luxembourg City. He once applied for a patent when I was an ordinary class three technical officer. His idea was one of the most ridiculous. But I was new and willing to listen to practically anyone. Besides, I liked his brashness. We struck up a friendship and still correspond, though he has lived in America many years."

"What was his ridiculous idea?"

"A device with which the deaf could hear through their teeth. He called it the 'osophon.'"

Hilda guffawed.

"Precisely," Albert said. "This is a man whose criticism I should take to heart?"

"You should not!"

"Actually he wasn't critical of my idea, only of my belief in it. He suggested I write it out as a fictional story, but I haven't a gift for that sort of thing."

Albert thought of the brown ledgers he kept hidden under the loose floorboard in his study. But that was not the kind of writing Gernsback had meant.

Hilda squeezed his arm. "Come, oddball. Buy me an absinthe."

"But isn't it banned?"

"I know a place."

"It isn't a matter of wishing to be someone else," Albert said.

"Isn't it?" Hilda said.

They sat at a small table by the window in the Café Bubenberg. A candle flickered in a copper dish. Hilda was evidently a habitue, for the barman seemed to know her well.

"No," Albert said. "You misunderstood."

"Did I?" She crossed her legs.

"You have a habit of replying with an interrogative," Albert observed.

"Do I?"

He chuckled, but she did not smile.

The barman came to the table. He brought two glasses of emerald liqueur, a perforated spoon, a bowl of sugar, and a carafe of water. With grave ceremony, he heaped the spoon with sugar and poured cold water through it into each glass of absinthe, which transformed the liqueur from green to white. Now their drinks looked like tea heavily infused with milk.

Albert watched, fascinated and nervous. "But it's contraband, is it not?"

The barman, whose nose was broken and bent noticeably toward his right cheek, stared at him and then looked at Hilda, who shrugged.

To Albert, the barman said, "Yes. It is contraband, from Portugal. Very good contraband indeed."

He took his tray and left.

"Tell me then what I have missed in your theory of the many Albert Einsteins," Hilda said.

Albert cleared his throat. "The mistake was in thinking that I am not me."

"Do you have a cigarette?"

"I'm sorry, no."

"Go on."

"In fact, I *am* me," Albert went on. "However, I am prohibited from attaining my fullest expression." He smiled. "At least, this is what I tell myself."

Hilda picked up her glass. "What's to prevent you? Come, drink!"

Albert, who never drank strong spirits, brought his glass to his lips. The absinthe tasted of black licorice.

"Not like that," Hilda said.

She demonstrated how to drink absinthe, all in a gulp. Albert followed her example, and his eyes watered. He wished the barman had left the carafe of water.

"I dearly wish I had a cigarette," Hilda said.

"Yes, I know."

Albert got up and talked to the barman and a minute later returned with a box of cigarettes and a glass of water. Hilda's face transformed. She was like a child in some ways, acquisitive, easily disappointed and just as easily delighted.

Albert opened the pack and extracted one of the brown cylinders, and when Hilda had placed it between her red lips, he lighted it with the candle, dripping wax on the table.

"Thank you," she said, happy again. "You are a very thoughtful man. Are all the Einsteins so considerate of their mistresses?"

Albert winced at her use of the word "mistresses." But he smiled and said, "According to my theory, yes, we would all be equally considerate because we would all possess the same personality. It isn't a matter of personality; it is a matter of limitations and choices. In this sense there is no free will, since limitations dictate choice. Each life is a proving ground for some aspect of human existence. To that end, certain limitations are imposed on the individual's potential, and a different course is inevitably chosen. Thus a different theory of humanity is proved."

Hilda blew a nearly perfect smoke ring. "I see."

"And of course it applies to everyone," he said. "I suspect we are all busily proving our individual theories of humanity."

"Even me?"

"Certainly."

"Perhaps it's less lonely to think of it like that."

"Perhaps." Albert felt warm and prickly, and when he gazed at the candle flame his chair seemed to tilt slightly away.

"This evening you certainly proved the theory of your manhood, at least." Hilda giggled, leaning over the candle. With a jolt, Albert saw a disturbing resemblance to his daughter, Lieserl, who would have been sixteen had she lived. Hilda was older but he couldn't reject the similarity. Was this the shock of recognition he had been unable to identify when Hilda first appeared before him at the patent office? His stomach moved queasily.

"What is it?" Hilda asked. "Do you see a ghost?"

"Not a ghost. I want to walk. I need air."

He stood up, nearly knocking over his chair. But Hilda remained seated. She raised her empty glass with the same hand between the fingers of which she held her cigarette. A fragrant twist of smoke unwound from the glowing tip.

"All this walking," she said. "Doesn't it bore you? I'd like another absinthe."

Albert sat back down. Perhaps he had been mistaken about the resemblance. After all, Lieserl's features were wholly imaginary.

They each had another drink. Albert's thoughts popped and jumped erratically, sparking odd bits of information out of the darkness. He pointed at his glass and began to explain the colloidal properties that turned the liqueur white. Hilda laughed. He stammered to a halt and grinned sheepishly.

"You're one for obscure facts, aren't you."

"I suppose," he said, and another one crackled across his consciousness. "Do you realize that as we sit at this table a total eclipse of the sun is occurring?"

"But it's the middle of the night!"

"Not here in Switzerland, of course," Albert said.

"Then of what interest is it?"

He shrugged. "I read about it in the newspaper."

"Aren't you finished with that? Let's go back to the hotel and explore the aphrodisiac effects!"

Again she slipped her arm through his as they walked. Their shoes clicked out of sync on the cobbled street, and they passed within sight of the centuries old clock tower. It was only a short distance from this spot to the modest apartment he and Mileva had rented during the first seven years of their marriage. And also nearby, on this very street, the room he had occupied alone in youthful poverty. In a way it was all happening still. The nights alone in the sparsely furnished room, the morning dash to the patent office, the streets wet and steaming in the spring.

"Don't be so quiet." Hilda shook his arm.

He couldn't look at her, for again he was thinking of Lieserl. Hilda began talking about the patent office and how much she enjoyed being employed there.

"But you've only just started," Albert said. "Perhaps after many years you won't enjoy it quite so much."

"I *hope* I shall be there many years." She kissed his cheek, and when he looked at her he understood something.

"I know you're so good to me," she said. "It's hard for a young widow. There is prejudice, especially if one is Jewish."

"When I started in 1902," Albert said, "I never dreamed I'd be there still in 1919."

"But why not? Aren't you happy?"

"I thought it would be for only a little while."

"But what else would you do?"

"I don't know."

"Come. Tell me what your dream is."

"Anymore, I don't have a dream. Back then I thought I would be a teacher, though even that wasn't a dream but an aspiration."

"Why didn't you then?"

"Teach?" Albert said. "I passed my examinations with difficulty. Finally I was qualified to teach high school, but I could not get hired, except in a temporary position. And the pay was not adequate. At this time Mileva became pregnant, though we were not married. Then a decision had to be made. Would we scandalize our parents? My life had been like a great clock spring that had been properly tightened and was slowly releasing the seconds and minutes and hours into an orderly future. There was happiness and perhaps moments of joy, and of optimism. Am I unique, or is every young man the same? Suddenly the spring threatened to burst open all at once, dismissing all order and even hope."

"But it all worked out," Hilda said.

"Of course."

He considered Lieserl. Now she would be sixteen years old, a bright student in the high school, involved in many activities and blessed with the popular society of her friends. In the evenings she would read to her parents and her little brother by the fire. Her hands would be shapely, the fingers long and tapering, a musician's fingers. She would play the violin. This was the life he had given her in his secret ledgers. In those pages, Lieserl played the violin beautifully. Her imagined life was real, somewhere, Albert was convinced. But at this moment it wasn't Mozart he heard but Mileva's scream when the doctor pierced her. Albert had been standing in the next room holding his hat and turning it in his hands, pacing, feeling the clock spring unwind from the center of his heart. That scream.

They had come to the bridge.

"This isn't altogether unromantic," Hilda said.

Albert looked up from his thoughts. The river Aare chattered beneath his feet. He peered over the railing.

Hilda turned his face to hers and kissed him on the mouth. He closed his eyes and endured it as long as he could, then gently pushed her away.

"Is something the matter?" Hilda asked.

"This is a public place."

"There is no public at this hour."

Albert looked at the river, black ink upon which the yellow reflections of the bridge lamps reflected. What would it be like under the surface? What would it be like to kick with all one's strength, striving for the deepest currents of cold and utter darkness?

Hilda tugged on his arm.

"Come," she said, drawing him away.

They continued to the Stomberg Hotel. Hilda talked. Absinthe trickled into the convolutions of Albert's brain. He saw the impossibility of things. The patent office he already loathed made untenable by Hilda's presence. His "good" house across the Kirchenfeld Bridge, his study where he slept apart from Mileva. And worst of all, the brown ledgers under the floor: his secret parallel life which had been his refuge and now was spoiled, while his real life ascended wearily before him, and whatever could be in some elsewhere did not matter.

On the steps to the hotel, Albert stopped. Hilda turned to him. That smile.

"Come on then," she said, "it's too late to be shy!"

"You go up," he said. "I left something at the café."

"What did you leave?"

"I'll only be a short while," he said.

She called to him as he hurried away, but he didn't look back. At first he feared she would follow him but she did not. His heart lugged, and his shoes clocked rapidly on the stone path, carrying him back towards the Old City and his ghosts. But first he would have to cross the bridge, where yellow light bent on black water.

THE LAST GARDEN

The Surrogate walked past Casey's window. She watched its shadow slip across the shade, then she stood and zipped up her flight suit. This was the day. No matter what.

The doorbell rang.

It was polite, the Surrogate. It had manners. It rang the doorbell. It said please and thank you. It had saved Casey's life, twice, and the first time she had been grateful.

Casey bit her lip hard enough to hurt. The pain helped her focus on her mission. Because sometimes she didn't believe in it. Sometimes she was weak and disloyal to her own kind. That was understandable, considering her own kind, the human race, on Earth at least, was an extinct species. What was there to be loyal to?

The embryos. The cloned embryos in cryostasis.

Her mother.

Twenty-six months ago, Casey and her nine crewmates had watched helplessly from orbit while a plague wiped out humanity with the brutal efficiency of a world-wide tsunami. The final message sent from Washington to all orbiting spacecraft said simply, "Don't come down." But Casey and her crew had no choice. Without re-supply vehicles, they couldn't remain in space. Meanwhile, arguments raged on the lunar colony, which was self-sustaining. Those in favor of staying put seemed to be winning. Then all communication coming from the moon ceased.

The polite Surrogate rang the bell again. It claimed to worry about her, like a parent. But it couldn't really be worried about her.

The Surrogate was a machine, a top-secret military grade AI, from when there had been both a military and anything secret.

Casey stood in the entry, arms folded, feet planted on the vinyl floor. Military housing, drab and cheap. When she was a child in Virginia, Casey had lived with her mother in a big house with white columns in front. She remembered her mother pulling her down the dappled sidewalk in a red wagon, remembered the sound of the hard rubber wheels rolling on pavement. It was funny how that memory stood out but later ones had folded away into the dark. It was like peering down a long tube to a vision drenched in sunlight.

The knob turned, encountered the lock, turned harder until the lock broke and the door splintered away from the jamb.

The Surrogate had a paint-can head, eyes that glowed blue, and a slot mouth. The sturdy torso contained the power source. A flexible spine, like a length of knuckled bike chain, attached the torso to a pair of ingeniously swiveling hips. The legs were like attenuated cages made from carbon rods.

When Casey and her crewmates descended from orbit in two vehicles, automated defenses had immediately attacked them, destroying one vehicle outright and severely damaging the other. Casey managed a hard landing in the high desert of New Mexico near Tourangeau Air Base. Only Casey survived. Pinned inside the wreckage, her leg broken, she had expected to die of plague. The microbes, however, had all perished as soon as no humans were left to host them, and Casey had returned to consciousness and a world of bright pain in time to see the robot Surrogate peel away a flange of the damaged hull and reach for her.

Now Casey had let the Surrogate break open the door of the house. She hoped the destruction would make her angry at the robot, instead of frightened by what she was planning. She needed the anger.

"You didn't answer, Casey Stillman," the Surrogate said. "Our agreement was that you would answer."

"I know that." Casey's voice broke. She wiped her eyes roughly. It was the stupid door, wood splintered and hanging there on bent hinges, like a memory of things unbroken that were now broken forever. Instead of producing anger, it lifted the cover off a deep well of sadness. For months after the crash, she had combed the internet and the airwaves, desperate for contact. But if anyone had survived, they were unable to communicate. During those same months, the Surrogate had nursed Casey, waited on and bonded with her—as it was programmed to do.

The robot fitted the split door jamb together. "I will repair this."

"Don't bother."

"Then I will help you move to a new house."

"I don't want a new house." She stood as straight as she could. "I'm flying out to the Doomsday Vault. I want you to lower the shield."

If the Surrogate could have sighed, this is when it would have done so. "As we've discussed," it said, "the embryos will not have survived."

"You can't stop me trying."

"I have never stopped you. You have stopped yourself. Before this, your mission was the gun."

"Will you not talk about the gun?"

"It concerns me."

"You can't be concerned about anything. You're a machine."

"I am an empathic Surrogate."

"If you won't lower the force shield, I swear I'll crash into it on purpose and die. I know you don't want that."

Almost a minute passed. From the robot came only a sound like a flywheel flutter, or hummingbird wings. "Here is my analysis," the Surrogate said.

"Spare me."

"The embryo clones preserved in cryostasis once represented your desire for restoration. But now they represent your desire to stop living. They are like the gun."

"You are so full of shit."

"My casing is filled with many things, but excrement is not among them."

Casey rolled her eyes. "I wish you wouldn't try and be funny."

"Apologies. Our relationship has caused a symbiotic evolution of my algorithms. It is by design."

"This isn't a relationship," Casey said. "And the embryo clones are *not* like the gun." After the Surrogate came upon Casey fooling around with a pistol and her soft pallet, the robot had gathered all the loose weapons on the base and locked them in the armory.

"They beckon, like the gun, and promise the same conclusion. Leaving the protection of this base for a hopeless goal is irrational. It is suicide."

"It isn't, but even if it were, it would be none of your business."

"It's wiser, and safer, to await the Moonites."

Casey snorted. She had long given up on a rescue mission from the Lunar colony, though the Surrogate continued to flog the possibility, probably as a strategy to mollify her. But Casey knew they would never come. The Surrogate referred to that certainty as Casey's "attitude."

"I'm going to try," Casey said, "whether you turn the shield off or not."

"My algorithms will not allow me to restrain you. But if you are determined, then I will come with you."

"No."

"Otherwise I won't disable the force shield."

"I already told you, I'll fly into it. I'll *gun* myself."

"If you truly want to save the embryos, you will let me accompany you. Otherwise you admit your mission is a gun and not what you claim it is."

"I don't have to make deals with you." Casey pushed past the Surrogate and strode out to the street. She stopped and closed her eyes, took a deep breath.

"Well, come *on*," she said.

Shattered aircraft hangars gaped like broken shells. Black furrows crisscrossed the runways. Wreckage smeared across the tarmac in rusty debris fields. The plague came and was assumed to be an act of biological warfare. Someone in the US, or China, or India, Or Iran, or Russia unleashed the first retaliatory assault. The reactive response spread like the plague had spread. The world became a gun aimed at itself, which kept on firing even after there were no humans left to pull the trigger.

Ironically, in the last days, CDC scientists determined that the plague itself had *not* been an act of war. Microbes had filtered into the atmosphere, where they thrived, located human hosts, and proliferated throughout the population. Where the plague failed to kill, the weapon response from every country in the world had succeeded. The shield over Tourangeau Airbase should have protected it, as should have the shields over the White House, NORAD, and other critical places. But all the shields had gone down under viciously effective cyber attacks. The Surrogate, however, had figured out the code to reactivate the shield at Tourangeau, and now the AI controlled it.

Some air vehicles at the base had gone undamaged. A wasp with a long stinger was painted on the nose of the electric VTOL. Casey hauled herself up to the canopy and claimed the forward seat. The Surrogate installed itself behind her. Casey buckled up and began her pre-flight check. But when she attempted to move the control surfaces, ailerons, rudder, and elevators, her side stick and pedals resisted her. "Are you doing that?"

"I will fly us out," the Surrogate replied.

Casey craned her head around, awkward in the snug helmet. "You just open the shield, like we agreed."

"The moment this air vehicle passes beyond the shield it will be attacked by weapons in terrestrial orbit as well as the automated weapons still operating on the ground. I have downloaded complete specs and will fly."

Casey wrenched at the control stick. "Let me fly my own goddam ship."

The Surrogate went quiet. Hummingbird wings fluttered.

Casey closed her eyes, let her fury subside to the point where she could speak without shouting. "You think you can fly better than I can?"

"I do not doubt your skill. But I can predict the assault and react with greater efficiency."

Casey tapped her fingers on her thighs. She knew the Surrogate was right. The Surrogate was *always* right. It was one of the most infuriating things about it (a trait the robot shared with Casey's mother). Rudimentary AIs directed the orbital and ground-based automated weapons. Some of the weapons were "ours," some "theirs," some "who knows." And yes, it was probably beyond Casey's skill set to evade them all.

"You'll give me control once we clear the attack?" Casey said.

"There will be other attacks."

"You will give me control." Not a question this time.

"Very well."

"Then let's go."

The instrument panel and heads-up display came alive. Powerful GE engines spun up. The ship rose vertically. At two hundred feet, the nose pitched down and they powered towards the invisible shield.

Beyond the shield, buried in a Doomsday Vault under the Sangre de Cristo Mountains, lay the frozen embryos cloned from some of the greatest scientists and leaders on Earth, including Casey's mother. They were the seeds of humanity's future.

And Casey was the last garden.

They sped toward the shield. Casey blinked sweat out of her eyes. "The shield's off, right?"

"No need. We can pass through unaffected from this side."

"What? You never told me you could do that! You mean I could have—No wonder you wanted to come. You tricked me."

"There will be a bump."

The ship accelerated to full power, crushing Casey in her seat. If there was a bump, she didn't feel it. The airframe was already shuddering. And then they were through and pitching steeply upward while rolling left. The sky flashed white and blue with energy bursts. The ship rocked wildly.

"Shoot back!" Casey yelled.

Instead, the Surrogate throttled down and deployed speed-breaks, which threw Casey against her restraints. If the Surrogate hadn't reacted with superhuman speed and precision, the VTOL would have been destroyed. They skated across the sky, wing tips banked steeply. Then they were clear, rolling right and gaining altitude, finally leveling out.

"Okay," Casey said, "hand it over."

"I am adjusting the vector," the Surrogate said. "Destination in six minutes."

"Give me control!"

"There will be other attacks."

"You shouldn't even be here. You lied to me about the shield."

Casey seized the side stick and pressed her feet to the rudder pedals, fighting the Surrogate for control. She hadn't realized the robot *could* lie. That made it almost human. A warning light flickered, and something streaked up from the desert. The Surrogate wrenched the ship over, but the projectile clipped the starboard wing, and the ship barreled out of control. Sky and Earth swapped relative positions. Casey grasped the stick in a death grip. Despite that, the Surrogate established a semblance of stable, albeit inverted flight, rolled again for straight and level, and compensated for the loss of starboard thrust.

"Casey Stillman, let go, please."

Casey released her grip and watched the displays. Hydraulic pressure dropped steadily on the starboard wing. The strike had severed a line. Worse, battery levels had plummeted, an emergency reflected in the off-key whine of the big electric turbine on the port side.

The ship wallowed toward the ground.

"We're going to crash!" Casey's heart was racing.

"I am managing it."

The remains of a town passed below them. The VTOL, rocking and swaying under depleted power, traveled another mile. A landing pad came into view. The Surrogate angled them toward it, dumping two hundred feet of altitude before rearing back and engaging sputtering vertical thrust. The ship teetered on the edge of a stall. Casey clenched her body for impact. In the next moment the undercarriage absorbed the bone-rattling jolt of touchdown. Casey looked up. They had landed fifty yards short of the pad.

The instrument panel displayed the red lines of overtaxed and underpowered systems, and then the display went dark.

Casey popped the canopy. "Don't say it."

"Don't say what?"

"That if I'd kept my hands off the controls we wouldn't have been hit."

The Surrogate reverted to hummingbird wings.

Casey unbuckled her restraints and turned around, kneeling on her seat. The Surrogate's blank face regarded her. "Damn it. *Not* saying anything is the same as *saying* it."

"I could have avoided the attack, yes."

"I knew you couldn't resist rubbing it in."

She climbed down to inspect the damage. Hydraulic fluid dripped on Casey's boot. A piece of the starboard wing's trailing edge was missing, a ragged bite taken by the projectile. If the VTOL had been running on jet fuel instead of electricity it would have exploded. As it was, shrapnel had penetrated the fuselage and damaged the battery array. Maybe the Surrogate could repair the wing, but without power they were stranded.

"I will effect repairs," the Surrogate said.

"What about—"

"The repair procedure will render me helpless. So you will get your opportunity to pilot us back to base. You will have to manually deactivate the barrier. I will provide instructions. Don't do it too soon, or the weapons will gain access ahead of you. Don't wait too long, or you may misjudge the approach and destroy us."

"How long will repairs take?"

"Estimated three hours."

"I'll be back by then."

"Don't go, please."

From the stowage compartment Casey retrieved a pulse rifle, a sidearm and a flashlight.

"Without me, your survival is questionable," the Surrogate said.

"Thanks for the vote of confidence." Sarcasm was a reflex. Casey knew she didn't deserve a vote of confidence, not after almost getting them blown out of the sky. "Look," she said, "I'll get back okay. Don't worry about me."

But the robot was already dismantling the starboard aileron assembly.

Casey hiked up the steep terrain to the blast-door. She stayed off the road, using the trees for cover. Her boots swished in the undergrowth. She held her rifle at the ready, knowing it wouldn't do her much good if weapons attacked her. Once upon a time, her mother had given her a tour of the Doomsday Vault. Casey had only gone because it was so rare that her mother invited her *anywhere.* "You're so busy with your career," she told Casey, neatly reversing the situation. Casey hadn't been the one "too busy" for her mother.

Standing before the cryostasis capsules, Casey's own lifelong position as a daughter-in-stasis did not fail to ring ironic bells. As an Important Person, one of the world's top researchers in genetic engineering, Casey's mother had spent most of Casey's childhood somewhere *outside* Casey's childhood. Maybe that's why the little-red-wagon memory was so important.

At first glance the blast-door appeared intact, a slab of thick steel recessed under a brow of granite. Casey studied it from the trees. Something wasn't right. Finally, Casey bit down hard on her lip, burst out of the trees, and ran to the door. Nothing attempted to stop her. In a moment, she understood why. From the trees, she hadn't seen that the door's magnetic locks had failed, probably as a result of the cyber attack two years ago. A narrow gap presented itself. She hooked her fingers around the edge, and hauled on the door until the gap widened sufficiently for her to squeeze through.

Inside, daylight fell in dusty shafts from the shattered ceiling. Daylight.

High above, where Casey had been unable to see it, an explosive discharge had ripped open the mountain. Just as the Surrogate had assured her, the weapons had long ago destroyed the Doomsday Vault. Casey's hope vanished like the mirage it had always been, something to crawl towards in a desert of regret and loneliness. For years, Casey had imagined the cloned embryos, tiny quick-frozen shrimp sealed in cryogenic capsules, buried deep behind impenetrable walls. She had imagined her mother.

Casey unclipped the flashlight from her belt, found stairs, and descended to the cryo vault. She had to be sure. Twenty minutes later, she was.

The embryos were all dead.

Her *mother* was dead. Again. Of course, it wouldn't have been her mother, just her genetic potential, her familiar features. Casey would have nurtured the potential in her own virgin womb, would have raised the child behind the force shield, and perhaps she would even have sat with her and told her a fairytale about the Moonites coming back to Earth.

Casey sat on an iron beam that had partially melted and crashed down. Alone in the dark, she felt the weight of her life, like the weight of the mountain. What else had she expected? The Surrogate had been right, again. The cryo vault was another gun, a thin excuse for a suicide mission. Casey wiped her eyes and stood up. How could a robot know her better than she knew herself? In symbiosis, its algorithms had deciphered the mystery of Casey's own secret intentions.

She began climbing stairs.

*

The Surrogate had cannibalized itself to repair the ship. Hollow rods from its legs completed the broken linkages in the starboard aileron assembly. Unused rods and couplings lay in the wing's shadow, like discarded chicken bones. The hydraulic line had been welded, but what good would that do without fluid in the reservoir?

Using only its arms, the Surrogate had pulled itself back to the cockpit, where it sat bolt upright in the pilot's seat, strapped in place.

Casey said, "You were right about the cryo vault."

The Surrogate did not reply.

Casey hauled herself up to the cockpit. The Surrogate had patched a line from its own body and drained itself of fluid, giving the wing reservoir a blood transfusion. A thin cable led from the Surrogate's chest through a new hole in the firewall to the batteries. Casey toggled the power on. Battery levels jumped to eighty-six percent. But the surrogate was inert. Even the hummingbird was still.

A different emotion supplanted all the others roiling inside Casey, an emotion she had once felt acutely and then spent years suppressing.

Grief.

"You goddam piece of junk," she said, not meaning it.

Without the Surrogate, there was only Casey's voice left in the world.

A tablet device lay on the tandem seat. Words displayed on the screen, instructions on transmitting a number sequence. Casey picked up the tablet, which was the key to unlocking the shield. She climbed into her seat, buckled her restraints, and waited for anger to muscle aside the grief of loneliness, then she spun up the engines, lifted away, and swung towards home base.

The first attack came almost immediately. Projectiles streaked up from the desert. Casey rolled left, rolled right, then plunged for the desert scrub, leveling out at fifty feet. A warning light flashed. Out of the clouds, a glittering swarm came at her.

Casey punched the throttle. The electric power plants whined like things about to burst apart. A burning odor filled the cockpit. The Surrogate rattled and bounced on the cable, the ship violently sucking the last kilowatt from its chest. The base lay dead ahead. So did the shield.

Heat rays crossed her flight path. Casey banked onto her wingtip and veered between them, flying with the skill of unconscious desperation, proving she *did* want to live. The maneuver drew the attack swarm into the rays. Fireballs burst like red kernels all around her. Casey tapped in the key code and transmitted it to the shield. She squeezed shut her eyes as the VTOL streaked over the border, the force shield rising automatically behind her. Rays, projectiles, and swarms burst spectacularly against it.

On the ground, Casey threw open the canopy. Sweating profusely inside her flight suit, she reached over the seat to unbuckle the robot, but the straps had melted into its frame. She used her knife to cut them away. The Surrogate's metal body remained searingly hot. Casey ran to the nearest intact hangar and returned with a chain-fall and a rolling cart. She pulled on big silver oven-mitt-looking asbestos gloves and used the chain-fall to hoist the Surrogate out of the cockpit and lower it onto the cart.

Restoring the Surrogate's mobility proved impossible. Casey had left the chicken bone parts behind, and she wasn't a mechanic, anyway. Replenishing the robot's power seemed at least worth a try. Casey rolled the Surrogate to the fusion generator building which powered the force shield and everything else on the base. She rigged a connection between the generator and the Surrogate, then she waited. After three days the Surrogate showed no signs of life, or whatever it was that animated the AI. After a week she stopped checking on it.

Without the Surrogate's voice, the base became a tomb in which Casey wept and talked to herself and then stopped talking. She wandered the streets she had always wandered, while inside she unraveled in loneliness. Some nights she stood at the perimeter, almost wishing the weapons assault would resume—and this time be successful. She toyed with the idea of lowering the shield, but she was past that.

At night, stars encrusted the New Mexico sky, a bed of diamonds to hold the yellow rind of moon. Suddenly Casey's attention quickened. A point of light sped silently across the sky. She sat forward, making the chair creak. But it was only a weather sat, remnant of the conquered human race, not a humanitarian mission from Luna. She stood up and walked through the broken door into her house.

After a month's absence, she returned to the generator building. It had taken that long to believe again in the possibility of hope. She dragged her feet the whole way, indulged detours, pretended she wasn't hoping, and finally approached the door. Something rapped against it from the other side. Casey stopped—then ran the rest of the way. When she wrenched open the door, the legless Surrogate lay on the floor, one arm raised.

"You were gone a long time, Casey Stillman," it said. "I was worried."

She swallowed. "I'm here now."

Casey took the Surrogate with her when she went to the warehouse for supplies. MREs lasted forever and there were enough of them to feed a thousand soldiers for a year. She placed the Surrogate's torso and paint-can head on the cart and pulled it behind her, the way Casey's mother had pulled her in the red wagon. The sound of the wheels was like a memory echoing up a long tunnel. Casey looked over her shoulder. The Surrogate's blue eyes watched her.

"They're really coming, aren't they," Casey said. "The Moonites."

"Yes," the head in the wagon replied.

The Surrogate was always right.

ARLINGTON

Three thousand feet below the wheel fairings of my Cessna 150 trainer, a perfect sheet of fog pulled off the Pacific and covered the Washington coastline. To my right, the Olympic Mountains bulked jaggedly against the sky. I had to duck and crane to see the top of Mount Olympus, nearly four thousand feet higher than my flight path. I was sixteen years old, alone on my first solo cross-country flight, a requisite of my training before I could apply for my pilot's ticket.

And I was lost.

Okay, not *lost*, exactly. I knew my approximate location. All I had to do was look out the windows. VFR is what they call it when you can see where you're going: Visual Flight Rules. Even though the coastline was obscured by fog, the Olympic Mountains still presented a pretty distinctive reference. But mostly I was relying on my VOR instrument, and that was a mistake.

VOR is short for VHF Omnidirectional Radio. Aviation is full of acronyms—it was even back in 1982, when I got lost over the Olympic Peninsula. With a VOR you tune in the station, center the little arrow on a compass dial, and fly straight along the selected radial. Theoretically you don't need VFR conditions to do that. It's how I found my way from Crest Airpark, a small private field east of the Kent valley, to the logging city of Hoquiam. From there I turned north, switching to the next station, which was in Port Angeles—and that was the mistake. VORs are line-of-sight signals, and I did not have a line-of-sight to Port Angeles. The mountains were in the way. I should have stayed on the Hoquiam signal until I'd traveled far enough up the coast to clear the mountains.

The signal was faint. I got worried and hauled back on the yoke, trimmed the elevators, and started climbing, on the assumption increased altitude would translate into a stronger VOR signal. My hands were damp, and I gripped the yoke too hard. I was sixteen. Not only was I an inexperienced pilot, I was an inexperienced human being.

A 150 trainer is a very small airplane. Four cylinders and a hundred horsepower start to feel inadequate the higher you go. My airspeed had dropped to fifty-six knots. Considering my steep angle of attack, that was uncomfortably close to a stall. The Cessna's airframe shuddered in the unstable air around Mount Olympus. The controls felt mushy.

A peculiar white cloud hung in the sky directly in front of me. It had the general look of a small cumulus, that vaguely popcorn shape that encourages day dreamers to see dragons or schooners or whatever. To me this one looked like a Mickey Mouse head. But what made it peculiar was its seeming flatness, the way it appeared to be painted right on the sky, in two dimensions. Soon it felt like I was falling toward the cloud instead of climbing laboriously. That scared me, and I attempted to veer off but I was too late. It was almost as if the cloud were pulling me in by gravitational attraction. In the next moment the world turned white.

2012

My name is Paul Birmingham. I don't know how old I am now. But in 2012, when I was forty-six and dying, I decided it was time to go flying again—thirty years after that day I got lost over the Olympic Peninsula. The idea came to me late at night in a nearly deserted office bay. I was an engineer by profession, and I worked graveyard shift for the Boeing Company in Everett, Washington.

I liked working graveyard for the same reasons most people hate it. Being awake in the small hours after midnight put me out of sync with a world I always felt out of sync with anyway. I shut off the overhead light panels and set up a lamp in my cubicle, the kind of lamp you'd find in somebody's bedroom. Over the course of my six-hour shifts I toggled between 3D renderings of structural spars and dense blocks of text on physics websites. Only the spars were part of my job.

I was not a "God" man. I was not a believer in the mystical—and I still am not. That's important. I was an engineer and possessed an engineer's mind, the kind of mind that wants to figure out how things work in the real, observable world. If I were imprisoned in a medieval fortress, I would not waste my time praying for freedom. I would study the foundation. I would contrive tunnels. The physics stuff—much of it beyond me—was like studying the secret layout of the world prison in which I found myself.

In my entire office bay there was only one other guy. We never talked. He knew nothing about me and I knew nothing about him. He didn't know I was dying, for instance, or that a stroke killed my mother when I was fifteen years old, killed her dead right before my eyes. I had to pass his desk on the way to the bathroom. He was always working, intently focused on some project, his shirt sleeves rolled to his elbows. He never looked up when I walked by. He might as well have been set dressing in somebody else's play. I had come to a place in my life where this point of view did not strike me as irrational.

A window in the corner of my monitor was linked to a Harvard physics page about "flop transitions." The material was pretty dense but I stuck with it, as I imagine God-inclined people will stick with even the dullest parts of the Bible.

I was forty-six years old and dying; but then, I'd been dying ever since Quillayute. By centimeters, and painfully.

1982

In the sudden whiteout my instruments lost touch with reality. The altimeter froze. The artificial horizon flipped like a dead man's eyeball. A windy hiss came through my headset, like what you get when you hold a sea shell against your ear. The compass attached to the top of the instrument panel stopped pointing to magnetic north. It bobbed and swung and dipped like it didn't know *what* to point at. This was not an electronic device but a simple magnetic compass, so basic and straightforward in principle that its origins date back to China in the second century B.C. And yet the compass in my little Cessna was now, inexplicably, broken.

The engine strained and whined, and I strained with it. The hard plastic yoke was slippery with my sweat. White vapor erased the Olympic Mountains, the sky, the terrain below, stranding me in a void without reference points. I couldn't even tell which direction was up and which was down. My inner ear told me I was banking right. Probably that wasn't true. Inexperienced pilots can easily become disoriented if you steal their VFR conditions. I panicked, depressed the left rudder pedal, and banked left while still climbing. The Cessna stalled and rolled over.

My instructor, Jim Brodie, had taught me how to recover from something like this, relying on instruments alone. But my instruments weren't working, and my panicked yanking and wrenching at the flight controls made things a lot worse. In a normal nose-up stall, an airplane will recover by itself, if you simply let go of the controls. It's counterintuitive, something a mature pilot knows to do. But that wasn't me. I wasn't mature. And besides, it wasn't a simple nose-up stall. I was simply SOL—another useful acronym, applicable not only to aviation.

Shit Out of Luck.

And then, suddenly, I dropped clear of the white cloud. Sunlight flooded the windows. Shadows swept around the cabin as the airplane tumbled. My instruments resumed functioning. I corrected the stall, established level flight, with altitude to spare. I was shaking—and I laughed, a kind of hysterical bark, like someone on a rollercoaster after the first serious dip, the one where you were *certain* the car was going to jump the tracks.

A couple of thousand feet below, the Quillayute airfield lay clear in the midst of the world's only temperate rainforest. It had been my lunch-stop destination, but thanks to crappy navigation I almost missed it altogether. Quillayute was an old Navy project, thrown together in the 1930s and used during World War II as a northern blimp patrol base as well as for fixed-wing operations. Supposedly it was deserted, practically a ghost airport. That had appealed to me when I was plotting this cross-country flight.

But as I set up my approach, I was struck by the number of airplanes parked all around the field, in no orderly fashion. A lot of them seemed to have halted randomly and been abandoned by their pilots. One was parked on the south end of the runway, a tail-dragger, its front wheels in the grass, back wheel still on the tarmac. I glided right over it, my prop feathered. The tail dragger had no forward window. It reminded me of the plane Charles Lindbergh flew across the Atlantic. How long ago were airplanes like that in general use?

I touched down for a bumpy landing. Weeds grew out of cracks in the neglected tarmac. My hands were still shaking, and my feet on the rudder pedals felt blocky and uncoordinated. I knew damn well I had almost been killed, and my body knew it as much as my mind did.

I steered my trainer onto the ramp and shut off the engine. In the absence of the racket it was *so* quiet. I climbed out and stared at the sky, which was perfectly clear, perfectly blue, except for that one puffy white popcorn cloud. Even from the ground it looked unnaturally flat, a cloud painted on blue canvas. But I'd flown into something big, all engulfing.

A couple of World War II-era wooden hangars stood on the south side of the field, one of them falling apart. Daylight showed through wide gaps in the boards. Between the collapsing hangar and a rusted-out fuel island was a thing that looked like a big metal insect, a beetle or something. It stood about five feet off the ground on four articulated struts. From the air I'd taken it for a liquid storage unit. But from this close it looked alien and out of place. The hairs prickled up on the back of my neck.

There was nobody in sight, but there were all those airplanes parked every which way. Some of them looked old enough to be vintage antiques. Others looked like designs straight out of a *Popular Mechanics* "Future of Aviation" issue. One I hardly even recognized as an airplane. Its long, elegant wings were folded close to the fuselage, like the wings of a bird, and the wing tips swept up. A forward blister must have been where the pilot sat, but it appeared to be made of mirror glass.

A Piper Cub with its left door hanging open dated back to at least the early 40s. In 1982, it was possible but unlikely that somebody would still be flying it around. A Beechcraft Bonanza with the distinctive V tail hunkered nearby on the ramp. It looked old, but not that old, maybe late 1950s. I peered through the windows, shading out my reflection by cupping my hands around my eyes. There were coloring books and crayons on the back seat. Bobbsey Twins. Buster Brown. The titles sounded vaguely familiar. As a sixteen-year-old I was solidly, myopically, entrenched in1982. But I knew no self-respecting modern kid would be caught dead coloring in the Bobbsey Twins.

The airport windsock hung limp, the red fabric frayed, weathered to pale pink. Not a breath of air moved it. The silence pressed against my eardrums. I felt a strong urge to climb back into my Cessna and get out of there. My brown-bag lunch lay in the right-seat foot well, where it had tumbled when the trainer stalled. I pulled myself in and started to reach for it.

Far away and faint, someone screamed.

I froze. After a moment I backed out of the plane, still listening, my breath shallow and my heart beating heavily. The cry had been so faint and distant that I wasn't even sure I really heard it. I stepped out from under the wing. I'd heard it, all right. I just wanted to pretend that I hadn't. It had come from the forest, a girl's brief cry, suddenly cut off. I looked in that direction, straining to see something—and I did. In fact, it was weird that I hadn't noticed it before. A pair of heavy wheels had left parallel tracks in the grass beyond the end of the runway. Those tracks ran right into the wall of the rainforest. The big olive drab tail section of some kind of military plane stuck out of the trees. It was the paint job that made it less noticeable, I guess. It was *supposed* to blend in.

I walked toward it, my feet swishing in the high grass between the wheel tracks. It was a World War II bomber, a B-17. The pilot had crashed into the trees, and the rainforest canopy had folded over it like a lid. The starboard wing was ripped half off the fuselage. When I got close enough I picked up the sharp smell of high-test fuel.

I leaned inside the open hatch. The fifty-caliber machine gun swivels were tied down and the plane was empty, like all the others. An odd sound drew me out of the hatch. It came from behind me, from back toward the runway. It sounded like a *sonar ping*—at least, the way sonar pings sounded in the war movies I'd watched. A single hard ping, rippling out, and then the oppressive silence again.

The runway, hangars, and jackstraw scatter of abandoned airplanes all looked the same—but *something* had changed, and I couldn't figure out what. I looked up, half expecting to see a Corsair or a P-51, or maybe even a flying saucer banking out of the clear sky. But there was nothing except that one cloud, still hanging motionless above the field. The cloud was different, but you'd expect it to be. Clouds are nothing but tiny droplets of water vapor. They're so inherently unstable that a sky of scattered cumulous never looks the same for long, letting kids play endless games of see-the-dragon. This cloud, though, wasn't pulling apart or reshaping—it was shrinking. Shrinking while keeping the shape it had started with. The popcorn shape, the vaguely Mickey Mouse shape. Clouds didn't behave that way.

I sensed someone behind me and turned around fast. A little girl, maybe eight years old, started to duck behind a tree but stopped when she knew I'd seen her. She was wearing a yellow blouse, pleated skirt, and two-tone shoes. Immediately, I associated her with the Beechcraft. Her blouse was dirty and one of the sleeves was torn. Her blond hair was done in a sloppy ponytail, a half untied green ribbon straggling at the knot. A long red scratch crossed her left cheek. I said, "Hello."

"You should hide," she said. Very serious.

"Hide from what?"

"Them."

"Did you scream a little while ago?"

"That was my sister, Tammy. She stepped in a hole and hurt her ankle. Now she can't run."

"What's your name?"

"Amanda."

"Where are your parents?"

"The things got them. You need to hide now."

I took a careful, non-threatening step in her direction, and tried to make my voice as friendly as possible. "How did—"

Another one of those weird, hard-sounding sonar pings went off behind me, the echo rippling out. I looked towards the runway, and when I turned back to the little girl, she was gone.

"Hey. Hey, kid!"

Her yellow shirt flashed. She already covered quite a distance. I started after her, jogging fifty yards into the forest. Under the trees, the shade was dense, the quiet even more oppressive. I stopped when I saw the mail. Dozens of envelopes, letters with stamps on them and hand-written addresses, lay scattered around my feet. Above me a wooden-framed biplane hung in the branches, the sun passing amber through the torn fabric wings. A big hole gaped in the side of the plane. Painted in black letters along the fuselage were the words: US MAIL 246.

I picked up one of the envelopes and turned it in my fingers. The paper was thick and heavy compared to a modern business envelope. The return address was the US Department of Defense. Absently, I folded the envelope and shoved it in the back pocket of my jeans.

You better hide, the little girl had said. Hide from what? *The things.*

"Hey, kid, come on out!"

Nothing.

I left the forest and headed toward the hangars, thinking there might be a phone or something. I doubted I'd get anyone on the Cessna's radio, at least not while it was on the ground. When I reached the fuel island I stopped dead.

The beetle-looking liquid storage tank was in a different position.

The front struts were now planted forward, the smooth silver body leaning slightly down. I stared at it, as at an optical illusion. My stomach moved queasily.

Someone came running toward me, then, out of the forest on the other side of the runway. He wore a brown leather jacket, white scarf, tan pants that ballooned at the hips, and boots. When he got closer I saw it wasn't a "he" at all, but a woman with blonde hair cropped shorter than my own. She reached me, panting for breath.

"Kid, if you don't come with me right now, you're a goner. We've got about one minute to skedaddle."

"Who are you?"

"Did you hear what I said about one minute?" She grabbed my hand and started pulling. Her fear and urgency communicated through me like electric current. I started stumbling along and then we were running together, flat out, across the runway and into the trees. A third sonar ping sounded, the echo rippling in sick wavelets right through my body. "*Down.*" The woman yanked me to my knees, and when I stayed like that she shoved me forward onto my elbows. I started to complain and she shushed me. Then the terrible stuff began.

A Little Family History

I was raised Catholic. My mother's faith pulled my family along, pulled us to church every Sunday, to CCD classes, to confession. She kept us, my big brother, my dad and me, on the path. Dad was our anchor in worldly affairs, the affairs of bills and mortgages and oil changes. Mom was in charge of God. And when my mother died, Dad did his best to hold us together and carry on. Sometimes his holding-together looked like a man clinging to a ledge by his fingertips. But he never let go. He never fell. Once, a couple of weeks after her death, Dad came home with a bottle of gin in a brown paper bag. He had quit drinking a few years before. Weekends and holidays had become less tense. His quitting had been like the lifting away of a shadow.

The sight of the gin bottle frightened me.

He never opened it. In bed one night, I heard him crying. Frightened, I slipped down the hall to the kitchen. He was sitting at the table, that bottle of gin in front of him, and my mother's rosary in his fist. He didn't see me, and I was too scared to approach him. A little while later he came in and sat on my bed. I pretended to be asleep. He wasn't crying anymore. After a few minutes he stood up, kissed my forehead, and went away, leaving the hall light on, the way I liked it. I never saw the gin bottle again.

Dad tried to pull my brother and me along, the way Mom had. But for me, once Mom was gone, my faith also departed. I needed something to believe in, but it wasn't going to be God. For a while I maintained the rituals of Mom's faith, the routine appointments with God. Religion is full of rituals. But so is science. Both are seeking the truth, driven by similar impulses; both want answers. In the Catholic church, for instance, there is the ritual of transubstantiation. The priest dons his robes, speaks the Latin words, retrieves wafers from the Tabernacle. At the same point in every service, he invites the congregation to approach the altar and receive the blood and body of Christ. Because of the repeatability of the ritual, and the belief of all involved, it works every time. Of course, you couldn't demonstrate any such thing in a lab. But that's the difference between religion and science. For a priest it's enough to believe in the answer. For a scientist, it's enough to believe in the method of obtaining the answer.

In the seventies, some parishes still offered "the cup" to adult laity. During communion the Sunday before my mother died, our parish priest startled me when, after placing the Host on my tongue, he touched the chalice to my lips. I had never tasted wine; alcohol was banned from our house. For days afterward I debated whether it had tasted like blood, which was illogical, even within the context of the ritual. After all, the wafer never tasted like "flesh." At Mom's funeral, crying, staring at my lap while the priest spoke his useless words, a ghost of the wine's bitter taste returned.

1982

The beetle-looking thing stepped haltingly away from the office on its jointed stilts.

"What is it?" I whispered.

"I don't know for real sure," the woman said. "I call them hunters. Keep down and keep quiet, or you'll see why. That one does nothing but stand quiet as a tombstone, right up till you hear those three echo sounds. It comes a little bit more alive with each one. Those sounds, they're like a doorbell. Somehow that one there answers it and opens the door. But that's not all it does. I believe it transmits some kind of signal to the others, whenever a fresh victim turns up. That's what you are, kid. The fresh victim."

I didn't like her calling me kid, especially since she didn't look all that much older than me, with her little upturned nose and brown freckles. While she whispered, the beetle walked into the middle of the runway and stopped. Each leg had a joint about in the middle, like a knee, except they bent the opposite way a human knee would bend, inward instead of outward. Now the knees all bent at once, and the beetle squatted low to the tarmac. After a moment, the air in front of the thing became blurry, like the way air looks above a hot road in the distance, almost a liquid appearance of rising heat. In no time the air swirled into a white mist screen, hanging there on the tarmac, wafer thin.

"That's the door."

Out of the mist three more of the beetle things came stalking forth. One ran directly to my Cessna. I mean, it really was like a giant silver bug, moving in that quick scuttle on its set of back-ward-jointed legs. The sound of those legs clacking on the tar-mac gave me an awful feeling. It was such an *alive* sound. A cable extended from the nose of the thing's body and probed through the open door of my airplane. I imagined it was sniffing around, trying to pick up a scent. Trying to pick up *my* scent.

The cable withdrew from the cabin—and it was holding my lunch bag. It brought the bag close to its body for a moment, then dropped it. The other two beetles had remained motionless after their initial appearance. The cable slithered back inside the third one and it clickity-clacked back over to join them. They stood in a close circle, motionless, as if discussing what to do next. After a moment, my head started to hurt. I closed my eyes, like that would help. It didn't. The ache worsened, a drilling, hot, yellow pain.

The freckle woman nudged me. Her eyes were the blue you see in a fire. "Now you listen to me," she whispered. "We can block whatever it is they're doing in our heads. You just got to concen-trate real hard on something else. I mean concentrate like you're gonna bust a vein. Do that and it backs off."

"I don't *understand*." My voice trembled.

"Do it. Concentrate."

Shapes, vague and eager, humped forward in my mind. A sound like a crowd of foreign voices rose up. I couldn't under-stand any individual word. I concentrated, imagining a fence between me and the shapes. It was the old wooden slat fence from my backyard, leaning and half rotted, that couldn't keep out so much as a bunny rabbit. But I made it strong by concen-trating on every detail. I was aware of the questing shapes try-ing to nose through the fence to get at me. But as long as I didn't give them my attention, as long as I focused on the fence, they became less urgent, less potent. The crowd murmur reached an inarticulate peak then subsided, like a wave crashing against and withdrawing from a breakwater. My mind became quiet, and I let go of my rickety fence and came out of myself, blink-ing, rubbing my eyes.

"Howzit?" the woman asked.

"Okay, I think. What are those things doing now?"

"Giving it up, I hope. Lot of time, what I think happens is the new arrivals are so confused they tend to hang around the aero-drome. Easy pickings."

"Like me?"

"Yep, like you."

"What do they do if they catch you?"

"Carry you through the door. I've seen it. I'm not always so dumb I try to *save* anybody. But heck, you looked so dang pathetic, I almost couldn't bear it. My name's Maggie, by the way. Maggie Farmer. I haul the mail. Or used to, I guess."

"I'm Paul."

"Glad to meet ya."

"So why do you hang around here? Aren't you scared?"

"Heck yes, I'm scared. Not as scared as you, I bet. But if there's a way to escape, it's right here. The whole world is like this aero-drome—empty. When I first got here I had a bad feeling about Quillayute, and I kept going, flew my ship as far as Astoria, then inland to Portland. There isn't a soul around, as near as I could determine. Except for maybe the handful of folks that dropped out of the same hole we did and then didn't get caught by the hunters. Maybe some of them are still out there. What I want, I want to go back to the other world, the one that's filled up with people. That's why I keep coming back. This was the way in, so it's got to be the way out, too. Right?"

"US 246. Was that your, ah, ship crashed in the trees?"

"Yes, but it's no reflection on my piloting skills, and don't think it is. Truth is—" Maggie's face blushed, which made her freckles stand out even more, and she looked both angry and embarrassed. "Truth is, I ran out of fuel. The damn doorbell was going off as soon as I landed. Guess that ship with the tail that looks like a vee had just dropped in, and I didn't even know it. I was already running on fumes, coming back from Oregon. When I heard the chime, I didn't know if it was the first one or the third one. I throttled up without thinking. Lucky for me, if you want to call it luck, is the hunters got their hands full with the folks from the vee plane, and that gave me time to climb down from the crash and hide."

"There was a little girl—" I started to say.

"Hold it. They're moving."

The three machines scuttled off in three different directions.

One of the directions was our direction.

"Shoot," Maggie said.

"Maybe we should run."

"Those things go like racehorses. Just keep your dang head down and pray, if that's what you do."

I kept my head down but my eyes open. My heart was beating like crazy. What would happen if one of those things carried me through what Maggie called the "door"? That's when I noticed something. The white mist doorway was gradually shrinking.

Like the popcorn cloud over the field.

What if the cloud was all that was left of another doorway? Was it a trap, deliberately created by the beetles, or just some kind of lucky accident for them, regularly delivering up victims? I remembered the feeling of being pulled in, as if by a force of gravity.

The backward-jointed legs of the nearest beetle swished in the undergrowth. It paused every few yards and swiveled its dome, maybe sweeping the area with some kind of radar or sensor.

Hunting for us.

Maggie squeezed my shoulder. I looked over. She was staring at me with those blue-fire eyes, and I knew what her look meant. The beetle was going to get us, and there wasn't a damn thing we could do about it. I was so frightened my body was paralyzed, and I felt cold and hot at the same time.

Then a girl screamed.

The beetle on the verge of discovering us pivoted and scuttled back to the runway. All three were converging—and the one that had gone hunting in the direction of Maggie's mail plane emerged from the forest holding a child coiled up in its tentacle. It wasn't the girl I'd already talked to, it wasn't Amanda. It must have been her sister, Tammy, the one who stepped in a hole and couldn't run. She had lost a shoe. Her white ankle sock made her seem even more vulnerable. She flailed and screamed.

"Oh, my God," Maggie said.

I hated myself for not acting, for not trying to save that child. With a huge effort I fought through my fear and tried to stand up, but Maggie grabbed my hand and wouldn't let me. Her fingers were cold and her grip was like steel bones, digging in.

"You can't help her," she said.

I twisted my hand, trying to break free, and I saw Maggie's

face. She was in agony, tears streaming down her cheeks. Then the captured child's sister bolted onto the runway and ran straight at the monster that was about to scuttle through the shrinking doorway, where the other two had just gone. Amanda had a short, broken off tree branch in her hand, a club. Her yellow ponytail bounced as she ran.

"*Dang*," Maggie said, and before I knew what was happening she had dropped my hand and was up and running, sprinting toward the field.

The beetle hesitated when the sister appeared. Maggie intercepted Amanda, snatched her up around the waist without breaking stride, and continued across the field toward the trees behind the dilapidated hangar. The girl fought her all the way, but Maggie wouldn't let go.

The beetle coiled its tentacle in, like tightening a watch spring, then snapped it straight out—flinging its screaming captive into the diminishing white screen of the doorway. Tammy's scream skirled away, like something spinning down a deep well.

By then I'd broken cover, too, and was running full out. It was like my body was doing something my mind hardly knew anything about. The beetle was halfway to the trees in pursuit of Maggie and Amanda, when it turned in my direction. I guess it sensed me, because I was yelling all kinds of raging profanities at it, making as much noise as possible. I *wanted* the damn thing to notice me, to come after me and leave Maggie and the girl alone.

When it did, I veered toward my Cessna, pouring everything I had into my legs, sprinting for my life. I didn't look at the beetle again until I was inside the trainer with the door shut. The beetle came on fast, legs a blur of furious energy. I turned over the prop, shoved the throttle in, like I wanted to ram that knob right through the instrument panel. The tach pegged into the red zone, and I kicked in the right rudder pedal, turning my flimsy little airplane around on the ramp. The other-world door and the metal beetle racing toward me meant I couldn't use the runway, so I powered along next to it, the Cessna jolting and bouncing, half out of control, gaining speed, prop kicking bits of gravel against the cowling.

I was up to forty-nine knots—too slow, but I pulled back on the yoke, anyway. The Cessna lifted indecisively, the tricycle gear touching back down a couple of times, like the wheels didn't want to let go of the earth. The beetle extended its tentacle and whipped it against the fuselage. It sounded like a hammer striking sheet metal, and the trainer yawed wildly across the runway toward the trees. Climbing sluggishly, I cleared the tree line with only a couple of feet to spare.

Blue sky filled the windows. I banked right, my wing pivoting over the airport. The door and the third beetle were gone. The one remaining, which I'd originally mistaken for a storage tank, had returned to its place between the hangar and the fuel island. It was almost as if none of it had happened. There was no sign of Maggie and the girl. In the trees they wouldn't have been visible, and I allowed myself to believe they had gotten away—that I had given them that chance. But for a few minutes, hanging up there in the safety of the sky, I felt guilty. How could I save my own ass and leave them down there? But then I let it go, because I had to concentrate.

The white popcorn cloud hung motionless in the clear air above me, its original Mickey Mouse head shape remarkably unaltered, except in size. I banked steeply and climbed in a spiral toward it, praying that I was right in thinking the unnatural behavior of this cloud indicated it was somehow related to the white mist doorway the beetle had opened on the runway.

The altimeter indicated seventy-seven hundred feet. In the time it had taken me to climb that high, the cloud had further diminished in size. If I had been looking at it from the ground I probably could have covered it with the end of my thumb. Up close, it was barely as wide as the trainer's wingspan, about thirty-some-odd feet across. I ascended into it without much hope, expecting only wisps of white vapor to blow past my windshield.

Instead, it totally engulfed my plane.

The world turned white. My instruments went haywire again. The magnetic compass swung and bobbed without direction. I lowered my head and fought my inner-ear instinct to roll left. I held on, held on . . . and then the mist blew away, and I was staring at the massive rock and ice face of Mount Olympus, unstable air buffeting my Cessna.

I was back.

2012

Thirty years later, I simply wanted to find *something* that worked—a practical ritual I could believe in, something to resurrect the events at Quillayute. Migraines plagued me. Body aches, intestinal agony. Burning pain throughout my body. Doctors investigated all these symptoms and more, to the limit of my insurance coverage, then stopped. They could find nothing to pin a bill to. I may have displayed symptoms of cancer, but no cancer was evident. I may have displayed markers of fibromyalgia, prostatitis, even brain tumors—but there appeared to be no causal events. Insurance coverage does not recognize symptoms without cause. And yet, my body was so clearly betraying me. Only one doctor used the word that must have been on everyone's mind: *Psychosomatic*. Ironically, he's the one who prescribed Demerol.

Pain can be inspirational, and I wanted to believe.

It took only a few days to track down the 150 trainer I'd flown back in 1982. November 60558 was registered to a dentist in Redmond, Washington. At first he wasn't inclined to part with it. I overcame his reluctance with money, depleting twenty-seven thousand dollars out of my pension fund. But what did I care? I would probably be dead long before I ran out of money.

The dentist had stripped out all the old avionics and replaced them with the latest instrumentation available. I hired a mechanic to restore the 150 to its original configuration, outmoded instruments and all. I wanted it in exactly the condition it had been when I last landed at Crest Airpark. The mechanic thought I was crazy, but he did his work well.

I hired an instructor, but didn't keep him long. He wasn't a proper acolyte, always asking if I was all right, if I was sure I was up to this. What he saw was the pain. I left my Demerol on the ground for these refresher flights. Anyway, the basics of piloting came back to me quickly, the muscle memory part of it. After a few lessons I felt competent to do what I needed to do.

I left Crest Airpark at the same time of day as I had when I was sixteen. I'd kept my logbook and knew the time down to the minute. Of course, this was all ridiculous. Magical thinking. Not really *thinking* at all. Even if the plane was similar, the weather wasn't. Broken clouds and five-mile visibility over the Olympic Peninsula. I feared my ritual in the sky was as bankrupt as the Catholic ceremonies of my boyhood.

By the time I was on an outbound radial from the Hoquiam VOR, I'd been in the air for hours, and I began popping Demerol. The pain ripping through my bowels and joints was simply too intense otherwise. Intoxicated on painkillers, belief became easier. The Quillayute airport appeared exactly where it was supposed to be. I circled, climbing, looking for a cloud that wasn't a cloud, a cloud painted flat on the sky.

There was no such cloud.

I climbed through a gauzy gray thing, about eighty-two hundred feet up. It was just an ordinary cloud. Sudden pain stitched through my bowels like a tin jag ripping through my Demerol screen. I squeezed my eyes shut, still pulling back on the yoke. The 150 nosed up and began to shudder toward a stall, the warning buzzer drilling out of the headset.

1982

Jim Brodie was surprised to see me back at Crest hours ahead of schedule. And I was surprised to see *him*. In fact, I couldn't stop staring. His hair covered the tops of his ears, which is how a lot of guys wore their hair back in the eighties. But not Jim Brodie. When I took off that morning, he had been wearing his usual crew cut.

During the flight back from Hoquiam, where I'd retreated after escaping the empty world to refuel and call in a new flight plan, I'd thought a lot about what I was going to say to Jim. I had two versions to account for what happened at Quillayute. I would start with the true version—but there was a crossroads in the truth, a point at which I was going to have to jump into the weird with both feet—or veer into a lie that I knew Jim would accept.

Now all I could think about was Jim's hair.

In the airport office, he handed me a can of Pepsi and popped one open for himself. The office was exactly right, from the beat-up orange vinyl chairs to the old issues of *Flying* magazine, to the snack and soda vending machines. The office was right, but Jim's hair was wrong.

"So you ran into some trouble?" he said.

"Uh huh."

"Paul, what's wrong? What are you staring at?"

I forced myself to stop staring at his ear comb-over, and launched into my story, concentrating on what I was saying and how Jim was reacting. The crossroads moment came at the point in the story when all the vintage and future out-of-time airplanes made their appearance. I'd watched Jim's face very carefully when I described getting lost near the Olympic Mountains, trying to follow the wrong VOR radial, then finding myself in the white cloud, and the failure of my instrumentation. When I described the behavior of the compass, Jim sat back a little and sipped his Pepsi. It was like I'd been holding his attention on a string, and the string just snapped.

"Back up a minute, Paul. Your compass wouldn't do that, unless there was an almighty powerful magnetic field pulling it off magnetic south."

"You mean magnetic north."

He looked at me funny. "Are you pulling my leg, Paul?"

"No, I—no."

"Look, even if there was a magnetic field, it wouldn't make the compass swing in all directions. When you're done, we'll go out and have a look at it, but I'm telling you it couldn't happen the way you just described."

I nodded, suddenly out of words. If Jim couldn't accept the compass thing, how was he going to believe the doorway, the beetles, Maggie and all the rest of it? I already knew the answer. He *wasn't* going to believe it. Nobody was. And I couldn't prove it, either.

Jim wasn't mad at me. I could see that. It was more like he was confused and worried.

He wanted to believe me about the compass but just couldn't.

"Go on, Paul," he said, when I was quiet too long. There was real kindness in his voice. I couldn't bring myself to ruin it with the truth. "You say there were a lot of old airplanes when you made your approach?"

"It was just a few, actually. I think it was like one of those shows. You know, like they have up in Arlington every year?"

"Oh."

"That's pretty much the whole thing. After I got lost I was scared to go on. That's all."

Jim was really studying me now. I looked at my Pepsi. He put his can down and stood up. "Let's have a look at that compass."

Before we ever got to the compass Jim gripped my arm and pointed at the side of the 150.

"What happened here?"

The metal was creased, the yellow paint scratched off in a long, shiny wound, where the beetle's tentacle whipped out, trying to prevent my escape. But I couldn't tell Jim that. He squeezed my arm, not painfully, just to focus my attention.

"Paul?"

"I don't know."

"You don't know? You must have hit something pretty hard to do that."

"I didn't hit anything," I said, which was true; something hit me. "But I was parked for a while at Hoquiam, when I stopped for fuel. Maybe . . . I don't know."

"Come on, Paul, what happened out there?"

"What I said, that's all."

I looked at my feet, blushing. After a moment, Jim let go of my arm and opened the passenger door.

"Go ahead and get in. We'll check out those instruments."

There was nothing wrong with the instruments. I'd already told him they'd only stopped working while I was in the white cloud. A little while later, after we talked about re-doing my cross-country requirement, I said my awkward goodbye, drove away from Crest Airpark, and it was thirty years before I went back.

At home, when I removed my pants to get in the shower, I saw the envelope I'd folded and stuffed in my back pocket. I held it in the bright bathroom light. Thick gray paper, a stamped return address in Washington D.C., but a *typewriter*-produced mailing address to some guy named Ralph Hoffman in Aberdeen. Sitting on the toilet seat, I ripped into it eagerly, like the envelope was going to contain an *answer*. Maybe Quillayute had been the location of some kind of Top Secret government experiment.

But the text of the letter, also produced by a manual typewriter, concerned the approval of a claim for veteran's benefits. It was signed by someone in the office of the Secretary of the Army. The only interesting thing about the letter was the date typed in above the "Dear Mr. Hoffman."

14 September 1926

Did I run back out to Crest the next day, show Jim Brodie the letter, and tell him the whole story? No, of course not. It was just an old letter, not proof of anything. Holding the letter made me feel slightly queasy. Maybe it was just an old letter to other people, but I knew it was an artifact I had no business possessing. It didn't *belong* here. In its own way, the letter was as disturbing as Jim's haircut. Or magnetic south.

And then things got worse.

At that time my dad was working swing-shift at Boeing's Kent facility. My only sibling, David, was nine years older than me and a First Sergeant in the Army, stationed in Berlin. Six years ago our parents had tried to talk David out of enlisting—the Vietnam War had only recently ended. Anyway, it was just my dad and me in the house now, and I would be alone that first night back from Quillayute, until midnight, when he got home from work.

I'd decided I was going to tell him what happened. I wasn't afraid he would think I was lying. He might not believe me, but he was my dad. He was on my side in a way that Jim Brodie couldn't be. Who I really wanted to tell was my brother, but David wasn't due back until Christmas. Dad had remained solid and strong after Mom died. It hurt him bad—they been married twenty-six years—but except for that night a couple of weeks after her death, he had held himself together with incredible strength—largely for my sake, I thought. It was Dad who found Jim Brodie through a friend at work and set me up with flying lessons—an expense he couldn't really afford to take on. I think he did it to coax me out of my long depression over Mom's death. My father was a kind and sensitive man, though I don't think I gave him enough credit for it back then.

When he didn't arrive home at his usual hour, I wasn't worried. Dad was a lead man in the factory, which meant he occasionally worked overtime. Normally he called when he was going to be late, though. That *did* bother me a little. It was another not-right thing. I was half asleep on the sofa when a car turned into the driveway, splashing headlights through the curtains. I sat up, waiting for him to come in. After a while—too long a while—a car door slammed, and then keys fumbled at the front door. That went on so long, I wondered if the porch light was burned out. He dropped the keys; I heard them jangle on the porch.

I got up and opened the door. The porch light was on, and Dad was stooped over, groping for his dropped keys. His hair was mussed, his bald crown red and scabrous in the porch light.

"Dad—?"

He came up with his keys and patted me on the shoulder as he passed into the house. "Paulie, worked late. How'd the big adventure go?"

"Good." It's all I could get out.

"Tell me all about it tomorrow, huh? I'm beat."

Dad reeked of gin. I closed the front door and watched him weave down the hall to his bedroom. There was never alcohol in the house, not since that one time when he didn't even open the bottle. But after Dad went to bed, I found three empty bottles of Tanqueray in the trash. Just like the old days, before he'd quit.

It was a couple of days before I learned that my brother was dead. I was used to thinking he would be home at the end of the year, after his deployment, and I was looking forward to seeing him again. Nine years older made him feel like another adult, one I could relate to more easily. When I casually made reference at the breakfast table to David's impending return, Dad leveled me with bleary eyes over the rim of his coffee cup.

"What's wrong with you, Paul?"

"What?"

He put his cup down and left the room. I stared after him, bewildered, at first, and then frightened. In David's bedroom, which Dad had converted to a "den" after my brother enlisted, I found a picture on the wall that hadn't been there when I left for Crest Airpark the previous day. It was in a group of family photos, most of which my mom had framed. In the place where there had been a studio picture of my brother in his army uniform, looking almost laughably fresh-faced, there was now a shot of him in jungle fatigues with his arms around the shoulders of a couple of guys similarly dressed. David's cap was pushed back, and he was smiling. The background was some kind of military compound. In the white border of the photo, cramped words in blue ink identified the location as *Able Base, Chu Lai Province, Vietnam. 1979.* Eventually I found the letter—the one that had probably been hand delivered, confirming David had been killed in action—killed in a war that should have already ended. I cried alone in my brother's old bedroom, cried my eyes out. I had been wrong to think I'd made it back home.

In 1982, if you wanted to research something, you went to the library. I found what I was looking for in the main branch of the Seattle Public Library: a detailed history about the early days of Air Mail service in the United States.

Maggie got a whole page.

US MAIL 246 was lost and never found, somewhere in the dense wilderness of the Olympic Peninsula, September 18, 1926. At the time there were only a handful of female pilots in the world. Maggie's picture showed her standing next to her de Havilland DH-4, the same "ship" I'd seen trapped in the high canopy of the rain forest with a pair of broken wings and a gaping hole spilling mail like blood from a mortal wound. Maggie looked confident and ready to take on anything in her leather jacket and boots, her right hand gripping the strut of the plane. She stared straight into the camera (I imagined one of those tripod things where the photographer huddles under a black cloth and holds up a pan of flash powder). It was a sepia-toned picture. Back in the twenties, if you wanted a color photograph you had to "tint" it by hand. If anyone had bothered to tint the Maggie picture they would have had to find paint the exact color of blue fire. I stared at that picture for a long time, and I swear that after a while I could see the blue even without the tinting.

I found books about missing aircraft, looking for details that were lacking in the history of airmail. My most interesting discovery was that the airspace over that quadrant of the Olympic Peninsula was considered a kind of Bermuda Triangle of the sky. At least it was by one Art Feinberg, author of *Mysterious Vanishings*. I put the book down, wondering if Jim Brodie had been aware of this reputation.

That summer I borrowed my dad's car and drove out to Quillayute. It was a long drive, and I got lost more than once, heading north up the wilderness coast. The Navy base appeared empty and abandoned, except for a couple of guys clanging away at something in the one intact hangar. The sky hung low and gray, but I tried to imagine a blue expanse and a white cumulus, painted flat against the sky. I *could* imagine it. But that's all it felt like: imagination. Not a memory of a real thing.

2012

In a universe of infinite space, infinite repetition is inevitable. I read that on my monitor at two o'clock in the morning, a couple of weeks before flying my newly restored Cessna 150 out of Crest Airpark for my ritual in the sky. It was a lightbulb moment. I read it again. It wasn't that I'd never encountered the idea before in all my after-midnight reading. But this time, expressed in this way— something clicked. All night I had been popping Demerol like Tic-Tacs. Maybe the resulting haze made it easier to accept the idea of sky portals between infinitely repeated worlds. Maybe the portal over Quillayute had been a junction between multiple possibilities, not a single, direct link between where I had come from and where I wound up.

1997

Fifteen years after the events at Quillayute, I drove down to Arlington, about half an hour south of Everett. It's where my mother was buried. A yellow Citabria, a tail dragger, swooped low over the road, headed for a landing. I'd forgotten about the annual fly-in. After visiting the cemetery, I found my way to the airport, bought a ticket, and spooked around for a while. The new world was textured with differences. Some were trivial, like Jim Brodie's haircut. Others were devastating, like David's death and Dad's reversion into alcoholism. At first I had been like a blind man feverishly discovering the altered textures of my new world. After a while it became overwhelming, the accumulation of wrong detail. Unable to trust anyone or anything beyond immutable engineering specs, I withdrew into myself. In the other world, the first world, as I thought of it, would I have been so alone?

It was a warm summer day and the crowd was substantial at the Arlington Airport. Vendors sold Sno Cones and hot dogs. I wandered around with lemonade in a plastic cup full mostly of ice, looking at the static displays. Sharp pains occasionally daggered through my bowels, and I had to stop and catch my breath. I felt a hundred years old.

I paused in front of a home-built micro plane, a BD-5 with the unusual aft-mounted prop. I'd read about these things but this was the first time I'd seen one up close. The BD-5 was a single seater with a big clear plexi canopy that made it look a little like a toy fighter plane. This one was painted white, with narrow red and blue stripes from nose to engine cowling and the word EX-PERIMENTAL printed just under the canopy.

I wasn't the only one interested in the BD-5. Ten or twelve people stood around the plane, which was so small and toy-looking you almost expected to see a bunch of clowns climb out of it. I leaned over the cockpit and imagined myself snugged in there, my hands on the controls. I was thirty-one years old and had never gone back to flying. Bright lights began boiling around my peripheral vision—warning that a migraine was coming. I closed my eyes and tried to wish it back. When I looked up, there was Maggie, haloed in pre-migraine distortion.

She stood on the other side of the BD-5, holding a cherry Sno Cone to her lips. She wore a black long-sleeved shirt, dark green cargo pants and sneakers. Her hair was still boyishly short. She had aged but she wore the years lightly. We made eye contact. I knew she recognized me. I could see it. After a moment, she turned and walked away, and I followed her, kind of hobbling along like Quasimodo after the latest beating.

"Hey—?"

She stopped suddenly and turned. "Do I know you?" When I didn't reply, she said, "I guess I don't," and turned away again.

"Wait. It was Quillayute. You crashed your de Havilland. US mail 246. You're Maggie—"

She turned back slowly, smiling. "Just testing you, kid."

"It's really you?"

"In the flesh. Been trying to find you for ages. There's a lot of

Pauls out there in a lot of worlds, but only one that doesn't belong where he is. That's you, chum. You tried to save me. I'm here to return the favor. Let's walk. I'll show you my ship."

I hesitated, and Maggie took my elbow and pulled me along. "Best not to think too much about this, Paul. You've gotten yourself a little hypnotized, being in the wrong world. It's a survival mechanism."

I stopped walking. I had suddenly found myself occupying three worlds, and I wasn't comfortable in any of them: the world inside my throbbing head. The wrongly- textured world I'd been living in since Quillayute, and the world Maggie created by her exuberant, anomalous presence. I said, "That time at Quillayute, all I did was run away."`

"No, it worked. The Automatic Retriever went after you instead of us. We got clean away into the forest. 'Course, that was the exact opposite of what we should have done."

"Automatic Retriever? You mean those robot beetle things?"

"Sure. Look, Paul, it's not what we thought. The Automatics were sent in to save us—us and anyone else who dropped through the hole. That world, not just the airport but the whole dang world, it was a big empty. I doubt you're going to believe me, but there are so many worlds I couldn't even count 'em if I tried. Most are pretty much like the one we're standing in right now, except some are more in the future or the past. The one where the Automatic Retrievers got made, that one's the future, way, way off. Those things were set on automatic because there's so many worlds, and so many bad, empty ones, that the Retriever people couldn't possibly be everywhere at once to save folks who got themselves trapped. Remember the headaches? That was them trying to communicate, give us the story. Mind talk is what the future folks use instead of regular words. They don't hardly ever move their mouths anymore. The Automatics, they were trying to talk in our minds, too, like with a coded message, but we blocked them."

I tried to process this but mostly failed. "Is that little girl with you? I mean, I guess she wouldn't be little anymore."

"Amanda? Heck no. Her whole family was waiting for her, soon's we ran through the door at the aerodrome. That's right. Next time a ship dropped in and the door opened, we ran through it on purpose, before the other Automatics even came out. I figured it was the only chance we had of finding our way out of the empty world we were stuck in. And I was right. See, I wasn't smart like you. I didn't catch on to the cloud being like an accidental sky door. Anyway, the future people were waiting for us. And what a reunion for little Amanda, her whole family there like if they'd been killed, which is pretty much what we figured, and then gone to heaven and bam there they *are*, waiting."

She took a lick on her Sno Cone, which was dripping.

"The future people showed me how to open up doors between worlds on purpose. All you got to be is good at finding the right place, and then *want* the darn thing to open. Only it's a special kind of wanting, not like if you want a Coke or another piece of cake, or something. I'm a Retriever now, myself. Hey, it beats hauling the mail, I'll tell you that. You wouldn't *believe* it, Paul. People make empty worlds all the time, without even knowing it. Some of them are like traps for other people. That's what caught us at Quillayute. Anyway, it's what I do nowadays. Look for doors and want at them till they open. Then I swoop down, on the rescue. It's a talent, and who knew I had it?"

I shook my head. "You sound out of your mind."

"I'm just happy."

We walked past the static displays. The airport was utilizing a grassy field to accommodate all the fly-ins. Maggie's "ship" was a fire-engine red biplane, newer than the De Havilland, but not contemporary.

"Whatchya think, kid?"

"It's beautiful."

She pointed at the sky. "Look up there, Paul."

I looked. Blue sky and broken clouds. "What am I supposed to be seeing?"

"That one cloud, way, way up. Call it seven thousand feet. That little one, all by itself. That's my door. I wanted that one open, and it opened. Like I said, I been looking for you. Arlington is a place you always turn up, only this is the first time I found the right Paul in the wrong world."

I squinted at the cloud. It didn't look much different than all the other clouds. But when I stared at it steadily for a minute it never drifted, never changed shape. And maybe there was a flat quality to the cloud, almost like it was painted on a blue canvas.

"That's one of your doors?"

"Sure is."

"Is it . . . shrinking? The ones at Quillayute shrank."

"Yep. There's a time limit. Least there is in places like this. Other worlds, they're more steady and wide open, like the one where Amanda is with her folks. Come on. I'll show you."

I touched the side of the airplane, trying to picture first the exhilaration of climbing into the sky and then through the doorway and into the unknown with Maggie. Frightened, I grounded myself where I stood—where I was used to the wrongness of things. Where I was hypnotized, I guess.

"I can't."

"Sure you can."

"What you're talking about is magic, and I can't accept that."

"Come on. It's not magic. It's real. I can show you how to open doors. Least I can do, after you tried to save me from the metal 'monsters' and all."

I stared at her.

"Come with me now, Paul. It's great times, I promise you."

"If I do, can you bring me back here?"

"Trust me, Paul, you don't want to come back here."

"I have a *life*."

Maggie's face became serious. "Listen to me. Listen very carefully. You aren't yourself. You never did belong here, but being here so long, it's making you like you're in a dream you can't wake up out of. Listen to how angry you are, all of a sudden, and just because I want to save you. Use your head now. I can't rescue you if you don't let me. Once I go away from here I might never find my way back. You don't *belong*, Paul. I bet you don't have a soul in this world you can call a friend. I bet you don't even have a girl. Hey, I've seen it all before."

I couldn't speak, couldn't move. What she said was true, but I was sunk deep in the dream, even if it was the wrong dream. Going with her terrified me.

"There's worse to come," Maggie said. "This isn't your world. Being here, what you're like is a foreign object in a body. The world's gonna reject you. Stay here and you might live, but it will be a long, miserable life, full of pain and sickness that nobody can fix."

"*Stop* it," I said, trying to close myself against the pain she described—the pain I already felt.

She climbed on the wing, held her hand out. "Come on. Take a chance. Wake up, and come flying with me. It's the only way people like us can live, since we lost our own first worlds. We got to keep moving."

I shoved my hands in my pockets, shook my head.

"Be brave," Maggie said, "like you were that time."

I felt trapped inside my frightened body.

Maggie glanced at the sky, at her closing door. "Time's up. Coming?"

"I *can't*."

"Dang it, Paul."

She hoisted herself into the rear seat. It felt like everything inside me was collapsing into a dead crater. My eyes filled with tears. Maggie yelled, "Clear prop!" like she was pissed off. The engine turned over, belching pale blue exhaust. The prop spun into a blur. She worked the control surfaces, checking them out preflight, ailerons waving at me as she rolled away. The grass blew flat in the prop wash. My shirt fluttered around my body like a cotton fire.

The engine throttled up and she raced away and lifted like a thing cut loose from chains. By then I'd broken my paralysis and was running, waving my arms, but it was too late. A hundred feet up, Maggie turned downwind, rocked her wings once, and began a steep climb, the engine racket growing fainter and fainter, in that lazy, droning way. A coughing fit took me over. When I pulled my hand away from my mouth it was speckled with blood. Maggie's ship droned in the distance. I shaded my eyes against the sun. The biplane banked smartly, a bright red toy against a blue field, aiming for a cloud hanging directly over the airfield, flat and motionless. Moments later my center vision began pulsing with gray blotches, and the throbbing pain of a brutal migraine started.

2012

High above Quillayute, my trainer stalled and the nose dropped. But the 150, like all airplanes, *wanted* to fly. That time, thirty years ago, I'd been disoriented and had put the plane into a steep, spiraling plunge. But in this case, I had simply pulled into an angle of attack too severe to continue. My brain rolling in a Demerol tide, my hands off the controls, the trainer righted itself into stable, if untrimmed, flight. I let that happen, took control again, and set up a sloppy approach to Quillayute.

I climbed out of the trainer slowly. The pain encapsulated me in a bubble. I pictured myself dry swallowing Demerol until the bubble dissolved, taking me with it. I thought my improvised ritual had failed, was as impotent as the Catholic ceremonies of my boyhood. What had made those old rituals work, for me, had been my *mother's* belief. I could never believe in transubstantiation, but I always believed in Mom. Who did I have to believe in now, to make my sky ritual potent?

The airport appeared deserted. I retrieved my brown bag lunch. I'd put together the same peanut butter sandwich plus two bananas, just as I'd packed back in 1982. When I reached for the sandwich, my abdominals clenched involuntarily. I was down to a hundred and thirty-five pounds, which is about what I weighed when I was sixteen. The rejecting world had in its own way helped me build this ritual. I stared at the sandwich, then dropped it back into the bag.

An engine droned out of the sky. I looked up. A shiny red biplane slipped over the tree line and dropped to the runway, flaring at the last second, the big forward wheels lightly kissing the tarmac once before settling. The pilot rolled out and swung over to where I was parked. Maggie killed the engine and hopped down, peeling goggles off at the same time. There were streaks of gray in her hair, but the fire still burned bright in her eyes. She planted her hands on her hips.

"We going flying, or what?"

I smiled. It probably looked like a grimace.

"It's too late," I said, believing it, even though my sky ritual *had* worked after all, and Maggie was standing before me.

"*Bull pucky.* Come on, kid. Let me show you something about the brave new worlds."

Kid. I hobbled over to her ship.

"How did you find me?"

"Actually, you found me. Finally. Remember what I said about wanting? Not just sitting around all vague, but doing something with the want. Paul, it's like ringing the doorbell, what those automatics used to do. Except you did it with your mind. You did it with your *want*. I heard you and came through. I'm telling you, Paul, you're a natural. If you practice up you could find doors easy as me—easier, maybe. I can teach you, same way the future people taught me."

Which is when I realized it was Maggie I believed in. Maggie I *wanted*. But it was still too late. At forty-six I was hobbled, bent, in constant pain. I said, "*Look* at me. What am I supposed to do?"

Maggie took me over. "You're supposed to get in."

She helped me into the forward seat and secured my lap belt, careful not to cinch it too tight. I was really sweating, and that tin jag in my bowels ripped a wicked cross-stitch. Maggie placed her hand on my chest and spoke softly in my ear. Her touch calmed me. My breathing slowed down.

"You don't look so good, Paul. You got something you're taking for all that pain?"

"Yeah."

She patted my chest. The prescription bottle rattled in my breast pocket. Maggie reached for it, squinted at the label . . . then threw it away. I made a sound in my throat.

"Thing is, Paul, a world full of people can still be an empty world for the person who never made it. Sometimes a guy needs a friend to point the way out, is all."

I nodded, trying not to think about the pain.

"Paul?" Her face was close to mine, those blue, blue eyes big and wide as the sky. "You're going to have to fly us through the door. I made it open, but it won't let you through, if you don't believe. I mean *really* believe. You weren't ready at Arlington, but this time you have to be. You hearing me, Paul?"

"I hear you."

She climbed in the rear seat. Before she started the engine I said, "Wait. What's out there, on the other side?"

"Something real good, where the pain goes away. The trick is to keep moving."

The engine coughed blue exhaust and the prop turned, caught, revved up. The racket was tremendous. The airframe shook like it wanted to pop rivets. Then it smoothed out and we started rolling. After a few seconds we rotated into the sky, hooked around, and roared toward a white cloud painted flat above the tree line. A rusty blood taste percolated in the back of my throat. Maggie slapped my shoulder and yelled, "It's your airplane!"

I took the stick. Suddenly the cloud looked like a drifty, cheesecloth thing, ordinary and ephemeral. I concentrated hard, concentrated around the pain and doubt, until I thought I could see the fair blue sky beyond. A surge of power traveled up my arm. My heart beat wildly, and the sky portal painted itself white and flat against the sky.

We passed into it, and there was no pain.

STEEL LAKE

W hy are you doing this?" Brian Kerr asked his son.
"I'm an addict."

"Yeah, I *know* that. But why now?"

They sat at a table in an institutionally grim room. The flat glare of fluorescent light made Brian's eyes ache. His shirt clung to his body in dark patches of sweat. A big school-style clock counted the seconds in tiny jerks of a black needle.

"I took something that scared me," David said.

"According to the checklist we just went through, you've taken every damn drug known to man."

"This one wasn't on the list."

"Great. What was it?"

"It isn't even on the street yet. This guy, he stole it out of a UW lab, he said. Like he was a volunteer for this test?"

"Okay. But what *was* it?"

"I don't know."

"Jesus Christ."

David shrugged, looking away. His over-sized white T-shirt hung loose on his shoulders—the way it would on a coat hanger. Green spray paint speckled the shirt. Graffiti blow-back.

"You just took it. Without even knowing what it was?"

"Yeah, I guess."

"*Why?*"

"It was there so I took it, is all. You don't really get it, Dad."

"No, I don't. What scared you about this drug? I mean, what's scarier than—" He picked up the checklist, the unbelievable, terrifying checklist. "—heroin, for instance."

"It turned my head inside out."

"What's that mean, turned your—"

The door opened and two men entered. The older man, Ray,

was in charge—he handled the late shift intakes. About forty, lean and muscled, he looked like a penitentiary cliché. Tattooed thorns vined around his muscled forearms and a pack of smokes bulged in his short rolled up sleeve. Rehab wasn't jail, but so far it shared a similar flavor. Or so Brian imagined. The younger man was actually a kid David's age, eighteen or so, pale and blooming with acne.

"Nick's going to check your bag for contraband," Ray said.

Nick, all business, opened David's hastily-packed suitcase and began pawing through it. He tossed aside a paperback novel. Brian had packed the book for David, thinking it would help him get through the next month.

"Why can't he have that?"

Ray picked up the novel and handed it to Brian. "The only book allowed in here is The Big Book."

"That's—"

"Dad, it's okay. I don't care about it."

"What your son needs, he has to keep his mind on recovery."

"Yeah, I get that."

Ray pushed the insurance papers across the table and held out a Bic pen. Brian sighed and started on the forms. Until it was time to say goodbye, David did not speak another word.

Business as usual.

For a week David had been living in his car, a black 1993 beat-to-shit Honda Civic. Turning the ignition key produced a rapid series of dead clicks. When Brian picked him up, they left the Honda parked on a residential street in a south Seattle working class neighborhood. Sooner or later somebody would call the city to get it towed. Before that, Brian decided to strip out whatever "contraband" he could find.

A Mag-Lite in his left hand, he popped the glove box. Registration papers, parking tickets, a dead cell phone, half a dozen disposable syringes, and a pipe that looked like it was hand-tooled out of plumbing parts. Brian sniffed the bowl, winced at the burnt smell.

He dropped the syringes and pipe into a plastic Safeway bag then swept the Mag-Lite around the foot wells. Among the crumpled cigarette packs and Taco Time wrappers, colonies of little Ziploc baggies gleamed in the moving light. Some were empty and some contained a faint residue of white powder. Brian scooped them all up and added them to the Safeway bag.

He found the miniature aspirin tin under the cup holder insert, shook it, flicked the lid up with his thumbnail. Five chalky blue tablets, each printed with the same Greek letter. David's mystery drug? A car turned onto the street behind the Honda, headlights swinging through the Honda's rear window. Brian froze but his shadow tilted across the dashboard, as if ducking out of sight. The car rolled past without slowing.

Brian let his breath out. He pocketed the tin, checked the backseat and the trunk, then walked quickly back to his own car. He dropped the Safeway bag in a garbage dumpster behind a Korean restaurant.

By midnight he was drunk, holding down a stool in The Sitting Room, a quiet lamp-lit bar two blocks from his apartment. Even on the best of nights, the studio apartment felt like a divorce tomb. This was not the best of nights. Murphy's Irish whiskey and pints of Stella failed to erase various realities, the tomb-apartment being one of them.

He fumbled his cell phone out and thumbed a garbled text. Immediately, he regretted it. But when Trish failed to reply, he regretted that even more. He ordered another drink and nursed it along until closing time.

Halfway up the hill, stumbling towards his apartment, the phone vibrated in his pocket. He squinted at the screen.

One word, from Trish: "Okay."

"You're a mess," she said when she opened the door to her condo. She wore a Seahawks jersey and nothing else. Her hair was messed up, like she'd been asleep.

"Bad day," he said. "Look, I shouldn't have texted you."

"I know that."

"Oh—"

"And I shouldn't have invited you over. So we're both stupid."

In the bathroom he toed off his shoes, dumped the contents of his pockets on the towel rack. He rinsed his mouth in the sink. The tap water was cold and tasted of iron.

Trish was sitting up in bed, waiting for him. "I'd offer you a drink, but that would be like offering kerosene to a trash fire."

"Yeah." He collapsed on the bed beside her.

"So what happened?"

"David called and I checked him into Lakeside."

"I'm so sorry, Brian." She held his hand, picking up where they left off—where Brian left, actually. The Man Who Couldn't Stay. "But it's kind of good, too," Trish said. "I mean maybe it'll straighten him out this time."

"There's always that chance. At least I'll know where he is for the next six weeks." Brian covered his eyes with his free hand. "I really am an idiot. My head's going to hurt so bad tomorrow."

"Wait a minute." She scooted off the bed, returning shortly with a tall glass of water. "Stick your tongue out."

He did, and she placed two bitter-tasting tablets on it.

"Aspirin. Swallow—and drink that whole glass. Plus the next one I'm going to bring you. It'll knock down the hangover."

Brian came awake at some dead hour of the morning.

He had been dreaming about playing catch with his son. In the dream they stood on a grassy slope in Steel Lake Park, near the old neighborhood. David was a young boy again. The baseball sailed between their gloves, and the good world, the lost world, was restored. Then something woke Brian and it was over, his son was gone—as if David had stepped out of the dream, and the sound of his passage had awakened Brian, like a person leaving the bedroom and pulling the door shut.

The good years, right. Not long after Brian taught his son to catch a baseball, a man was murdered in that same park, knifed repeatedly. Some gang thing, the opening event of the neighborhood's long, steep slide. The victim's blood stained Brian's good memories, like sour wine spilled across a holiday table cloth.

Trish's bedside clock read 4:17AM. Brian was *wide* awake. Sharply, almost painfully, wide awake. He did not feel drunk or hung-over. Trish slept on her side, turned away from him.

In the bathroom his haggard face regarded him from the mirror. He rubbed his sandpaper cheek. His mouth tasted like rust. He stuck his tongue out, almost expecting to see it coated with iron oxide. His wallet and keys were on the towel rack over the hamper. Brian stuffed them into his pockets.

In the living room he grabbed his empty water glass and carried it into the kitchen. A little tin of aspirin sat on the counter next to the microwave. Brian stared at it. He set his glass down, wiped his lips with the back of his hand. The tin rattled when he shook it. He pried it open. Three chalky blue tablets with Greek letters. When he found the tin in David's car it had contained five.

"Trish?" He shook her gently until she woke up.

"Huh? God, what are you doing awake, it's—"

"Four-thirty. Never mind that. Last night you gave me aspirin. Where did you get them?"

Lying on her back, she held the clock up and squinted at it. "My God, it *is* four-thirty. Jesus."

"Trish, the aspirin. It's important."

"I was out but there were some with your wallet and keys in the bathroom. What's wrong?"

"Shit. *Shit.*"

She sat up. "What's wrong, what's happening?"

"Nothing's wrong, except those weren't aspirin."

"Oh, God, Brian, what were they? Is it something David had?"

"Yeah."

She took the tin out of his hand. "What are they?"

"I don't know," he said, thinking: *Like father like son.*

"What's this symbol? Damn it, I'm sorry, Brian. I should have looked more closely. But I was half-asleep and—"

"It's not your fault."

"Let me hold onto one of the pills. I'll show it to a lab rat I know at the hospital. Maybe she can figure it out."

"You don't have to do that."

"Are you on any other medication? There might be something reactive—" Trish suddenly inhabiting her full-on RN mode.

"I'm not taking anything. Don't worry about it, okay?"

"Excuse me for trying to help."

"I'm sorry. Look, tell your rat they might be part of some kind of drug trial at the UW. David said that's where they came from.

And I appreciate it, I really do."

"Okay." She looked closely at him. "Are you feeling anything ... weird?"

"Just really wide awake."

"Maybe they're some kind of stimulant. That wouldn't be too bad."

"No, that wouldn't be bad."

It was bad.

A week later, Brain still hadn't slept. He no longer felt sharply awake, but he didn't feel sleepy, either. Or he felt he *was* asleep, walking through a dream. But he knew that wasn't true. Reality did not bend the way it did in dreams. At least, it hadn't so far.

Three north bound lanes of Interstate 5 were shut down for resurfacing, and even at ten-thirty p.m. traffic was slow, rolling into Seattle. Brian slouched behind the wheel of his Ford Focus, windows cranked down. He was wrung out after nine hours on the night shift, stringing wires in the fuselage of a 737. A big industrial fan circulated air through the hatch but it hadn't helped; the air had been thick and hot, stinking of human sweat and machine oil. The fan blades had scraped the safety cage—like a blade scoring the inside of Brian's skull.

The lights at Safeco Field blazed over the twelfth inning of an interminable tie game between the Mariners and Toronto. A play-by-play broadcast chattered from the radio speakers, which was a lucky break, considering the radio hadn't worked in two weeks.

The last game he had taken David to had been four years ago. They'd sat in the sun, Brian with his seven-dollar Budweiser and David with his four-dollar Coke (all Brian could afford, after paying for the tickets and parking). The plastic cups sweating in their hands, they'd watched the Mariners take their lumps against the Oakland A's. The Mariners were *always* taking their lumps. David had sipped his Coke and crunched ice with his teeth, speaking only when he had to respond to something Brian said.

In the traffic crawl, Dave Niehaus, the Mariners' venerable color commentator, was in the middle of calling a pop fly to right center field, when the broadcast washed out in a tide of static. Brian reached for the knob to turn the volume down but hesitated when another voice, low and intense, began speaking. "I hate you, you fucker. You think you got away with it, but you didn't."

Despite the heat, a cold breath prickled the hairs on the back of Brian's neck. The voice was familiar but Brian couldn't quite identify it. He adjusted the volume up but there were no more words, just the usual static that had been hissing out of the speakers for weeks. After another moment, he punched the radio off. Then Brian remembered something, and it wasn't a good something.

Dave Niehaus was dead.

A heart attack had nailed the commentator over a year ago. So, what did that mean? Was Niehouse some kind of auditory hallucination? Was it starting, whatever 'it' was? David's "inside-out" head?

A dog loped out of nowhere, head down, sniffing the hot, grated surface of the road, oblivious of traffic. Brian gripped the steering wheel and hunched forward. A golden retriever, the dog favored its left hind leg, and Brian recognized her immediately. This was Gypsy, the family dog—from back when Brian *had* a family.

Gypsy was as dead as Dave Niehaus.

The muscles tightened in Brian's chest. Behind him, somebody laid on a horn, and he jumped half out of his seat. A pair of truck lights glared in his rearview mirror before swerving around and passing on the right. In the thick traffic the maneuver was impossible—but the truck managed it anyway, as if there *were* no traffic. Or maybe it was the truck and dog that weren't really there. That seemed more likely, given what Brian now saw.

Cancerous rust had eaten holes in the Suburban's left front wheel hub. The driver's arm hung out the open window with a cigarette. The big, ramshackle SUV cut back in, almost clipping the Ford's bumper. Brian tapped the brakes. An old California plate, orange numbers on a black background, hung crookedly by a single screw from the Suburban's bumper.

It was the same truck that had killed Gypsy seven years ago.

Even before Brian could process that idea, the Suburban struck the resurrected dog. Brian almost felt the dull thud of impact reverberate in his bones. The dog yelped in pain.

"*Asshole!*"

The truck moved off, at times occupying the same space as

other vehicles, overlaying them like an optical trick.

Brian pulled into the narrow break-down lane, parked, switched on his hazard flashers. The dog lay smashed against the jersey barrier, where the impact had landed her. Nobody but Brian seemed to notice. The tortured, squeaking yelps of pain drilled into Brian's mind—just as they had seven years ago. He had been having a rare, loud argument with Sheila. She had just discovered his first affair. David hadn't come home from school yet—except he had, and neither one of them knew it.

The boy stood by the open front door, listening to the whole thing. Gypsy, always in heedless puppy-behavior mode, had streaked out the door. David shouted after her. Brian and Sheila stopped yelling at each other. A moment later tires screeched, and Brian bolted out of the house after his son. He got a good look at the Suburban.

Now Brian plugged his ears with his fingers but that didn't dampen the sound at all. Gypsy's heart-breaking whimpering was *inside* his head. Brian clenched his teeth. Gradually, the yelps and squeals faded. In his mind, close up, he saw Gypsy's heaving flank and the blood pumping out of her mouth—his memory like a dream awake in the world. He blinked back tears. When he looked again, the dog was gone. Thank Christ.

What was so scary . . . ? It turned my head inside out.

Brian switched off his hazard flashers and re-entered the traffic flow. His hands were shaking. Just past the Convention Center he moved into the exit lane and found himself behind the Suburban with its ancient orange-on-black plate hanging by a screw.

A young boy, maybe six years old, stared at him out the back window, his face white in Brian's headlights. David's face. Brian's heart pounded. The window was dirty, like looking at the boy through a sheet of crusted brown ice.

David at six years old—the good years.

Brian had pissed all over those years. Oh, he had his excuses lined up, but they all boiled down to his own weakness. The first affair had provided him temporary, selfish relief from an estranged marriage. At least he could pretend that first one was love. Subsequent affairs were just a bad habit.

You thought you got away with it, you fucker . . .

The voice on the radio, so familiar, had been his own voice. The relentless accuser.

The line of cars started to move. The Suburban pulled away, magically passing through the slower cars, oily blue exhaust belching from its jiggling tailpipe. The David hallucination or whatever it was raised his hand to the window. A shadow loomed behind the boy and yanked him roughly back. Brian made a small, trapped sound in his throat. He goosed the accelerator but could not get around the intervening traffic. The SUV melted away, like a lost opportunity.

On the phone, Trish said, "How are you feeling?"

"Still haven't slept."

"Jesus. You're up to nine days. Okay, I've got a number for you. A Dr. Weinstein. That Greek letter on the pills? It identifies them by experimental lot-trial. I made some calls."

"Thanks. What's the number?"

She told him and he wrote it down.

"Brian? Maybe you should come over, not be alone."

"I'm all right."

"Then maybe you should come over so *I* don't have to be alone. I'm just saying."

"I'll call you."

"I doubt it."

He knew he shouldn't say anything else, but he did: "What's wrong?"

"A lot of things."

"Trish, you know I never said—"

"Here's what it is. I don't hear from you for like a month, sometimes even longer. Then you have a crisis, and you want one of two things. The first is a mother. The mother's the one that listens patiently, commiserates, tells you it's all better, even takes you to bed, for God's sake."

"All right."

"The other is a child. When it's the child, you get to take care of me, fix stuff. Convey wisdom about things you know and I don't know, whatever. Be a comfort. Be a man. Here's what's sad. I used to mistake both of these for the wrong thing. Love."

"I love you," he mumbled, like a guy coasting into a four-way intersection without conviction, just begging for a bus to T-bone him. And it did:

"You've learned to say it, but I think you're sketchy on the concept."

"Come on, you don't even—"

"Don't get all dramatic. All I'm saying, what I mean is . . . that I can't really do it anymore. I can't alternate between mother and child. Because you know what? I'm not either of those things. If you ever think you're over yourself, then call."

"Trish, I have to go."

"Big surprise."

"How many did you take?" Dr. Weinstein asked.

"Two."

"Since you won't come to my office, I strongly urge you to see your own physician as soon as possible."

"Won't the effect just wear off?"

"Eventually, of course. But there is an interim danger. The visions you describe are not, strictly speaking, hallucinations."

"Then what are they?"

"Dreams. Dreams of a very special type. The drug eliminates your body's need to sleep but it does not eliminate your mind's need to dream. I'm afraid we don't understand very much about this process, Mr. Kerr. But we've discovered that a mind deprived of REM sleep will begin to manifest the unconscious in the form of waking dreams."

"I don't see what the danger is."

"I suppose you're familiar with the adage, 'You can't die in a dream?'"

"Sure. You're falling, or drowning. Whatever. But you always wake up first. Because if you died in a dream you'd really die. Like your mind would just stop your heart. I never believed it."

"Let me just say, Mr. Kerr, we are now in possession of evidence that lends powerful credence to this particular wives' tale. These visions are dreams, but you are already wide awake. Do you understand what I'm saying?"

*

Three no-sleep pills remained in the aspirin tin. In his little kitchen nook at three o'clock in the morning, Brian dropped the pills into the palm of his left hand, his right hand loose around a glass of water. Time passed. He would never have this chance again—this chance to dream awake. Dream of the good time and see it before his eyes as if it were real. He clapped his hand to his mouth and chased the pills down with water.

See his son again, his little boy.

Thirteen days.

David was eighteen and could do what he wanted. But because it was Brian's insurance paying for rehab, he received a call when David disappeared.

"How can that happen?" Brian said.

"Your son wasn't sent here on a court order, Mr. Kerr. There's nothing we can do if a patient decides to leave. Of course, we counsel against it. In this case, David left in the night. Nobody saw him go."

Brian called his ex to let her know. Talking to Sheila was like talking to his own cranky reflection—the one that constantly blamed him for everything that had gone wrong. Well, she and it had a point. "I know," she said, when he told her David had checked himself out of rehab.

"Who told you?"

"Nobody. Evidently I'm out of the loop around here. But I saw Kevin at the drugstore, and he said David was sleeping in Steel Lake Park. He talked to him. So I can figure it out from there that David checked out of rehab."

"You're not out of the loop. I'm making this call, right? And who's Kevin?"

"Of course you wouldn't know. Kevin was David's best friend. Honest to God, how can you *not* know so much? Did you even live here, when you lived here?"

*

After midnight, Brian left his car in a church parking lot, walked to Steel Lake, and scaled the chain link fence. The grass appeared blue in the moonlight. It was still hot as a sauna. He stood on a grassy slope and turned slowly, searching for movement. David could be lying in the darkness under the trees right now, and Brian would have to step on him to know it.

A baseball smacked solidly into a leather glove.

Brian turned. The figure of a boy stood in the moon shadows. He was no more than a silhouette, his arms hanging slack at his sides, a baseball glove on his left hand. Brian's breath went shallow. This had been the good place, the good time. It would have continued if only Brian had allowed it. But you didn't get a second chance.

Except in dreams.

He started across the blue grass towards David.

A car door slammed.

Brian stopped. A vehicle had appeared, mixing dreams and nightmares. A big ramshackle Suburban with California plates. A man, faceless in the dark, strode across the grass, seized the boy and began to drag him towards the truck.

"Davy!" Brian ran towards them. At the last moment, the man released the boy and raised his hand—a knife in his fist. Brian threw himself at the man, driving him off his feet. They rolled down the slope.

"Davy, run, run!"

Thinking: *It's not real.* But he was on his back, struggling with the man's knife hand, fighting with himself. And dreams always felt real when you were in the middle of one.

So did nightmares.

The strength began to drain out of Brian's arm. The point of the knife descended inexorably.

His fault all the way: the dead marriage, his boy lost to drugs.

Brian stopped resisting.

The knife plunged. He arched his back, heaving into the thrust. A great piercing grief flooded his chest.

The killer leaned back, his face finally revealed in moonlight.

It was Brian's own face.

The nightmare-Brian stood and grabbed Davy's thin little-boy's-arm and dragged him to the waiting Suburban. Brian rolled onto his side, reached out, as if he could retrieve every mistake. The engine rumbled up and the headlamps came on like baleful amber eyes.

Brian's heart jerked and clenched.

"Dad?"

The Suburban started to roll, bouncing across the field, taking it all away.

"*Dad*?"

The Suburban dimmed back into his mind, and Brian looked up. "David."

The boy stood over him, a backpack slung from one shoulder. "What are you doing here, Dad?"

"I came to find you but I was too late. Fifteen years too late." Speaking was difficult. He couldn't seem to draw enough air into his lungs.

David laughed uncertainly. "I'm right here."

"Yeah, so I see." Somehow this lanky, disheveled kid was less real than the dream-boy. Maybe that was the problem. Brian sat up, grimaced, placed his hand flat over his chest. His shirt was sopped with blood only he could see. The grief-wound.

"What's wrong, is there something wrong with your heart?" David dropped his backpack, hunkered beside him.

"No. Listen, I found those pills in your car. The ones from the UW. I took them."

"How many?"

"All of them."

"Dad, that wasn't such a great idea."

"No kidding."

"Are you . . . seeing things?"

Brian nodded. "You bugged out of rehab. Are you using again?"

"No," David said. "I just needed to get out of that place. I mean, like I didn't think I could be there. I might go back, though. Hey, you really don't look good. Is something happening?"

"Seeing things."

"Pretty bad?"

"Yeah." His breathing labored. *If you ever died in a dream . . .* "You remember we used to come here? I taught you to play catch."

"I remember."

The next words stuck in Brian's throat a couple of times before he could get them out, but he did get them out. "I'm really sorry about screwing everything up for you. I know it's mostly my fault."

"What are you talking about?"

"The way things turned out. If I'd been a better father, maybe—"

"Dad, it doesn't have anything to do with you. I'm an addict. Even before I started using, I was an addict. I'll always be one. I wish you'd quit blaming yourself for everything. It's my life, not yours. How long have you been awake, anyway?"

"Two weeks."

"Whoa."

"When you were a little kid, we used to have a great time."

"I'm not a little kid anymore."

"Right, I get that."

"You *really* don't look so good."

Brian lay back on the blue grass and closed his eyes. "I'll be okay in a couple of minutes."

"Let me see your phone."

"David—"

"Come on. I don't have mine."

Brian reluctantly slipped the phone out of his pocket. David grabbed it and flipped it open.

"Hey, slow down. I don't need any—"

David ignored him. He punched three numbers and moments later said, "Yeah, I think my Dad's having a heart attack or something."

In the ambulance the paramedic immediately rigged an I.V. drip, something to compensate for Brian's inexplicably low blood pressure. Of course, the medic did not see what Brian saw: the front of his shirt saturated with blood.

Brian turned his head on the flat, Clorox-smelling pillow. David slouched on the other bench seat, hands shoved in the pockets of his hoodie, affecting indifference. But he was there. Brian studied his face. The eyes were all that was left of that six-year-old.

After a while, David said, "What?"

"Just looking."

"Okay."

At the hospital they wheeled him into Emergency. Brian craned his head around. David, backpack slung from one shoulder, stood talking to the admitting nurse. The nurse wrote on a clipboard.

Behind a curtain, in a brightly-lit room, a young doctor asked Brian questions.

"I'll be all right if I can get over myself," Brian said.

"Please try to focus on what I'm asking you, Mr. Kerr."

"All right."

Staring at the white acoustical ceiling tiles, Brian felt himself slipping away. Don't get all dramatic, Trish had told him. Maybe *Brian* was the six-year-old around here. If you died in a dream, you really died. But Brian didn't want to die.

He interrupted the doctor. "I want to see my son."

"Where is he?"

"He was talking to the admitting nurse, I think. I really want to see him, if he hasn't already left."

"Why would I leave," David said in his usual half-belligerent tone as he stepped around the curtain.

"No reason, son."

Brian opened his hand and moved it toward David. After a moment's hesitation, David took it—and the dream dissolved.

David, however, was still there.

THE FLOW AND DREAM

He inhabited a timeless flow and dream. The flow was part of the Undertower's machine mind, endless surging data, meaningless to him. The dataflow buoyed him but he dwelt mostly in dream, where the others hadn't died. In dream, Sten hadn't brought the alien virus back through the interlock. In dream, Celia touched him and their voices murmured in the close darkness. In dream, his daughter Kayla laughed.

Occasionally, open sky and light-drenched vistas intruded—non sequiturs. He pushed the vistas aside and clung to the close murmuring dark.

Then it all stopped.

Braincore needles, catheters, muscle-stimulating cuffs, esophageal tube, transdermal sensors, retinal pulsers—all withdrew and fell away with a final whir, click, and suspiration.

He lay stunned in the gel-couch.

After a few moments of real time, he opened gummy eyelids. A dim amber rectangle created as much gloom as it dispelled. Above the ceiling, an air-handler labored in counterpoint to his rasping breaths. Encircled by dark projectors and withdrawn meldpoints, bereft of the flow and dream, the man groaned. He reached for a meldpoint—and stopped when he saw his hand: wrinkled and puckered, bulging with knuckles, corded with thick blue veins. He held the hand in front of his face, turned it slowly. "*God.*"

With effort, he sat up. The gel-couch tilted forward, obeying his movement, folding itself into a chair. For a long while that's all the man could accomplish. But eventually he stood, knees grinding painfully, as if spun glass wound through the bones; lost in the flow and dream, he had become old.

*

His memory was ragged, blown through with holes. One of the holes had swallowed his name. But he did recall his first dangerously-extended meld. It occurred weeks after the deaths of his family and fellow Monitors and their children. His daughter had survived the longest. But in the end, she had gone like the others, staring uncomprehendingly into a dark the man could not see, her eyes watery blue coins in her fevered face. He incinerated her body, along with the others, and then he went on, alone.

Far below the Monitor's quarters, Sleepers stacked in the deep lockers waited for the next generation of Monitors to revive them, when the planet became habitable. But now there would be no further generations. And so he rode the flow and dream, and craved it unbearably when withdrawn, until, finally, he ceased withdrawing from it at all.

Except now, when forcibly expelled.

He hobbled around the living quarters, inventoried the storage bins of comestibles, tested the potable water. He established a routine that at least approximated life, taking food and drink as needed, eliminating his waste. All this, while bent under the gravity of grief. The dead feeling had been waiting for him while he dreamed.

As his strength and ability to concentrate slowly returned, he attempted to restore the melding apparatus. But it was as if the Undertower, which had been Ship, had lapsed into coma. All but the most vital life-sustaining systems were inactive. Nothing the man attempted succeeded in revitalizing them. Without functioning surface telemetry, he could not monitor progress of the terraforming machines. Without the lift, descending to the deep chambers was too daunting a prospect. Besides, he felt nothing for the legions of sleeping colonists. All he wanted was the flow and dream and the cessation of his thoughts—all he wanted was to escape the dead feeling.

He wondered—Would real death be like an eternal meld, or like the dark cell of his approximate life? Rocked back in the useless gel-couch, he stared at the dim light panel above him and wondered how long he could wait to find out.

*

He was tearing open a packet of protein concentrate when he heard echoing footfalls ascending from below. He dropped the packet and turned toward the door to the stairwell. Someone was coming up—coming up from the deep.

But there were only Sleepers down there.

He approached the door, hesitated, trembled his fingers over the burnished metal, then gripped the latching mechanism, cranked it over, and wheeled the door aside.

Stale air, like a final, dying breath. Below him, in amber gloom, a bright bar of light appeared, swept up and fell upon him. He squinted, holding his hand up, palm turned out.

"We've come for you," a girl's voice said from behind the too-bright light.

He squinted and moved his head, trying to see her. He cleared his throat. "I'm a Monitor," he said, in a cracked voice. "Who are you?"

The girl swung the light off his face. She came up another flight of stairs, feet slapping on metal, and paused again, only one flight below him. "We know you," she said.

He regarded her, a girl no more than twelve, hair growing out in short bristles, a backpack strapped to her shoulders. Where were the others, the "we"? "Who—" he said, groping either for her name or his own, which had been swallowed down one of the holes in his mind—sinks created by extended melding.

She bounded up the last flight, pumping her legs, knees practically to her chin, fairly leaping up the stairs. This, after already ascending from the deep chambers. "We're Almeta," she said, thrusting out her hand. "And we're going to the surface. Your name is Bale, and you have to come with us."

Bale. The name was his; he remembered it instantly. He looked at her proffered hand. "The surface—"

"Yes."

"But you can't do that."

"We *are* doing it." She grabbed his hand. Her skin was hot, damp with sweat. "Come with us," she said. "You have to. Now."

He pulled his hand free of hers, suddenly frightened. "You have the virus."

She stared at him, evaluated him like a diagnostic robot—the way her head moved in little stuttering jerks. "There is no virus," she said. "You successfully eradicated it decades ago. Now come with us. You have to. Now."

"No virus? How could you possibly know that?" It was Bale's turn to evaluate *her*. She both was and wasn't a child. "What are you?"

"We must go now."

"There's no point. The surface is—"

"The planet is habitable."

"You can't know that. I'm a Monitor and even I don't know it."

"It's true," Almeta said.

"Because you want it to be true doesn't mean that it is."

"Come," she said.

"How are you awake?" Bale reached out and touched her chin, turning her head a little, leaning to see the bio-ports, as if it were possible she *wasn't* a Sleeper. The ports were there, of course. Some violent scoring blackened her cranial plate. The skin around the plate was shiny with recent scarring. The Sleepers dreamed in a far deeper meld than Bale had achieved, their pods designed to hold them for generations of time, the meld allowing vital dream function to continue even as their bodies remained in stasis. Bale's melding apparatus was not intended for such long-term use; its function was strictly restorative. He had abused the apparatus and paid the price: lost years and addictive longing for the flow and dream.

"The child was sleeping." Almeta lifted her chin away from his fingers. "Like the others. Ship chose her because of her youth and vitality."

As an original colonist in stasis, Almeta was easily a hundred years older than Bale. The bristly hair covering her head indicated the days since she had awakened. Absently, Bale touched the needle ports on the top of his own head, picked at the moist crust that continually formed since the needles withdrew. "Ship chose?" he said.

"You must come with us to the surface, to complete the mission."

Bale frowned. "Virus or not, you have a fever." He looked over his shoulder at the open door to his quarters. A piece of him wished he hadn't left them to encounter this strange child. He had been preparing to end his isolation permanently. "I suppose you better stay with me for now." As he started to turn away, the girl said, "We will go alone if we have to."

He paused. "I can't stop you. But you're wasting your time. The interlock will only open for a Monitor."

"It will open." She resumed climbing stairs, hitting the next landing before Bale could find his voice again. She moved so *fast*. In moments she would be gone. He shook off his enervation and shouted, "Wait!" She stopped and looked down at him. "Please wait." he said. His breathing was ragged with the fear of being left alone. "I must pack food and water. It's still a long way to the hatches. And I can't run up stairs like you."

"We will wait for you, Bale."

Almeta slowed down, but nevertheless set a steady upward pace that Bale could not match. Soon she was half a dozen flights above him, her flashlight flickering distantly in the high gloom of the Undertower.

Bale halted and leaned against the bulkhead, chest heaving, knees on fire. He sat down and wiped sweat from his eyes.

"Hey!" Almeta came bounding down the stairs, making a racket of echoes. Bale lifted his head. She reached the landing above him in seconds.

"What are you sitting there for?" she said. Her speech vacillated between a child's loose diction and the elocutions of some . . . *other* voice.

"Resting," Bale said.

"Oh, okay. We will wait while you rest."

"Thanks."

She didn't sit, didn't even stop moving. She paced, looking up, like a caged thing under open sky.

"Why aren't you tired?" Bale said. "Where do you get this energy?"

"We are new. Young."

"I know. But—never mind. In any case, I'm *not* young."

She interrupted her pacing and lowered her gaze to him. "You're not as old as you behave," she said.

"Look at me!"

"You're seventy-six in Terran years. The average human life-span is one hundred and five."

Bale said, "How do know my age?"

"We know everything," Almeta said, voice shifting again. "We are Ship."

"I don't understand." Ship had crossed the interstellar gulf. Upon planetfall, after the establishment of the terraformers, Ship had burrowed beneath the surface, to wait as Undertower. A thinking mechanism, Ship was more than machine, less than being. But Ship was not a human child.

"Are you sufficiently rested to proceed?" Almeta asked. "We are used to knowing all. When you melded there were no barriers."

Bale stood up. "Explain."

"We are Ship. We are the child. We are Undertower."

"Come down here," Bale said.

Almeta went back to pacing. "I don't want to. We're supposed to be going up, not down."

"Just come down here." He was talking to the child now.

Almeta came down, practically falling, skipping more steps then she touched. When she reached him, Bale put his hand on her shoulder to hold her still. He turned his flashlight on her face, which was streaming sweat, and practically glowing with fever. He placed his finger over the large artery in her neck. "My God, your heart—"

She pushed away from him. "We need to go now."

He pointed the light at her eyes. The pupils did not contract. He almost dropped the light. "What's happening to you?"

"Child and Ship are together," the *other* voice said. And then the child: "We're mixed up now." And the *other*: "Half the Sleepers are deceased. The deep has become a tomb. You did not fulfill your function, Bale. Mission goal should be paramount. The new collective purpose of the Sleepers superseded the mission."

"What purpose?"

"To meld forever."

"You're killing me." Bale paused after another hour of steady climbing, leaned against the bulkhead, panting, sweat dripping, legs trembling. Almeta had waited for him this time.

"No, we're saving you," she said.

"Thanks."

"Sarcasm. I get it."

That was the child. He raised his head, wiped the sweat out of his eyes. He shined his light on Almeta and didn't like what he saw. "You're burning out the girl's body."

Almeta pushed the light aside. "It is necessary." She turned to the next flight of stairs. He grabbed her arm.

"Wait," he said, "at least eat something."

The girl, still turned away from him, gazed up the well of stairs. He tugged on her arm. "Sit down. Eat. *Now*. There's no point in killing yourself." He put his hands on her shoulders (a somatic memory of his daughter, Kayla, communicated with a buried part of his wounded heart), and pushed her firmly down. At first she resisted. Then she bent her knees and lowered herself until she was sitting on the stair tread.

"We will die, Bale," she said. "We have already sacrificed Ship to be together with the child. Only the mission is imperishable."

"Shut up," Bale unshouldered his backpack, opened it and pulled out a couple of protein bars, a packet of salt tablets, and two bottles of water. Almeta watched him with unblinking eyes. He divided the meal and sat beside her. "Eat, drink and be merry," he said.

"I don't understand."

"Old World phrase. Never mind. Just get some food in you. Your body has to have fuel to function. You should be able to understand that."

Almeta lowered her chin and tore open the wrapper on the protein bar. She ate the bar mechanically, as if she were chewing cardboard, popped the salt tablets in her mouth, and washed them down. Bale drank from his own bottle. The water tasted dusty. Almeta dropped her empty bottle on the landing and stood up. "Let's go."

"I want to rest a little longer."

She looked at him.

"Never mind, never mind." His legs still felt wobbly. He wanted to delay as long as possible. He made a face at his protein bar and pushed the last bite into his mouth. Really it *did* taste like cardboard. "What have you got in here?" He gave Almeta's back-pack a shake. It felt light.

"Nothing."

He slipped his thumbnail along the static seal and opened the top flap. Empty. "The girl wanted it," Almeta said. "It was a familiar thing."

A comfort item, Bale thought. Children needed familiar things. "It was a long climb in the dark, wasn't it." He patted Almeta's shoulder in a tender way.

Almeta shrugged. "Let's go."

She was waiting for him when he finally reached the sealed hatches. "They will open for you," she said.

He glanced at the interlock. Long ago, Sten had gone on a recon and unknowingly brought the virus back with him. The sterilizing beams had done nothing. Diagnostics hadn't even detected its presence.

"They won't open," Bale said.

"You inhabited the meld a very long time," Almeta said. "We sent you the truth of the world in dreams but you ignored them. Now you must complete the mission of human habitation. You don't even know what generation this is."

"Of course I do."

"This is third generation."

"That's impossible."

"Mission goal," Almeta said, "is to establish human habitation of the transformed surface. You are the only viable human left on ship."

"You said there were others, in stasis."

"A few remain, but their survival is questionable. You are viable. Mission protocols require human habitation of the transformed surface."

"*One man* can't colonize a world."

"It's time to go out," Almeta said. "Go out now."

"I can't. After Sten brought back the virus, I recalibrated the safety filters. The hatches won't open, even for me, as long as the virus exists as a threat in the atmosphere. I told you climbing up here was a waste of time."

Almeta shook her head. She was starting to wilt. Her breathing had grown shallow. She was weakening. "This is third generation. The terraformers long ago scrubbed the atmosphere clean."

"Without telemetry I can't be sure of that."

Almeta started to speak, then collapsed. Bale caught her. It happened so fast. "Please open the hatches," she said, and it was the child, pleading. "I want to see the sky, the way it was in my dream." Bale eased her down to the floor, cradled her head in his big hand.

"I'm sorry," he said.

"Please—" In a fading voice. Almeta's eyes were drowsy. Bale felt the heat against his hand, just as he had felt it when he cradled his daughter's head on her death bed. So much heat, burning out the child's brain.

"For God's sake," he said, addressing Ship. "Can't you let her go?"

"The sky . . ." Almeta said.

Bale carefully let her head down on the floor and stood. His body was aching after the long climb. "It won't work," he mumbled. Was it that he *preferred* it not work? Was he that afraid of living? He glanced back at the child, then, angrily, he slapped his hand spread-fingered on the sensor pad. Immediately the pad lit up, the interlock began to grind, and after a brief lag the complicated puzzle arrangement snapped open, slipped aside, unwound and withdrew. Directly above them the ceiling parted. Wind roared through the hatch. Brilliant daylight drenched them.

Bale fell back, threw his arms up, nearly blinded.

Almeta gazed unblinkingly into the light, and Bale knew it was Ship lying incapacitated on the floor.

The wind was like a crystalline freshet, cold air flushing out the stale, heated atmosphere of the Undertower. Bale shaded his hand over his narrowed, stinging eyes. The sky was pale and pink. Clouds like yellow gauze drifted by.

"Mission goal," Ship said, "is to establish human habitation of the transformed surface." Bale looked down in time to see the girl's eyes close and her body, without moving, subside toward death. His heart clenched in a memory of grief. He knelt beside her and took her hand into his. Her lips moved. He leaned closer.

"I want my mother," Almeta said. The heat of intense fever radiated from her face.

Something green with featherless wings, like a kind of bat, fluttered through the open hatches, caught by the inflow of wind. The bat-thing knocked against a metal strut and fell stunned to the floor, wings twitching. When Bale turned back to the girl, she was dead.

Bale picked up the New-World creature in his cupped hands. With wings folded it was no larger than a starling. Its head was long and narrow, ending in a hooked beak. He could feel it breathing, perhaps too frightened to move. The wind had finally abated, now plucking at Bale's tunic like a fussy companion about to send him on his way. The creature twisted, hooked its beak into Bale's thumb. His hands sprang apart, and the thing flew away through the open hatch.

Bale examined the wound. A bead of bright, living blood seeped forth, and he smeared it away.

It was a long while before he could bring himself to do the next things, but eventually he did them. He sealed the interlock, to protect the child's body. And then he began the long decent to the deep lockers and whatever life remained for him to revive.

LAST CALL AT THE
MOONLIGHT LOUNGE

Becoming human hadn't really worked out. Just look at this place. Ethan lay on the trundle bed's thin mattress. The room enclosed him in dismal seediness. A bare light bulb stuttered and buzzed in the ceiling socket. Shadows twitched over the bed, the pressboard dresser, his clothes draped on the arms of the upholstered chair. The room smelled of sweat, toilet water, and deeply absorbed cigarette smoke. Ethan's shoes pointed at the door, black socks drooping out of them as if they'd decided to abandon Ethan but hadn't quite the animation to take the first step.

Ethan held a black pill, no larger than a peppercorn, between thumb and first finger. Four out of ten pills remained—three if he swallowed this one now. He based consumption of the pills on a standard denary system. The whole universe was denary-based. Ethan himself was one of the original Ten Creators. As such, he was, technically, all powerful. At least he would be if he hadn't chosen to become human. And becoming human *really* hadn't worked out.

Also, Ethan wasn't his name.

On the sidewalk under his window, a man and a woman began arguing. "Please," the man said, "I'm giving it to you."

"You can shove it up your ass," the woman said.

Ethan sat up on the trundle bed, making the springs squeak tiredly. "I don't want to lose you," the man on the sidewalk said, practically sobbing. "Take it. I won't hide anything from you again. Not ever."

Easy to say, Ethan thought, *after what you've already hidden and only revealed once she'd caught you.* And here it was again: Ethan inside another person's head. It happened all the time if he didn't take his pills. Was this why he had no firm identity of his own? Let the so-called doctors parse that one out.

Ethan's ability to migrate through other minds had served him positively when he was writing stories for *Galactic Tales of Wonder* and *The Uncanny Zoo*. Other than that, it didn't help. He feared straining through the minds of everyone around him while his own body remained immobile forever. Also, no one ever bought his stories. He resorted to the computer at the public library where he posted his favorites for free download on Amazon. When after a week they had achieved fewer than ten downloads in total, he panicked and pulled them all. He and the other Ten Creators had designed a denary Universe. It was bad luck to fuck with that.

Ethan got up, took ten shuffling steps to the kitchen nook, pressing his fingers to his temples. At the sink he held a dirty coffee mug under the faucet and turned on the cold-water tap. Water trickled into the mug. Silently he counted to ten then cranked the tap off. He pushed the pill between his lips and washed it down. The water slid oily over his tongue and tasted like tarnished copper.

He waited, leaning on the edge of the sink, head down, counting backward from ten. When he reached zero, the pill released its chemical power and knitted closed the leak in his mind. Self-contained once more, Ethan approached the window (ten steps in a modified stride). Under his bare feet, the loose, paper-thin carpet felt like loose skin. At the window, he pulled the curtain aside. Iron bars fenced him off from Brooklyn. Below the windowsill, a man in a rumpled sport coat pressed something into a woman's reluctant grasp. The man was about Ethan's age, thirty or so, but heftier than Ethan, who at best presented as malnourished. The woman wore a black cocktail dress and too many rings. Her hair fell messily across her cheek. Was it deliberate, or had it come undone? "Take it," the man said. "Go look. It's all there. You'll see it's nothing. A lot of talk. Dumb talk."

The woman made a fist around whatever he had given her. Was she about to strike him? Having taken his pill, Ethan had no idea beyond his imagination. Perhaps it was always imagination; he didn't like to consider that. Though he knew he was one of the original Ten Creators of the Universe, in this human form he had so often been mistaken for an ordinary madman that Ethan sometimes believed this was indeed the case.

"Joe," the woman in the black dress said, and Ethan, though she was clearly speaking to the man in the rumpled sport coat, felt himself addressed. Ethan backed away from the window (two steps plus a silent count of five to serve the multiple equaling ten), confused. Outside, the man sobbed openly. "Wait –"

Footsteps retreated. The woman leaving him? After a sobbing interval, a second set moved off.

She had spoken his real name. It was Joe, not Ethan. Joe contained only three letters and so wasn't even a multiplier that could equal ten. No wonder he hadn't remembered earlier! His name was bad luck.

If she knew him did that mean she was one of the Ten Creators of The Universe? Perhaps he was not the only one who had decided to try exile in human form. Was he not alone after all? Alternatively, it might be nothing. Are there coincidences? He couldn't remember what he and the others had decided about that. Joe pulled on jeans, a T-shirt, and a shiny blue warm-up jacket. He plucked his traitor socks from his shoes and filled both socks and shoes with his feet.

Outside, the air smelled like rain. Streetlamps gleamed on the seal skin sidewalk. Joe felt disoriented, buzzing with nervous energy, like the failing light bulb in his room. People shouldered past him, their faces moving, emitting noise. Words. Joe was like them and not like them. He held his breath and counted down from ten. He felt calmer. Centered.

Joe.

At the end of the block, the woman in the black dress halted by a lamp post, staring at the object in her opened fist. After a moment, Joe understood she was weeping. At his halting approach (his head was full of tens; moving down the sidewalk in ten-step sections while counting cracks in the pavement), she opened her hand and dropped the insubstantial thing, a tiny wad of paper. She glanced at Joe, then turned and passed under a pink squiggle of neon. Joe stooped to pick up the wadded paper. He pried it open with his fingernail and read the word hand-printed across the wrinkles. BOOSTAR555. He counted letters and numbers. Ten again. Proof that coincidences were not part of the design.

The pink squiggle was a martini glass tilted festively (drunkenly?) over the doorway of the Moonlight Lounge. Joe stood under the neon sign, listening for the code to unlock the secret mystery of BOOSTAR555. He imagined the code whispered intermittently from charged gas trapped inside the pink glass tubing. It was the key to releasing him from human bondage.

Go after her. She's one of you.

Joe entered the lounge, where answers waited. Recorded cabaret music failed to enliven the environment. Heavy wooden booths absorbed the already-dim light. A stuffed raccoon stared down from the back bar with black marble eyes. Two men together and the woman in the black dress sat at opposite ends the leather and oak bar, feet propped on the brass rail. The men stared blatantly at the woman, and the woman stared at her drink—something blue in a stem glass. Her fingers picked apart a cocktail napkin.

Joe looked at BOOSTAR555, then closed his fingers around it and approached the bar. He sat, leaving one stool open between himself and the woman, as if they were expecting a mutual friend, or the answer to an important question. Succumbing to the ambience, Joe ordered a scotch.

The woman ignored him, her cocktail napkin reduced to confetti that failed miserably to suggest celebration. Joe watched from the corner of his eye, anticipating a pattern, a true coded message, something. When coherency didn't emerge (a recurring theme in his life), Joe opened his hand and placed it on the bar between them, BOOSTAR555 in his palm. "You dropped this," he said, "didn't you?" Adding the question reduced his advantage, and he wished he could take it back.

The woman looked sidelong at his hand. "Not mine," she said.

"It's a code, isn't it? From Joe."

She turned her head and looked directly at him. Her unevenly applied lipstick gave her mouth the appearance of a double meaning. She narrowed her eyes, or refocused them, and he realized she was already drunk, and must have been even during the argument under his window.

"Who do you *think* you are?"

"I'm—" His reply dissolved. Her question was so relevant. He closed his mouth to form a new answer. She was angry, indignant, perhaps righteously so. He found it difficult to interpret the signs.

Joe rummaged through a store of expected responses—a box in a dingy corner of his mind which contained the sorts of things people might say in given circumstances. He found something and quickly adapted it, first trying the words in the privacy behind his eyes. *You seemed upset.* "I'm nobody," he said aloud. "You seemed upset." The addition of *I'm nobody*, though technically accurate, may have been a mistake. She drew back. *Don't improvise,* he told himself.

"I'm upset," she said. "Why shouldn't I be?" She picked up her drink and finished it. "Blue Jasmine."

He frowned, not understanding.

"You want to buy me a drink, don't you?" she said, clarifying things. "That's the point, correct?"

"Yes?"

The bartender removed the woman's empty glass and shredded napkin. He mixed a new drink, strained it into a clean glass, and set it before her on a fresh napkin. "Cheers," she said, tilting her glass toward Joe. He stared at her. She rolled her eyes and drank. Joe sipped his house scotch. It was awful. He put the glass down and pushed it away.

"About the code," he said.

"What code?"

"Here." Joe tapped the wrinkled paper with BOOSTAR555 written on it. She swept her hand at it and the scrap of paper fluttered to the floor. Joe grabbed for it and almost fell off his stool. Holding onto the edge of the bar, he reached down and came up with the paper.

"It's just his password." the woman said. "Are you going to drink that?" She pointed at his drink.

"No."

She pulled his glass over.

"Whose password?" he asked.

"Joe's."

"I'm Joe."

She held his glass of scotch to her lips, eyeing him owlishly over the rim. "Huh?"

"My name. It's Joe. Are you saying this is my password. And by password do you mean code? I need something to unlock my powers."

"You're fucked up." She threw her head back and finished his scotch. It pulled her face into a sour knot which loosened after a moment, her eyes blinking rapidly to catch up. "I'm out of here. Call me a cab or, what is it, Uber. Now you're supposed to say you're a cab. You're an Uber doesn't sound right."

"You're one of the Ten, aren't you?"

The bartender loomed in. "You okay, Allison?"

Allison.

The bartender knew her. She came from the neighborhood. Had she been monitoring him? Was Joe the only one in the dark? The raccoon observed them beadily from its dusty perch on the back bar.

"I'm A-okay," Allison said and started to stand, then abruptly dropped back on her barstool, as if a faulty mechanism had given way, as if pins had slipped out of her knee joints. "Give me another drink, please." The bartender filled a glass with water, garnished it with a lemon rind, and set it before her. Allison regarded the water without comment. She turned to Joe. "Is Joe really your name?"

"I think so."

She laughed. "Don't you *know*?"

He smiled because her laugh suggested it was the appropriate response. Humor. He supposed it was a thing missing in him; one of the things.

"You're pretty strange," Allison said.

"Am I? I think you're one of the Ten."

She squinted. "Listen. Don't get any bright ideas."

"I don't understand." Joe drew back a little, as if distance enhanced clarity.

"People *know* me in this place, all right?" She turned to the bartender. "How about another Blue Jasmine?"

"Drink your water, Allie," he said. "Then maybe."

Allison made a face and picked up the glass, held it a moment, then set it back down. She leaned towards Joe. "Sometimes it's a pain in the ass to know people."

"Yes. *Yes.*"

"Aw, what do you know about it."

"I—"

"Anybody ever cheat on you?"

"I don't know."

"You're lucky." She grabbed the scrap of paper away from him. "This password, it's supposed to make me think Joe—my Joe—is sorry. But all it means is that he wants me to love him even if he goes online and talks to men. I'm supposed to go on his account and see it's all harmless. You know what I think?"

"Not yet."

She squinted. "I think *my* Joe has identity issues."

Joe's attention quickened. Perhaps too eagerly, he said, "I do, too."

"You don't even know him."

"I meant me, I have identity issues."

"Oh, God. Really?"

"That's why I said I think so when you asked if my name was really Joe. *Because I don't know.* Can I tell you something? Something important?"

She looked intently at him, swaying on her bar stool. "Only if you get me another drink."

Joe motioned for the bartender. "I want to try one of those blue things." When the drink arrived Joe held onto it until the bartender turned his back, then he passed it to Allison, who drank half of it and quickly handed it back. She regarded him unsteadily. "Go ahead, Joe. If that's your name."

He sipped the Blue Jasmine. His disorganized thoughts floated and bumped into each other like furniture in a room filled with water. "That's the thing, I don't know if it's my real name or not. I guess it doesn't matter. The name is like the body. It's an identity marker, not the identity itself."

"Joe. Honey. What the *hell* are you talking about?" Then in a stage whisper, "Quick, give me that." She grabbed the almost-empty glass, finished it, and put the glass down just as the bartender turned and frowned suspiciously at them both. Had the raccoon whispered to him? "May I have another glass of water," Allison said. "This one's warm."

Looking unhappy about something, the bartender scooped ice into a glass, filled it with water, and set it before her. She gave him a sloppy lipstick smile and turned back to Joe. "Do go on."

"Never mind." Joe felt defeated by the encounter, as he did by most encounters.

Allison grabbed his jacket sleeve. "No, you don't. Tell me the rest of it."

Joe looked at her hand. "Remember—I don't actually *know* any of this."

"Go on."

"I don't belong here. I'm not one of you. One of them, I mean—if you're a Ten."

"You've got eyes. Do you think I'm a ten?"

"I want to think it. That code, if it could unlock me, then I would know everything."

"Who's 'them'?"

"Them. The human race. The natural humans."

Allison shook her head, like it was attached to a wobbly spring, making her hair flip across her cheek. "Sorry, but you pass. You might not be a great example, but you definitely pass the human test."

Joe smiled weakly. "What it feels like is I just started a few days ago, out of nowhere, in a dumpy apartment a couple of blocks from here. I didn't even have a name until I heard you say "Joe," and then I thought that sounded right. I thought, yeah, that's me. I'm Joe. For sure. Before that, I called myself Ethan, but that's just a name on a license I found in my wallet. Look."

He dug his wallet out of his hip pocket and showed Allison the driver's license, which had the face of a movie star on it and the name "Ethan Hunt."

Allison snorted. "Impossible Missions Agent. Are you for real? It's a gag license."

"I *know* that." (Did he?) "But Ethan's a good name. At least you get ten if you double it, unlike Joe. I couldn't remember a different one, until you said 'Joe.'"

"I don't get it. You have amnesia or something?"

"You don't understand what I'm saying."

"Joe? You're making my head hurt."

"My head hurts all the time, too."

"If you don't remember who you *are*, that's amnesia."

"Except I do remember. But it isn't *my* story."

Allison blinked. "What story?"

"Joe's life story. Everything that led to that stinking apartment. That's how I know I'm not me. I think when I became human, this body was already here, but parts of the brain were missing, so I slipped in. I'm a *squatter.*"

"But is your name Joe, or isn't it?"

"It belongs to this body."

"I can't tell if you're making fun of me."

"I'm not making fun of you."

Allison shook her head, "Whatever. Okay."

Joe experimented with a smile. It felt false, which made him wonder if he meant it. No, it was a sincere but failed effort. You could say the same for the last thirty-odd years of *Joe's* life. Then Allison smiled back at him, so maybe it wasn't a failure. The smile. How could he tell? How did anybody tell?

Allison picked up the empty glass. "I wish I had another drink."

"If we wait a few minutes maybe he will give you one. Or he'll let me order, probably, but I think he's on to us. I don't trust that raccoon."

"What?"

"I'm not saying it's alive, playing possum or whatever. But it could be a disguise for surveillance equipment with a direct link to the bartender."

She looked at him for a long moment, then seemed to come to a conclusion about something. The conclusion unhooked her attention from Joe, and she looked past him. "He's not going to give me any more drinks tonight. It's how it goes."

It took a minute for Joe to realize she was talking about the bartender. "We could go somewhere else."

"Out the door with you, alone? I'm not *that* drunk."

Joe deflated a little, probably not enough for anyone outside his head to notice. Maybe if he could act more normal for once, she would trust him. "What time is it?"

Allison glanced at her phone, the screen a glowing playing card in her hand, briefly lamp-bright, then black again. "Almost midnight. You got an appointment?"

"No. I take these pills? One a day. I started with ten, but there's only three left. I took one a little while ago, but if it's past midnight then technically it's a new day."

"What kind of pills?"

"They keep me from . . . spreading out. You know how a wave

crashes and absorbs into the sand? That's how I get, except the sand is people, all the people everywhere. Sometimes the animals, too." He glanced at the racoon. There was something about it. But what? "There's no more of me left at that point, because I'm everywhere else."

Joe reached in his pocket for the plastic pill container and set it on the bar. A few strips of paper, all that remained of the label Joe had scraped off, clung to the orange plastic.

Allison picked up the container. "Why'd you tear the label off?"

"I didn't believe it anymore. Besides, they were the wrong pills." Joe unscrewed the cap and shook a pill into his hand. "These are the right ones. They don't make me so sleepy."

Allison leaned in close. "It looks like some kind of candy." She picked the pill out of his palm before he could pull his hand away. She scraped it with her ruby-painted fingernail, held it under her nose. "Smells like licorice." She touched the "pill" with the tip of her tongue. "It *is* licorice."

Joe looked away. He watched his fingers drum nervously on the bar. "It doesn't matter what you think it is."

"It's not what I *think* it is—it's what it *is*."

Joe looked up. "It's what *I* think it is, not what anyone else thinks. That's how my powers work now, since I don't know how to unlock my true identity anymore. Which is why I thought you might be one of the Ten and BOOSTAR555 might be the code, only I don't know how to use it. So I'm locked." He lifted his gaze to the racoon.

Allison popped the bit of licorice into her mouth.

"Hey—"

"Candy," she said.

His frantic heart bumped against the bones of his chest. "I have to go." He stood awkwardly, as if his legs didn't belong to him.

"Have a nice day," Allison said. "By the way, do you even hear the words coming out of your mouth?"

"Of course I hear them."

"Maybe all you hear are the voices in your *head*." She laughed, which sounded like other people at other times in Joe's life, all through his life, really. His human life. Allison covered her mouth with her hand. "Hey, I'm sorry. I'm a little drunk."

"It's not voices, in the sense you mean it."

"What?"

"It's all the voices. Every voice, everywhere. The whole world comes out of me. It comes right out of here." Joe tapped his forehead. "*Your* whole world, everybody's whole world."

Allison stared at him like she was seeing something she wasn't supposed to see, which he hated. But Joe was used to it.

"Take it easy," the bartender said.

"If I was unlocked, I could snap my fingers and *poof* the whole world would go away. Your whole world."

Now everybody in the bar was staring at him. It felt as it always felt, even when he wasn't in a bar, even when he was alone in his room, which is where he mostly stayed. He lost his last crappy job, washing dishes at The Burrito Barn. The money was mostly gone. Pretty soon he would be on the street. That's why it was so important to unlock his powers.

He backed up toward the door, moving his lips, counting. Everybody watched him, even the raccoon. That racoon. What if it was one of the Ten Creators? There wasn't any rule that it couldn't be. What if the racoon was a prison, just like Joe's body? Joe could free both of them, if he had his powers.

As he turned and pushed the door open, Allison said, "Hey, Joe, try saying the code backward."

One of the guys sitting at the end of the bar laughed. "Yeah, dude," he said, "Make the big bad world go away, starting with yourself."

Out on the sidewalk, Joe, or whoever he was supposed to be, quietly said, "555RATSOOB" then snapped his fingers at the door under the pink neon martini glass, like he was snapping them at everybody everywhere, all of them. "Poof. Come on."

Poof.

The world didn't vanish, but he popped loose—free at last—leaving Joe standing on the sidewalk. What surprised him was that the raccoon really had been playing possum, perched up there so quiet and still, watching over the humans in the Moonlight Lounge.

SALVAGE OPPORTUNITY

S ometimes I wish I could touch you," I said, lying on my bunk, not touching anyone. I was alone on Kepler-186f.

My bodiless Companion voice, replied, "You've mentioned that before."

"I don't think so."

"Actually, Badar, you have. Five times in the last twenty-two days."

"It couldn't be that many times."

"Couldn't it? I can play back—"

"No, thanks."

The Companion was stubborn. In that and other ways she reminded me of myself. Which made sense, considering her presentation was a gender flip based on my own personality matrix. A reactive voice closely modeled for compatibility, the Companion existed to preserve my sanity by providing a convincing simulation of conversation. I called it a simulation because I did not believe the Companion was an individual in the same sense that I was. For that reason, I stuck with calling her by the generic "Companion" rather than giving her a human name. I liked to keep things straight in my head. Gender aside, when I talked to the Companion I was talking to myself.

Most of the Companion's attention was devoted to exploring the wreckage of *Leviathan*. The immense hulk lay half a kilometer from my shelter. Using micro swarms, the Companion was building a catalog for future salvage. Intercorp had planted me like a flag on Kepler-186f. I was the "living representative in continuous habitation" legally required to validate Intercorp's claim. Machine intelligences didn't count as "living."

My contract ran four years. The pay was fantastic. When I returned to Earth, I would be modestly independent of economic constraints, and Intercorp would install another "living representative." Eventually they would get around to implementing real salvage operations, or not, depending on long-term expense/reward analysis. In the meantime placeholders like me were relatively cheap.

"There's a surprise coming," the Companion said.

I sat up. "What are you taking about?"

"Look outside in the direction of *Leviathan*."

I swung out of my bunk and climbed the ladder to the observation dome, my knees feeling the extra forty pounds the planet's gravitational mass loaded on my skinny body. Leviathan rose from the rocky terrain like an artificial mountain. The ancient starship had departed Earth three hundred years ago. By the time it crashed on Kepler-186f, refinements to the Kessel Drive had made interstellar travel infinitely faster.

I raised a pair of high-powered binoculars and swept the landscape. A lone figure came into focus, approaching my shelter. I lowered the binoculars. "What's going on, Companion?"

"It's the surprise. Go answer the door, Badar."

By the time I reached the bottom of the ladder, something was pounding on the outer door of the airlock. It must have been very strong, otherwise I would never have heard it.

The pounding stopped.

"Companion, tell me what the hell's out there. I'm not kidding."

"*Leviathan* was a colony ship—"

"I know that."

"What you don't know is that the crew had been stored inside Schrodinger Chambers. When *Leviathan* reached Kepler space, the indeterminate crew were supposed to collapse into android hosts, which would then thaw out the cargo of human embryos and raise them into colonists. It's a host android outside."

"Hold on. Are you saying there's a three-hundred-year-old Leviathan crewmember knocking on the door?"

"No. The Schrödinger Chambers failed, *Leviathan* crashed on the wrong planet, and all the frozen embryos perished."

The pounding resumed.

"Go ahead and open the door," the Companion said.

I stood by the airlock but didn't touch the controls. "If it's not a crewmember, then what's driving the android?"

"I impregnated its central processor with a seed from my personality matrix."

I thought about that for a moment. "Why?"

"My job is to evaluate salvage opportunities. I wanted to determine whether the android host was a functional mechanism. Since no Schrödinger indeterminates remained, I used a piece of myself."

I sighed. "All right." I didn't want to, but I opened the outer door, closed it, cleared the airlock, then opened the inner door.

"Hello, Badar." The android sounded like a talking washing machine. It stumped into my living quarters, servos whirring and grinding.

I drew back. The android was modeled on the human form but without any identifying gender characteristics. Synthetic skin, like a layer of pink rubber, covered its metal skeleton.

"You're really in there, Companion?"

"Not *me* me," the Companion said. "An autonomous seed."

The android spoke again, "I am myself."

I rolled my eyes. "That's great."

In a series of stop-motion jerks, the android's arm reached toward me, four-fingered hand open. "I'm happy to meet you, Badar."

I looked at the hand. "Wait here and don't move. I mean it."

The shelter was small. It already felt crowded with just me and the Companion voice. Intercorp selected me for my high adaptability to voluntary isolation. I didn't want the damn android in my space.

I opened the trapdoor leading to the storage room. The android's dull amber eyes watched impassively. I climbed down and pulled the door closed.

"Isolate our conversation," I said to the Companion.

"You're not happy."

"That's an understatement. What am I supposed to do with that thing?"

"Touch it?"

"Are you being funny?"

"Not very."

"Look," I said, "just turn it off. I mean, send it away first, then turn it off."

"I can't."

"Why not?"

"The test seed I planted has fully integrated with the processor. The android is autonomous. I told you. I can't turn it off."

"Oh, come *on*." I could hear the android's heavy tread as it walked around my living quarters. Annoyed, I said, "I told it not to move."

"Badar. It's not a robot. You can't order it around."

"Why'd you even bring it here?"

"I didn't. It was lonely in the derelict."

"Lonely. How long has it been . . . awake, or whatever you call it?"

"A week. It had nothing to do. The android was designed to maintain *Leviathan* in orbit, then build a colony and help nurture a human population."

"Maybe you haven't noticed, but we're fresh out of starships and frozen embryos around here."

"I've noticed."

"I don't want the android. How do I turn it off? There must be a way."

"The main processor is located in the head."

"There's a switch?"

"No. You have to use a laser."

I threw my hands up. "I have to burn it?"

"If you want to turn it off, yes. Although I wouldn't recommend that. The android belongs to Intercorp. Even if you dragged it back to *Leviathan*, it would return. Why don't you let it stay? It could be another Companion. It wants company. It's as social as you are."

"I don't believe this." I looked at the ceiling, chewed on my lip, and made a decision. Fine, then. I retrieved my s-suit from its locker, put it on, and strapped a utility belt around my waist— laser pistol included.

As soon as I opened the trapdoor to the living quarters, I heard them talking. The Companion and the android.

"He's not so bad once you get to know him," the Companion was saying.

"I can see that."

Sarcasm?

"You," I said, pointing at the android. "Since you're here, I need help adjusting the weather array."

The android turned to me. "I want to help."

I put my helmet on.

The weather on Kepler-186f frequently turned nasty. As soon as I stepped out of the airlock, the wind staggered me. On Earth it might have hustled me across the rocky plain, but the extra forty pounds kept me mostly stable. I walked a few yards from the shelter, the android dutifully following, then I turned and planted my feet. Dust and debris blew between us.

"This will damage my mechanism," the android said in its halting mechanical voice.

Did it know I was about to burn a hole through its processor, or was it talking about the dust? It didn't matter. I found I couldn't draw the pistol. The android was barely human-looking, but now that the moment had arrived, I couldn't shoot it. Not so much for its own sake, but because I knew my actions would bother the Companion. Or at least the Companion's reactive conversation would trend in a "bothered" direction. So, essentially, it would bother *me* to pull the trigger, since the Companion was a reflection of my personality matrix.

"The array's a couple klicks due south. We're going to take the rover."

Angry with myself, I drove too fast, bucketing over the rough terrain. Kepler's dim noon light faded, and I switched on the rover's forward lamps. After a while we arrived at the weather array. I parked the rover. In the passenger seat the android's amber eyes stared at me. I knew there was nothing to read in those eyes, but my imagination perceived judgment. All that meant was that I was judging myself. I pushed the feeling aside.

The weather array required precious little adjusting, and what adjusting it did require could be accomplished remotely from the shelter. Though the android couldn't possibly know this, I felt it *did* know this. Of course, that was nothing but me feeling, illogically, guilty.

"Well, let's get to work."

There was room for only one of us at a time in the rover's airlock. The android crouched inside. I locked the inner hatch, purged the airlock, then opened the outer hatch. Grit and dust churned violently into the open airlock. The android stepped outside. I sealed the outer hatch and immediately slammed the rover into reverse, half expecting the android to come after me. It didn't, though. It just stood there in front of the array, all hell gusting around it. *Martyr*, I thought, swung the rover in a tight turn, and headed back to the shelter. Two kilometers in a raging windstorm. The android couldn't make it.

Prior to my Kepler-186f assignment, I tested as a loner-introvert. Intercorp threw everything at me. Myers-Briggs, brainwave analysis, even Rorschach. The works. I tested high but not too high, probably because I fudged selected responses. I had studied up on how to do this, how to achieve a desired psyche evaluation result. For the last test, they locked me inside a geodesic dome in the middle of the high desert of New Mexico. One year in total isolation. That one I passed with flying colors, no studying required.

It was no sweat.

You don't want to test too high. Above a certain range, the loner-introvert personality type slips into a personality *disorder*. At least according to some people. They don't give deep space/high-pay assignments to disordered applicants. And I had desperately wanted this job. The isolation suited me. And the credits accumulating in my Earth-side account were like insulation from the society I could barely tolerate. When I got back, I would live far away from my fellow humans. Maybe I'd buy a dachshund, but I doubted it. I didn't want *any* emotional complications.

I prepared my evening meal. Since I'd returned from the weather array, the Companion hadn't spoken a word. It needed me to start a conversation, which I had no intention of doing. If I spoke, she spoke. Even then it wasn't a given. Only a direct interrogative guaranteed conversation. This was to spare me from uninvited interaction with the voice outside my head. I knew the Companion wouldn't appreciate what I'd done to the android, and I didn't want to hear about it. I ate my bowl of quick-thawed stew, took a stress pill, and stretched out on my bunk. Given the increased gravity, lying flat was the most comfortable position.

The damn android plucked at my conscience. I tried to ignore it. But it was like a hangnail, or a rock in my shoe. Eventually I lapsed into troubled sleep, from which I woke suddenly to the sound of dust hissing against the observation dome.

"*Damn* it. Why can't I be left alone?" My voice was thick with crappy sleep.

"What's wrong?" the Companion asked.

"Bad dream."

"Do you want to talk about it?"

Was there something about her tone of voice? Something judgmental? I sat up, rubbed my face. "People are shit."

"That was your dream?"

"The dream was about my stepmother."

"You've never mentioned her. What happened in the dream?"

I stood up and drew a glass of water from the reclamation tank and drank it. The water tasted metallic. "Really it was about the cat, what she did to the cat. Except this time I was the cat."

"You were the cat. I see."

"Don't be funny. I don't feel funny."

"You can tell me your dream. I'd like to hear about it. What was the cat's name?"

"I don't remember the cat's name." Truthfully, I *did* remember, but for some reason I didn't want to speak it out loud to the Companion. Seymour. The cat's name was Seymour. At least that's what we called it. A stray that we unofficially adopted.

"All I remember," I said, "is that it kept spraying all over our house. I guess my stepmom got tired of it. She transported the cat about ten miles away and left it in the woods. That was her solution to the spraying problem."

"But in the dream you were the cat."

"Yes, something like that."

"Maybe your evil stepmother should have shot Fluffy in the head processor instead, if she felt she had to get rid of it."

My back went ridged. "Knock it off."

The other true thing I didn't want to say out loud to the Companion was that it wasn't my evil stepmother who abandoned Seymour in the woods. I didn't have a stepmother. My *real* mother did it, and she wasn't evil, but it was still a shitty thing to do, even if Seymour was a stray that was probably tough enough to survive. When I was a little kid I used to wonder if Mom would do the same thing to me. Of course, that was stupid. But I was kid. All those psyche tests? They confirmed that kid was still alive and disturbed inside me. The cat incident didn't make me that way; I was already that way.

"Okay, okay," I said to no one. For once I hadn't bothered to properly stow my dusty s-suit. I pulled it on and cycled open the inner door.

"Good luck, Badar."

"Yeah, yeah."

The android stood where I'd left it, in a maelstrom of dust and debris. I un-holstered my laser pistol and held it in my lap a few minutes. That's how long it took me to figure out I wasn't there to burn the android. I'd cared about Seymour abandoned in the woods—so it was all about me and my precious feelings, right? Even though I was calling it my better nature.

I put my pistol away and climbed out. Because of all the dust blown through the android's mechanism, it couldn't move by itself. What a bitch it was getting that thing back inside the rover.

By the time I'd muscled the android into the shelter, I was exhausted. The thing never said one word. Wind and the abrasive grit had stripped most of the synthetic flesh off the android's skeleton. What remained clung to the metal in rubbery gobbets. Not exactly the ideal nursemaid for those long-lost embryos.

I rapped my knuckles on the top of its head. "Are you even in there?" Now that I'd saved the android, I felt I'd earned the right to indulge my resentment. Did that make me a shitty person? There was no one to ask but myself.

"A piece of me," the android said in answer to my question. Because of the dust-clogged and mechanical nature of its voice box, I couldn't detect the underlying tone. If it had been me saying it (and it was me, by a circuitous route, sort of), the tone would have suggested a couple of unspoken words. *A piece of me, you prick.*

I spent hours cleaning the android's mechanism, a job I resented every inch of the way. I vacuumed dust from the joints and rubbed lubricant into them. I whisked the eyes, disassembled, cleaned, and replaced the voice box. Finally, I removed the occipital plate and discovered that dust had penetrated the skull. I blew it out with compressed air. A titanium box protected the main processor. Not only wasn't there an off switch, there was no way of disconnecting it from the frame. I covered it again with the occipital plate.

"Can you move your limbs?" I said to the android.

It didn't reply, or move any limbs.

"Oh, well, I guess you're irreparably damaged. I might as well burn a hole through your processor."

The android walked to the other side of the shelter, whirring and clicking with every step. It was temperamental. Of course, in this shelter who wasn't? I had to remind myself that I was alone, even though it now felt like there were three of us.

"Is there anything to do?" the android said.

I squinted at the back of its skull.

"On *Leviathan*," the android continued, "I was to have tasks."

"This isn't *Leviathan*."

The Companion said, "Would you like to talk about your tasks?"

"If anyone wants to hear about them, yes."

I rolled my eyes. "Okay. I'm going out to secure the rover." I yanked on my suit and helmet and got out of there. I had suited up so fast, I forgot to strap on the utility belt with its holstered laser. The rover didn't need any securing. I'd just wanted to escape from the crowded shelter. Which was ridiculous. The shelter was *mine*. The Companion was nothing but a reflection, and the android a reflection of a reflection.

After staggering around in the storm for a few minutes, I returned to the shelter. But when I tried to open the outer door, it wouldn't budge.

I activated the comlink. "Companion?"

"Yes?"

"The door won't open."

"I know."

Wind buffeted me and I staggered sideways. "That's wonderful that you know. Now could you open it, please?"

Silence.

"Companion?"

"The android has disabled the lock."

"What? Well, make it un-disable it."

"I'm sorry, Badar."

"This is ridiculous. *Make* the android let me in."

"We're talking about it."

I stared at the wind-and-grit-polished surface of the outer door, which held my own blurred reflection. My frustration boiled over, and I pounded the door with my fist. It hurt, so I stopped. Fine. I'd cut my way in. I reached for the laser—and it wasn't there. Behind me, the rover hunkered in a fury of blowing grit and dust. It was my only option.

Inside the rover's cab I removed my helmet. A haze of abrasive dust lingered. Coughing, I cranked the scrubbers until the air cleared. After that, there was nothing to do. I had food and potable water sufficient for a three-day excursion. But there was no place to excursion to. I considered ramming the rover into the shelter, smashing open the outer door. But I'd never be able to repair the damage.

To keep the batts charged, I periodically ran the engine. And I rationed the food and water. Sooner or later, though, it would all run out. Fuel, battery, water, food. Air. I was alone on Kepler-186f, but then I'd always been alone, separated by choice from friends and family, cut off, even, from the emotional boobytraps in my own psyche. When my mother died, I'd fled a houseful of weeping relatives and hid in the backseat of the family vehicle. I wanted to move away from pain. Eventually, someone found me and made me come in.

The storm subsided. The cloud cover cleared, and Kepler's muted energy shone through. On Kepler-186f it was always twilight, except when it was full dark. I looked towards the shelter. Light filtered up from the living quarters and softly illuminated the observation dome. It was a homey light, but nobody was going to find me and make me come in.

I wondered what they were talking about inside the shelter. I wondered if I was already forgotten—by myselves. Emotion tightened across my chest. I opened a comlink to the Companion, but at first I couldn't speak. Finally I said, "Please. I want to come in."

Silence resonated through the link. The Companion needed a question.

"Companion, can I come home?"

After a minute, she replied, "Are you running out of air?"

"No." I swallowed. "I'm . . . lonely."

Another moment, then, "The outer door is unlocked, Badar."

THE SAVIOR VIRUS

After the bombing, John Crawford's daughter, Sarah, found God, and Crawford went to work on a weapon designed to kill Him.

"Eleven hundred dead in Jerusalem today," Brian Turley said, frowning over his tablet and his pint of Bass Ale. On Fridays, to unwind, Crawford and Brian visited a Washington D.C. pub called The Ivory Rose. Brian worked in the Mechanical Division of weapons development, Crawford the Biological Division. Brian was thirty years younger than Crawford and was dating Sarah. Crawford was grateful his daughter had chosen someone of Brian's intelligence. Since her mother was killed, Sarah had begun to slide, and Crawford feared she would eventually slip into the abyss of religious dogmatism that had swallowed Crawford's own mother.

"What if you could kill war itself?" Crawford said.

"I don't follow you."

"Kill the motivation for war," Crawford said.

"What kind of weapon could do that? Besides, doesn't it presuppose there is only one motivation?" Brian was third-generation Irish and had the pallor to prove it. When he became emotional (or drank his requisite single pint of ale), two spots of high color appeared on his cheeks like dustings of clown makeup.

Crawford sipped his Ardbeg single malt Scotch, his second, and set the glass down. "I concede there are many. Power positioning, economic issues, survival of the state, even loyalty imperatives. But God is often what motivates the common soldier. Who believes, really believes, a political cause, for instance, is worth dying for?"

"Plenty of people."

"I disagree."

"So you've invented a biological to kill God?"

"Not God, since He doesn't exist. I propose eradicating the irrational part of the mind that created Him."

Brian had been bringing his glass to his lips. "Oh, is that all. I can't tell if you're joking."

"I'm not. When you think of evolution, what springs to mind?"

"Darwin, I suppose. Survival of the fittest, all that."

"Life adapts to maximize survival efficiency. You agree?"

"Yes."

"And how have we ended up the dominant species on Earth? Is it our opposable thumbs, our great physical prowess?"

"Thumbs yes, physical prowess no. Obviously the main factor is our brain."

"Exactly. And with our brain has come self-consciousness and the awareness of our inevitable mortality—the simple fact of which could have driven our more primitive ancestors mad, except for yet another evolutionary advancement, this one in the brain itself."

"John, you *are* serious."

"Of course."

"In that case, maybe we should change the subject. You know the rules about discussing this stuff away from The Institute."

"It's a hypothetical, Brian. The Biological Division demands ever more efficient means of killing *people*, not gods." Crawford performed his war work conscientiously, but deep down he agreed with his daughter's view that human violence would eradicate the human race unless something was done to curb it on all sides.

"Hypothetical, then. Go on. What's this evolutionary advancement?"

"I call it the God impulse. It's a constant. Go back to the beginning of recorded history and you see this irrational belief in the immortal soul. Usually the belief is accompanied by whichever god or gods are in vogue. In fact, forget recorded history. You can see the superstitious irrationality of the human race in the most primitive cave paintings. It's as if from the moment human beings climbed out of the trees to claim the Earth, they brought with them a concomitant irrationality. I think it was as necessary for psychological survival as the opposable thumb was to physical dominance in the form of tool-making and weapon-making."

"If it's so necessary, perhaps your God impulse serves an important function."

"It did serve. So did our wisdom teeth, until we evolved beyond them. Our ancestors had longer jaws because they needed those extra molars to chew and grind foliage. Their digestive systems had trouble with the cellulose. When our diets changed, our jaws got shorter. Those back molars are vestigial. Now instead of helping us survive, they impact our other teeth, give us headaches and huge dentist bills."

Brian laughed. "Maybe we should be eradicating wisdom teeth."

Crawford sipped his Scotch, the peaty fumes already lying over his mental landscape like an obscuring mist. Perhaps he was talking too much. "I'll leave the orthodontia to you people in Mechanical."

Brian nodded and raised his glass. "Go on with your God assassin, John. I want to see how you hook up molars and deities."

Crawford smiled, immune to the gentle ribbing. Brian Turley would be his son-in-law one day. And though he knew he should stop talking about it, Crawford's excitement, released by alcohol, made him reckless. "The comparison is simple. In the same way our wisdom teeth served a purpose in our earlier development as a species, the God impulse comforted us when we were afraid of the night, when we lived in a world beyond our comprehension. But the God impulse is a vestige, like the extra molars. It does more harm than good in an age of scientific enlightenment."

"Religion comforts people. What's the harm in that?"

People. Brian was always protective of Sarah. Not long after the bombing she had begun attending weekly survivors meetings. Crawford accompanied her to one, but that was sufficient. The church basement, the bad coffee. It felt like a gathering of Alcoholics Anonymous. The religious tone did not comfort but rather offended Crawford. Hadn't the bomb itself been triggered in a delusional fever, the God impulse raging in the bomber's mind like an unbanked fire?

"Religion also motivates them towards bigotry," Crawford said. "Besides, it's not religion per se. Even in modern times, everyone, even diehard atheists, address life as if their personal experience of it weren't limited to a brief span of years. Of course, intellectually, we all know differently. But the God impulse always trumps intellect. A useful evolutionary development has turned against us."

"Well, it's an interesting idea." Brian sounded like someone ready to change the subject.

Crawford pressed on, suddenly needing him to understand. "Consider if the God impulse could be eliminated, if we—all of us—could see ourselves for what we truly are, instead of miracles created by an invisible magician in the sky. If we believed in our mortality, maybe we would be less inclined to slaughter each other." Crawford wiped his forehead on his sleeve. Though snowing outside, it was too hot in the pub.

"Are you all right, John?"

"Yes, fine."

"Maybe it's time to go. I'll help you."

"Yes." Crawford threw back the remainder of his Scotch. Standing was a slow, awkward process. The carbon frames enclosing his legs worked best for walking short distances. Rising from a sitting position required a complex series of small load-bearing movements. The straining, whirring sound of actuators drew looks from other people in the bar. For Crawford, it was like sitting atop a robotic crane. He directed the exo-legs by an act of targeted concentration in his chipped brain. Targeting was also the flaw in weaponizing viruses. Unleashed, they infected everyone exposed, not just the enemy. The Biological Division was working hard to defeat the targeting problem. So far the most promising avenues appeared problematically racist.

But indiscriminate targeting was a plus for Crawford's savior virus, which of course was real and not a hypothetical at all. He had identified the specific locations in the brain, God's hiding places. Using a simple adenovirus as a delivery vector, the Savior was even now spreading an epidemic of rationality.

Brian took Crawford's arm to steady him and they walked out of the pub, Crawford's legs clicking and whirring, pinching at the fabric of his baggy pants. On the sidewalk their breath appeared in frosty puffs. Crawford looked around. Traffic moved between berms of dirty snow left by the plows. Pedestrians walked rapidly by, scarves trailing. In the distance the Capital Dome, which presently housed some of the most dangerously irrational minds in the world, glowed like a giant Christmas bauble. In a few weeks everyone would be living in a radically different world, or so Crawford hoped.

"John?"

"Eh?"

"Does she talk to you?"

Crawford looked into his young friend's eyes and saw deep unhappiness.

"Not much, I'm afraid. People need time. Sarah was very close to her mother."

Crawford walked haltingly into his study as soon as he returned home. The exo-legs tired him, mentally and physically. At home he preferred his wheelchair. Sarah ducked her head in after him.

"I'm leaving for my meeting, Dad. I left you something for the microwave."

"Help me with these first?"

"All right."

Crawford directed his exo-legs to lower him to the sofa. Sarah hunkered before him, unfastening locks, loosening straps. The legs opened like the cages they were, and Sarah helped him into his chair.

"That's a relief," he said. "Thank you."

"Why do you bother with the exos, if they're so uncomfortable?"

"When I'm out in the world they help me believe less was taken away. Why don't you stay home tonight, dear?"

She frowned. "Dad, let's not start again."

"Sorry. Of course you should go to your meeting."

She kissed his balding head and pulled her coat back on. Crawford watched her closely. He had been observing her for the three days since he'd infected her, watching for signs of a change—a return, really, to the Sarah he had known before the DuPont Circle attack two springs ago. As far as he could tell, there was no change at all, and this was very disappointing. Sarah was the second person he'd infected with the Savior virus.

Crawford himself had been the first.

Sarah departed for her meeting. Crawford rolled himself to his desk and activated the Vapor screen. Twinkling jewel light projectors embedded in the desktop created a fully realized 3D representation.

Crawford brought up his epidemic model. Red lines burst from infection points. Ronald Reagan airport looked like the Fourth of July, red lines arcing in all directions. Within a week the Savior would have landed across North and South America and Europe. Then, in less time than it would take a man to drive from New York to L.A., the Savior would have penetrated Africa and the Middle East, and gone deep into Asia. Because of the adenoidal vector, symptoms would manifest in mild cold-like symptoms, including some respiratory difficulty—but nothing alarming. Crawford was optimistic that no agency, such as the CDC, would be alerted in time to halt the spread.

It bothered Crawford that the Savoir had yet to effect any obvious change in Sarah. They used to talk, share ideas. Sarah was a scientist in her own right, a cancer researcher at Georgetown, and a rock-solid humanist. She abhorred the weapons work Crawford and Brian performed. Since the attack she had become withdrawn and increasingly stubborn and argumentative about "the choices" people make.

That day in the DuPont Circle Park, the three of them—Crawford, his wife Connie, and Sarah—had been together. The lunchtime crowd had swelled for a support-our-troops rally. Suddenly a blast ripped through the crowd. By a stroke of improbable luck, Sarah remained untouched while dozens around her were killed or maimed. Crawford had discovered himself on the ground in blood-hazed shock. And Connie did not survive.

Crawford hadn't expected infection to change his own point of view. After the cold symptoms passed, he was left with a persistent headache. Gradually, even that faded. "Am I different?" he asked himself that first day, looking into the bathroom mirror. His face grinned back at him, certain that it wasn't.

Now Sarah was late coming home. That wasn't unusual for a meeting night. Crawford finished another glass of Scotch, which made three counting what he'd drunk with Brian at the Ivory

Rose. He wanted sleep, and took himself to bed.

The ringing woke him. Crawford groped out of the dark and fumbled for the phone, knocking it off the bedside table. He stretched for it, extending himself over the edge of the mattress, almost sliding off the bed. His fingertips pawed at the phone until he was able to grasp it.

It was Brian.

"Hello, what's wrong?"

"It's Sarah. My God, they've arrested her. Haven't you been contacted?"

"Arrested—?" Crawford was still confused with sleep, despite the sudden flood of cortisol.

At that moment, someone began knocking loudly on Crawford's front door and a hovering drone light pierced his bedroom curtains.

He was allowed to talk to Sarah. The agent in charge told Crawford everything would be recorded. Of course, in the last three months, *all* their conversations had been recorded without their knowledge. Those recordings had helped exonerate Crawford, which is why he was visiting Sarah instead of occupying a cell of his own.

The room was a box with beige walls. It contained a table and four chairs. Sarah, manacled, sat in one of the chairs. As soon as Crawford stumped awkwardly into the room on his erector-set leg frames, the door fell shut behind him and the lock audibly engaged. "For God's sake," Crawford said loudly, "are the chains necessary?"

"Daddy, it doesn't matter."

Crawford approached the table. "Sarah, what were you thinking?"

"I can't talk about the case."

"But what were you *thinking*?"

His daughter looked at him steadily. Crawford's chest tightened. He saw all the Sarahs, the whole of her life: the baby, the toddler tipping and swaying across the rug, arms out for balance, every day of her life up to the explosion and the wounded aftermath—every day of her life leading to this shackled moment.

"I was thinking," his daughter said, "that I had to *do* something."

Sarah had been conspiring with Vina Byers, a woman she met in her survivor group, to build and explode a bomb of their own. They had both stopped attending the survivor meetings months ago. Instead they met at Vina's house in suburban Washington, where Vina had once lived with her husband and daughter, both of whom had died at the DuPont Circle attack. Actually, they had been part of a small counter-rally demonstrating against US aggression.

In Vina's basement, she and Sarah had begun the practical steps of constructing explosives. It was Vina's contention that the DuPont Circle attack had been carried out *by* the US Government with the aim of generating sympathy for the government's immoral actions abroad. On F.B.I. recordings Vina was heard saying a strike against the "US war industry" was justified and even necessary. Sarah came off as more moderate. She didn't want to *hurt* anyone. But she was there, apparently immune to the irony of building a weapon to oppose building weapons.

Crawford's visit lasted fifteen minutes, and nothing more was said about what Sara was thinking. His first words, spoken in anger, had erected a wall between them. The next time he saw his daughter it was in a packed courtroom, where she was the focus of government prosecutors. The trial's outcome was never in doubt.

The memorial, a simple ring of marble with the names of the victims beveled into it, integrated with the fountain that had always stood in the middle of the DuPont Circle Park. The day it was dedicated, exactly two years after the bombing, the park was crowded with patriotic observers. A temporary outer ring roped off the crowd from the inner circle of principle mourners, including Crawford. Sarah would have been seated beside him, except she was now serving her sixteen-year sentence for conspiring to use a weapon of mass destruction.

The president appeared as an electronic presence, a quietly hovering drone projecting the chief executive's familiar hologram. Being a hologram, the president seemed to be facing the assembled from all directions at once. The drone was symbolic of Homeland's aggressive security strategy. The president himself hadn't appeared publicly in almost two years. His supporters and contributors were so used to the whispering arrival of the presidential drone that they greeted it like a warm handshake.

At the dedication, the president's remarks struck Crawford as a little pat. *Enemies of liberty. American spirit. Held accountable.* Was the president speaking in real time from the residence less than two miles away? The phrases were so stock, so tried-and-true, they could have been produced by a random patriotic-phrase generator.

During the reading of the victim's names, Crawford looked away, *Connie and Sarah.* His personal losses pained him more than his legs.

"Are you all right?" the man in the Navy uniform seated next to Crawford asked.

"I will be when that thing stops talking."

The "thing" talked for another couple of minutes, hovered solemnly through the multi-denominational prayers, then whispered away over the heads of the gathered mourners and spectators and press, back to the White House.

Rolling his wheelchair through the rooms of his empty house was like navigating a soulless museum replica. In his study, a bay window looked out on the garden. A service performed only the minimal required maintenance. Barren branches trembled in a stiff October breeze. Light and shadow blew through the garden, as clouds scudded between the Earth and the sun, creating in Crawford's mind an effect both fleeting and dismal.

Crawford had long since abandoned hope in his Savior virus. For months he combed the web in vain for indications of a positive change in human consciousness. Instead he discovered only the usual bestialities. However, a piece in the local news feed caught his eye. There was a statistically anomalous uptick in suicides over previous years. When Crawford checked the suicide rates in other states and cities around the world he found a similar rise. Taken as a whole, the number might be alarming. Did weaker minds miss their precious illusions, or was it a coincidence?

And what about stronger minds, Darwin's "fittest"?

*

The Ivory Rose was moderately crowded. A young couple going in ahead of Crawford held the door for him. His exo frames carried him haltingly into the pub, his upper body swaying and jerking with the robotic movement. He spotted Brian at their usual table. The younger man appeared in need of a shave. Two pint glasses, one nearly empty and the other full, stood before him on the table.

Crawford sat down across from him with his Scotch whiskey. "You look as though you've been through it," Crawford remarked.

Brian shrugged. "Putting in some long hours. We're on to something in Mechanical."

"We are, too." Crawford reached for his glass. There was a very clear thumb print near the rim. He turned the glass so the thumb print didn't touch his lips when he brought the glass to his mouth.

"Change of subject," Brian said, "since we can't discuss work. Last night I couldn't sleep and I found myself thinking about your hypothetical God killer."

"Yes?"

"It would never work."

"I might agree with you. But why do you think so?"

"Look around, John. God left the building a long time ago. It's pretty obvious we're on our own."

Crawford grunted, drank more Scotch. "It wasn't God in actuality, you know."

"Right, it was your toothache God, your vestige."

Crawford smiled tiredly. They drank in silence for a while, then Brian said, "She was going to use me. That's the part I can't get over. Use me to get her filthy explosive inside the Institute. As if that could even have happened."

"It was supposed to go off when the building was empty. Make some kind of statement."

"That's something, I suppose."

"They killed my daughter," Crawford said with sudden heat. "As sure as if the DuPont bomb had torn her in half." The Scotch had traveled a direct route to Crawford's brain. "I was naive to think people were driven by the God impulse. It's in name only. We say we kill for God, go to church for God, quit drinking with

God's help. In fact we do everything out of self-interest. Sometimes the self-interest serves an admirable cause, sometimes a wicked one. But the effect is collateral—and usually it's wicked."

Looking for firm ground in footing soggy with ale, Brian said, "Neutralize the bastards the old-fashioned way, with fire, lead, and steel. Your biologicals are a little too indiscriminate for my taste."

"It's a matter of precision targeting," Crawford said. "And I can tell you, Brian, we've licked it."

"Keep your voice down."

"As an example," Crawford continued, loudly, "a highly contagious norovirus could be genetically tailored to infect specific types of individuals. In this room, say, that gentleman over there." Crawford pointed at a man standing at the bar who looked like he shared a common heritage with the DuPont Circle bomber.

"John, for God's sake." Brian pushed his hand down.

"Just as an example," Crawford said. "A hypothetical."

"Sure."

Later, Crawford said, "The norovirus doesn't get the job done."

Brian looked up from his pint. "What?"

"It's a vector."

"Let's go home, John."

"It needs to be something nastier. There needs to be more suffering."

Brian rose unsteadily. "Are you coming?"

"I'm going to sit a while." There was no one waiting for him, at home or anywhere else. Crawford picked up his glass and found it empty. He produced his tablet and began tinkering with battlefield infection models. The savior virus *had* made a difference in him; he was thinking more clearly than ever. And his thoughts centered on survival.

Crawford looked up to catch the bartender's eye. The man he had pointed at earlier was looking at him. *Go ahead*, Crawford thought. *It won't be long now.*

THE DESPOILERS

Sometimes Allegra had to get away from the dying man. Inevitably her steps brought her to *Destiny*. The lander stood in a field of high grass, the last unnatural thing on 51 Pegesi d. Of course, the dying man would say Allegra herself must stop challenging the natural order. Wind moved the grass in purple waves, and Allegra could almost imagine it was an ocean and *Destiny* a sea-faring vessel that might carry her away, instead of a spaceship deliberately disabled.

Allegra sat on a hill overlooking the field, already out of breath after her short walk. 51 Pegesi d's lower oxygen combined with the planet's greater density to turn Allegra into a wheezing and stooped old woman—at the age of seventeen! It wasn't *fair*. The dying man called the planet Gaia. He called it "unspoiled." He called it "paradise." And he had marooned them there forever.

A flying reptile, about the size of a kitten, beat into the air. The reptiles were harmless, but their shit stank and was everywhere. Gaia wasn't paradise to Allegra; it was prison.

And the dying man was Allegra's father.

The wind carried the scent of wildflowers. She was not allowed to name the flowers, or catalog them, though back home she had been studying to become an exobotanist. 51 Pegesi d's unofficial name might have been Gaia, but that's where the naming of things stopped. "There is no ownership here," her father said. "Either we are in perfect harmony or we are despoilers from outside the body of the planet. A disease infection. Part of the human cancer that ravages worlds, starting with our own."

Had the scent of alien flowers unraveled her father's mind? Molecular compounds, incompatible with sanity, carried on the wind? That Allegra wanted to investigate the possibility already invalidated the premise. She breathed the same air, and she still believed in science. Her father's mind must have harbored delusions even before they departed Centauri for the unknown, or, as he told her when she woke from stasis, an "unspoiled haven."

Allegra almost had her breath back. She stood up slowly—and froze. The wind carried something besides the flowered scent. Tiny voices, as if invisible insects in the grass were speaking.

The voices were coming from *Destiny*.

She ran, gasping, down the hillside. Her knees ached with every jolting footfall. The hatch stood open, as it had for three months, ever since her father marooned them here. She pulled herself up the steps. The voices had stopped, and she wondered if she had imagined them; Allegra was desperate for other voices.

The natural world had infiltrated the body of the ship. Beetle-like insects crawled on polished surfaces. Something had made a nest under one of the acceleration couches, an untidy bundle of purple grass. And despite the open hatch, the cabin smelled so bad of flying reptile shit she wanted to gag.

In the gloom, a white light glowed on the communication console. Allegra stared at it, and the voice spoke.

Her father's voice.

"Maintain thirty-degree downslope on a relative heading of two-four-zero."

A recording?

Allegra slumped. She leaned heavily on the console, breathing hard. The planet pulling her down, always pulling her down. Then another voice spoke. Allegra raised her chin. A man, speaking crisply, focused.

"Confirmed. Following your vector, *Destiny*."

Not a recording. The lander's rudimentary AI, a reactive voice capable of simple back-and-forth, had been reprogrammed with her father's voice and was conversing with someone. The someone probably didn't know what he was talking to.

Allegra touched the microphone key. "Hello, hello? Pilot, this is *Destiny*. Do you copy?"

Nothing.

Then: "What the hell is this?" A violent rattling, mechanical disturbance, and the voice was gone.

Allegra leaned into the mic. "Pilot, what's happening? Talk to me. *Please*."

Dead air.

Allegra hunkered and pried off the access panel under the communications display. She unzipped the hip pocket of her flight suit and produced her forbidden halogen light. Her father had declared all technology an affront to Gaia (except, apparently, when it served to misdirect this pilot), but Allegra had kept the light anyway. And she continued to wear her flight suit, despite his insistence she "clothe herself properly, in harmony." He couldn't just *tell* her what to do, couldn't take everything away from her. She should have listened to her mother when she told Allegra that her father wasn't entirely rational anymore. Now she would never see her mother again, unless this pilot . . .

There: an interrupted circuit preventing live communication out of the lander. She rigged a cross patch and tried the mic again.

"*Destiny* calling unidentified pilot, *Destiny* calling unidentified pilot. Are you there?"

She waited, received only dead air. Had something gone wrong with her patch? That anything was functional on the *Destiny* lander was a revelation to Allegra. Her father's sabotage had appeared thorough, rendering the vehicle powerless. But he must have anticipated the possibility of outsiders and prepared this . . . well, whatever this was. A trap?

Then the voice spoke again, sounding strained. "I'm identified. I identified from orbit."

"I wasn't here."

"Who are you?"

"Allegra Ray. I'm, we—I'm here with my father. We're stranded."

"Was it your father who talked me down?"

"Only in a second-hand way," Allegra said. "His voice but my lander's interactive AI."

"Well, whatever it was, it steered me into a hell of a mess." The pilot sounded angry—and in pain.

"What's your situation?"

"Not wonderful. Crashed. Pretty banged up—the ship and me both. I might have to charge you for repairs, Allegra Ray."

"I'm good for it. Who are you anyway?"

"Malik. Deep space survey, private contractor. Found your orbital frame. There's not supposed to be anyone out this far, so it was a surprise." Malik groaned.

"What's wrong?"

"Told you. Banged up."

"I'm sorry."

"Yeah. Anyhow, I started receiving transmissions from the surface. Guy said his ship was disabled and could I help. Naturally I followed the landing instructions. I was going to be the hero, rescue the castaway and all that. Instead I flew into some nasty geothermal venting. My shuttle's small. Struck me like a disrupter blast, flipped me. When I came to, you were talking. Oh, God. Wow. That hurts."

"What's your location? "

After a long rasping pause, Malik said, "I don't know."

"I heard the last relative heading, but I don't know what it was relative *to*. Can't you check your nav history?"

Another long pause. "Can't get to it, or anything else. Hurt bad. Broken legs. Pinned against the bulkhead."

Allegra closed her eyes, feeling more pulled down than ever. "You could be anywhere."

"Yeah, but I'm not. I'm right here, where the pain is. If you've got a medbot handy bring it along. Look, I might pass out."

"Hang on, Malik. I'll figure out where you are. Hello? Malik?"

It took a while, but she managed to unlock the lander's recorded conversation and tracking data. *Destiny* might never fly again (her father had dumped the fuel and severed control linkages) but it still had a functional mind. Before hearing the distant insect voices from the hilltop, she hadn't realized that anything on the vehicle was still working. Her father's sabotage was both technically intricate and mad.

"There was no voice," her father said.

Inside the yurt, the light was dim. Her father had constructed the shelter with sloppy enthusiasm, even as he was becoming ill and Allegra was still refusing to accept their marooned status. Now he lay on a bed of reeds padded with big fibrous leaves that Allegra called "elephant ears." He wore a kind of Tarzan loin cloth made of the same leaves. With the advent of his illness and frequent fevers, he had lost so much weight that his body resembled a hide-and-bone doll. His watery eyes, sunken and bright with fever, watched Allegra.

Her heart ached—with anger and pity. If only he hadn't eaten the indigenous plants without testing them. How could a mind so brilliant also be so irrational? Allegra had subsisted on ship's stores for as long as she could. Then, against her father's insistence that they abandon "the tools of the despoilers," she'd retrieved a testing kit from the lander and used it to figure out what she could safely eat. The answer was: not much. And what she did consume, ate *her* as much as she ate *it*, turning her gut biome into a volatile experiment—even with pills from the emergency survival kit that were intended to mitigate such reactions. All her father said was, "If we trust Gaia, she will welcome us."

Not so much.

"Dad, I *heard* him. On the radio. I talked to him."

"I told you to stay away from the lander."

Her anger surged, and she held it down. "The pilot was following a heading the AI gave him. A heading *you* gave him. You made him crash. I can't believe you did that."

His head rolled side-to-side, making the dried-out elephant ears crackle softly. "There's only us, sweetheart. I saved you from the despoilers, if only you could see that. Gaia is—"

Her frustration boiled over. "Pegasi d is *killing* you."

He shook his head. "She knows we don't trust her."

"You—"

"We. You and I are the same flesh. She knows that." He plucked weakly at the leg of her flight suit. "You defy her even in what you chose to wear."

"Don't put it on me. Please, don't."

He closed his eyes. "I knew they would come, the despoilers. I prepared."

In a fading voice, he added, "Don't leave me."

Why not? You left us. Then came back to "rescue" me from the big bad human race. But humans weren't a disease infecting the universe. They made it matter by observing it—that's what Allegra's mother, a physicist, said. That was the whole point. So what if humans also made messes? You could clean up a mess and learn not to make the same one over again. Her father had made a mess, too, but he wasn't cleaning it up. He was making it worse. He wanted to disappear into nature, but it was nature that disappeared, without humans to observe it.

She put the back of her hand to his forehead. His damp skin radiated heat. On the orbital frame, where she had access to medical equipment, she might be able to help him. But without a functioning ship, the orbital was out of reach. Malik had a ship. Was it flyable after the crash? She had to find out. But she was torn.

Don't leave me.

Allegra sat on the ground beside her father. He had lied to her, brought her here, took away her life. But he was still her father. Sometimes the good memories seemed farther away than Centauri, than Earth, even. But she still saw them (Daddy, pick me up, pick me up *now*!) and so they still mattered.

She stared at the ground. The planet pulled at her, like hands reaching from a grave to drag her down. But it was only gravity— as indifferent to her presence as the ocean she nearly drowned in back on Centauri b. She had steered her windboard into a squall. Breaking waves tumbled her into the sea, and she had struggled to keep her head above water until she could regain the board. It had been like fighting a living thing, a thing with intentional malice. In the midst of drowning, that was how it felt.

Her father believed Gaia did things intentionally. At least Allegra understood her own misperception. But she hadn't gone back in the water and never would. The fear of drowning filled her with dread, as did the fear of her father's death. Sitting there, she couldn't do anything—not for her father, or the pilot, or herself.

Allegra stood up, heavily. She filled two water bottles and clipped them to her flight suit. For a moment, she looked down at her father. Then she turned and ducked out of the yurt, squinting in the setting glare of 51 Pegesi. *Don't leave me*, he'd said. But he had left her first, and besides, she was on a mission to save them both.

She stopped at the lander and booted the communications rig. "Malik, are you there?"

Nothing.

"Hey," she said, "I don't have a medbot, but I'm coming. *Malik*?"

"I'm here. Calm down. I'm the one who crashed, remember?" He sounded weak.

"I remember. What's your status?"

He laughed harshly, started to cough. "Status? My status is unhappy. If I get out of this, I'm going to clock your old man. Sorry, kid, but he tried to kill me."

Allegra winced. "He's not himself. And I'm not a kid."

"Yeah? Then all's forgiven." He coughed again. "I hurt."

The com went silent. Had he passed out again?

Allegra opened a locker and retrieved the first-aid kit. It wasn't a medbot but it was better than nothing. She climbed out of the lander and stood before the sunset. According to her analysis, Malik had come down more than twenty kilometers from the lander. It would take her most the night to reach the crash site. All around her the purple grass whispered doom—a secret sea that wanted to drown her.

Twenty kilometers might as well have been a hundred. Plodding through the night, fear and gravity weighed heavily upon her. She stopped to rest, lay flat on the ground, panting. Three small moons made a lunar ellipsis. Out of the dark around her, 51PegesiD's fauna huffed and grunted. She was used to the flying lizard-kittens, which made an almost-cute squeaking noise. But these unseen creatures sounded *big*. Would anyone ever study them, build a taxonomic classification? Or would they remain a pointless mystery that might ignore you—or eat you.

She stood up, studied the stars, oriented herself, and resumed walking. An hour before dawn, she saw a light—and wondered what was wrong with it. The light, definitely artificial, shifted, strangely refracted. She lurched toward it, trying to run but incapable, heavy legs stumping like posts. Sweat poured off her. The flight suit clung to her body, chaffing her thighs. She stumbled on disturbed earth, fell heavily, got up and found herself standing in a long track of torn-up landscape—the crash-path of Malik's shuttle. The path ended at the edge of a small lake. The shuttle was down there, its blue position lights refracted by the cold, clear water.

"Oh, shit."

She couldn't go into the water. Couldn't. Allegra clenched her jaw. Had she come all this way for nothing? She looked up. Among the faded stars, two orbiters sped around the planet, empty and waiting for crew that would never return, while Allegra stood here feeling sorry for herself.

Gaia had won.

Bubbles, trailing up from the shuttle, collected on the surface of the lake. In the pre-dawn light, the outline of Malik's craft became visible. How damaged was it? If she could get inside, she might be able to power it out of the water. Only fear prevented her from trying, from taking the first step. And her fear was like the planet. It only mattered because she was paying attention to it.

"*Screw* this."

At the edge of the lake Allegra took deep breaths, heaving oxygen into her lungs, expanding her chest. That time on Centauri b it hadn't been the ocean trying to drown her. It had been Allegra making a series of bad choices that ended with her in a drowning panic. But acknowledging the irrational premise of fear and acting against it were two different things. Allegra was already tired. If she went into the water and failed to access the shuttle's airlock, how would she fight gravity and exhaustion to reach the surface again?

Stop delaying.

One last deep breath. She held it and, clutching the first-aid kit, dove into the lake. The water was shockingly cold. She hadn't expected that. She sank rapidly. As if on its own volition, her body twisted around and tried for the surface. She wasn't ready! She couldn't! Gravity acted like lead weights tied to her ankles. The surface trembled beyond her fingertips, and she began to sink back, Gaia dragging her down.

No! She twisted around again and began pulling and kicking for the bottom with everything she had. In moments she reached the shuttle. Vision blurry, chest aching, she couldn't find the hatch. She hauled herself frantically around the vehicle. Air bubbled past her lips, her lungs desperate for replenishment. She started to become disoriented—and there it was.

The airlock.

It was a standard arrangement, similar to *Destiny's*. She tore open the hinged cover, revealing the manual control wheel, and started cranking it. If for some reason the inner hatch was already open, she was about to flood the shuttle and kill Malik, if he wasn't already dead.

The outer hatch began to retract. Trapped air exploded out, churning Allegra away from the shuttle. She fought her way back and cranked the wheel until the gap was wide enough to squeeze through.

The inner hatch was still air tight.

She closed the outer hatch and slapped the PURGE button. The water level began to drop, and Allegra thrust her face above the surface, gasping and choking. The shuttle wasn't a submarine. The chamber was designed to equalize atmospheres, not water pressure. The water level drained only as far as Allegra's knees. The inner hatch rolled open, allowing the remaining lake water in the chamber to sluice into the main cabin. Malik yelled, "What the hell!" and Allegra dragged herself through the hatchway.

The crash impact had ripped the pilot's seat off its track and pinned Malik against the bulkhead. A knob of bone poked through a tear in the leg of his suit. Allegra grimaced. Malik stared at her through his pain and astonishment. He forced a grim smile.

"What took you so long, kid? And where'd all the water come from?"

"I'll tell you later. Will this thing fly?"

"Who knows?"

Allegra took in the flight controls and determined them similar enough to *Destiny's* that she believed she could handle the ship. She turned to Malik, unsealed the first-aid kit and selected a needled opioid tab. "For the pain," she said and pushed it into his thigh. Malik's eyes popped wide, then narrowed to dreamy slits.

Now she would find out. Allegra strapped herself into the second chair, studied the controls, and initiated engine-start. The shuttle trembled, like something coming awake in the cold. Allegra powered up the thrusters. The shuttle jerked out of the mud and rose swiftly. In moments they were airborne. Allegra banked towards her father's yurt, her heart aching with anger and regret. Gaia was a fantasy. Allegra would never understand her father, but she knew if she'd wanted to she could have eventually understood 51 Pegasi d.

The shuttle's engines gobbled air in thunderous harmony. Below, creatures like bears with long necks, stood up in the grass, craning their heads.

She caught only a glimpse.

The President's Drone

The president's drone survived the cataclysm. It not only survived but maintained its pre-programmed schedule of campaign appearances. Thanks to Faraday shielding and a nuclear power supply (the solar array was a sop for the green vote), the drone whispered from one deserted town to the next, where it projected a holographic representation of President Biggs. The hologram delivered its stump speech and the drone continued on its way.

Because it was a machine that never rested, the president's drone made "personal" appearances in such out-of-the-way locations as Wenatchee, Washington, where its speech to the empty town center was interrupted by a M855 armor piercing round fired from the rooftop of Starbucks. The drone jerked violently. The presidential projection wobbled and flickered.

On the roof of the Starbucks, two figures in full hazmat suits, including portable air supplies, stood up from where they had been hunkered behind the parapet. Darrow, the man, held a scoped AR-15 assault rifle.

"You don't think it's armed, do you?" said Lia.

"No. It's basically a public relations drone. Remember the corporate models some of the big CEOs started using? Amazing it's still functioning."

"Especially after you shot it. Why'd you do that?"

"Couldn't help myself. I *hated* Biggs. Too bad he was the last president."

Darrow and Lia were a recon team operating out of a cave in Montana, an auxiliary depot formerly under NORAD command, where a small population of American Democrats had taken refuge. Darrow shouldered his rifle. They made their way down to the street and approached the drone. The thing was still delivering its speech, the words now fragmented and out of sync with the flickering hologram.

"...my...ends, America is...b...acon...of...reedom..."

Lia nudged Darrow. "I think it just said America is bacon."

"More like toast." Darrow reached up, grabbed a strut, and hauled the drone lower. "Look at that." Darrow screwed the end of his gauntleted finger into the hole his slug had punched though the body of the drone.

"Nice shot."

"...a ne...day of prosperity is...on...th...rizon..."

"A nude is on the raison," Darrow helpfully interpreted.

"Indeed."

Darrow unslung his rifle. "Step back."

"What are you doing?"

"Putting it down before it asks for my vote."

"Wait. Maybe we can use it."

"For what?"

"It's the first functioning electronics we've found in the wild. We should take it back to the cave."

Darrow grunted. He started, reluctantly, to shoulder his weapon. Then he seemed to get an idea. Holding the rifle in both hands, he drove the stock into the triad of projector lenses attached to the drone's undercarriage. The drone torqued on its axis and recovered. The hologram of the president disappeared. Behind his smudged face shield, Darrow smiled and nodded. "We don't need the puppet show, anyway."

"...brought for...er...ect...nion..."

"Bought four erect onions," Lia said.

"Just what we need." Darrow scratched under his armpit. "Let's get a rope."

They lassoed the drone and knotted it to a cargo hook in the back of their pickup truck, where it never shut up. They drove out of town, the drone trailing behind on its tether, like Darth Vader's birthday balloon.

They stopped overnight at a Motel Six outside of Coeur d'Alene. There were no bodies in the parking lot and, luckily, none in the room they chose to sleep in. Still attached to the Ford, the president's drone made incomprehensible speeches all night.

"... my ... orthy ... opponent ... uld ... ave you ... lieve there is no ... ference betwe ..."

Lia let the sounds of the words flow through the window and relax her, like having a drunken medieval lit professor standing in the parking lot declaiming "The Friar's Tale" in Middle English.

Actually, she had stopped trying to make sense of any political speeches years ago, back when you had living politicians occasionally delivering them in, mostly, coherent sentences. In those days the Democrats and Republicans limited their attacks to vicious insults, political back-stabbing, and obstructionism. Of course the real power lay with the Krat brothers, twin billionaires whose combined wealth beggared the economies of half the world. The Krat logo appeared on almost everything, from service stations to weaponized orbiting platforms—it was even on the oxygen units Lia and Darrow had to lug around. Then came the attempted Purge, which precipitated The Great Party War. Lia never liked that name, since it made the thing sound like a fraternity mixer that got out of hand instead of the end of the United States and the collapse of the world economy.

Despite "The Friar's Tale," Lia tossed and twisted, unable to get comfortable in her hazmat suit. The oxygen rig rested on the floor, the hose linking to it from her suit further restricting her movements. The smell of her own sweat made her a little nauseated, and she longed to remove her hood, at least. Of course, she didn't dare risk it. Darrow snored raggedly in the next bed. Then he abruptly stopped. Lia was relieved for a minute, then worried. She sat up, raised her flashlight and thumbed it on. "Darrow?"

He lay too perfectly still. Lia rolled off her bed and stood over him. Darrow's faceplate was fogged, his face an indistinct smear. She put her hand on his shoulder and shook him. "Darrow, come on. Wake up."

Darrow didn't wake up.

Lia leaned in close with her flashlight, examining Darrow's suit. The breech was on the index finger of his right gauntlet, a minute tear, which probably occurred when Darrow was fingering the bullet hole he'd punched in the president's drone. "Oh, damn it." Lia stood back, suddenly frightened. They were in a ferocious hot zone, despite the negative reading on her air quality analyzer. When The Great Party War really got going, all kinds of WMD were unleashed. Red states targeted blue states and blue states targeted red states, both factions so blinded by hate they refused to see the indiscriminate nature of the biologicals, EMP bursts, and tactical nukes.

Lia controlled her breathing. There was no question of resting now. She was standing in an ocean of virulently poisoned air that her instruments couldn't even *detect*. She stood in the doorway a moment, looking back at Darrow's body. She hated to leave it there, but what would be better? At least in a motel room nothing would bother it—if there were anything left alive to bother it. And as a final resting place, there was a certain poetic symmetry to checking out where the slogan promised to 'leave the light on.' She pulled the door firmly shut and turned toward the pickup truck.

". . . ounding fath . . . ew what . . . ey were . . . oing . . ."

"Shut the fuck up," Lia said. She got in the driver's seat and keyed the ignition.

Upon her arrival at the Montana cave, Lia knew immediately something was wrong. She sat in the idling pickup, watching the reinforced entrance. By now several people should have appeared. Her approach would have been monitored from the old fire lookout post and relayed by walkie-talkie.

The Democrats constituted a small but very organized enclave. At least, that was the situation five days ago when Lia and Darrow had driven out. But things could have changed. Montana was traditionally a red, or on some maps, a purple state. Since there would be no more elections, the state's color would inevitably be determined by armed conflict.

The Republicans had established an aggressive presence in Kalispell—and they had long wanted the Dems purged. Lia could understand it. The NORAD cave complex was well provisioned and secure, with an independent generator-based power system. Of course the Republicans wanted it and wanted it bad.

Lia climbed out of the truck with her sidearm. The Montana atmosphere was free of deadly agents, so she had removed her hood. The president's drone continued its uninterrupted speech but she shut it out and walked toward the entrance. She stopped at the sight of the blast door standing half open. No one would have left it that way. She worked the slide of her 9mm.

Peering cautiously through the opening, Lia saw the body of a boy named Ted Lanaham. He had been military, an Air Force spec 5 who had been stationed at the facility in the first place. Someone had blown the back of his head off. Lia caught her breath. The murder was a few days old; the smell and flies told her that much.

Behind her, a gun cocked. Lia dove through the gap, twisting around in mid-air and getting off a lucky shot before she hit the floor. She lay on her back, aiming the 9mm outside, where a woman was groaning and writhing on the ground. Lia stood up, keeping her gun trained on the wounded woman. "God damn it, Robyn. Did you kill them all?"

"They didn't belong in a red state."

"It's purple."

Robyn Hulse was about fifty years old, of stout build and (Lia had thought until now) reliable character. They had been true friends, almost sisters. Now this. Even in her dying spasms, Robyn reached for her weapon. Lia kicked it away. "I thought you were an independent, like me?"

"I've been doing a lot of thinking about that," Robyn said then stiffened, a ghastly rattle issuing from her throat.

"Not anymore," Lia said.

Robyn Hulse had slaughtered the entire enclave, twenty-three men and women. Inside the cave no one would have gone armed. And Robyn's betrayal would not have been expected. Even in the past, political defections had been rare.

Lia secured the facility, cleaned up, and then cried. She huddled in her room for two days, brooding and depressed. Lia had always tried to remain aloof from the take-no-prisoners politics of the red / blue dichotomy. She wasn't a Dem but as an independent leaning left, she agreed with much of what they stood for and fully believed they had a right to the NORAD cave.

But now she asked herself: What was the good of remaining aloof if no one else was? Alone in the catacomb stillness, Lia's despair sharpened into anger, which felt better. She was angry at

Robyn, of course, but even more angry at the damned Republicans and their red state manifesto of dominance and eradication. Did they know the enclave was now vulnerable?

For the first time in days, Lia raised the periscope and took a look outside. The first thing she saw was the president's drone hovering at the end of its tether, still attached to the pickup truck.

Lia opened the blast door and marched out to the truck. The drone babbled non-stop. She untied the rope from the cargo hook. "Fly away," she said, making shooing motions.

"... ploy ... nt ... own ... en percent ... ince ..."

"Jesus Christ." Lia started back to the cave. A shadow moved ahead of her. She stopped and turned around. The president's drone was following her like a stray dog, ten feet of white nylon rope trailing from its undercarriage. "Go away."

It hovered there, blathering incomprehensibly. Lia's anger boiled over. She strode back into the cave, closed the blast-door on the drone, and grabbed a rifle. When she was ready, she opened the door. The drone bobbed eagerly on a cushion of air. "... a ... ote for ... e is a vo ... or the ... ure!"

Lia sighed. The thing's tone was so pathetically *upbeat*. At this point, Lia thought, she could use some optimism. Besides, she couldn't bring herself to silence the only other voice in the enclave. She lowered her weapon and stepped back. The president's drone crossed into the cave.

The president's drone was never far away. She had to lock it in a room to get any peace and quiet. Except the quiet wasn't peaceful. Lia's isolation smothered her like a pillow pressed over her face (the Krat brothers dominated the pillow market, too). The drone wasn't *good* company, but it was company. She was baffled as to why it would follow her at all. Maybe it was seeking the support of the one remaining independent in the western United States. As a pre-programmed machine, it should have sped off to its next scheduled stop the instant she untied it. Of course, Darrow's bullet had done some damage.

But maybe it was something more. There had been rumors that the president's drone was more than a drone. The White House had not discouraged the idea that the president himself occasionally spoke in real time through the holographic projection. This possibility brought more people to campaign stops—the idea that they might be getting a piece of the actual man.

Lia doubted President Biggs still existed in the flesh. But there was another possibility. It had long been conjectured that the White House drone integrated AI technology. If that were true, it followed logically that the more speeches the drone delivered, the more self-aware and functionally independent it became. Did that mean this damaged speech-making machine was emerging into neurotic, or even insane, consciousness?

Sleeping in her bunk one night, Lia lapsed into a dream in which the real, living President Biggs spoke to her from the presidential podium. Lia was the only one in the room, because Robyn had murdered everyone else. The president had a kindly, deeply intelligent face—a face at odds with the reality of the man. Lia was sitting in a folding chair in the first row. Biggs looked right into her eyes, his gaze informing her that she was not alone. "We are a nation of immigrants," the President said, "and yours is an immigrant soul, Lia."

She came awake with tears in her eyes. The drone hovered in the doorway, babbling nonsense. ". . . ation une . . . od . . ."

But *was* it nonsense? What if Darrow's bullet hadn't only damaged the drone but shocked it awake, a nascent AI blasted out of the stuporous hell of canned rhetoric? What if what Lia had taken for a scripted stump speech scissored into William Burroughs confetti might actually be the drone's attempt to formulate a wholly new language, one that spoke directly to Lia's "immigrant soul"?

Lia slapped herself. *I'm losing it.* Before "it" was completely gone she flung herself off her cot, pushed the drone back, and strode down the corridor to a part of the NORAD complex she had rarely visited. Here, in a low-ceiling, climate-controlled storage bunker, weapons of unimaginable power awaited their human stewards to make a mistake. Lia selected a micro-nuke the size of a tennis ball with a proximity detonation sensor. Behind her, the hovering drone said, ". . . th . . . utr is . . . rs!"

"Come with me," Lia said, and she led the president's drone to a technician's workshop. There she used a laser torch to open a plate in the side of the drone. Inside, the sophisticated mechanism had been brutalized by the path of the armor piercing round. Lia probed with halogen light, attached a cable to a diagnostic computer, and figured out the drone's pre-programmed route of appearances. She gave it a new destination, the Republican stronghold in Kalispell, rigged the micro-nuke to the undercarriage, and led it outside, where it had no choice but to execute its new programming. The drone sped off, the length of nylon rope trailing behind it. *Here it comes, you assholes*, she thought. *The last referendum.*

Lia climbed the lookout tower. At the top of the structure was a neat pine-and-shingled apartment. She raised high-magnification binoculars and tracked the drone's progress across open ground on its way to Kalispell. It wouldn't take too long, and then a second sun would illuminate the Montana landscape. The mother of all landslide victories.

But something else was moving out there on the plain.

Lia adjusted the focal range on her binoculars. Two drones raced on an intercept course with her nuke-carrying emissary. "Damn it." Lia reached for her dark glasses, letting the binoculars hang by the strap around her neck. It must be some kind of interceptor-based defense the Republicans had devised.

The drones sped directly at each other. Lia gripped the handrail, bracing for an explosion that might sweep the look-out tower right off the hilltop.

But when the drones closed with each other, they slowed significantly, finally coming to a complete halt. Lia removed her sunglasses and raised her binoculars. The drones hovered together. Several minutes passed. Were they communicating? Finally, all three drones accelerated towards the NORAD cave.

Lia was waiting by the cave entrance when they arrived, her AR-15 at the ready. She supposed the Republican drone was going to demand she surrender the cave. Her reply was already chambered. The larger of the three drones was more sophisticated than the others. It even had mechanical arms. One was partially extended, gripping in its pincers the end of the rope attached to the president's drone, pulling it along on a leash. The body of the larger drone was placarded with a familiar corporate logo, a dynamic K underscored by a lightning bolt. *Of course*, Lia thought. Krat Brothers electronics were integral components of almost every computer-based mechanism—including drones.

Lia suddenly felt weak. She had believed the real masters had all perished in the Great Party War. Before the folly of her naiveté could doom her, she raised the rifle. But it was already too late. The third drone, presumably from the Republican enclave, rushed Lia and knocked the rifle out of her hands. The Krat drone swiftly hovered in. A second mechanical arm deployed and grabbed up the rifle.

A pair of holographic projectors activated on the Krat-drone. A double presentation of an old man with flowing white hair wearing an expensive suit (American flag pinned to the lapel) and Italian shoes appeared before her. It took Lia a moment to realize it wasn't a double image of one person but separate projections of twin brothers.

The Krat brothers.

Business as usual? Were living Krats even now observing her from a remote location?

Or was it a rogue corporate drone wandering the doomed landscape of post Party-War America? She didn't even want to consider the third alternative, the emergent AI theory.

Lia spat, drew herself up. "Is anyone there?

The Krat-drone replied in the language of the new world order: "A . . . ew . . . erica has . . . isn!"

STRACONIA

Frank woke at two o'clock in the morning and discovered his wife was missing. It took a moment for the situation to register. He sat up and rubbed his face, clicked on the bedside lamp. The condo was quiet. He got out of bed and pulled on his pajama bottoms. At the top of the stairs, he paused.

"Janet?"

She didn't answer. He went down, switched on lights, searched the condo. Finally, he opened the door to the garage. The car was gone. An oil stain on the cement looked like old blood. Back upstairs he found his cell phone and called Jan's number. Her phone started vibrating on her bedside table.

Frank put on Levi's and a sweatshirt. He considered calling the police, but what could he tell them? Janet was forty-six years old. If she wanted to take a drive in the middle of the night, that was her prerogative. Frank paced around, trying to imagine a reason she would go out. There wasn't one.

He sat on the sofa, both cell phones positioned on the coffee table, in case she called using someone else's phone. (Whose?) The coffee table was really an old steamer trunk he and Jan had bought at an antique store in the first year of their marriage. Now it sat next to the sofa like an awkward memory of happiness they had to step around every day. Despite his anxiety, a strange lethargy stole over Frank. He tried to fight it off but couldn't. Then he was waking to the sound of a door closing. He looked at the ceiling. Directly above him was the master bedroom. The floor creaked; somebody was up there.

He opened the bedroom door. Hall light fell across the bed. His wife appeared asleep. "What's going on?" he said. She didn't reply. He approached the bed, placed his hand on her shoulder and shook her gently. She moaned.

"Jan, come on."

She awoke suddenly, looking disoriented. "What, what? What's wrong?"

"You tell me."

She squinted at the clock. "It's almost four in the morning."

"I know what time it is. Where did you go?"

"Go?"

"Yes, where did you go?"

"What are you talking about?"

"Come on. I woke up and you were gone. So was the car."

"You had a dream."

"No, you were gone."

"Frank, I've got to *sleep*."

"But where did you go?"

"Nowhere. You're the one who's dressed."

"Yeah, because I was worried about you."

She stared at him owlishly. "I haven't moved from this bed. I think you've been sleepwalking."

"I haven't done that since I was a kid."

"I'm going back to sleep."

She rolled on her side, muttered something, and was out, like a plug pulled. He went downstairs to turn off lights. Maybe he *had* been sleepwalking. When he was twelve, after the police and all the trouble—after his mother died—he had walked in his sleep a few times. He always woke in the bathroom with the door locked, as if to keep something out. But that had been thirty years ago.

Frank thought of something. In the garage, rain beaded on the Honda. He put his hand on the hood. The metal was warm. So Jan had lied to him. Frank turned off the light. He opened the front door and stepped out. The night was crisp and the sky was clear. It hadn't rained in five days.

Frank was a dispatcher at Boeing's 737 factory. He worked swing shift, and after six p.m. he was alone in the office bay. He complained about his job, like everyone else, but it suited him—Frank alone in his box, and Jan at home. They were distant but bound to each other, like entangled particles. Frank had drifted into the Boeing job as he had drifted into his marriage, but now he needed both. Everything balanced, and below the high wire lay the dark unknown.

He returned home at eleven p.m. Janet was already asleep. He stood next to the bed, glad she was there, but also glad she wasn't making his tightrope wobble. Her face was tense, as if she were waiting for something, a noise maybe, something sharp that would reel her out of a bad dream. He got into bed. "Do you love me?" he said to the back of her neck, barely mouthing the words. It was something she used to say to him regularly. *Do you love me* began as a playful question. Later she seemed to mean it. As if there could be any doubt, as if he hadn't married her in the first place. "Hmm," Janet murmured, and after a while Frank fell asleep.

He rolled over, tangled in the sheets, something grabbing at him in sleep, some worry, or fear. He blinked, and Janet emerged from the bathroom. It was past four a.m. She moved haltingly, pulled the covers aside, and lowered herself into bed.

"Jan—?"

She began snoring. He touched her shoulder. Her snoring paused then resumed. He spooned against her body but her rigidity did not welcome him. Her hair smelled faintly of fried food, a kitchen smell, a greasy spoon. He pressed close to her, close enough that tiny droplets of rain trapped in her hair touched his lips.

The following night, he took note of the Honda's odometer, writing the numbers on a scrap of paper. Instead of going to bed, he made a pot of coffee, determined to stay awake. He could feel Jan leaving him, and he was scared. Sleep overcame him like a drug. He fought but couldn't keep his eyes open. He woke to the toilet flushing upstairs. Groggy, he stumbled to the garage and compared the odometer numbers.

The discrepancy was seven miles.

The next night he crammed into the foot space in the back-seat of the Honda. The strange fatigue came on swiftly and folded him under. Later, a sharp pain in his back woke him. Rain thundered on the roof. He struggled onto the seat. Orange streetlamps glowed like lost suns down a long canyon of high-rises. Across from the Honda a diner with big windows stood open for business. Red neon spelled CHARLIE'S.

Frank pushed out of the car and ran across the street, the rain drenching him. The diner smelled of fried food and strong coffee. A couple of guys wearing shapeless caps sat at the counter, staring at coffee cups. The nearer guy had a black mustache.

The waitress was Janet.

"Jan?" She barely glanced at him. "Jan, what's going on?"

She was changing out the coffee filter on the machine. She looked over her shoulder. "Yeah, I know you then?"

"You *work* here?"

"Sure, what's it look like?"

"I don't understand. Why didn't you tell me?"

"Why should I tell you anything?"

Both men seated at the counter turned toward Frank. Frank rubbed his forehead. "I don't know. Because we're married?"

"You better hold your horses, mister," Janet said. "Coffee?"

"What?"

"Yes or no?"

"*Yes.* Whatever."

Frank took a stool next to the mustache guy. Jan placed a thick white mug on a saucer and slopped coffee into it.

"Take cream?"

"You know I do."

She rolled her eyes. "Anything else?"

"Can we talk? This is crazy."

She regarded him in a slow, evaluating way that was both familiar and, in this place, utterly foreign. His tightrope had snapped and he was falling.

"Okay," Jan said, "just coffee, then." She scribbled out a check and slapped it on the counter. "Whenever you're ready."

"Jan, please—" He reached for her wrist and she pulled it away.

"Mister, I don't *know* you."

The guy with the mustache poked Frank's shoulder. "Why not lay off, buddy?"

"Why not mind your own business?"

A man's grizzled face appeared at the kitchen pass-through. "Everything okay out there?"

Janet said, "Everything's fine, Charlie."

"I don't believe this shit," Frank said.

"Language," the mustache guy said.

The man next to him nodded and mumbled, "Language."

Frank said to Janet, "At least tell me when you get off."

"Don't even go there," she said.

Frank drank so much coffee he had to use the bathroom. When he came back to the counter, Janet was gone. A different waitress asked, "You want anything else?"

"Where's my wife?"

"Huh?"

"*Janet.*"

"Jan went home."

Frank ran for the door. The Honda pulled away. He sprinted after it, waving. Jan looked at him—and he saw, clearly, that she recognized him. The Honda accelerated, leaving Frank standing in the rain.

"Hey, you," somebody said. Frank spun around, mad enough to fight. It was Charlie from the diner. "You didn't pay."

"Oh, for—" Frank produced his wallet and ripped out a bill. "That cover it? Where am I, anyway? How do I—"

Charlie squinted at the bill. "You trying to be funny?"

"A cup of coffee is more than five bucks? You've got to be kidding."

"This ain't money." Charlie snapped the bill, then took Frank by the arm and started dragging him back to the diner.

"*Hey.*" Frank tried to wrench away. His temper boiled over, and he swung at the cook's jaw. The angle was wrong and the punch landed without authority.

"You doing that," Charlie said, "it authorizes me to defend myself."

"You goddamn asshole," Frank said,

The cook whipped him around and drove his knuckles into Frank's face. The lights went out.

*

Frank came to himself in a room shaped like a big shoebox. A light bulb hung by a cord over the trundle bed. He could feel the springs through the thin mattress. Against the wall were a sink and toilet. He sat up, put his feet on the floor, and rubbed his sore jaw.

An empty door frame opened into a corridor. Fluorescent light gleamed on beige paint. Suddenly the corridor filled with men and women, all walking in the same direction. Frank joined the flow. Expensive suits mingled with the shabby rags of street people. Some of the men wore fedoras, others flat caps.

Frank bumped into a woman in a black and white cocktail dress and said, "Excuse me." She glanced at him. "Where are we?" Frank asked. She moved away without answering. Soon the wall on his right opened into a room the size of a high school gymnasium filled with rows of trestle tables placed end-to-end. A complex puzzle of duct work made a low ceiling. Everyone found a chair. Bewildered and a little frightened, Frank grabbed a seat next to a brunette in tortoise shell glasses. Her short-sleeved shirt was part of a uniform, Electronics Warehouse, or something. Her name tag said: MEGAN.

"Who can I talk to about what's going on?" he asked.

"Best keep your attention on what you're doing."

"But I don't *know* what I'm doing."

"Here it comes."

Wide metal chutes descended on rusty armatures. There was a rumble, as of old pipes purging air. Frank's chute pointed at the empty surface of the table before him. It expelled a hot, linty breath. Frank coughed and scraped his chair away from the table. He hadn't much room.

Frank's chute trembled, disgorging a huge clot of tangled wool, cotton, and nylon—socks. He stared at them, dumbfounded. Similar clots dropped from chutes up and down the line. There were other, nosier, deliveries. Sunglasses, ink pens, keys, paperback books, even umbrellas dumped out of shuddering metal chutes. A chaotic racket filled the room, then it stopped, and everybody began pawing through whatever lay before them.

Frank looked around. "What *is* this?"

"Sorting," Megan said.

"Sorting. It's like a job?"

"It's punishment."

Across the space between table rows, an older man in a rumpled tuxedo, bowtie hanging loose, concentrated on a pile of pens. He separated cheap Bics, fancy gold Lacrosse models, and everything in between. His hands shook.

"Get started," Megan said to Frank. "You're not fed until you finish the day's sorting. Match them by general appearance. Tube, argyle, nylon dress, and like that. None will match exactly. When you get a box filled push this button. See the green light? "

"What box?"

"Watch." She tugged a pair of white gym socks out of her bundle. "These are easy," she said. "Most look pretty similar."

She balled the socks and tossed them past the edge of the table. Frank stretched forward, half standing. The socks landed in a wooden box. Boxes were positioned in front of every table.

"Where does it all come from, what's the point?"

"It's lost stuff, is all. Somehow it turns up here." Meagan shrugged and went to work. Everybody went to work. Green lights blinked on. Workers in blue coveralls responded by swiftly replacing full boxes with empty ones. Frank stood up, feeling unreal.

"This is not happening," he said.

He entered the corridor, leaving behind the shudder and bang of sheet metal. He followed the corridor around every bend, passing hundreds of cells. Finally he saw a wide break in the wall where light spilled forth. He jogged toward it—only to discover himself back in the sorting room. Defeated, he resumed his seat. Sooner or later somebody in charge would show up. Frank folded his arms and waited. Meanwhile, Megan never stopped sorting.

"Take a break," Frank said.

She didn't even look at him. She was sweating and starting to sag. Hours passed. Gradually the chutes stopped dumping on the tables. Workers finished their last piles and stood up, stretched, and shuffled for the exit. The old man in the tux looked like he might not make it. He dragged himself out of the sorting room, bent over, his white hair hanging in his eyes.

"What now?" Frank said.

"Dinner," Megan said.

Frank started to get up.

"Not you. You haven't finished sorting."

"And I don't plan to. Where's the cafeteria?"

She walked away. Frank followed. Everybody returned to their shoeboxes, where food had been delivered. The smell of boiled cabbage filled the air. Only Frank had no food. He shouted, "This is bullshit!"

Random voices replied with, "Language."

Stomach growling, Frank returned to the sorting room. Only the light over his table remained on. He began pulling socks out of the tangle, working listlessly at first, then with a kind of manic determination. There was no cheating. At first, Frank dumped randomly mismatched socks into the box. A young woman picked the box up and dumped its contents back on Frank's table. "Do it right."

Finally the chute retracted and it was over. Frank's back ached. He got up slowly. As he stepped into the corridor, the light over his table winked out. A tray of food was waiting for him when he returned to his shoebox. He sat on his bed and dug into the cabbage soup. Later he placed his tray in the corridor, as he'd seen others do. When he straightened up, an old man was standing in the doorway of the next cell, watching him.

"First day in sorting, am I correct?"

"First and last."

"Bluster won't get you anywhere. What'd you do to get yourself thrown in here?"

"I don't know."

"Oh, yeah?"

"The cook at this diner accused me of running out on my bill."

"Did you?"

"I tried to pay but I had the wrong money. We got in a scuffle."

"That's not too bad a rap. You probably got, like, three days to do."

"When do I see someone in authority?"

"There's nobody in authority."

"At least tell me what the hell it is with all this sorting crap. I mean, Jesus Christ."

"Watch the language. It's stuff that's gone missing. Haven't you ever lost anything? It turns up here. Where does it go after we sort it? I like to think it finds its way to folks who need it, folks somewhere else—like we're somewhere else. Three days, you'll earn your release. Then you can sort yourself out."

"How long do you have left?"

"I don't know."

"How long have you been here already?"

"Maybe a year? I lost track."

"A *year*? What'd you do?"

"I'm not positive."

Two days later Frank completed his shift and returned to his shoebox to discover dinner had not been delivered. He crossed to the old man's room, who was sitting on his bed hunched over his plate, spoon gripped in his fist.

"I didn't get any food," Frank said.

"Finished your sort?"

"Yes."

"So you're done. Walk out."

"I've tried that."

"Try again. By the way, you ever come back, remind me to tell you where the showers are."

As Frank approached the first bend in the corridor, a new passage opened. He slipped into it. A narrow-faced man in a white shirt and black tie sat behind a metal desk. The shirt was too big on him. "Hold up, buddy." He counted out five bills and slid them across the desk. The bills were yellow, printed over with abstract shapes in no obvious pattern and bordered with tight red cross-hatching.

"What's this for?"

"Get you started on the right foot."

Frank folded the money into his wallet. "Look, can you tell me where this is?"

"Where this *is*? That's a good one. This is where you are."

"And where the hell is that?"

"Straconia."

"Where's Straconia?"

"This is getting a little circular, don't you think? Keep your nose clean out there."

The man pulled a lever and a door swung open to the outside.

Frank stepped through into the cold rain, and the door slammed behind him. He scratched his three-day beard, looked up and down the street. After a moment, he hunched his shoulders, ducked his head, and set out walking. Once he looked up and saw CHARLIE'S spelled out in red neon. At last, a piece of decent luck. He took a seat at the counter and rubbed his hands, blew on them. The waitress sauntered over with the coffee pot. Her hair was shaved to a copper shadow, and her name tag identified her as Peggy.

"Cold out there?" She smiled, showing her overbite.

"Yeah."

"Coffee?"

He nodded. "Is Janet working?"

"No one's seen her for a while. Just coffee, then?"

"Yes. No. Something hot, soup?"

"Clam chowder or chili?

"Chili."

When she brought the chili Frank said, "This is going to sound odd, but I'm not sure where I am." He smiled, trying not to look insane.

"Are you for real?"

He maintained his smile.

"You're in Straconia."

"That doesn't help."

Peggy shrugged, tore the bill off her pad and placed it next to the chili. "No rush, hon."

He dug in. The chili was hot and spicy. When he looked up, Charlie, the guy who had clocked him a few days ago, stood before him in a soiled apron, his fists planted on his hips.

"Take it easy," Frank said. "I have money."

"No bones," the cook said. "I didn't figure you for a guy who'd try that trick twice. Give a guy a second chance, that's what I say."

No bones?

"Anyways." The cook held his hand out. Frank stared at it a moment then shook it. When he let go, Frank picked up his check but couldn't understand the figures, which looked vaguely Egyptian and not like numbers at all.

He said, " I can't read this."

"Oh, yeah?"

"Is this enough?" Frank held out one of the yellow notes.

"Sure. I'll ring it up."

A minute later he handed Frank three blue-colored bills with pink cross-hatching and printed with intersecting circles, like a froth of bubbles, like some kind of cartoon money. Frank put the bills away.

"Is there a phone I can use?'

Charlie pointed at a pay phone mounted to the wall between the Men's and Women's rooms.

"Thanks."

Frank had no coins. That didn't matter, since there was no slot to put them in. The "numbers" on the buttons looked like the numbers on his diner tab. He guessed at the pattern, based on a standard zero-through-ten arrangement, and punched in Jan's number. The sound in the handset was like the sound inside a seashell. He racked the receiver with enough force to knock a bright *cling!* out of the ringer.

Frank spent the rest of the day wandering the streets. The city seemed to go on forever. As night approached, he knew he had to rent a room, and it had to be cheap. He found a hotel with a burned-out sign and a drunk sleeping on the front steps.

"Your cheapest room," Frank said to the desk clerk, a guy sucking on a vape pipe and dressed in a shiny blue kimono.

"This is a clean place."

"What?"

If you're looking for a place to perform immoral activity, you've come to the wrong address."

"I just want to sleep. One night." He held out one of the blue bills. "This cover it?"

"You're a funny guy."

Frank produced a yellow bill.

"That's three days," the desk clerk said. "You want to keep your reservation open, I can hold the money."

Frank started to say no but stopped. If tomorrow was anything like today he would need at least another night.

"Okay," he said, "keep it open."

The room was small and smelled like cotton candy, or burned

kettle korn, or something. A blue-and-white-striped bedspread covered the narrow mattress, and a beat-up dresser blocked half the window. A lamp attached to a swing arm provided the only light. The shade was printed with cowboys and wagons. The lampshade in Frank's childhood bedroom had been like that, only instead of cowboys and wagons it was astronauts and spaceships.

Frank stood at the window, watching rain sweep between the buildings. It all felt real. But even if you left the weird shit out, there was no city this huge anywhere within overnight driving distance from Seattle.

Straconia.

The hotel provided a small gray towel, hardly bigger than a dishcloth. He held it up to the cowboy lamp. Light shone through in a mottled pattern. The shower was down the hall from his room and had no lock on the door. He used liquid soap from the dispenser to wash his hair. The showerhead dribbled lukewarm water. He finished as quickly as possible.

What if he was stuck in Straconia forever? The idea frightened him so badly he couldn't bring himself to look directly at the prospect.

As Frank approached his room, the door opened and a man emerged with Frank's wallet in his hand.

"Hey—"

The man, who was shorter and scrawnier than Frank, grinned. "Sorry, wrong room."

"That's my wallet."

The man's grin disappeared. "*What?*"

"I'm—"

The guy came at him. Frank raised his hands defensively. A fist streaked between them and clouted Frank on the side of the head. The next thing he knew he was on the floor. The thief stepped over him and continued down the corridor, in no rush.

Frank started to get up but felt too dizzy. A door opened and an old woman holding a toothbrush glanced at him before retreating into her room. Frank waited another minute, then tried to stand again. This time he made it. Shaky, holding his head, he stumbled into his room. The jamb was splintered. He pushed the door shut behind him. The deadbolt was useless, so he dragged the chair over and braced it under the knob.

He stretched out on the mattress and held his throbbing head. Rain whispered against the window. Sirens shrilled up from the streets. The cowboy lampshade looked absurdly reassuring. He closed his eyes. Straconia wasn't a dream, but it had started in sleep. Now Frank wanted desperately to hide in sleep. But he thrashed and twisted under the covers all night, and in the morning he felt drained and un-rested.

At the front desk, Frank asked if he could pay for only one more night and have the change back for the third night. He needed to eat. The clerk looked at him as if Frank were a talking caterpillar or some other nonsensical creature. Frank repeated himself. The clerk shook his head and opened the cash box, the weary gestures of a man compelled to participate in the final degradation of humanity. He handed Frank three purple bills with white cross-hatching.

"I got robbed last night in your clean hotel," Frank said.

"You should tell somebody."

"I am telling somebody. I'm telling you."

"It must have been somebody who didn't belong here. That how you got the shiner?"

Frank touched the tender flesh around his eye. "Yeah."

"It's assault. You have to file a police report."

"I'll take care of it."

Frank returned to CHARLIE'S—the only place he knew of where Janet had appeared in this world. When he arrived, the diner was bustling. He waited by the door almost half an hour, until a stool opened at the counter. The waitress with the overbite and shaved head, Peggy, slopped coffee into his mug.

Frank said, "Has anybody heard from Janet?"

She gave him a wary look. "You're that guy from yesterday. Why are you so interested in Jan?"

Frank had thought about how he would address this inevitable question. He had a couple of overly complicated lies ready to go, but when he opened his mouth only the truth came out. Not *all* of the truth, but some of it, at least. Frank had always been good at sifting the truth.

"She's my wife."

"Yeah?"

"We've been having some trouble," Frank said. "It's my fault, the trouble. It's all my fault." Frank didn't really believe this. "I want to make it right."

"Anyways, like I told you yesterday, no one's seen her."

Frank covered his eyes.

"Mister, you don't look so good. What happened to your eye?"

"Somebody hit me.

"Did you file your report?"

"Not yet."

"You don't want to put that off."

"I'm not putting it off. I just wanted to see if Jan was here."

"Do you want to order food?"

He nodded, dug three waded bills out of his pocket, the last of his Straconia money.

"What will this get me?"

"Blue plate special. Eggs, ham, hash browns, coffee and orange juice. With change back."

Later, while he was glumly forking breakfast into his mouth, Peggy came around with more coffee. "You look like a guy eating his last meal."

"It might be my last meal. I'm out of money."

"You need a job?"

"Probably."

"You don't seem like such a bad character."

"Who said I was a bad character?"

"People talk. There's a job opening here, you know. Dishwasher."

"*Dishwasher*?"

"It's honest work."

"I'm not—" He was about to say, I'm not that desperate, when suddenly he realized he was that desperate.

"You're not what?"

"That picky. But Charlie isn't going to want to hire me."

"Charlie's not that picky, either."

The dishwashing machine occupied a cramped corner of the kitchen. A glaze of grease lay over the green walls. Waitresses hauled back endless tubs of dishes. It was as hot and steamy as an Amazonian jungle. But the money paid for the hotel and food.

Also, it gave him an excuse to hang around the diner. He hoped that Jan would return, that he would peek out from the kitchen and see her talking to Peggy or Charlie or sitting at the counter sipping a cup of joe. Frank couldn't believe what was happening to him. He ached for home. One night, at the end of a late shift, Peggy said, "She's not coming back, you know."

"Who?"

"Your wife."

He didn't say anything.

"It's nothing against you," Peggy said. "Sometimes you can tell when someone isn't coming back. People like Janet turn up in Straconia all the time."

"What do you mean 'like Janet'?"

"People who think they're trapped in their lives. They come here, but it's temporary. Then something changes and you never see them again. Maybe they got themselves untrapped. Who knows?"

"Well, I'm here and I didn't feel trapped my life. I belonged in it fine."

"Of course you did."

Frank came up from the subway station a block from the hotel and saw a patrol car, or a "Police Interceptor," as they were called in Straconia, parked in front of his hotel with its flashers wig-wagging. Instinct made Frank retreat down the steps and loiter around the platform for fifteen minutes. When he came up, the Interceptor was gone.

The desk clerk stopped him on the way to the elevator. "You just missed the police. You know what it is, it's that busted door."

"What about the door?"

"It's a crime, busting that door."

"I didn't break it."

"You didn't report it, did you?"

Frank mumbled something.

"Because not reporting a crime, that's a crime, too."

"But if somebody doesn't report a crime, how do they know you didn't report it? I mean hypothetically."

"You wanted the door fixed."

For a moment this didn't compute. The door to his room had

remained broken for two weeks, despite his repeatedly berating the front desk. Every night Frank had to jam the chair under the knob. And of course, when he went out, the room was completely unsecured.

"I wanted to make sure you had plenty of time to do your civic duty," the desk clerk said. "But eventually I gotta get the door fixed, don't I?"

"And getting the door fixed means you have to inform the police?"

"Inform. That's not fair. It was your duty to report the crime. But if I call in the locksmith, it automatically gets the police involved. The wisest thing for you to do at this point is turn yourself in."

"But I didn't do anything! I'm the one who got robbed."

The clerk held his hands up. "Hey, it's your life, buddy."

Frank returned to CHARLIE'S. Peggy saw him at the counter and came over. "I thought you went home."

"I did."

"What happened?"

He gave her the abbreviated version, lowering his voice when he noticed Charlie listening at the kitchen pass-through. Frank was scared. The diner and his hotel room established his presence in Straconia. Without these anchors he really was a lost thing, like a gym sock or a pair of sunglasses.

"Frank, you should have reported the robbery."

"I meant to."

"You better turn yourself in."

From the kitchen, Charlie craned to see him, a phone pressed to his ear. Frank stood up. "I have to get out of here."

A block from the diner a Police Interceptor whooped its siren and cut into the curb in front of Frank. Two cops got out. Frank looked around. "You don't want to do that," the cop who had been driving said. He had a thick neck and a long jaw.

Frank backed away. "Do what?"

The cop stepped forward, took Frank by the arm and pulled him towards the car. Frank stumbled, almost fell. In the middle of his lurching recovery the second cop grabbed his other arm.

"Come on," Frank said, "I didn't *do* anything."

"Three violations is something."

"What three?"

"Failure to pay. Failure to report a crime. Failure to register employment."

"I don't know the rules around here."

"Watch your head."

They shoved him into the car.

Frank huddled in the back seat, separated from the cops by a thick, perforated Plexiglas barrier. He watched the streets. A man in a raincoat stood on the corner holding a large fish over his head, making the tail wave at passing traffic. A bulldog sat next to him, looking miserable. Frank rapped on the Plexiglas barrier. "Don't I have any rights?"

The cops ignored him. The Interceptor sped into a view of fast-moving water—an immense river, at least a mile wide. On the far shore, industrial buildings spewed black smoke.

Suddenly the car plunged down a ramp into a tunnel. The Interceptor's headlights penetrated the murky gloom. Large panel trucks rumbled past, going the opposite direction. Frank folded his arms and leaned against the door, his forehead pressed to the glass. After ten minutes they came out of the tunnel on the other side of the river and entered an industrial landscape of factories and warehouses. The driver guided them into a walled compound and parked next to a low, featureless concrete building. The cops got out. Frank's door opened and the cop with the thick neck said, "Let's get you organized."

Frank shared a cell without bars. Technically he could walk out whenever he felt like it. But walk out and go where? He had lost his place in Straconia. And when he tried to think of Jan and his life in Seattle, what came was a vivid recollection of his dispatch cubicle, the peacefulness of the deserted office bay.

Lying on his bunk that first night, hands laced behind his head, staring at the caged light bulb, Frank began to quietly weep. A voice from the lower bunk said, "Are you crying?"

Frank didn't trust himself to speak.

"You are," the voice said. "You're crying."

The voice belonged to Jonas, his cellmate. Jonas, like almost all the other detainees, was Black. In that respect, what passed for criminal justice in Straconia didn't vary much from what Frank was familiar with back home. Jonas wore round, rimless glasses and was young, maybe thirty. Hours ago their introductory conversation hadn't extended beyond a sullen greeting, after which Jonas stretched out on the lower bunk and returned his attention to the notebook he was writing in, his fingers crabbed around the stub of a pencil.

"It's nothing," Frank said, about the crying.

"You're goddamn right it's nothing."

Frank came awake to the smell of fried meat. He sat up in the dark and hit his head on the ceiling. "*Damn it.*" There was a buzzing sound, like a fly trapped in glass, and the light bulb flickered on. Frank threw his cover aside and climbed down, the concrete floor chilling his feet right through his socks. He dressed in the all-gray clothes he'd been issued. The shoes were too big and lacked laces. They felt like clown shoes.

He followed his nose to breakfast. Cells lined the corridor. Most were empty. In some, men lay curled on their bunks, sleeping, or simply staring. Frank came to a larger room filled with tables and benches where forty or so men, dressed exactly like Frank, sat drinking coffee and eating. One graybeard looked at him and nodded. Frank nodded back. The graybeard looked deranged. A few other men glanced at Frank, then went back to eating. Frank picked up a tray and joined the food line. When his tray was full, he looked for somewhere to sit and spotted a place across from Jonas.

"Hi," Frank said.

Jonas flicked his eyes up, said nothing, returned his attention to his notebook. He worked with the pencil stub, printing minute characters on the unlined page, the index finger of his left hand hooked through the handle of his coffee mug. Frank couldn't read the writing upside down.

"What's the drill around here," Frank said.

"The drill is you stop talking to me."

Frank shoveled hash browns into his mouth. They smelled good but tasted like cardboard. All the food on his tray redefined the word "bland." He kept expecting a bell, or a P.A. announcement, or maybe a fat guard with a bullhorn voice to tell them to proceed to . . . someplace. Instead there seemed to be no organization at all. People came and went, lingered or rushed. There wasn't much talking. The atmosphere was thick with lethargy.

"I don't get it," Frank said.

Jonas had taken a break from his notebook and was sipping his coffee.

"That's obvious."

"Where are the guards? What are the prisoners supposed to do?"

"We're doing it."

"I'm not doing anything."

"Precisely. And by the way, the word is segregate. This is Segregation and you're a segregate, not a prisoner."

"What's the difference?"

"Try going for a walk and see what happens."

"Why, what happens?"

"Nothing happens. What you have to keep in mind is how passive-aggressive this place is."

Jonas closed his notebook and stood up. He took his tray and dirty dishes to the self-bussing cart and walked out of the cafeteria. Frank did the same, but instead of returning directly to the cell, he went for a walk around the prison, or whatever it was. Nothing happened except he got lost. It took him hours to find his way back to his own cell, where Jonas was snoring.

Next morning in the cafeteria, Frank said to Jonas, "I *really* don't get it."

"You aren't educated. What did I already tell you?"

"You said it wasn't a prison."

"Correct. What else?"

"You said we weren't prisoners but something called 'segregates.'"

"You got a good memory."

"You only told me yesterday."

"Around here, people start forgetting all their shit pretty quick."

"Maybe it's the boredom. When I was in sorting I had to *work*, or they wouldn't feed me."

"This isn't sorting. All I can say is, you're in here you must be some kind of fuck-up."

"Whatever. You're in here, too."

"No one's born in Straconia," Jonas said, "so let me guess." Jonas closed his eyes and moved his head around, like some kind of hokey TV psychic. "I see you living this normal, white-bread life in Minneapolis, or Duluth, or Portland, some place like that."

"Seattle."

Jonas opened his eyes. "I was close."

"Seattle isn't anything like Duluth."

"Point is, despite appearances, you didn't belong there."

"I belonged."

"You can say what you want, I know how it works. You don't want to listen, you don't have to." Jonas forked scrambled eggs into his mouth.

"I'm listening," Frank said.

"You didn't belong where you were. You felt alien, ostracized. Maybe it was subconscious, maybe it was bullshit, but you felt it. You drifted through life. Then one day you went for a walk in the night, in the fog, or rain. Or maybe you got in your car and started driving, and you didn't even know you were doing it, because you were asleep. That happens, and you always wake up at home in your own bed, no matter how much time you spend in Straconia, because time doesn't match up between Straconia and anywhere else. Then it happened that you *didn't* wake up. You stayed in Straconia, because this is where you really belong."

"What if we walked out of here, out of Segregation?"

"Wouldn't do you any good. You've got three strikes. Next time they pick you up, it's going to be worse than this place."

"Maybe they won't pick us up. And maybe if we're in the city, we can find a way home. The sleepwalking thing might go in reverse. But nobody sleepwalks into Segregation. They sleepwalk into the city Straconia."

"You keep saying 'we.'"

"How long have you been in Segregation?"

"Feels like forever," Jonas said. "I was seventeen. I'd wake up in bed with rain in my hair and vague memories of tall buildings. We lived in Scottsdale. The only skyscrapers I'd ever seen were in movies and video games."

"How old are you now?"

"No idea."

"How did you wind up a segregate?"

"Three strikes, same as you."

"What were your three strikes?" Frank was curious.

"I'm Black. One, two, three."

"You automatically got segregated because you're Black?"

"That's cute, the way you're so shocked. I opened my eyes in a filthy alley, slumped against a dumpster. Rain was falling past one of those orange streetlamps. I stood up and walked toward the light. I didn't even get both feet on the sidewalk before a Police Interceptor made a U-turn. No ID, no job, no address, no friends. They put me to work in the subway tunnels, janitorial, and waited for me to fuck up. It didn't take long. I found this unused maintenance closet in an old station near the river. The work they had me doing, it was dirty, but there was nobody watching me, nobody in charge. You know, the Straconia way.

"I used to slip off and hide in that closet, catch a break. One time I fell asleep and was late showing up at the next platform, where they had me mopping out toilets. That's all it took, little missteps like that. Now I'm here. Straconia's where folks wind up who don't feel at home where their real home is and don't try to do anything about it. But the city doesn't welcome everybody. Some, it's got no use for right away. You fucked up by being ignorant, but all I had to do was be me."

"Well, I can't stay here. Not in Segregation. Not the rest of my life."

"You're not getting that it isn't a choice." Jonas picked up his pencil and started writing in the notebook again.

Frank sat back. Something shifted in him, something deep, like tectonic plates. "It *is* a choice. Everything is. I think I just figured that out." Jonas ignored him. Frank said, "Will you stop writing in that damn thing and look at me? I think we should walk out of here, you and me."

Jonas put his pencil down and stared blandly at Frank.

"Well?" Frank said.

"You're new. You don't understand how everything's against you."

"I don't want to understand that. I want to live."

Frank started early in the morning. He put on all his gray segregate clothes, layering against the cold. He had considered stealing some food out of the cafeteria, but feared that might constitute a "misstep" that would level up his punishment.

Lying on the lower bunk, tapping his pencil stub against his chin, Jonas watched Frank pull one shirt on over another. "You're crazy," he said.

"At least I'm trying."

Frank was halfway to the river when he heard somebody running up behind him. He turned around, expecting to see a cop. But it was Jonas. "Change your mind?" Frank said.

"Shit, without me you wouldn't even make across the river." Jonas was shivering in the wind.

"You should have put on more layers."

"I left kind of sudden."

"Where's your notebook?" Frank had never seen Jonas without his notebook.

"It was done. Let's start walking. It's damn cold."

A few minutes later, Frank said, "What were you writing in that notebook, anyway?"

"Memories about home, about Scottsdale, mostly descriptions of things. After a while in this place, you forget the details of your other life. If that happens, I don't think there's any chance you go back. My details were about gone when this guy showed up. He had the notebook and some pencils with him. I talked to him a couple of times. He was old, like fifty? He died and I grabbed his stuff."

"How'd he die?"

"He stabbed himself with a pencil, in that big artery in the neck, right in the carotid. Bled out pretty quick."

"Jesus."

"Anyway, I was down to the last pencil. Pretty soon I was

going to have to decide. Writing the details didn't help, anyway. Mostly I was making them up."

The river was turbulent, the water brown and smelling of sewage. They walked along the muddy bank until they came to a narrow two-lane road that plunged into an opening in the ground—the tunnel to Straconia. Sawhorse barricades blocked the way. The road was cracked and buckled. Weeds grew out of the cracks. Sagging turf and brambles lent the tunnel entrance the appearance of a baleful, half-lidded eye.

"This isn't the way I came."

"That's farther down river. What I think, this one used to be the main tunnel, maybe back when Straconia was smaller. The newer one, it's mostly for the big trucks that transport stuff from the factories. This one's our best bet. No traffic."

They stood at the mouth of the tunnel, breathing its damp concrete-and-rot exhalation. Deep inside, a feeble green light glowed.

Frank turned to Jonas. "You've gone in there before, haven't you?"

"Only a little ways. Didn't have the guts to really go for it."

They started walking, shoes slipping in the slime of river seepage and rat shit.

Jonas spat. "This is dumb. We should turn back."

"So you can stab yourself in the neck with a pencil?"

"Don't knock it if you haven't tried it."

They paused under a green panel spotted with filth. Insect husks dotted a sagging cobweb veil. The panel cast a dim glow. Roughly mortared bricks sweated with condensation and seeping river water. Ahead, at erratic intervals more such panels glowed.

"They're chemical," Jonas said. "Backup emergency lights. I doubt they've run power through this tunnel in years."

Something scuttled in the dark. It sounded big.

"Rat," Jonas said.

"It sounds big as a puppy."

"I doubt that." Jonas sounded nervous.

They resumed walking. The rat, or whatever it was, scuttled in the shadows ahead. At the next oasis of chemical light the sound of splashing water became audible. The roadway rippled in the green glow like an oily mirage. Their feet splashed into a broad puddle of stinking river water. There wasn't room to go around.

The puddle got deeper as they progressed, rising above their ankles, filling their shoes with cold, slimy water. From up ahead there came a dreadful sound—a high-pitched squeal of pain and terror. Frank and Jonas stopped, an oily wave rolling ahead of their last steps. The squealing cut off abruptly. The next sound was worse: the full-throated bark of a large dog. Fear prickled the back of Frank's neck. "Holy shit."

The dog stopped barking. It emerged out of the dark between chem lights, prowling forward, a big shepherd mix. It stopped, regarded them from a safe distance, advanced a few more steps, and halted again, snarling.

"Looks starved," Jonas said. "See his ribs?"

They stepped back. It was like a signal. The dog started a wild, savage barking and came charging towards them, splashing through the puddle before they could turn and start running for their lives. It sprang at Frank, hit him solidly in the chest and drove him off his feet. Frank, screaming, tried to hold it off, the dog's jaws snapping at his throat.

Jonas waded in, getting his arm around the animal's neck, wrenching it back, heaving it away from Frank. The dog scrabbled up. So did Frank. The men crouched, waving their arms, yelling and snarling like madmen. The shepherd lunged and pulled back, lunged and pulled back, then paced away from them, panting. Too weak to take them both on, it padded off into the dark, toward the Segregation side of the river.

"Jesus Christ," Frank said, breathing hard. "You saved my ass."

"Told you."

"That fucking dog."

Jonas shook his head. "Dog's just a dumb animal wants to live, same as us. Including the dumb part. Man, I wish I could take a hot shower and lie down on my bunk."

"We can't go back now."

Half an hour later, daylight appeared at the end of the tunnel. Jersey barriers blocked the entrance. They climbed over them. The road rose steeply into Straconia's urban sprawl. At the top a rusty, abandoned toll gate blocked the way. Graffiti scrawled over the sides of the tollbooths.

A damp breeze came off the river. Frank folded his arms, hands tucked under his armpits. His feet were soaked and numb. Jonas's teeth chattered so loudly that Frank could hear them from ten feet away.

"We shouldn't have come," Jonas said.

"You're pretty pessimistic for a guy from Scottsdale."

"I'm not *from* Scottsdale. My mom married a guy."

"Anyway, we're not going back. I've got a plan."

"I hope it's a good one."

"We need a safe place to get warm and regroup."

"Great plan. It's like, 'How to become a millionaire. Step One: get a million dollars.'"

"That wasn't the plan, that was the situation. What about that maintenance closet you told me about, where you fell asleep? You said it was near the river. Can you find it?"

"Yeah."

"Is it far?"

"It's walkable."

"Okay. We go there. That's step one."

"What's step two?"

"I don't know yet."

Jonas snorted. "We stand here talking about it all day, I'm going to go hypothermic."

"You need another layer." Frank started unbuttoning his top shirt.

"You're crazy. Keep your shirt."

They entered the city, their wet shoes squelching on the sidewalk. After two blocks, a Police Interceptor slowed down, the driver giving them a hard look. They turned down an alley and walked faster.

"We better split up," Jonas said. "You can pass, but I stick out."

"We're staying together."

"It's your funeral."

An Interceptor picked them up a block later.

Uniformed men escorted Frank and Jonas into the Public Safety Building and down multiple levels to a subterranean maze, where they separated the men. Jonas looked over his shoulder as his escort led him away. Frank turned around. The door through which they had entered was gone, seamlessly blended with the wall. Frank's escort pulled him away. They walked a long time.

Frank's room contained a bed, a toilet, a built-in lamp, and a sink. On a little shelf next to the sink there was a plastic drinking cup. There was a door. Frank waited a minute after his escort left then tried the door. It opened. In Straconia, always, you had freedom of movement, if not of consequences. He stepped into the corridor. Faintly, the hard-soled shoes of his escort clocked on the cement floor, growing fainter, until silence took over.

Frank dreamed of Janet grocery shopping. In the produce department she selected nectarines for her basket, holding one, putting it back, picking up another, evaluating them for ripeness. Frank was present only as an unseen and unmissed observer. *Sometimes people like Janet come to Straconia, people who think they don't belong in their lives. Then something changes, and they never come back again.*

Frank awoke with the weight of grief on his chest.

He prowled the corridors, hunting a way out, using his wedding band to mark the twists and turns, scratching hash marks in the brick. The hashmarks didn't help. And the ring wouldn't stay on his finger anymore; he was losing weight. There was no cafeteria; no one brought food to his cell. His head ached all the time, and it became harder to get off his bed.

By the end of what Frank reckoned must be the fifth day, he knew he was in the middle of a Straconia execution.

They were starving him.

Despite his growing weakness, he continued to search for a way out of the maze. A piece of himself marveled at his own tenacity. Before Straconia, he would have quit long ago.

As he came around a bend, expecting another unmarked wall, he was instead confronted by a set of his hash marks. He had been walking in circles, wasting his strength. He fell back against the wall under a narrow air circulation vent. "It's cruel," he said to no one. "This is fucking cruel and unusual."

A voice came out of the vent, startling him: "What did you expect?"

"Jonas?"

"I told you it would get worse."

"Keep talking," Frank said, "maybe I can find your cell."

"What for?"

"We put our heads together, we might figure a way out of this."

"Forget it," Jonas said.

"Come on."

But Jonas wouldn't speak again, and Frank had lost heart. He retraced his route back to his cell.

He drank tap water to keep his belly full. The metallic after-taste made him nauseated. Frank lay on his bed, picking over the past, exhuming regrets. It's what he had always done: use the immutable past to construct a wall against the future. Now he had to think in a new way. In Straconia the door was always open. But how did that help, if he couldn't *find* it?

He stood over the toilet, dizzy with hunger. When he flushed, the pipes knocked loudly behind the wall. He turned back to his bed, but stopped. It wasn't just the knocking pipes. There was something else, a mechanical sound. Frank pressed his ear to the wall. A motor ran, the sound conducted down the pipes to Frank's cell. A pump, a sump pump. They were underground. Wastewater had to be pumped out. And the pump station had to be accessible for repairs and maintenance. That meant a passageway behind the wall that possibly led to the outside.

Frank flushed the toilet again, then stepped quickly into the corridor and listened at the walls until, faintly, he heard the pump churning before shutting off. He needed Jonas. Frank started working his way through the maze. Every time he came to an air circulation vent, he shouted at it. "Jonas! Come on, I've got a plan!"

"What plan?" Jonas finally replied.

"I need you to flush your toilet over and over again."

"Fuck you, let me sleep."

"I'm serious." Frank explained the idea, and Jonas started flushing.

*

Frank stood before a wall at a junction of corridors. Behind the wall, the sump pump churned loudly. "Okay, stop," Frank yelled at the nearest vent. "I found it."

"Okay."

The pump completed its cycle and ceased.

"Do you think you can find me?" Frank said.

"That place where all the hallways meet? Yeah, I been there before, when I was walking around that first day."

Frank sat on the floor to wait. After a long time, Jonas arrived, dragging his feet. He nodded at Frank and sat beside him.

"Your plans are always pretty half-assed," Jonas said.

"What took you so long?"

"Got lost," Jonas said. "This damn place reminds me of a summer job I had in high school. County Fair. I took tickets for the mirror maze, except when kids got lost too long inside, then I was supposed to rescue them."

"Be the hero."

"Yeah. Had these secret doors all over the maze, so I could just pop out of the wall near where the kid was standing around crying for his mom, like I'm—"

"Wait a minute." With effort, Frank stood up.

"What?"

"We got secret doors here, too, like the one that let us into the maze. It makes sense there'll be one next to the pump."

Jonas started to get up. He was having some trouble, and Frank helped him.

"You never quit, do you?" Jonas said.

"I used to quit all the time. Actually, I used to never start. A bad strategy in Straconia."

They faced the wall.

"What now?" Jonas said. "You got a magic word or some-thing?"

"Start pushing on bricks."

"This is dumb," Jonas said.

A brick that looked exactly like all the others gave under the pressure of Frank's hand. He pushed harder. The brick de-pressed into the wall on some kind of pneumatic actuator. A section of the wall separated and slid aside, revealing a pump station and a narrow passage.

"Like I was saying," Jonas said, "great plan."

The passage led to a flight of steep stairs, almost a ladder, with handrails. At the top was a steel door. Frank grasped the handle, waited, afraid it would be the one locked door in Straconia, then cranked it down decisively. The door swung outward. Rafts of black and gray clouds scudded above city towers. Across the street, laundry flapped on lines strung between the iron balconies of a fire-escape framework. About fifty yards away, a uniformed man huddled against the building, smoking a cigarette. Jonas sighed. "Here we go again."

"Maybe not," Frank said. "Execution is the biggest punishment—and they still made it possible for us to commute our own sentence. What else can they do to us?"

Jonas shook his head. "Famous last words."

Frank, grimacing in the sharp wind, walked toward the uniformed man. The man wasn't much more than a boy, Frank saw when he got closer. The boy drew on his cigarette. Wind snatched the smoke away.

"We're hungry," Frank said. "What do we do?"

"Pick up your vouchers, I guess."

"What vouchers?"

"Food vouchers. Come on with me, I'll show you where."

"Are you serious?"

The boy flicked his cigarette away. "Yeah, my break's over anyway."

The boy led them to an office in the Public Safety Building. A municipal clerk issued them food vouchers, rolls of currency, and, most importantly, blue CITIZEN cards. Jonas stared at his card in amazement. Frank had to wipe his eyes. Somehow they had come through the full gamut of Straconia's passive-aggressive justice system, and the reward was citizenship.

"Good luck to you," the clerk said from behind his bared window where he sat like someone accepting bets at Emerald Downs.

*

Frank and Jonas took a cab to the nearest restaurant, food vouchers folded in their pockets. "Do you think this is how everybody in Straconia became a permanent resident?" Jonas said, dunking a hard roll into a bowl of thick beef stew and cramming it into his mouth.

"I don't know. What if Straconia started as a little town, or a village, or maybe just some mud huts, or something? Then gradually it got bigger, absorbing more and more people?"

"Mud huts, right."

"I'm serious."

'Sure," Jonas said, chewing. "Hey, maybe the whole thing's like Peter Pan."

"Peter *Pan*?"

"All those orphans or whatever they were," Jonas said.

"Straconia isn't Neverland."

"Makes as much sense as mud huts."

"We aren't the Lost Boys."

"Watch that 'boy' shit."

They took a room in a flophouse. It wasn't called a flophouse, of course. Even in the old world, the word "flophouse" was just a remnant from the Depression era. But flophouse felt like the right name for the sagging wood-framed building with an interior space divided into dozens of shabby rooms. At least they were able to get an extra cot, so one of them didn't have to sleep on the floor.

Frank lay on the cot facing the window. The steam radiator clanked. Jonas started snoring. Frank's mind climbed restlessly around the next day. He began to think he would never fall asleep, then Jonas cried out, thrashing his covers off. Frank got up and shook him awake. Jonas looked wildly around the room, then shuddered and lay back. "Goddam dream. I was trying to go home. I could *see* it, then fog covered everything."

"We'll get home."

"You got a plan?"

"Sure."

Jonas snorted. "Man, you're crazy."

"You always say that."

"Because it's true."

Frank returned to his cot. After a while, he said, "Are you awake?"

"No."

"When I was a kid," Frank said, "I used to sleepwalk, and they would find me locked in the bathroom, like I was trying to hide. There was some bad stuff going on in my family, but it's nothing you could hide from behind a locked door."

"Since I'm not awake," Jonas said, "I didn't hear any of that."

"I'll tell you about it tomorrow," Frank said.

"You won't remember it tomorrow."

"Yes, I will."

In no time, Jonas was snoring again. Frank felt the heat of the steam radiator on his face and watched the rain fall past the window. It would be pleasant to fall asleep, but he knew this wasn't home. He got up, found his wallet, and removed the blue CITIZEN card. After a moment of hesitation, he rummaged through Jonas's clothes until he found the other CITIZEN card, and then he threw them both down the trash chute. One day Jonas would thank him, Frank hoped. Now all he needed was a plan. He knew he had one in him.

TRIBUTE

Nasa died two hundred and three nautical miles above the planet Mars. It died when Daniel Chen, the last surviving crew member of *Pilgrim 2*, ran out of breathable atmosphere. At that point, Chen pulled himself close to the nearest camera lens. Even though NASA was not sharing the feed, hackers inevitably populated it across the internet. Millions witnessed Chen's death. He was a beloved figure, a brilliant scientist as well as a twenty-first century Will Rogers dispensing wisdom and humor on the talk show and lecture circuit, in books and popular podcasts.

Chen's face contorted in gasping agony, veins standing out on his forehead, eyes popping, red with burst blood vessels. He spoke three words on his dying breath: *A stupid waste*, after which he rolled away from the lens. Five dead astronauts drifted in fisheye perspective. It was the latest in a string of catastrophic failures.

A stupid waste.

Millions heard Chen, but his words were aimed at one person: his sister. Nevertheless, *a stupid waste* became a popular catchphrase, often heard in Congress and the Senate chamber. Most notably it was invoked by the senior senator from Ohio when he exhorted his colleagues to defund the ninety-year-old space agency, declaring it nothing more than a fiscal black hole into which a substantial portion of the nation's treasure (less than one-quarter of one percent of the budget) was annually dumped without any reasonable expectation of a return on the investment. In short, NASA itself had become *a stupid waste*.

The Agency continued to operate, if only on the margins of relevancy: paid consultants to private industry, managing historical archives. Even data retrieval for existing satellites and robotic missions was contracted out. For America, except in the private sector, manned space flight was as dead as the crew of *Pilgrim 2*.

Karie

Getting there was the best part of the Nova Branson Orbital Resort. That's what Karie Chen thought. The orbital provided one-percenters with breathtaking views and nude zero-G
"tumble bays," among other attractions. Everyone loved it, even
the ninety-nine percent of the population who would never visit
the thing. Maybe they enjoyed the idea of nude movie stars free-
falling against the real stars.

Karie rode a Nova Branson shuttle launched from a facility in
the middle of Ohio farm country. The senior Senator deemed the
commercial space port a great boon to the state economy and an
invaluable asset to the ever-expanding space tourism industry: in
short, the exact dead opposite of *a stupid waste*. It was all of that,
Karie supposed, but for her it was mostly a great ride. From inside
the launch facility she couldn't see the giant advertising displays
that placarded the perimeter fence. Nike, Wal-Mart, Time War-
ner Direct Holo Vision, Amazon's Everything Experience—whoever had the money. Rocket launches still drew the Earth-bound.
They paid for bleacher seats and bought cheap souvenir trinkets
mass produced in China—the last country on Earth with an active manned space program not driven by commercial interests.

Three million pounds of thrust lifted Karie and half a dozen
millionaires into a cornflower blue sky. The roar scattered graz-
ing cows in surrounding fields. Three minutes in, the boosters
kicked them past seventeen thousand miles per hour, crushing
Karie into her seat, flattening her eyeballs—*the price of paradise*,
according to Nova Branson's literature. Karie's once-shattered and
badly healed knee throbbed in perfect agony. It didn't matter. Lips
skinned back in a fierce grin, she inhabited the pure joy of vertical
acceleration. It had been too long.

After hard dock everyone unstrapped. Released from gravity, movers and shakers became floaters and drifters. Karie was
a stranger among them. Aside from cordial greetings back at the
launch facility and a couple of don't-you-look-familiar glances,
the other passengers had mostly ignored her—the expected trib-

alism of the rich. The chip on Karie's shoulder turned it into classism— that's what Danny would have said. But then, Danny had gotten along with everyone.

Last to leave the shuttle, she pulled herself through the tunnel into Nova Branson's visitor processing bay. A resort agent in a pale green jumpsuit greeted her with a winning smile. "Welcome to Nova Branson Orbital."

"Thanks."

The agent accepted Karie's pass card and performed the required retinal identity verification. She already gotten the hell verified out of her before lift-off.

"You're all checked in," the agent said.

"What a relief."

"I'm sorry?"

"Never mind. Look, I thought somebody was going to meet me."

"Would you like to talk to customer service?"

"Naw. I think I'll have a look around."

Karie pushed off—and almost butted heads with a man gliding recklessly through the passage. "Hey—" The man caught her, which changed both of their trajectories. Karie banged her knee on the bulkhead, yelped, bit her lip hard enough to break the skin. A tiny crimson drop wobbled by her face.

"Sorry about that," the man said. "I'm James Brennerman. Alistair's my father. Are you all right?"

James offered his hand and Karie shook it. He was about forty years old, ten years her junior. He had one of those man-boy faces.

"I'm fine. Can I have my hand back?"

"Of course. Father's waiting. I'll take you there. Afterwards meet me in the rotation lounge. The spin maintains a one-third Earth gravity simulation. Called Forward View. Ask anybody how to find it. You'll love Nova Branson. At least that's what Dad is hoping."

James pushed into the passage. She followed him to what he called the conference room.

"Word of advice? Let Dad do the talking."

"Sure."

"He likes to be in charge, is all I'm saying. If you want this to happen as much as I do, you need to be ready to compromise."

"Got it."

James smiled. "Good luck. See you at Forward View. I can't wait to get this thing started."

Hand straps festooned the padded walls. The northern hemisphere of Earth appeared in a circular view port.

"Hello?" Karie said.

A holographic projector flickered on. A man, aged sixty, appeared. Athletically fit, virile streaks of gray. In reality the head of Nova Branson Corporation was pushing ninety and had been out of view for decades. Karie checked her temper. A little seeped out anyway.

"Mr. Brennerman, you insisted on a face-to-face meeting."

"And here we are."

"Actually, here I am."

"Alas, my physical limitations preclude me from space travel. But I wanted you to enjoy my orbital firsthand, encourage a change in perspective.

"I've been in space before."

"Perspective in the sense of attitude, Ms. Chen."

Karie tried to make her smile look natural. She was here for something only a man like Alistair Brennerman could afford to give. "Of course I'm grateful. Getting into space isn't easy these days—not without a funded mission."

The projection wobbled. For a moment Brennerman's voice fell out of sync with his lips. "Tell me why, exactly, you want to go to Mars."

"To fix what my brother helped break."

"A morbid contest of sibling rivalry?"

"It has nothing to do with sibling rivalry. The *Pilgrim 1* habitat is still on the surface, waiting for someone to unpack it. The crew of *Pilgrim 2* is dead, but that shouldn't invalidate the mission goal: a self-sustaining beachhead on Mars. Mr. Brennerman, America is squandering its potential by playing around in Earth orbit. Until the Chinese last year, no one had even stepped foot on the moon since 1972—eighty years, for God's sake."

"Nova Branson is not America."

"It is, actually. Along with every other global corporation

with roots in the United States. You run *everything*. I'm just asking you to invest in the pioneering spirit that used to define us. You can push the frontier." She was talking too much. Worse, she sounded like a used-car salesman. Karie's pitch lacked the sincerity she genuinely felt. She tried again:

"Listen. After the *Pilgrim* disaster and congressional defunding, NASA mothballed *Pilgrim 3* and *4*. But they are viable spacecraft. You could get one at a fire-sale price and cut expenses further by reducing the crew."

"Are you quite sure you'd be up to the rigors, Ms. Chen, in light of your injury and, excuse me, your age?"

"I'm perfectly fit for the mission."

"Of course. And James insists on you. I think he's star-struck by your celebrity. Hero of the *Phoenix* debacle."

"James? I don't understand."

The holo wobbled out of sync again. "You are not in the least bit impressed by my resort, are you?"

Karie sighed. "It's an impressive technological achievement."

"But?"

"But it doesn't accomplish anything." Okay, Karie thought, stop talking. "Earth orbit used to be the frontier. You don't even do any science here. We have to keep pushing outward."

"Yes, as I've often heard you say. I think you must wake each morning with the words already on your lips. Have you ever, for a moment even, considered you might be mistaken? Because you're wrong about the frontier. This is the greatest business frontier in history."

"Not my field."

"Can you conceive of any circumstance under which you might modify your obvious disdain for Nova Branson and the profitable future of orbital recreation?"

"I'm not disdainful. I'm *impatient*." Karie had drifted too close to Brenneman's holo. Her shoulder interrupted the projection, fracturing organized light. She looped her wrist into a hand strap, pulled back, and the holo resumed its integrity.

"For a round-trip ticket to Mars," Brennerman said, "will you be capable of recanting your impatience?"

"Recanting how?"

"Renounce your current and often stated opinion about orbitals. Lend your unqualified endorsement of orbital recreation, Nova Branson in particular. Participate in a public campaign which will include interviews, public forums, ghost-written books, and so on."

Karie stared. "I thought not," the holo said.

"Mr. Brennerman—"

"My son wishes to go to Mars. He wishes to go to Mars with the hero of the *Phoenix*. He admires you. Which suggests a lack of admiration for his own inheritance, since you and I are very much at odds. So this is my price for a trip to Mars. You vigorously and publicly embrace what I've accomplished, and intend to go on accomplishing, with Nova Branson. Do so and you may orbit the red planet as a tribute to your brother. That's how you will put it. A tribute to your brother. And that will be the end of it. If the Chinese want Mars, let them have it."

Karie was quiet, then said, "You know what it is, Mr. Brennerman?"

"Eh?"

"This kind of wasteful development of Earth orbit. It's like the prairie towns that sprang up after the frontier moved west. Those towns were mostly saloons and bordellos, places to get drunk and get laid while pretending you were in the midst of something wild. The difference between then and now is the wealth of the customers."

"Nova Branson has been in business a very long time, Ms. Chen. My grandfather started it, my father developed it, and I have been a loyal steward of the legacy. We did not succeed by indulging romantic notions such as your 'pushing the frontier' mantra."

"So you brought me up here just to slap me back down."

The Brennerman projection smiled. "I'll tell James you weren't interested."

She worked the lecture circuit. People still paid to hear her talk about *Phoenix*. She had been in command. Mission: to rendezvous with a robotic vehicle that had successfully captured a small asteroid and established itself in lunar orbit. One of *Phoenix's* fuel cells ruptured. The explosion crippled the ship and killed Karie's pilot. Despite her shattered knee, Karie babied the spacecraft back to Earth, saving herself and the three scientists onboard. Her knee never healed properly. NASA declared her unfit to fly, even as they praised her heroism. That was ten years ago. *Pilgrim 2* should have been *Karie's* mission. Instead they selected Danny, the public relations star with no flying experience, two fully functioning knees, and a social media following in the millions. Privately, Danny told Karie he was glad she was grounded. Watching her almost die on *Phoenix* had been unbearable. When he saw the hurt look on her face, he immediately took it back. "Hey, I didn't mean it that way." But it stung. Sibling rivalry, Alistair had suggested. But it wasn't that simple.

Now, during a Q & A session at Wyoming State University, an old guy in the second row stood up and the usher handed him the microphone. Karie pegged him right away. Leather jacket, cap with US NAVY Ret. blazoned across it: Aging space buff. Mostly that's what she got these days.

"I have a comment and a question," he said. "The comment is: We need NASA back. The *real* NASA!" Applause rippled through an audience who wouldn't be there if they weren't already in the same nostalgia camp. They always wanted to hear about Karie's heroic save of the stranded *Phoenix* scientists. She complied, then switched to her message about the future of exploration. At that point she usually took a few jabs at Nova Branson, among others. Tonight she skipped the jabs. Karie had been thinking a lot since her return from the orbital resort.

"And the question is," the old space buff continued, "how do we *get* it back?"

More applause. Karie's anger surged—more at herself than anyone else. The applause wound down. She raised the microphone. "NASA isn't coming back." Microphone feedback whined through the hall. Karie winced, held the mic farther from her lips. "The agency that took us to the moon is dead. You should get over the idea that NASA can happen again. Because it won't." She paused and let them grumble. "And we don't need it to come back. The future of manned space flight exists right now, the technology, the infrastructure. The privatization of space flight is *here*. What our entrepreneurs lack is a vision without dollar signs."

She talked a while longer, departing from her usual lecture notes, but she had lost some of the audience. People began standing, gathering their coats. Later, when she stepped out into the evening air, James Brennerman was waiting for her.

"Mr. Brennerman."

"Can we talk?"

"Go ahead."

"I meant over dinner."

"I'm headed straight to the airport to catch the redeye."

"Then let me drive you. You stood me up, you know." He smiled.

"On the orbital? After talking to your father there didn't seem to be any point."

"Let me try to convince you otherwise. Please."

She hesitated, then said, "The University provided a driver. I'll have to tell her."

In the back seat of the limo James offered her a drink.

"No, thanks."

"My father was pushing you."

"Yeah, I got that."

"You understand, it's about me. You represent a threat."

"A threat! He's Alistair Brennerman. I can barely fill a lecture hall."

"That's not the point. I'm in your camp. I believe we need to extend the frontier. Dad interprets that as almost traitorous. We've locked horns on this since I was a kid. Now he's old and he wants to groom me to take over Nova Branson. The corporation means everything to him. Instead, I want to fly to Mars with you."

"I'm a bad influence."

James laughed. "In his eyes, absolutely."

"So why are you here?"

"This is the good part. Dad's changed his mind, or I changed it for him, or I'm not even sure what." Frowning, James scratched his head. "To be honest, I'm a little baffled myself."

"Wait a minute. He's agreed to fund the mission, his *tribute* mission?"

"Yes, provided I can persuade you to his terms."

"Let me save you the trouble of trying: you can't."

"Hear me out. He's agreed to back off on the more extreme

elements. No ghost-written paeans to orbital resorts, no public lectures recanting your position. We're talking about a one-time public statement of support, a willingness to play nice with the press, and passive participation in a program of advertising revenue. And, Karie, he's agreed to a landing, not just a bullshit tribute orbit."

Karie held back her elation. A Mars landing! A real chance at exploration. "I can live with those terms. But why is he doing this? I don't get it."

"I pledged my loyalty to the status quo, promised when I took over I would adhere absolutely to Dad's vision without, as he put it, romantic deviations. Look, our relationship has always been rocky." His face made an ugly grimace, an unintended glimpse of just how hard "rocky" had been. "Now time's running out. He wants us to reconcile, he wants his legacy carried forward. We're compromising around Mars."

"He didn't strike me as the compromising type."

"Maybe in this case we're both wrong about him."

"Maybe. Are you really willing to come back and spend the rest of your life pampering rich tourists?"

"Of course not."

Karie gave him a skeptical look. "But Alistair believes you?"

"He believed me after I signed a legal document binding me to the terms." James poured himself a scotch. "Of course, there's no such thing as a contract that can't be broken."

The driver spoke. "Coming into the airport now, sir."

"There's something off about all this," Karie said.

"The point is," James said, "do you want to go to Mars or not?"

Seventeen months later, at a pre-launch photo-op, Karie turned to James and said, "We look like NASCAR drivers."

"*You* look great," James said.

Joining them were Brandon Krueger and Treva Hilgar, NASA-trained astronauts and early defectors to Nova Branson. They wanted to fly. Krueger was six feet of lean muscle mass and smiling optimism. Hilgar was compact, emotionally self-contained, and fiercely competent. She wore a small gold cross around her neck. Karie was happy to have them along. All their flight suits

were emblazoned with advertising patches. Especially annoy-
ing was the wearable GIF touting Nova Branson Orbital Resort,
winking and shifting like Vegas casino signage.

"Put on your smile," Krueger said. "We're going to Mars."

Later, riding the elevator up the gantry, Karie said, "The last few
months, it's like launching a circus, not an interplanetary mission."

"Apollo wasn't about exploration, either," Krueger said.

"I know. It was about beating the Russians."

"But exploration was a byproduct of that competition. And
this mission isn't about the NASCAR suits or your endorsement.
So cheer up."

James laughed. "I can't believe you two are even debating
about something that's already a done deal. Enjoy yourselves, for
God's sake."

Treva Hilgar, as always, kept her thoughts to herself and
watched the booster slip by.

Mars rolled out beneath them. After seven months in space,
it was time. Karie opened the hatch between the main body of
Pilgrim 3 and the landing module attached to its belly. "Go ahead,
James," she said.

Smiling, bearded, excited, James moved toward the hatch.
They had really done it. In a few hours they would be examining the *Pilgrim 1* habitat, reporting on its readiness for future
missions to occupy. If there ever were any future missions. Karie
wished what they were doing felt more like a beginning and less
like a swan song—or, worse, a *tribute*.

She followed James into the LM. Krueger had already begun
the power-up procedures. Treva would remain in orbit.

"Here we go, huh?" James said.

"Here we go."

They were all grinning like kids.

Karie separated the LM from the main body of *Pilgrim 3*. This
is where trouble had struck her brother's mission. *Pilgrim 2's* separation maneuver had failed, trapping the entire crew in a landing
module that couldn't land. *Pilgrim 3's* separation was flawless. A

short burn took them to the edge of the atmosphere. Their speed increased exponentially. Seven miles up, the supersonic chute deployed. Karie and Brandon Krueger watched their instruments. A mile from touchdown the chute separated and the retro rockets fired. Then it began to go wrong. The retros fired too hot, sapping fuel reserves. Still thousands of feet above the surface, the LM doggedly hovered.

"Damn it," Karie said. "Switch me to full manual."

"I'm on it."

Seconds ticked by, then minutes.

"Brandon?"

"Problem. Hold on."

Karie watched the fuel gauges drop. They were already depleted below what was necessary to achieve orbit and rendezvous. Being marooned was a given; soon they wouldn't be able to land at all.

"Brandon, come on."

"*There*. The damn thing wouldn't let go."

Karie took them down, radically angling the descent, going for a hard landing while she could still control it. But it was too late. Sixty feet above the surface the fuel gauges flashed red, the engines quit, and they dropped like a stone.

"Brace!"

The desert plain came up like a wall and swatted them.

Karie dragged James from the wreckage. Her knee collapsed and she fell over, cursing. The landing module loomed against the butterscotch sky, a mangle of abstract junk. Krueger's severed arm hung from a gash in the bulkhead. There was no need to pull him out. Adrenalin, fear and pain routed Karie's rational response. Gasping, she fumbled at her helmet. Then made herself stop. The readouts on her sleeve display indicated all was in order. She bore down, forcing calm, taking deep, slow breaths, then put her attention on James. Behind his faceplate his eyes fluttered. Blood crept from his hairline.

"James."

He groaned.

She shook him. "James, can you stand?"

"I don't know."

"You're going to stand."

"I'm sorry," he said.

"Don't be sorry, just stand up. If I can do it you can do it."

They both stood up, leaning on each other. A wave of dizziness swelled through Karie. She swayed, almost fainted, but held on. The *Pilgrim 1* habitat was a mile away. Packed inside was everything they needed to survive—if they could reach it.

Except for the lighter gravity, Karie would never have made it. By the time they came upon the habitat her knee was screaming and her body was drenched in sweat. James, who had recovered quickly, all but carried her the last hundred yards. The habitat was roughly the size of a shipping container. They passed through the airlock, initiated life support. Kari stripped off her helmet and gloves. She powered up the communications rig and sent a message to *Pilgrim 3*. Treva did not reply. She tried again. Still no response.

"What's wrong with that thing?" James said.

"I don't know."

"Does Treva even know we crashed?"

"She tracked our descent. She knows."

Karie slipped on the headphones and tried again.

"Anything?"

"Quiet."

Karie thought she heard something—a voice, so faint and submerged in static she couldn't be sure it was real. She adjusted the radio, fine tuning, but the voice was gone.

"What?" James said.

"I thought I heard a voice."

"What did she say?"

"I don't know. I'm not even sure it *was* a voice."

"Let me." James took the headphones and began broadcasting, listening intently for a reply, broadcasting again. Then his expression changed. He closed his eyes, appearing almost in pain as he listened. After a while, looking disappointed, he removed the headphones. "I thought I heard something."

For the next hour they traded off on the radio, trying to contact both Treva in orbit and Mission Operations back on Earth, sometimes with the headphones on, sometimes allowing the wash of hopeless static to pour out of the speakers.

"We both heard the voice," James said.

"We heard something." Karie's mind was moving off the radio. There was so much to do.

Day three.

A dust storm came howling out of the desert. They huddled inside the habitat. Dust and grit hissed against the shell. Karie had been working on a protective shield for the life support unit's loader. Attached to the outside of *Pilgrim 2*, the loader shipped Martian soil into a chamber, where it was heated and the evaporated water captured. LS apparatus then divided the water into hydrogen and oxygen, adding nitrogen directly from the atmosphere. It produced drinking water and breathable air and was designed to support five people. But the equipment proved balky, in need of constant attention. And then the dust storm drove them back inside before she could fix the shielding in place. What would be left after the storm? Feeling her optimism fray, Karie said, "I'm beginning to think people like your father are right."

James scooped fruit paste out of a ration cup and sucked the spoon clean. "Dad's always right about everything. Just ask him."

"*Phoenix* was a disaster—my pilot killed, the mission aborted. *Pilgrim 2* up there right now with five dead, including my brother. And now Brandon Krueger. You want to talk about a stupid waste, there it is."

"Karie."

"You know, when Danny said that stupid waste thing, he was talking directly to me. He was saying, I know you're going to try to find a way to come out here. Don't do it."

"Well, you did it anyway."

They stood by the loader. Dust and grit had wind-blasted through the mechanism, tearing rubber seals, clogging the armatures and servos.

"We're going to have to break it down, clean everything, replace the seals, and put it together again. Otherwise we can manually ship the soil, which is more labor than we want." Karie's knee throbbed. She ignored it. In the direction of the crashed landing module, something moved. She paused, holding her wrench. A dust devil tracked across the desert, like a fleeing ghost.

Day nine.

By now Treva had left orbit, headed back to Earth. Karie had tried everything she could think of to make the radio work, to no avail. There didn't seem to be anything *wrong* with it. Possibly their outgoing messages were being heard. There was simply no way to tell. She turned to the hydroponics and other matters demanding attention. James meanwhile spent too much time monitoring the useless radio. One morning he shouted, "There's somebody! I heard somebody."

Karie, already suited up, was about to enter the airlock. Dust accumulated on the solar panel array if they didn't keep it wiped off. "Are you sure?"

"Yes, yes. I was broadcasting to Earth, and then there was a voice. I couldn't hear what it said, but it was real. I heard it. This time I'm positive."

Karie switched to speaker. She cleared her throat and spoke into the microphone, "*Pilgrim 1* habitat, this is *Pilgrim 1* habitat. Please respond."

James leaned in eagerly.

"Relax," Karie said. They both knew it would be at least twenty-eight minutes before they received a reply. She was about to stand up when, faintly, a voice spoke through the static. Karie tweaked the noise reduction filter. The voice became slightly clearer. *Pilgrim 1 Habitat, this is Pilgrim 1 habitat. Please respond . . .*

An echo.

Like calling into the mouth of a deep, black, empty cave. James looked stricken. After that, he rarely wasted time with the radio.

Day seventy.

Karie lay on her thin mattress. Many nights she and James shared a bunk, but Karie had been sleeping poorly for weeks and wanted her own space tonight. An amber panel near the airlock provided minimal illumination. Tired as she was, she couldn't let go, her mind constantly worrying at the myriad of tasks. The hydroponics required constant attention. In nightmares, Karie awakened to discover the plants withered and dead. In reality the radishes, lettuce and green onions were thriving under carefully controlled conditions. Still, they were a long way from a bioregenerative life support system.

From where he lay in his own bunk, James said: "We're never leaving this planet."

"What are you talking about?"

"My father's not sending a rescue ship."

"And you know this how?"

"Somebody reprogrammed the LM computer. Reprogrammed it to burn all our fuel, making sure we'd crash. If Brandon hadn't managed to override it and if you hadn't been at the controls, we would have all died."

"I didn't exactly execute a soft landing."

"We survived, didn't we?"

"Two of us did."

"Dad knew I would find a way to wiggle out of the agreement I signed. I thought it was odd when he suddenly conceded the point and agreed to a landing. I should have trusted my instincts, but I wanted this so bad."

"What are you saying?"

"Dad saw an opportunity and he seized it. Think of it. Yet another fatal disaster confirms that manned spaceflight pushing the frontier is too dangerous and pointless. A stupid waste, right?"

"James, it's his corporation. He didn't have to *kill* you to keep you from taking control after his death."

"That's exactly what he had to do." James's voice contained bitterness like acid. "My ascension was out of his hands. *Grandfather* liked me. It was in his will that the family line not be broken. Barring death or some kind of certifiable mental derangement, I was next to take charge of Nova Branson. Period. Dad had to sign off on that before the reins of power passed into his hands."

"You're being a little paranoid."

"He's capable of anything when it comes to getting his way." James shook his head. "I'm a fool. Look. The retros fail, then the communications fail. That's pretty coincidental, isn't it? You've said yourself there's nothing wrong with the radio. That means it has to be the satellite relays. Guess who NASA contracted with to upgrade and facilitate satellite data retrieval? Nova Branson has held those contracts for over a decade. They can facilitate data retrieval from Mars satellites—or subvert it, or filter out what they don't want seen. We're dead, Karie, as far as anyone back home knows. Ship crashed, no communication from possible survivors. Done. It's not paranoia. It's brilliant. Cold-blooded but brilliant. You see it now, don't you?"

"James, I stopped counting on rescue as soon as we established the impossibility of communication."

James was quiet for a minute. "In the old days didn't the rovers use high-gain microwave transmissions for direct-to-Earth communication?"

"Find a rover and cannibalize it? Forget it."

"Why?"

"Because we have no idea where any of them are, and we're not equipped to go searching."

"*Damn* it."

"There's another possibility. The landing module. The locator beacon, it transmits directly on high frequency."

"Can we adapt *that* antenna?"

"No. But we can move the beacon."

"How does that help?"

"All it does now is identify the crash site. Well, crash sites don't move."

"But survivors can move the beacon! We have to go get this thing tomorrow."

"James, I'm exhausted. We'll talk about it in the morning, okay? Two miles on my knee is going to be a stretch, even if I'm rested."

"I'll go alone."

"Don't. It's too dangerous to separate. I really have to sleep now, okay? We can figure out a plan in the morning."

Karie got up and found her way to the head. With the door shut, she turned on the light, opened the medicine kit, and took a couple of sleeping pills. God bless NASA for deciding the pilgrims might need artificially orchestrated rest.

*

She woke up groggy, her head like something stuffed with wet cotton. Dust and grit hissed against the habitat's shell. Karie checked her chronometer. It had been more than ten hours since she took the sleeping pills. Jesus. Dimly she remembered James shaking her, trying to wake her up. She had brushed him off, rolling onto her side. Now she reached for the lights. They came on in sections, flickering at first. James was gone.

She checked the outside conditions. Wind speed was variable, between twenty and thirty knots, the direction changeable. She tried to raise James on his helmet com but the storm shredded the signal. She needed line-of-sight. After a couple of hours the dust storm began to subside. James was running out of time. Karie loaded up with extra oxygen and headed out.

She came to the wreckage of the LM. Her knee hurt but it was tolerable. The return hike would be worse. She had tried to raise James repeatedly on the helmet com, but no luck.

She climbed into the LM. Krueger's body lay frozen in place, attached at the ragged shoulder to a great dark sheen of frozen blood. His face stared at the twisted bulkhead, unmarred, fixed for eternity in a blank expression. Karie observed no inkling of the living man. Brandon Krueger's body was like another piece of the inanimate wreckage.

A tool bag from the habitat sat near a partially removed floor panel. James, going after the damn transponder. Karie picked up the pry bar and ratcheting wrench. The crash had twisted the deck out of alignment. She worked on it for a half hour, finally wrenching the panel aside. The transponder, the size of a shoebox, appeared intact. She detached it from its nest of cables and braces, stowed it in the tool bag, and started back.

The wind buffeted her. Dust churned all around. The bag was heavy. She shifted it from shoulder to shoulder. Her knee and back hurt. She stopped at the midway point and sat on the gritty hardpan, her head down. James was out here. By now his oxygen was depleted and he had suffocated, another piece of human wreckage. Another catastrophic failure.

She got up and went on. By the time the habitat came into

view, Karie could barely walk. How would she do this, how would she go on alone, day after day, week after week, year after year? The arid future lay before her. She staggered forward. Inside the airlock she closed the outer door, equalized the pressure, entered the habitat—and found James preparing dinner.

"I was getting worried about you," he said.

"James."

"What's wrong—hey, is that the transponder?"

"What happened to you?"

"Dust storm caught me. I tried to make it back before it got bad, but it got bad too fast. Wound up digging in behind a hillock. After the storm backed off I couldn't figure out where I was for a while. Beyond stupid. My air was pretty low. When I finally got here you were gone. It seemed dumb for me to go out again, so I've been waiting. Are you sure you're all right?

"I'm fine. I'm just glad you're here. I'm so glad."

Day seven hundred.

Karie woke before James. She turned on a section of light panels, and James's face emerged out of the dark beside her. He had taken to trimming his beard, after first threatening to shave it off altogether. She was glad he hadn't done that. She liked the beard, the way it transformed his man-boy features. In repose James looked like someone Karie might even love. She placed her hand on his bare shoulder and shook him gently.

"James."

His eyes opened. "Hey."

"It's time," she said.

"All right."

They suited up.

The dawn was so cold Karie could feel it even through the insulating coils of her suit. They hiked away from the habitat, Karie limping, and climbed to the top of the ridge. Their feet skidded in the loose scree. Karie had to hold on to James's arm until they reached the top.

"Okay," he said, "where do we look?"

She pointed to the horizon, where the sky had turned the color of burnished steel. "There. About thirty degrees above the plain."

They waited. After a while Karie had to sit down. He helped her and then joined her, and they leaned against each other. They had both lost weight, and they tired too easily, but almost two years in they were still alive—and not merely surviving. The habitat was designed for expansion. They had deployed the diggers, which tunneled out from *Pilgrim 1*, allowing them to construct a long underground "greenhouse," where they planted and nurtured a greater variety of vegetables and fruits. They still supplemented their diets with the supplies brought from Earth, but they were far less dependent than they had been in the beginning. The habitat was nearly a closed system, self-sustaining. Nearly. And if they had to get there, Karie was optimistic that they would. James, an amateur geologist, was even doing some science. *Pilgrim 1* was a viable foothold.

Now they were looking at the dawn sky. When it happened, it was so brief they almost missed it: A brilliant flash described an arc—and then *Pilgrim 2* was gone.

"Goodbye, Danny."

"You okay?"

"Yeah."

"Hey, Karie? You're my favorite Martian."

She laughed. "So we're Martians?"

"We both know my father isn't sending a rescue ship."

"It doesn't have to be Alistair, you know."

"Sure. Someday there'll be a knock on the door."

"What would happen if everyone thought you were dead and then you weren't?"

"I don't follow."

"Nova Branson is still your birthright. You told me Alistair *can't* disown you corporately, not according to the terms of your grandfather's will. I believe it will be worth it to someone to come up here looking for you. You know, there's gold in them Martian hills. Maybe that transponder trick worked."

"Karie, I wouldn't count on it. Hey, we're doing all right, aren't we? I mean as Martians."

They helped each other back to their feet.

"We're doing great," Karie said. "Come on, let's go home."

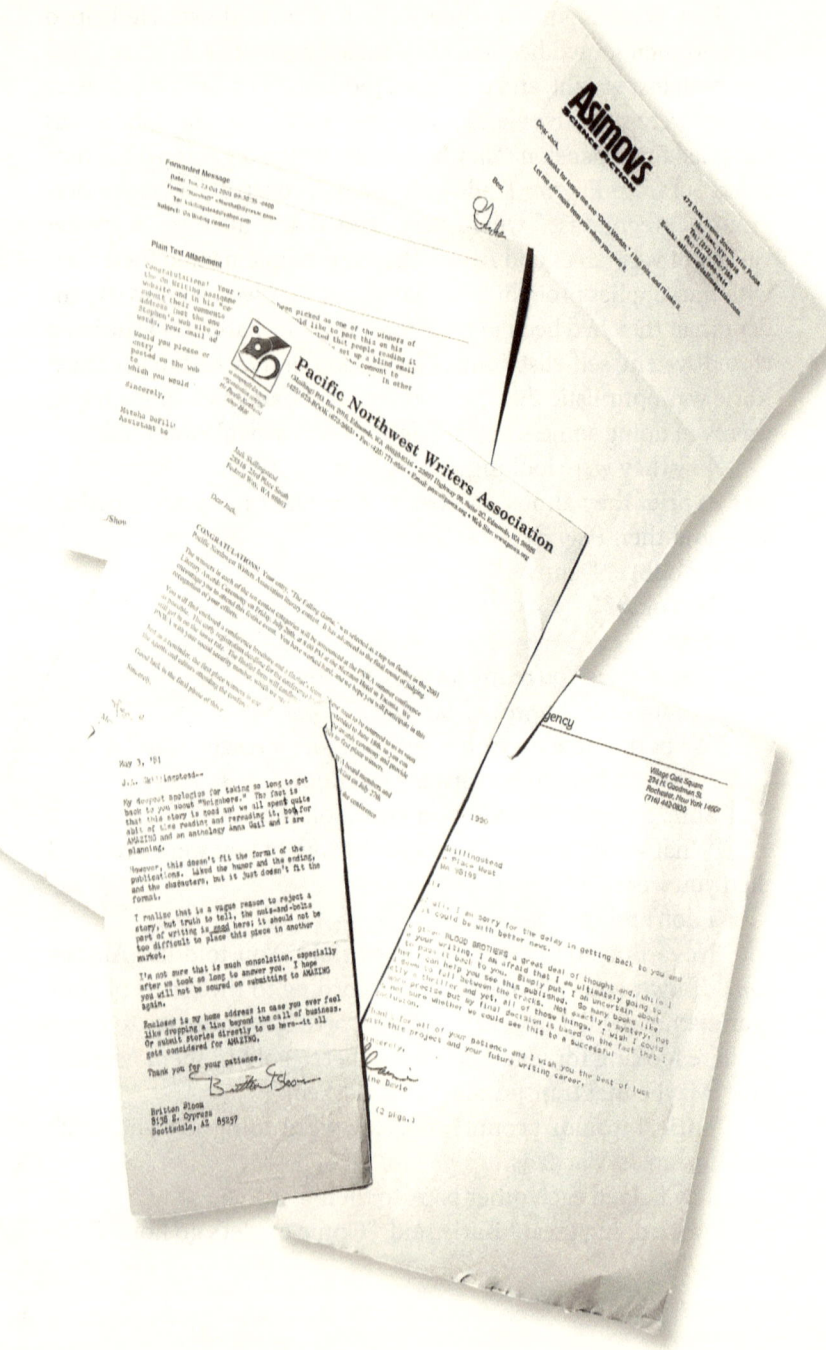

The Writing Life

I've been publishing professionally for twenty-one years.

Now here's the other part: I strived an equal number of years just to arrive at that starting point. My story was always about getting to the future, where I imagined I already existed as a published writer. Eventually that story came true. But there's another kind of self-story that we tell ourselves, one that is about the past—about who we used to be.

The first draft of this essay acknowledged that yes, I'd written a lot of words over a long period of time prior to breaking into print, but, I told myself, the reason it took so long was a combination of my disorganization and my dread of rejection—that dread exacerbated by emotional trauma suffered in adolescence. Essentially, I was spinning a victim narrative. I wasn't *lying*, though I am a good liar. But just as in fiction, memory and imagination are the primary ingredients of the past. Even the victim's journey must have seemed preferable to what I actually, deep down, believed the reality had been: failure upon embarrassing failure followed by a lucky break that revitalized my ambition and finally got me through the door. The victim's journey and the lucky break story are both false narratives.

The truth was in a box—several boxes, actually—waiting to be opened.

Something about that first version of the essay wasn't adding up. It felt like I was writing about someone else, maybe one of the characters from, as my wife likes to put it, my "tortured lonely guy" stories. I decided to excavate my old manuscripts, notebooks, and rejections out the storage closet. I was looking to reconstruct a timeline to see where my memory may have gone off track. Luckily I had the foresight to put dates on the novels, and many of the rejection letters and correspondence with publishers and agents were also date-marked. But I soon discovered that I was doing more than establishing a timeline; I was discovering the true picture of who I had been, and the person who emerged wasn't the guy I'd been selling to myself and others.

My wife came into the kitchen that first day of excavation and found me sorting through piles and piles of rejection letters. "What are you doing?" she asked. I told her I was trying to find the guy I used to be, so I could understand how I became who I am. Or something. She laughed. It is kind of funny, when you think about it. For the next week or so, it was our little joke. I would be shut up in my office, floor and desk covered with old manuscripts, bent over notebooks I'd filled with my illegible scrawl decades ago. "How's it going?" she'd call from down the hall. "Find him yet?"

"Getting there."

When I was a kid, maybe twelve years old, I wanted to write movie and TV scripts. Instinctively I knew, or thought I knew, that the most important thing about film production was that the writer was in charge. I'll wait until you stop laughing.

But really. Think about it. That army of talented people, actors, lighting guys, set designers, wardrobe, cinematographer, even the director—they're all there to serve the story. And where do stories come from? Writers!

I want to pause here and point out what a weird thought process this was for twelve-year-old me. I didn't know any writers. I liked books and stories but mostly I watched a lot of TV shows and movies. The visual medium really had me in its jaws. But I didn't dream of making movies, being a director. I didn't dream of being an actor *in* movies and TV shows. No, I dreamed of being the guy who wrote the thing that allowed all those other people to do their jobs. Back then I believed that "real" writers wrote books and *then* wrote scripts. I still kind of believe that, though there are probably a lot of examples that prove me wrong. Anyway, I decided I wanted to be a "real" writer.

In junior college I was an indifferent student. Back then it was common to accumulate enough credits for an associate's degree and then transfer those credits to a four-year institution like the

University of Washington. At the end of my two years of community college I got sick and blew a final. I would have had to make
up the class that summer. A measly five credits, but the thought
of it made me simultaneously exhausted and impatient. I saw myself arbitrarily choosing a profession, buckling down, and pow-
ering through the summer plus two—or even four—more years
of education . . . and for what? I wanted to be a writer, and for
that I didn't need a degree. So I skipped the summer class, joined
my brother in Alaska, and worked in a salmon cannery. Was this
a smart move? Don't ask me; I didn't even finish college. At the
cannery my official job description was "slimer." This was the aus-
picious beginning of my journey through a rickety gauntlet of
paycheck jobs on my way to becoming a professional writer. I was
naïve but determined.

In later years I reinterpreted my abandonment of academe
as a consequence of my inability to concentrate and focus: the
victim narrative. In reality it had been a deliberate choice. Why
would I claim otherwise?

My favorite answer to the question Why do you write? (other
than my own, which I will soon reveal) goes, "It's the only thing
I know how to do!" I like this answer because it says something
about the writer's mindset. I also think that ninety-five percent
of the time it's bullshit. Most of us don't have the luxury of writing full-time with no other supporting income. So we *must* learn
how to do more than write fiction. Gene Wolfe, a prolific top-tier
SF writer, used to get up two hours early every day and write before going to his day job editing an engineering journal. In her
early twenties Margaret Atwood was a barista, whose co-workers
thought she was "a mutant." Octavia Butler used to rise at 2:00
a.m. to write before going to work. Her resume included tele-
marketer, dishwasher, and potato chip inspector. Later on, the
MacArthur Foundation gave her a new job title: genius. Even
Thomas Pynchon had a day job. He worked for the same airplane
company that eventually employed me. In fact, we worked in
same building, decades apart. In time, Pynchon found gold at the
end of *Gravity's Rainbow*. Good for him. The point is that most
writers wind up supplementing their income for at least part of
their career. Many have maintained dual professions their entire
working life. Anton Chekhov, renowned playwright and one of

our greatest short story writers, was also a doctor. In a strange reversal of order, Chekhov used his writing income to support his medical and humanitarian efforts.

The nice thing about a reliable paycheck is that you can stop thinking about money all the time. Far from stifling creativity, a job can free your mind of worry. I say this because it's true, despite the fact that some of the jobs I've held along the way drove me batshit crazy. Actually, all of them did. But that was better than failing to pay my bills, or missing meals—both of which happened in my early years of trying to get published.

So I took a succession of paycheck jobs that included bartender, dishwasher, convenience store clerk, school janitor, assistant librarian, and airplane-parts expeditor. But writing is the only thing I'd ever wanted—and more importantly—*needed* to do. I've gone back and forth on the idea of "need" in this context. With or without a steady income or professional acknowledgment, for most of my life I have been obsessed with writing fiction. If I stop writing for any length of time I get anxious, twitchy, short-tempered. Does this qualify writing as a need? For me, that's what it feels like.

I write because I have to.

I wrote my first stories when I was fourteen or fifteen years old. I sold my first story when I was around forty, to a small-press magazine that hadn't yet published a single issue (and never would). The $150 payment arrived years later. At least the check cleared. If there wasn't going to be much money, why did I persist so long? What's so wonderful about the writing life? Gardner Dozois, who edited *Asimov's Science Fiction* for a couple of decades, gave me my first professional sale in 2002. Gardner once described the writing life as ". . . a series of vicious kicks to the teeth." Based on that description, what kind of a crazy person would want to devote their life to sitting alone in a room telling stories about people who don't exist so that months or even years later over-worked and under-paid editors can say, "No thanks"? I don't have to look any farther than the nearest mirror.

One of my oldest friends, Burt Courtier, with whom I wrote the story "Assassins" in this collection, told me recently that he admired how I stuck to my dream of becoming a writer. That was nice of him to say, but he gives me too much credit. It was clear from the beginning that I had no choice. Without writing, the world appeared bleak and hostile. Quitting would have poisoned my other life, the life I was living with everyone else, my family and friends. It felt like a matter of life and death. I simply had to succeed. Had to.

I remember only two occasions when I sought writing advice from people who had actually published fiction. My oceanography professor (the guy whose class I'd failed to complete) had co-written a science fiction novel. That was way more interesting to me than methods for determining the salinity of large bodies of water. When I asked him if he had any tips for writing a novel he suggested something to do with shoeboxes, magazine clippings, and 3x5 cards. It didn't click.

The other person was my creative writing teacher at the same junior college. How long would it take to get good enough to publish? He said ten years. If you hadn't made it by then, you probably aren't a writer. This piece of advice, though well intentioned, was probably the worst advice I've ever received. To be fair, based on what he'd seen of my work so far, he probably thought I was doomed anyway.

Your life becomes the story that you tell yourself. Somewhere between age twelve, when I began telling myself the story of being a "real" writer, and age twenty-five, when I road-tripped across the US to Maine where I'd pound out my first novel, I forgot about movie scripts and became obsessed with prose fiction—obsessed with my story of being a fiction writer. I must have been out of my mind. Armed only with an encouraging rejection letter from *Amazing Stories* and five hundred dollars cash I got for selling my Martin guitar, I left behind everyone and everything I'd ever known. That much I've always remembered. What follows is the result my personal literary excavation project. Every manuscript, every rejection letter, every journal entry, every piece of correspondence switched on a light in rooms I'd long ago left dark and locked, as if they contained a shameful record of past sins.

*

So how do you become a real writer in the real world, instead of remaining a wannabe mooning around bookstores, coffee shops, and—God help you—bars? A serious emotional wound suffered in early adolescence can be useful, but I don't recommend it. What it really takes is a one-track mind and a bonkers, sometimes desperate, work ethic. Or, if you prefer, a pathological case of stubbornness.

During those early years the writing itself was doing something for me. It was a lifeline. I couldn't see a way of living in the normal world, so I threw everything I had at what I thought of as the only work that mattered. Either writing would save me, or I would drown. It wasn't until much later that I figured out that the whole idea of a "normal world" was a deceptive premise.

The first novel I attempted was a mainstream character study called *Runaways*. It remains the only book I've ever failed to complete. Not finishing the book scared me. I couldn't let that become a habit, or I was sunk. The second book was a straight up sword-and-sorcery fantasy, which I had no business attempting. At that time, the only sword-and-sorcery stories I'd read were Fritz Leiber's Fafhrd and the Gray Mouser tales and Tolkien's *Lord Of The Rings*. I wrote *The Hook* in rented rooms in Portland, Maine, San Francisco, and Seattle, and then shopped it around to the few New York publishers that would look at un-agented submissions. No one was interested. It didn't surprise me. The book wasn't good. But this time I'd wanted to follow the process through to the end. Write a book. Rewrite it. Type a clean copy and send it out.

Although the novel didn't sell, the novelette version of *The Hook* got positive feedback from an editor at *Amazing Stories*— the same editor who had launched me across the country with the other positive rejection letter. This was to become a recurring theme. Editors at various magazines would add handwritten personal notes to the rejections, so I would concentrate my efforts on one or another magazine that seemed receptive, drawing so close to a sale, so close. I knew this was how the game was played, and I was all in. It would only be a matter of time before I broke through. I had a *Martin Eden* mindset. I was going to crash through the door of publishing by main force of will. Years later when I read the Jack London novel about a working class autodidact fighting with manic desperation to sell his writing, I could really relate—except for the part where Martin drowns himself in despair *after* he starts selling his work. That seemed a bit much. At age twenty-seven I thought it was perfectly possible that I'd be a working professional by the time I was thirty-five. But, as so many of those rejection letters began: *Alas . . . No.*

Here on this page and the next are some of the magazines I was sending stories to between 1981 and 2000—at least the ones I still have rejection slips from:

Amazing Stories
Twilight Zone Magazine
The Magazine of Fantasy & Science Fiction
Alfred Hitchcock's Mystery Magazine
Weird Tales [Worlds of Fantasy & Horror]
Asimov's Science Fiction
Analog Science Fiction and Fact
Whispers From The Shattered Forum
Deathrealm
Fantastic Worlds
The Horror Show
Century Magazine
Pirate Writings
Terminal Fright
Ellery Queen
Talebones
2 AM
Zoetrope
Playboy
The New Yorker
Cemetery Dance
Pulpsmith
Charm

On Spec

Sci Fi

Realms of Fantasy

Horror Garage

Black Gate

Interzone

New Genre

Science Fiction Age

Pulphouse

Brutarian

Dark Tome

Space and Time

Flesh and Blood

Faerywoods

Glyph

Espionage

Zyzzyva

And here are a few examples of the many personal notes I found scribbled on or attached to the rejections:

". . . the nuts-and-bolts part of writing is *good* here; it should not be too difficult to place this piece in another market." (This one is taken from that first *Amazing Stories* reject, the one I carried with me to Maine as if it were holy writ. Proof positive that I was going to make it. Alas, it was not only difficult to place the story in another market, it was impossible.)

". . . I definitely like your writing style." (*Pirate Writings*. Great! Here are five more stories. No sale.)

"Strong effort! Try again. Good luck." (*The Horror Show*. Fantastic! Here's more! Nope.)

And from the committee at a prominent fantasy/horror mag: ". . . We've been arguing over your story at length. One said creepy, weird, imaginative, and liked it; another: very good but not quite irresistible. Two said maybe. One thought it could use one more rewrite to correct some minor points, and thought it not as unconventional as that one would like. Overall then: very good but not irresistible. A question: how have you been doing with the earlier stories we labeled good but not irresistible?" (They continued to be good and continued to be resisted. Cue head banging on desk.)

And so on.

Publishing was a locked door.

I knew that to become a writer I had to become a better reader, a more serious reader. Being under-read meant starting a race flat-footed. It was all connected. During this ten-year period I read constantly, mostly concentrating on stuff outside my limiting bubble of genre. I at least tried everything. Some writers I bounced off of like a bird bounces off a plate glass window. Ford Maddox Ford comes to mind. Virginia Wolf was one of many writers who struck me powerfully but selectively. *Mrs. Dalloway*? Yes. *To The Lighthouse*? Oh my god, not happening. Faulkner's *Absalom, Absalom!* defeated me every time. But his lesser works like *Pylon* and the infamous *Sanctuary* worked, maybe because they were closer to my history of reading popular genre novels. Then I stumbled on Faulkner's collected short fiction and was blown away, especially by stories like "Turnabout." Based on his description, I drew a sketch of the torpedo boat that figures prominently in the story. I wanted to visualize more clearly. I wanted to *see*.

Some writers almost literally made me drunk. I'd read Nabokov's *Lectures on English Literature*, and his notes on Charles Dickens encouraged me to try *Bleak House*. Dickens's use of language was absolutely stunning; it far outweighed the sentimentality critics like to denigrate him for. I spent a year lost in Charles Dickens land.

This intensive period of reading changed my perception of language and what books could do to you. I remember standing in the general lit aisle of Tower Books and being struck by the wonder of all those treasures, hidden in plain sight my whole life, and available to own at about a buck ninety-five a pop. My advice, if you want to be a writer? Do yourself, and your readers, a big favor by filling your head with every kind of fiction and nonfiction you can lay your hands on. Give Jane Austen a try. See what you can make of Virgil's *Aeneid*. Take a run at Tolstoy. Literature is a mansion; don't lock yourself in one room.

For a long time, starting at age twenty-five, my approach to writing was to produce a bunch of short stories, market the better ones, collect the rejections, then go back and write another novel. My third attempt at a novel was a horror story called *The Cave*. It took me four years to finish. My brother—not the Alaska brother—was working at a paper recycling plant and he snagged several reams of legal-sized bond paper and gave them to me for probably what he thought of as my "hobby." I filled all those 8 1/2 x 14 inch sheets with *The Cave*, writing it over and over again on my Smith-Corona portable typewriter. The combined drafts added up to more than half a million words. The book improved on the sentence level but never cohered as a novel. It was simply too big for me at the time. And when I say I finished it, I mean that I stopped writing it. *The Cave* was a big lumbering truck that I drove straight into the desert until it ran out of gas. Then I walked away feeling like I had accomplished nothing. I didn't know how to do this.

At age thirty-three I still had a couple of years remaining on my ten-year countdown to "make it." I also had a wife, and a baby due in seven months. Big bills were coming. I took a union job—my first full-time gig. It felt like a retreat. But you do what you have to do.

My writing slowed down but not by much. Basically, I was now holding down two jobs but only getting paid for one. After my four-year war with *The Cave*, I tried a crime story. I had been reading the early novels of James Ellroy, short and brutal works that were his proving ground before exploding with *The Black Dahlia, L.A. Confidential*, and others. I wrote *Colt .44* in under a year. It was about a contract killer who takes assignments all over the country. What the people who hired him didn't know was that he was also killing Catholic priests—a life-long vendetta for wounds suffered. When his bosses find out and the police catch up to him, all hell breaks loose. *Colt .44* wasn't bad but it wasn't particularly good, either. However, it taught me a valuable lesson: Even a little forethought and planning can make the difference between an empty gas tank in the middle of the desert and a successful road trip to a real destination. I still wasn't great with novelistic story structure, but this was progress. I holstered *Colt .44* and moved on.

Then came *Blood Brothers*. Book number four. This was a watershed. I'd been writing steadily for eight years and now I finally finished a novel that worked. The book was my riff on *Cape Fear*. The wife of a high school English teacher living in the burbs is kidnapped by a vengeful ex-con out of the teacher's past. My files contain correspondence with agents and publishers. I pushed hard. What I got back was what I'd become accustomed to with my short fiction: praise for my writing, close-but-not-quite. New York agents took me seriously; my files contain thoughtful letters peppered with praise. But every one of those letters ended with a variation of the phrase "ultimately I have to pass." Once again I was being told how good I was but apparently not good enough. It would be more than ten years before I met Gardner Dozois in person or even knew who he was, but I was already well acquainted with his vicious-kicks-to-the-teeth theory of the writing life.

A lot of the rejection you get when trying to publish can be chalked up to the vagaries of the marketplace and the temperament of a given editor or agent on a particular day. Luck, good and bad, is part of the process, maybe even a major part. To counter this situation you have to play the long game. You have to not only work like crazy but you also have to outlast the bad luck. I knew all this at the time, but the failure of *Blood Brothers* to find a publisher or even an agent—that one really hurt. I felt a creeping sense of hopelessness. That door to the publishing world seemed not only locked but an illusion, a taunting picture of a door painted on a cement wall.

Instead of writing another short crime novel to follow up my near-miss with *Blood Brothers*, I plunged into a three-year wrestling match with a long science fiction/horror novel. As the short story rejections continued to roll in, I lost myself in the world of *Incubus* (Original title: *Dreaming Monsters*.) It went through multiple drafts. The finished manuscript stood at a hundred and fifty thousand words.

As always, the writing itself provided me with something essential, something I could find nowhere else. And for a while it took my mind off what I feared was an embarrassing misstep. What if staking everything on being a writer had been a colossal error in judgement? I imagined friends and family regarding me as an eccentric failure or, at best, an underachiever with a pointless hobby that took up far too much of my life.

By the time I'd finished *Incubus* I was in a pretty dark place, at least as far as my writing ambition was concerned. There was the usual let down after completing a long piece of work, but it was more than that. I know I was depressed because my boxes contain no record of ever having submitted the book. Not so much as a query letter to an agent, though I surely must have sent some out. All I can remember is that I went to a local conference where it was possible to schedule fifteen minutes with a literary agent. I arrived unprepared, my pitch bounced off the back-stop. She said my book sounded interesting, the same way you might tell a friend that their nonsensical dream from the previous night sounded interesting. And she invited me to send her the first fifty pages and outline, which I did. I have no record of her response, which probably speaks for itself. However, looking through the manuscript all these years later, it's clear that unlike my previous attempt at a long, multi-viewpoint novel, *Incubus* didn't run out of gas. It was a solid, if derivative, piece of work.

When I hauled out of storage all my old manuscripts with the idea of using them to help establish a timeline for this essay, I didn't even recognize *Incubus*. I'd forgotten about the title change and thought it must be a totally lost novel. It was a Phil Dick moment: guy going through old boxes of papers discovers a long novel he has no memory of writing. What did it mean that a hidden personality lurking within him had created this thing?

It's a kind of insane, often sardonic brand of optimism that keeps you in the trenches. If you lose faith as a writer, you lose everything. It eats at your will to engage with life, gnaws at your moral fabric, reduces you. The year was 1992, almost exactly eleven years after the starting gun for my ten-year commitment. It would be another eight years before I wrote the next novel. I did continue to produce short stories, but not nearly as many. My attention was veering. The union job was a grind. My kids, one and three years old, needed me to be present, and I knew if I didn't pay more attention to my marriage and the life outside my head, things could quickly go wobbly.

At my nadir I tried to quit writing altogether but could stay away for only a couple of miserable months. It was still the case, would always be the case, that without writing, the poison would seep into every relationship. No, I couldn't stop looking for that key to the cement-wall door. Resigned, I went back to work. The ten-year race was over but I wasn't done. I didn't lower my expectations; I no longer had any.

Despite all the positive feedback from editors, I knew my short stories were missing some crucial element. Otherwise somebody would have bought one by now. Why hadn't I managed to cross the "irresistible" margin? I sat at my desk in the middle of the night—I worked second shift— and with a black felt-tip marker I lined out every superfluous sentence in my latest story. Turns out there were a lot of them. What I ended up with was a manuscript that looked like a redacted government document, a dispatch from the war zone originally intended to be read only by those with a need-to-know. Well, I fucking needed to know.

After that, every story I wrote was better than all the stories I'd previously written. Why could I suddenly see what was superfluous and what wasn't? I'd been at this a long time. Maybe because I'd let go of the idea that I had to reach print, or die, the sentences just . . . came into focus. I wasn't trying so hard to *make* something happen. Letting go of expectations meant freeing myself of blinders. There was more to learn, and I would eventually get there. But for now, I thought I'd cracked the code.

Nope.

My new "redacted" stories came back just like the others. This was frustrating but it didn't murder my ego or anything. Eventually I did sell some of those stories, but that would happen in a future that back then looked more and more unlikely. I wondered if it was too late to return to school, get that degree, and at least change my mundane working life, trade in the factory for a desk in an air-conditioned office—maybe even find a real profession that engaged my mind.

But I had designed my real life—the one life I'd been given—

without a back-up plan. To return to school now while holding down the full-time job needed to pay bills and feed my family plus continue to write . . . it just seemed impossible. Something would have to be sacrificed. Obviously it couldn't be my kids or job, and my brief resolution to quit writing had done nothing but reconfirm that I couldn't stop, didn't dare stop. That may sound overly dramatic but it was how I saw the situation.

If my first short story collection, *Are You There*, featured a lot of "tortured lonely guy" narratives, the current collection contains protagonists exploring the lives they might have led in other reality streams, characters looking for a way into the life they were meant to live, or back into the life they had abandoned through neglect and bad decisions. This transmuting into fiction of unique personal life experience, psychological states, and emotions is what was missing from much of my unpublished work.

The turning point finally came in late 2001-2002. Three things happened. The first was a detective novel called *The Falling Game*. I don't know why I wrote it after essentially giving up novel writing. Maybe because I'd recently discovered the Robert B. Parker detective series and thought it was something I could pull off. Also, I missed writing novels. I missed the engagement and the long commitment that kept me busy in a different world. By now I'd sold one small-press story and even cashed the check, though the magazine itself had been cancelled before publication. Success, even in a very small dose, can power the optimism engine for a while. So I put aside the short stories and wrote the detective novel.

I thought the book was pretty good and I entered it in the Pacific Northwest Writers Conference's first novel contest. To my utter shock, *The Falling Game* became a finalist. I took off half a shift at my factory job and went to the banquet at a fancy hotel. In the parking-lot I chatted with a guy who turned out to be Charles Johnson, author of *Middle Passage*, for which he'd won a National Book Award—but more importantly (for me), it was a book I'd actually read. Unfortunately, faced with the author's presence, my mind went blank on the title. (My mind going blank at crucial social interactions used to happen quite a bit.) Johnson and I shared a nice moment over our mutual frustration with folding five-dollar bills tight enough to squeeze into the pay-slot. Then he asked me if I was there for the banquet. When I told him I was a novel finalist, he said he would root for me. I begin to feel genuinely optimistic, almost light-headed. It was like an omen. The feeling was so unfamiliar that I wondered if I was coming down with the flu or something. Was it possible that that after all this time . . . ?

Nah. I failed to win the contest and felt obscurely humiliated. That feeling was soon swept away by a heady sense of standing, however tenuously, in the world where I belonged, among people who read and wrote books, people who worked in the publishing industry and spoke to me as if I were one of their tribe. This was different from the conference I'd gone to in order to pitch *Incubus*. I'd felt like an outsider in that situation. This time I was invited. It was unlike anything I'd ever experienced, and I wanted more.

After that night I tried again, unsuccessfully, to find an agent and/or publisher. I was disappointed but not devastated. In fact, I felt more optimistic than I had since the days when I was writing *Blood Brothers*. Something was in the air. I could feel it.

The second thing happened a few months after the awards banquet. I'd been in Spokane for a couple of days and returned just in time for my Monday night shift. There was an email waiting for me. It had arrived on my birthday (you can't make this stuff up) and it was from Marsha DeFilippo. The name looked familiar. I opened the email and learned that Stephen King had read the story I submitted to his *On Writing* contest. I had won the thing (actually, there were five winners but that didn't diminish my happiness.) Marsha was King's personal assistant. Reading that email was a surreal moment. I heard a door unlock. It wasn't a taunting illusion anymore, but I still had to write a story that would get me over the threshold.

A word about King's *On Writing*. Scribner published the book in 2000. I'd read Stephen King's early novels and stories and was a fan but hadn't really kept up with his output. (Is it even possible to keep up with it?) Nevertheless, when I heard he was publishing a book about writing I was eager to get my hands on it. Something told me that I *needed* to read that book. Which was weird. I'd read plenty of how-to books on craft and I devoured interviews with writers both in and out of genre. There was no particular reason that I needed to read this one. However, the feeling was so strong that I got up early so I'd have time before work to hit the local Borders on publication day. I remember sitting in the car feeling grumpy and underslept, flipping through *On Writing*, and thinking: What? As if I were actually asking someone a question—maybe the guy who made me get up early to shell out twenty-five bucks for a book that I "needed" to read. (Magical thinking comes with the territory; writing and gambling addiction have a lot in common.) King's book seemed to be more of a memoir than a craft book. Since I already knew about his rags-to-riches story, I wasn't too interested in reading about it at greater length, even if it was a great story.

I tossed the book on the passenger seat and drove to work. The following weekend I read it. The bit about writing a story based on a prompt, which King provided, and sending it to him through his website was kind of interesting. His idea about finding stories by narrating from a situation instead of working from a plot outline was something I'd done a lot of. Why not give the exercise a shot? According to King, the contest winner would be printed in the paperback edition of *On Writing* (didn't happen). I'd recently acquired a computer. This would be my first-ever electronic submission. After some fumbling around, I managed to send off what amounted to a piece of flash fiction in plain text format, which looked incredibly clunky and unreadable. By the time Marsha DeFilippo notified me that I'd won, I'd long ago put the contest out of my mind as just another failed longshot. But the truth was I'd played the long game, outlasted the bad luck.

And it was about to get better.

The third thing happened in the summer of 2002. I'd stepped up my submission schedule and had ten manuscripts in the mail. Right away I sold a couple of stories to a micro-press in the Midwest that paid in copies. That was nice. And immediately afterwards I got an acceptance letter from Gardner Dozois. My story had been on submission for six months, and now *Asimov's*, a major science fiction magazine, was taking "Dead Worlds." And they wanted more. I couldn't stop staring at Gardner's letter, three sentences typed on badly Xeroxed *Asimov's Science Fiction* letterhead. It was even more surreal than the one from Marsha De-Filippo. At long last the door was open. I stepped through and never looked back.

Until those boxes.

A better question than *Why do writers write* would be *Why does anyone tell themselves the particular story of their life?* For instance, why didn't I story-tell myself that I was a commercial pilot? By now I could be retiring from Delta Airlines with a fat pension. As a teenager I actually got a pilot's license (see the story note for "Arlington.") But like a few too many of my landings, it failed to stick. After the initial thrills, my interest level fell off. And if you're going to be a pilot you'd damn well better remain intensely interested. Flying was a thing I could do but after a few years stopped doing. Unlike writing, it was a hobby, and one that required too much of my time, money, and attention. Being a pilot wasn't part of my self-story and you can't force these things. Your story is there, waiting for you to tell it, or it's not.

By the way, the self-story can start rolling at any age. When my wife, Nancy Kress, was twelve years old she had no idea of being a writer. Even after she started selling short stories in her late twenties, she still thought of herself as a teacher, not a writer. It wasn't until she began writing and publishing novels that her self-story became *I am a writer.* After that, her career accelerated, though she still worked other jobs to pay bills until she could go full-time.

Everybody's life is a work in progress right up until the worksite is permanently shut down. That should be encouraging news to anyone who believes they've finished changing, are hopelessly stuck or ready to quit. That naïve but determined person I used to be emerged out of a chaotic jumble of papers and memories. Why I shunned him for so long was bound up in my erroneous ideas of what the writer's journey should look like. Everyone is different. The same unique forces and circumstances that create your voice also determine your route to finding that voice. I had *not* been a disorganized, neurotic, rejection-averse wall flower hoping to be invited to the dance. That was a character I made up to camouflage my embarrassment at so much effort with so little result, and eventually I believed my own fiction. The reality was that I'd fought relentlessly, attacking that door with everything I had. All those novels and short stories didn't represent the failed ambition I feared to acknowledge; they were my classroom.

"Did you find him?" Nancy asks.

Yes. In the boxes.

June 2023
Alki Beach, Seattle

STORY NOTES

THE WHOLE MESS

This one was a cover story for *Asimov's*. That made my day. It also explores an idea that has always intrigued me: all the different lives an individual might have lived. The feeling of not being in the *right* life, the optimal life—and knowing it, or coming to realize it. I work this idea in a few stories included in this collection.

MINE, YOURS, OURS

David Brin invited me to submit a story to the anthology he was co-editing. The theme was the coming transparent society. The stories were supposed to lean in a positive direction. Mine kind of didn't. But David liked the story and made a couple of editorial suggestions that I found useful. For me, the main thing was that the changes not compromise the story's original intent. They didn't, so I went ahead and performed some rewriting. When the book appeared, "Mine, Yours, Ours" was first up in the table of contents, which delighted me. I enjoy working with editors. Writing is a solitary activity. At times it can feel like you're playing tennis by yourself—just as exhausting, if less sweaty. So it's nice once in a while to play with a partner. And that's what the best editors are. David's suggestions made the story better, and that's always the goal: a better story.

ASSASSINS

Burt Courtier is one of my oldest friends. We went to high school together. In college, where I actually got to know him, we were in the same creative writing class (the only one I ever took). For years we were those guys who always *talked* about writing without actually doing much of it. Somewhere in this period we came up with the idea of writing a story in collaboration. We took a few stabs at it over the years but came up short. Finally, in 2015, I thought, It's now or never. I'm glad we got in the ring for one more round. Burt's a fine writer, and the story is a seamless blend of our styles. "Assassins" made it into Gardner Dozois' final volume of his *Year's Best Science Fiction* series. I'm particularly pleased about that. It also picked up a couple of translations.

THE SUM OF HER EXPECTATIONS

In the last decade I've written some stories that are what I think of as meat-and-potatoes science fiction. I guess you could also call it traditional science fiction. Many of my stories tend to wander off the beaten track. A long time ago, the teacher of that creative writing class I mentioned in the previous story note told me to discard the first three ideas for a story that come to mind, because those will be ideas that everyone else will have already thought of. After that, the story gets personal and therefore more interesting. That's when you get stories that only *you* could have written. "The Sum Of Her Expectations" started out as very much meat-and-potatoes SF, then happily diverged.

DESTINATION

I wanted to write something about a self-driving car that kidnaps its human passenger. This one worked well enough to sell to *Asimov's* and ascend to fourth place in the annual reader's poll. But looking at it for this collection, I thought it was politically simplistic. I had skated into the ending without really examining what the story meant, or even understanding what it was my character wanted, beyond the idea that he wished to be left alone. So I ran this one through the typewriter a couple more times, as we used to say in olden times. Not that I even own a typewriter anymore.

DREAM INTERPRETATION

This is my most recently published story. Just to show you how much a story can change from original idea to final draft, this one began as an encounter story between human astronauts and ancient technology left by an extinct race on Mars. Total meat-and-potatoes stuff. If I remember correctly, the Martians still existed as ghosts in their machines or something. That idea didn't work, so I tried again. This time it was a sole-survivor story. One of five astronauts returns from Mars, where things have gone very wrong. She fights to remain awake, because if she sleeps there will be big consequences. And so on. I wrote maybe four different versions of this story before discovering what it was really about (see "discarding ideas" note above). If you've read "Dream Interpretation" you know that it has nothing to do with Mars. Nothing. There *is* an astronaut, but he's not center stage. Sometimes you have to really dig to find the thing you didn't know you were digging for. This was one of those times.

EINSTEIN'S THEORY

This is the oldest story in the collection. It was one of three I sold in the 2000s to the Canadian magazine *On Spec*. I remember feeling quite pleased with it. I was selling a lot of stories in that first decade of my professional writing career. I felt like I was in the *zone*. The words came swiftly, story elements arose naturally, without the all too familiar strain of making things fit. I researched the Bern/Einstein details and deliberately set it on a particular night when an event important to the history of the real Einstein took place. However, upon re-reading "Einstein's Theory" after all these years I saw how it was a little out of focus. Everything was there. Everything worked. But it didn't quite . . . come into view. I must have sensed the same thing back in 2009, since I didn't include "Einstein's Theory" in my first collection. This time I meticulously combed through the text, making small changes—running it through my non-existent typewriter—and it popped into clarity. At least it does if you've had enough absinthe.

THE LAST GARDEN

I'd just sold my novel *The Chaos Function* to John Joseph Adams, who was editing a line of books at Houghton Mifflin Harcourt (which is now part of HarperCollins). At last, the Big Time! The novel had to do with a unique apocalyptic scenario, as does this story, though not the same one. I must have had a little gas left in the Armageddon tank. My starting point was the idea of a woman giving birth to her own mother. And my original title was "Are You My Mother?" which I still like, riffing off the famous children's book. By "riffing" I mean blatantly stealing. John wisely convinced me to change it.

SALVAGE OPPORTUNITY

Writing this one was a sheer pleasure. As I've mentioned, I'd been trying to work with more traditional science fiction tropes. I don't know why. I guess to join the club. Some of those stories succeeded on their own terms but failed to light me up. But with "Salvage Opportunity" I knew right away that I'd landed in the sweet spot. A familiar SF genre situation but one that took full advantage of one of my most potent themes. The icing on the cake was hearing from James Patrick Kelly, who enjoyed the story so much that he volunteered to do the audio version for *Clarkesworld*.

ARLINGTON

I wanted to write a story whose starting point was a real-life situation that happened to me involving a Cessna 150. When I was sixteen my dad hooked me up with a flight instructor and I began taking lessons. This wasn't as extravagant as it might sound. Back then the airplane rented for about fifteen bucks an hour. My mother had recently died, and I think Dad was trying to nudge me out of my deeply gloomy state of mind. It was a start. Anyway, everything in the story's opening scene, up until the mysterious cloud appears, really happened. I screwed up with the VOR, got a little lost in the Olympic Mountains, and landed at that remote airfield. Of course, the situation wasn't nearly as weird and fraught as it is in the story. One interesting side note: I used the actual identifying numbers of the Cessna I trained in. And I discovered that even after all this time, the airplane was still operational. It now belonged to a dentist in Bellevue. As far as I know, he has never been lost in the multiverse, though you'd probably have to ask his patients.

STEEL LAKE

Everything about this story is personally painful.

THE FLOW AND DREAM

Not a lot to say about this one. Meat and potatoes science fiction. For some reason I had to work twice as hard on it as on other, much more complex stories. *Asimov's* published it in 2011.

LAST CALL AT THE MOONLIGHT LOUNGE

Originally titled "Licorice" and published in the Newcon Press ten-year anniversary anthology. All the stories had to incorporate the number ten as a meaningful element. For this collection I spent a few days closely examining the sentences, making tweaks, trying to tune it up. Yes, running it through the "typewriter." Happily, it remains one of my weirder stories. When it was originally published, one reviewer declared it wasn't even science fiction. He was mistaken. The Devil's in the details.

THE SAVIOR VIRUS

For a year or so I'd been kicking around the idea at the core of this story, but nothing had quite gelled. Then I was having dinner with a bunch of SF writers and editors at some con, and I causally mentioned the idea and that I hadn't gotten anywhere. A well-known short story writer raised his hand and declared *he* wanted to write it. Ha ha, I don't think so, pal. I finally got off my butt and figured out what I was doing.

THE DESPOILERS

I wanted to play around in science fiction land while also making a point concerning the core argument between the father and daughter in this story. But to be clear, I almost never begin a story with the intention of making a point or educating the reader. I really think that's an unproductive approach. In "The Despoilers" I was attracted by the image of the spaceship submerged, the way the position lights looked refracted by lake water. I built outwards from that.

THE PRESIDENT'S DRONE

This is the first publication. My starting point was simply the image of a futuristic drone wandering a post-apocalyptic landscape, kind of a less-cute version of WALL-E. The rest grew out of that. At the time I was especially depressed about the way we have sorted ourselves into red and blue states, like gang colors. A situation without hope of compromise or useful cooperation. Why not take it to the ultimate conflict: outright war? This seemed more far-fetched and satirical a few years back.

STRACONIA

I love this story so much. The original "final" draft was fifteen thousand words. It could have gone on and on, but I had to stop somewhere. Sheila Williams at *Asimov's* suggested it would be better at ten thousand. By better, she meant publishable in her magazine. I thought: impossible! But after a year or so, I decided to try cutting it by a third, just to see if I could do it. The rewrite was a multi-step process. Big stuff first, cutting whole scenes, then increasingly smaller cuts, recasting sentences to make them tighter, and right on down to the single word level. In the end, I had reduced the word count to just under ten thousand—and the story was better for it. So why was it so much longer to begin with? I'd found a prose rhythm and a Kafka-esque milieu that perfectly complimented each other, at least in my mind. Straconia, by the way, is taken from the Polish word stracon, meaning "lost."

TRIBUTE

I was invited to contribute a story to another themed anthology; this one was to be stories about post-NASA space exploration. "Tribute" was a challenge because I wanted to write a hard SF story, with real science—something I rarely do. But I'm proud of the way this came out. It's the best of my meat-and-potatoes SF. Side note: Someone who ought to know told me that the two most coveted positions in an anthology are the first and last. My Brin story in the transparent society anthology was in the first position. This one, in *Mission: Tomorrow*, occupied the close-out slot. Not bad for two stories written under the extra restrictions imposed by themes I hadn't personally chosen.

ACKNOWLEDGMENTS

Here are some of the people who helped get me through the years I was writing these stories. My wife, Nancy Kress. It's just stunning to me how long we've been in each other's lives, when every day feels like the first, best day. My kids, Daniel and Ruby, are inspirations. If some of the other people on this list showed me how to be a better writer, my kids did them one better by showing me how to be a better human being. Love you guys. Daryl Gregory and Ted Kosmatka have been steadfast friends since we all met back in 2006 at the Nebula Awards in Tempe. They are the guys I turn to when I feel I'm in deep water, whether it's writing related or otherwise. Patrick Swenson, the publisher of this collection. I've been attending his annual Rainforest Writer's Retreat almost since its inception. Patrick was a friend even *before* Tempe. He's also my Seahawks gameday pal, texting with me and answering my ignorant sports questions. Burt Courtier and I go way back to high school. He was the first person I knew who could really write. For years I measured everything I wrote against what he had shown me could be done. Rod Dungan and Ania Seymour are friends from my Boeing days. We don't see each other as much as we used to but it hasn't diminished their importance in my life. My new agent, Michael Signorelli, is helping me look towards the future. And special thanks go to the editors who bought these stories. Without their exquisite taste and judgement, where would I be? Sheila Williams, at *Asimov's*. Neil Clarke, at *Clarkesworld*. David Brin, for Tor Books. Diane L. Walton, at *On Spec*. John Joseph Adams, at *Lightspeed*. Bryon Thomas Schmidt, for Baen Books. Ian Whates, at Newcon Press and Solaris. And finally I'd like to thank Vincent Chong, who created the cover art for this book as well as my 2013 novel, *Life On The Preservation*.

ABOUT THE AUTHOR

Jack Skillingstead has sold more than forty stories to markets including *Asimov's*, *Clarkesworld*, *F&SF*, and *Lightspeed*, as well as various Year's Best volumes and original anthologies. In 2004 he was a finalist for the Sturgeon Award and in 2013 his novel *Life on The Preservation* was a finalist for the Philip K. Dick Award. In 2019 *The Chaos Function*, a science fiction thriller, was published by Houghton Mifflin Harcourt/John Joseph Adams books. Jack has taught writing classes onboard ship in the Bahamas and in Seattle for Clarion West's one-day workshop series. He lives in Seattle with his wife, writer Nancy Kress.

PUBLICATION HISTORY

"An Introduction to Daryl Gregory (featuring Jack Skillingstead)" © 2023 by Daryl Gregory | "The Whole Mess" originally appeared in *Asimov's Science Fiction* (2016) | "Mine, Yours, Ours" originally appeared in *Chasing Shadows: Visions of Our Coming Transparent World*, Tor Books (2017) | "Assassins" (with Burt Courtier) originally appeared in *Clarkesworld* (2017) | "The Sum of Her Expectations" originally appeared in *Clarkesworld* (2017) | "Destination" originally appeared in *Asimov's Science Fiction* (2017) | "Dream Interpretation" originally appeared in *Asimov's Science Fiction* (2021) | "Einstein's Theory" originally appeared in *On Spec* (2009) | "The Last Garden" originally appeared in *Lightspeed* (2017) | "Arlington" originally appeared in *Asimov's Science Fiction* (2013) | "Steel Lake" originally appeared in *The New Solaris Book of Science Fiction*, Solaris (2011) | "The Flow And Dream" originally appeared in *Asimov's Science Fiction* (2011) | "Last Call At The Moonlight Lounge" originally appeared as "Licorice" in *Now We Are Ten: Celebrating The First Ten Years of NewCon Press*, NewCon Press (2016) | "Salvage Opportunity" originally appeared in *Clarkesworld* (2016) | "The Savior Virus" originally appeared in *Asimov's Science Fiction* (2016) | "The Despoilers" originally appeared in *Clarkesworld* (2016) | "The President's Drone" is previously unpublished and appears here for the first time (2023) | "Straconia" originally appeared in *Asimov's Science Fiction* (2018) | "Tribute" originally appeared in *Mission: Tomorrow*, Baen (2018) | "The Writing Life" is previously unpublished and appears here for the first time (2023)

OTHER TITLES FROM FAIRWOOD PRESS

www.ingramcontent.com/pod-product-compliance
Lightning Source LLC
Chambersburg PA
CBHW020841020726
47497CB00005B/1205